M000215587

Amish Knit
Lit Circle
Smicksburg
Tales 3

Karen Anna Vogel

He restores my soul

Amish Knit Lit Circle: Smicksburg Tales 3
© 2012 by Karen Anna Vogel
Second Edition 2013 by Lamb Books

Contact the author on Facebook at:
www.facebook.com/VogelReaders
Learn more the author at: www.karenannavogel.com
Visit her blog, Amish Crossings, at
www.karenannavogel.blogspot.com

ISBN-13: 978-0615926643 (Lamb Books)

ISBN-10: 0615926649

DEDICATION

To Karamarie Farnam and Maryann Roberts, my companions in talking about all things Jane Austen, Anne of Green Gables and Little Women. You provided lots of inspiration for this series. Thank you 'Pauline and Anne-Girl.

My wonderful husband Tim who patiently listened to me fret that I couldn't pull this series off.
You are my Rocky.

To Jesus Christ who keeps me knit together in His love
Psalm 139: 13

INTRODUCTION

Pickwick Papers (Charles Dickens), *Adventures of Sherlock Holmes* (Conan Coyle)*,* and Anne *of Green Gables* (Lucy Maud Montgomery), have two things in common; they started as continuing short stories and became classics. I've always felt we should learn from the best, and to me, a continuing short story invited readers to participate in the storyline, helping the author see their blind sides.

This is how *Smicksburg Tales* was born, and this is the third novel to be formed from episodes. So, why knitting and literature together? Well, the Amish are avid readers, especially when the earth rests from its labor, winter brings rest and lots of books into Amish homes.

Also, when readers told me their knitting circles were reading episodes of *Amish Knitting Circle: Smicksburg Tales 1* and then *Amish Friends Knitting Circle: Smicksburg Tales 2,* and then making the dessert recipes included, an idea popped into my head. Granny loves Jane Austen, so why not have the women read classic literature and discuss it at their circle?

So, in *Amish Knit Lit Circle,* all winter, Granny and her circle, now consisting of Amish and English friends, knit for the homeless and discuss books. As these women reach out into their community, they share what they've learned. Missy Prissy, a snobby rich woman, reads *A Christmas Carol,* but will it change her Scrooge heart? The single moms at Forget-Me-Not Manor read *Anne of Green Gables*, and can identify with this lonely orphan, being formerly homeless and on the streets, and share their stories for the first time, bringing healing. Mona reads *Black Beauty* and images of past abuse haunt her dreams and this could not possibly be a good thing, or is it?

Visions of romance dance in the women's heads, too. After reading *Pride & Prejudice*, they swoon over Mr. Darcy telling Elizabeth, *"You must allow me to tell you how ardently I admire and love you."* Some start to write love letters to their husbands, others wonder why their husbands just can't spit out "I love you." Marriage problems come to the forefront, but will they be swept under the rag rug? With their wives being so touchy-feely, will their husbands dive for the nearest rock to hide under?

Some readers are participating in Granny's circle in the comfort of their homes, not having to travel to Smicksburg. If you'd like to read these classic books along with the women in the circle, here's Granny's reading list:

Pride & Prejudice Jane Austen

Little Women Louis May Alcott

Anne of Green Gables Lucy Maud Montgomery

A Christmas Carol Charles Dickens

The Life of our Lord, Charles Dickens

Emma, Jane Austen

Black Beauty, Anna Sewell

Pilgrim's Progress, John Bunyan

The Secret Garden, Frances Hodgson Burnett

Enjoy dear reader friends!

TABLE OF CONTENTS

AMISH-ENGLISH DICTIONARY

Ach – oh

Boppli – baby

Daed - dad

Danki – thank you

Dawdyhaus – grandparent's house

Dochder – daughter

Ferhoodled – confused, messed-up

Gmay - community

Goot – good

Jah - yes

Kapp- cap; Amish women's head covering

Kinner – children

Nee- no

Mamm – mom

Oma – grandma

Opa –grandfather

Ordnung – order; set of unwritten rules

Wunderbar – wonderful

Yinz – plural for you, common among Western Pennsylvania Amish and English. A *Pittsburghese* word, meaning 'you ones' or 'you two'

Karen Anna Vogel

EPISODE 1

Pride & Prejudice

Granny poured freshly ground coffee into Jeb's mug, and then sat down for breakfast. They joined hands as Jeb asked for a blessing on the food and for strength for this day.

"My neck's still sore, Jeb. It hurts to knit."

"Well, you're not a spring chicken anymore, and running a wedding like you did yesterday would tucker me out."

"You? Of course it would. You're older." She grinned at him. "Old man."

Jeb took a sip of the hot liquid. "That I am. As old as the hill, *jah?* But I don't plan weddings and have knitting circles and whatnot."

"My girls all helped with the wedding and we'll have leftover dessert at the circle like last year. *Ach*, I can't believe the circle started last wedding season, can you?"

"And look what *goot* came out of it. How many of the girls got married?"

Granny raised one, then two, then three fingers. "I think three. Lizzie and Roman, Fannie and Melvin, and Lavina and Nathan." She smiled with delight. "And with every wedding, I was right, and you were wrong."

"Huh?"

"I made Roman come to his senses about Lizzie, when you thought I was meddling. Fannie's inner beauty came out from the scriptures and compliment box —"

"Now hold on now. I gave Melvin the idea for the compliment box. It worked for you, remember?"

Granny pursed her lips. "*Ach*, Jeb, it did, and I'm ever so thankful. And it's the Lord who puts people together, not me." She took a bite of scrambled eggs, but when she turned to look out the window at the rain pelting against it, the pain in her neck got worse. *Stiff neck, again. Hope I can knit later on today.*

"Knitting circle is this afternoon. Well, our new book club and knitting combined. Suzy calls it our knit-lit circle for short. But I'll be starting it with a heavy heart."

"Why?"

"Ella's moved on to New York....and Mona's coming." Granny tried not to grind her teeth when spitting out that woman's name, but she couldn't help it."

"What are you reading, or talking about reading, or however it goes?" Jeb asked.

"We picked a book most of us have read, being so busy with the wedding. Promise not to laugh."

"I'll try."

"*Pride and Prejudice.*"

Jeb's expression didn't change. "What's so funny about that?"

"You always tease about my love for Jane Austen."

He put a hand up. "I'm used to it now. And I see the *goot* the woman writes about. You only need to stop trying to be like that Emma. The matchmaker." He winked. "God is the matchmaker, *jah*?"

"*Jah*, He is. I sure hope Mona learns a *goot* lesson from *Pride and Prejudice*...."

"Huh? You think she's proud or prejudiced?"

"She's not a *goot mamm*, like Mrs. Bennett."

"Deborah....."

"What?"

"Did you pick the first book because Mona is coming? To point out her faults?"

"Everyone's read it, like I said. But if we're to learn from great literature, *jah*, I hope Mona learns something."

Jeb sighed. "God knows how to fix her. Don't go weeding someone else's garden if you have weeds in your own."

Granny's brows furrowed. "Never heard that saying."

"Saying? I just made it up. With us working in the garden and all, it just popped into my head. But you understand my meaning, *jah*?"

"You're saying those without sin cast the first stone?"

"*Jah*." Jeb chuckled. "Don't take stones out of someone else's garden until the dirt in yours is fine as silt."

"Jebediah Weaver, stop while you're ahead. And all these proverbs you're saying apply to you, too."

He grabbed her hand and kissed it. "I know, but I have an easier time with it."

Granny withdrew her hand and slapped his arm. "What? Why? Being the bishop doesn't make you better, only more dependent on God for answers. God lifts up the humble and —"

"I have you, Deborah Weaver. You help carry the burden of all my faults, *jah*? I lean on you; you know that."

Trying to hide the smile forming on her lips, she took a sip of coffee. "And you help carry mine, too, Love."

"How much does Mona weigh? Think I'll hurt my back."

Granny snickered. "I love you, old man. My leaning post."

"I love you more…and need you more….Love."

~*~

Mona sat in the rocker in her room, struggling to learn how to follow the pattern Suzy had given everyone who joined the new circle. *Knit for charity…and for the English?* How many times she'd go to this knitting circle, read secular books, she did not know. It all seemed mighty carnal to her. Deborah Weaver always tested the limits, and now that her husband was bishop, did she think she could get away with more?

Well, she'd go to be a good influence on Deborah. The woman was just too friendly to outsiders.

~*~

A buggy pulled in and Mona stood up and looked down on her driveway. *Maryann? Ach*, she wished it was anyone but Maryann. The woman was a model mother, raising eight *kinner* in a house always spotless. Every church service in that house always made Mona's husband question her homemaking abilities, or laziness as he implied.

Mona set the black yarn down and slowly got up from her rocker. She heard Maryann enter though the side door, and call her name.

"I'm coming down. Just a minute." Mona quickly slipped out of her night clothes and put her black dress and apron on. No other Amish family knew how much time she spent in her nightgown, except Fannie. Ever prodding Fannie, who gave too much advice, given to her by Deborah Weaver. Twisting her hair up, Mona shoved pins to keep it in place before putting on her *kapp*. Granny, indeed. When Fannie said that she wanted to call Deborah *Mamm* , she knew it was out of spite. Why was Fannie spiteful, and not sweet, like Eliza?

Mona slowly descended the steps and moseyed her way over to her kitchen to meet Maryann. "*Goot* morning."

"Morning's almost over. It's eleven o'clock." Maryann's eyes bore into her. "Mona, are you alright?"

"*Jah*, sure. Just upstairs knitting the pattern Suzy gave us." Mona rolled her eyes. "Maryann, am I the only one who thinks getting together regular like with the English is downright...I don't know...sinful?"

Maryann flinched. "Sinful? We're to love. How could it be sinful?"

"Thou shalt not tempt the Lord thy God."

"And how is this knitting circle doing that? You do know that it was the English woman, Marge, who helped me while I recovered from surgery, when I had breast cancer. So glad she decided to join the circle."

"But we're a people set apart from the world," Mona blurted.

Maryann lifted the pie she had in her hands up. "Marge is a Christian and not worldly. Will some pie cheer you up?"

"Who said I needed cheered up? Fannie?"

"*Nee*. At church you seemed so sad, and I know how thick clouds can make people feel heavy in the heart."

Mona felt tears form, but they never spilled out. She had self-control, one of the fruits of the spirit. *So unlike Deborah Weaver who showed every emotion she felt.* Mona took the pie from Maryann and lifted it to her nose. "Pumpkin. *Danki*. Fannie told you."

Maryann collapsed on the long oak bench that sat parallel the oak table. "Fannie said nothing. Mona, I'm tired. Tell me what's wrong."

"Fannie knows my favorite is pumpkin..."

"We can so many pumpkins, it's lots of folks' favorite pie. Michael can eat a whole pumpkin pie for breakfast. Now, sit down and let me help carry that burden you're carrying around."

Mona sat at the table opposite Maryann. "Want some tea?"

"*Nee*, I'm fine."

"Well, I'm reading that *Pride and Prejudice* book, and don't like it. Why are we reading something other than the Bible, The Budget, or Family Life Magazine? I can tell you why. Deborah Weaver always gives in to the whims of the English."

"Whims? *Pride and Prejudice* was written a couple hundred years ago. I learned a lot."

"Huh?" Mona wanted to put her hands over her ears, not wanting to hear yet another woman sing the praises of Deborah Weaver.

"I was a snob like Mr. Bingley's sister. Thought I was better than others....better than the English. Sorry, but I must speak the truth. It's what I learned." Maryann's face lit up. "And Michael is my Mr. Darcy."

"Mr. Darcy is proud. I don't like him."

"Have you read the book, Mona?" Maryann pointed a finger at her.

"A few chapters. Enough to know he's not a *goot* friend. He treated Mr. Wickham real bad."

"*Ach*, Mr. Wickham is the one who's bad. You need to read it until you finish. It reminds me of Roman and Lizzie, just like Granny always said."

Mona ground her teeth. *Just like Granny always said.* Fannie repeated that over and over, like the tapping of the woodpecker outside.

"What's wrong, really?" Maryann was persistent, gazing deep into her eyes.

"*Ach*, Maryann, you're making something out of nothing. Don't borrow trouble."

Maryann got up and shrugged her shoulders. "I'll see you at three?"

"Most likely, since Fannie will give me no peace until I say I'll go."

"She'll have her *boppli* in three months and is emotional."

"Born that way. Has nothing to do with being pregnant. It's just Fannie being....*Fannie*."

~*~

Marge raced into the parking lot of Millers Variety, her red car slashing up water as she made no attempt to dodge mud puddles. If she was going to be a part of this knitting circle, she needed to stop parking down the road from her old house, wondering why on earth they moved back to Indiana, PA. How did they fail so miserably at living off the grid? According to Granny, they were a success. They found out it's wasn't *Little House on the Prairie,* and got a clear picture of what living off the grid was like. So why was she so sad? Joe, too. Was he really happy that she got pregnant or was he faking it? Or was it his father's constant criticism since they refused to go to his church, and attend Smicksburg Baptist? Or was she imagining everything because she was two months pregnant?

Marge watched her step as she exited the car and headed into the store. Why they hadn't changed the name yet was a mystery, but she bought all her dry goods here since they were half the cost. The bell attached to the door rang, and she saw Fannie sitting behind the counter, her nose in a book. She didn't even look up. "Now, I call this customer service at its best," Marge teased. "What are you reading?"

Fannie looked up, waving a hand to cool her face, tears pooled in both eyes. "Elizabeth loves Mr. Darcy." She hugged the book as tears streamed down her face. "She almost didn't secure him, like I did with Melvin, thinking him too grand."

"Secure him? Too grand?" Marge chuckled. "It's odd to see an Amish woman talk British."

"What?" Fannie asked, lowering the book.

Marge took off her jean jacket and picked up a jar of pickles. "They are tolerable, I suppose, but not enough to tempt me." A laugh escaped her. "Come on. No one talks like that. It's British, and old-fashioned British, I think."

Fannie smiled. "I get so caught up in it. Maybe too much, being pregnant and all. You came for my exam?"

"Yes, and to buy a few things. But let's get your exam over with, alright?"

"Sure. Come on into the house and have some tea."

"I'm sorry Fannie. This is just a quick physical for you, and to hear the baby's heartbeat. I've been delayed today."

"Are the roads icy?"

Marge sighed. "I keep driving past our old place and...daydreaming. Why didn't we stay?"

"You didn't like farming, and you're pregnant."

"Joe and I didn't know we shouldn't have named the animals. Too hard to kill something that's become like a pet. Oh, well, what's been done is done, but living down the road from Joe's dad is taking its toll."

Fannie shifted. "So, Joe and his *daed* don't get along?"

"Oh, his dad's so critical of Joe, and Joe can't seem to speak up. But he is reading his Bible now, and it helps." Marge took Fannie's wrist to take her pulse.

Fannie's green eyes mellowed, looking as fresh as springtime. "I can't wait to see her."

"Her? So you went to get a sonogram? How could you afford it with no complications?"

Fannie bit her lower lip. "I can just tell. We had no sonogram."

Marge took her blood pressure, and then listened for the heartbeat with her Fetal Doppler. "Just listen to that...."

Fannie pursed her lips and tears fell on her cheeks. "It's...a miracle."

Marge nodded. "And your 'little girl' is just fine. Do you have a name for her?"

"Deborah, for sure and for certain. If it wasn't for Granny, I don't think I'd be married to Melvin. Granny helped me recondition my mind."

Marge looked up, brow furrowed. "Recondition your mind?"

"Renew it. Transform it. I always thought I was fat and ugly, but the Bible has a lot to say about such thoughts. Granny had me memorize, *'For You formed my inward parts; You covered me in my mother's womb. I will praise You, for I am fearfully and wonderfully made....'*" Fannie put her head down and pat her stomach. "I'll be teaching Deborah that verse."

"That's what Joe needs to get deep inside of him. I'll tell him about this reconditioning." Marge lifted up two hands as if in despair. "He's getting hard to live with." When she met Fannie's eyes, the pain in them was evident. "What's the matter?"

Fannie sighed and then started to cry. "If I had a *mamm* like Granny, I wouldn't have had to recondition my mind. Eliza got all the praise. My *mamm* can be cruel, but I have Granny."

Marge was taken back. Was Joe's pain as deep as Fannie's? And Fannie lived down the road from her mom, just like Joe. Was it too much for him? She'd talk to him after church tonight. Working all day in Indiana County, going to knitting circle and then church would be a challenge, but she missed her Amish friends. Marge's heart sank. She missed Granny living right down the road.

~*~

Colleen was making her stitches of the shawl she was knitting too tight, and she knew why: her nerves. *How can I tell Hezekiah I think Lavina's wedding was...weird? You marry in a new apron and dress? No kissing the bride afterwards?*

"Tired from the wedding?" he asked, sitting next to her on the bench. "Or is the light not right in this little *dawdyhaus*?"

"What?"

"You're squinting and hunched over."

She put her knitting in her lap. "The lighting's fine in *here*. I love this little house, snug as a bug in a rug."

"Yep. So what's wrong then?"

Colleen was touched that he was so sensitive, picking up on her mood. Living plain wasn't that hard until she read *Pride and Prejudice*, and remembered the movie she'd watched over and over. It was more painful not to have a fancy wedding than she'd thought. Lizzie and Jane had wedding dresses...beautiful gowns. Colleen cleared her throat. "I'm surprised by Lavina's wedding...getting married with an apron on."

"You knew what she was wearing, since you were one of the attendants. Why so surprised?"

Colleen's heart plunged. "Not very romantic. How come Nathan could wear a nice black suit and tie? It doesn't seem right."

"I think they both looked *goot*. Lavina got to pick her favorite color for the dress." He took off his black wool hat and fidgeted with its rim. "How did you think it would be?"

"I don't know. I've never been to a wedding with no flowers…" She glanced over at the bookshelf, her heart sinking further. "Aurora can't read fairytales about princesses. I got rid of her book to please my grandma, but Aurora's too young to understand. *I* don't understand."

Hezekiah took her hand and stroked it. "Everything you give up will be filled with something else, in time. How about I get Aurora some books about farm animals? And I'm sure she likes her Pathway Reader at school."

"She does, but it doesn't have colored pictures."

The little room grew so quiet, Colleen thought Hezekiah could hear her heartbeat. There was usually noise coming from Iva's big house next door. But all the kids were in school, and the laughter was gone.

"Colleen. Are you having second thoughts about being plain?"

How could she tell him *yes*? But no doubts about marrying him, that she knew for sure. She'd never met a man so handsome who was so humble. A man who's big, blue, understanding eyes helped heal her self-hatred, and accepted the scars she still carried. Scars self-inflicted by cutting. No, if being Hezekiah's wife meant being Amish, she'd be the best Amish wife to him.

"Colleen, you're not answering my question. Maybe it's that book you're reading. Putting fancy notions in your head?"

"No. Jane Austen was a Christian. Her characters are women who somehow see their faults and change…"

Was she being challenged by Jane, too? To stop being so proud?

"Well, I know Jeb tolerates Granny reading all sorts of things, as long as she reads the Bible just as much. Can't say I understand it." Hezekiah shoved his hat on. "We best be going."

Colleen slipped her arm through his. "Hezekiah, are you upset with me?"

He shook his head. "A little concerned. Since you started reading that book for knitting circle, you don't seem like your content self."

"So many things are running through my mind. Baptismal classes, Aurora starting school and my worries about her. Do you think it's safe she walks to school?"

He put his arm around her. "She walks with the other *kinner*. And the school's only across the field."

Colleen leaned her head on his strong shoulder. "Maybe I need to pray more casting off prayers, like Granny."

He lifted her chin and planted a tender kiss on her lips. "I can help carry you're burdens, too. Your struggle to turn Amish."

She looked up into his eyes, searching. "What makes you think it's a struggle?"

"*Ach*, every Amish person has been through it. You're making a vow to the whole community that can't be broken, like a wedding vow. Who wouldn't be nervous?"

Colleen locked her arms around his neck. "Oh, I have been miserable. Keeping it all inside. Yes, I'm having doubts and thought you'd be upset."

Hezekiah stroked her cheek with his hand. "When I said I'll always be here for you, I mean your struggles, too. Remember how we talked at your secret garden?"

How could she forget? She tried to tell him her scars were from berry picking, but he was too smart for that. Too caring, and she told him her life's story. Being a single mom, homeless, hiding from crazy parents who were on drugs. "I remember it was in that garden I found the love I've always yearned for, but got more than I ever dreamed...or deserve."

He stole another kiss. "And you're what I've dreamed of." He took her hands and squeezed them tight. "Promise me that you'll be more open, not hide your feelings like you used to."

She nodded, and marveled at the unconditional love that this man had for her. He surpassed Mr. Darcy by far.

~*~

Lizzie popped a cherry pie in the oven, the girls' favorite. Thank you for my girls, Lord, she quickly said as the same feeling of hopelessness threatened to overwhelm her. No *boppli* yet, but she would give thanks in all things, like the Bible said to do. Like Granny had instructed.

She arched her back and rubbed the back of her aching neck, then slowly went to finish the end of *Pride and Prejudice.* She always did this, saving the last few pages as if a fine dessert. But when she was done, to her surprise, sadness pulled at her heart. The Bennett sisters may not have all gotten along, but they had each other. Being an only child was so rare in the Amish community, and she had no one to share Sister Day with. And she no longer had a natural *mamm.* Even though Mrs. Bennett wasn't the ideal mother, she was there for her daughters.

As Lizzie's heart sank into self-pity, fear overtook it stronger. Was self-pity something that grew like cancer? She'd been battling self-pity over not being pregnant yet, and now as sisters got together for special Sister Day activities, she felt sorry for herself. But she had Granny for a *mamm*, being that she was now married to her son.

Thank you, Lord, for Granny, who is like a mamm to me. Thank you that I may not have physical sisters, but I have close friends at the knitting circle. God give me grace to not sink into self-pity, but let me see all the blessings all around me.

~*~

Granny cut into the milk chocolate bars that were left over from Lavina's wedding, thankful she didn't have to bake today as she felt the change in weather in her bones. *Getting as old as dirt,* she thought. Jack barked in the driveway, but the noise did not compare to the high pitched yap of Beatrix. Poor little thing was afraid of people, never being able to trust anyone.

She bent down to scoop up the black and brown Pomeranian and nuzzled her nose against its soft fur. "No one's going to hurt you," Granny said, trying to sooth the creature, but when the door opened, and Fannie and Mona appeared, the dog's heart raced so, that Granny gently rocked the dog like a *boppli*. "It's alright, Bea. Hush, now. *Shh.* "

Fannie tip-toed over to the dog. "Hi, Bea. Remember me?" She put out her hands. "Can I hold her?"

"Not now. Her heart's fluttering faster than hummingbird wings."

"Aw, poor little thing." Fannie pat the top of Bea's head. "You just need to learn how to be loved." She looked up at Granny and smiled. "We humans do, too."

A *humph* echoed around the room, and Granny slowly looked over at its source: Mona. The woman stood like a frozen snowman beside the door, not making an attempt to take off her cape and hang it on the peg board.

"You must be cold. I have hot chocolate simmering on the stove, and brownies on the table."

Still no movement and Mona's glare seemed to bore a hole through Granny's soul. How she loved this knitting circle, but would she have to tell people not to come back if they didn't bring harmony to the circle? "Mona. Did you hear what I said?"

"*Jah*, I did. But I'm used to being welcomed into someone's home, not ignored…"

Granny shifted Bea's weight so the toy dog lay against her and she pat the dog's back, trying to calm herself.

"Are you burping that dog, Deborah?"

"What?"

Fannie put both hands up. "*Mamm*, Granny loves animals and can give the dog a bottle if she wants."

"Well," Mona sniffed, indignant. "God gave animals fur so they could stay outside, where they belong." Granny took a deep breath, not knowing if what she was about to say would only provoke more criticism.

"All things bright and beautiful,
All creatures great and small,
All things wise and wonderful:
The Lord God made them all.

"Mona, don't you remember singing that as a *kinner*?"

Mona whirled off her cape and plunked it on the hook. "*Jah*, but I'm a grown woman now."

"And how does it feel?"

Mona gawked. "What? Being a grown woman?"

Granny knew her brows were furrowing into one grand frown, so she raised them. "My *grandkinner* are cheerful. And the Bible says to be childlike in spirit." She stroked Bea's back. "Actually, they gave me the idea of taking Bea. They have a pet rabbit that they keep *inside*."

"I know. It's ridiculous." Mona pursed her lips and glared as if challenging Granny.

"Well, the rabbit would die if they let it outside. Has never learned to hunt or defend itself, since it was raised in a pet shop." Granny wanted to scream, *What we do is none of your business. Why are you so disagreeable a woman?* But she bit her lip and decided to talk to Jeb about this new predicament: having someone in her knitting circle that made her so nervous, knitting couldn't even calm her down.

The door opened again and Marge and Maryann let in a cold chill. Marge immediately clasped her hands without saying hello. "How's Bea? Can I hold her?"

Granny shook her head. "She's nervous and she'll be staying in my room. I best put her down now."

"You sound like her *mamm*," Maryann snickered. "I think it's cute."

Granny just couldn't resist looking at Mona's reaction. Another Amish woman was putting her stamp of approval on having an indoor pet. Mona rolled her eyes, and Granny walked out of the kitchen into the living room, stifling a chuckle as she buried her face in Bea's fur. She opened the door to her bedroom, happy that Jeb had decided to move it to her quilting room. The craft room that doubled as a bedroom for Nathan, her nephew. She was ever so thankful that he lived right down the road, with his new wife, Lavina.

Granny placed Bea in the new checkered bed she bought at Punxsy-Mart, then turned to leave, but ran right into Fannie.

Fannie lowered her gaze. "I'm sorry for my *mamm's* behavior."

Granny slipped her arm through Fannie's. "*Ach*. It was nothing."

"*Jah*, it was. She's getting worse."

"It's not your fault. Makes me appreciate *yinz* all the more, since you're a burst of sunshine."

The two came into the living room, smiling, and Granny asked everyone to help themselves to dessert. Janice was at the door, along with Ruth, Suzy, and Colleen. *Too big for one circle.* If Lavina came next week, it would make ten women. Truth be told, Granny didn't like quilting bees since so many women were crammed in one room, and gossip seemed to prevail. No, she liked the one-on-one closeness, and being like a granny to all the girls. Would Suzy understand?

Janice raised a book above her head. "Who all finished the book?"

Several hands were raised and Janice seemed defeated. "I'll admit, I didn't have time, but I've seen the movie."

"Me, too," Suzy squealed. "All of them."

"What do you mean, all of them?" Granny asked.

Suzy put her knitting bag next to a chair and sat down. "I think there are four versions. Not sure. But none of them compare to the book. You really get inside someone's head in a book."

"I agree," Lizzie said. "I don't go to movies, but I did cleaning in an English home ages ago, and something was missing. *Pride and Prejudice* made me... happy and sad at the same time."

Suzy stood up. "I think our new knit-lit group has started as Lizzie is about to share what she got out of the book." The women all took a seat that formed a circle. "Go on, Lizzie. You can all just knit scarves with the yarn you have. Homeless people can use them for hats, too."

The women got out their knitting and then looked at Lizzie. "Go on," Marge encouraged Lizzie.

"Well, the book made me realize how important a *mamm* is. Since I lost mine while courting Roman, I see her guidance could have saved me a lot of pain."

All the women leaned forward, eager for more information.

"You see, Roman and I were courting since we were very young. But when the assault happened, I had no woman to talk to."

Granny's eyes blurred. How she wished Lizzie would have come to her.

"What are you talking about?" Marge asked. "Did someone hurt you?"

"*Jah.* A hunter came by and saved me before, well, any damage was done." She lowered her head. "I felt so ashamed, I couldn't tell Roman, so I left a message in our woodpecker hole. But he didn't find it, and I needed time alone, so I thought. But time alone wasn't *goot*, and I became bitter." She raised her head. "It's not *goot* to be alone when you're in pain. That's why God says to carry each other's burdens. If you're in pain, open up to someone. Anyone. Someone in this group. We've all been through hard times."

Granny couldn't contain herself. So proud of Lizzie, who was hurt, but now trying to help others who were hurting. And how she loved Roman and his girls, forgiving Roman for being so proud, feeling spurned, and marrying someone he hardly knew. What the English called a rebound. But Abigail was like the scent of springtime, and like spring, her life was too short. But she left Roman three *kinner*....

"*Mamm*, are you alright?" Lizzie asked, breaking into her thoughts.

"*Jah*, I am. And Lizzie is right. We started this knitting circle last year. I was spinning wool and noticed how strong the new yarn was. Could hardly break it. And I thought of different women in my *Gmay*, I mean church. Women who needed to be built up by other women." She looked over at Maryann. "Women who I didn't know needed help, but the Lord did."

Maryann's eyes mellowed, tears pooling. "God knew I needed help to get through cancer." She turned to Marge. "He went before me in the most surprising way. Granny and I met Marge in the waiting room of the Indiana Hospital. She's a traveling nurse, just what I needed."

Marge leaned towards Maryann, who sat next to her on the bench. "And I got to see people have a real faith in God, and started to go to church again." She looked over at Janice. "And Janice was so transparent and real, Joe and I saw a real God working in her life. In all of your lives, and I rededicated my heart to him." She leaned again towards Maryann. "So you helped me as much as I did you."

Suzy smiled as a tear slid down her cheek. "We're supposed to be talking about *Pride and Prejudice*. Anyone else want to share what they got out of it?"

Ruth cleared her throat. "Last year, my marriage was not *goot*, and I couldn't read any book with happy couples. But when Elizabeth and Mr. Darcy got married, I was thrilled. And it made me realize my heart, my marriage, is healed."

The women "awed" in unison.

Ruth grinned. "I got something else out of the book, too. But you'll all laugh."

"We will not," Granny said, as a warning to the girls.

"Well, the letters written by Mr. Darcy to Elizabeth." She picked up her book that was on her lap. "I put a bookmark in the spot." She opened the book and read:

"In vain I have struggled. It will not do. My feelings will not be repressed. You must allow me to tell you how ardently I admire and love you."

Ruth put the book to her chest. "I love that, and started to write love letters to Luke."

Silence. All eyes remained on Ruth. No needles tapped against each other.

Granny could see Ruth become uncomfortable, and she knew why the women stared. "*Ach*, Ruth, I've read *Pride and Prejudice* several times, and never thought of writing such a letter to Jeb."

Maryann nodded. "I'm going to write one to Michael tonight."

"Me too," Fannie blurted. "I need to tell Melvin how much I ardently admire him."

Marge's giggle made her body jiggle. "There you go again. Talking like someone in a Jane Austen book."

Mona sat up straight. "Fannie always gets carried away."

The joyful fellowship in the room just had cold water thrown on it, and Granny's stomach tightened. Why did Mona seem to take delight in belittling Fannie? She put down her knitting. "I know what I got out of the book," she said, looking across the room at Mona. "Mrs. Bennett had her favorite daughters. I'm sure if she put as much love and attention towards Mary, she would have turned out to be a happier woman. Words can build up or tear down."

Mona didn't flinch. "What are you saying, Deborah."

Granny looked around the room. "All you girls understood my meaning, *jah*?"

"I sure do," Janice raised her hand. "Like most of you know, my tongue was like a sword towards Jerry. I was hurt and feeling neglected, since he was finishing his doctorate. And all along, he was doing it for me, so we could move back down South. Like the saying goes, 'hurt people, hurt people.'"

"What?" several women asked.

"When you're hurting, you tend to hurt others. Misery loves company."

Granny looked over at Mona. Was it her imagination, or had her stone-chiseled countenance softened? Was she cracking, becoming broken, that led to healing? *Lord forgive me for being so abrupt and spiteful, but I love Fannie so. Help me with this woman.*

Suzy continued to knit, but didn't need to look down, being an accomplished knitter. She looked over at Colleen. "You're being quiet. What did you get out of the book?"

Colleen's amber eyes seemed troubled. "It was hard for me. I know this sounds vain, but I saw the movie at the theatre. All the beautiful gowns made me realize I won't have a wedding dress. Is that so wrong?"

Suzy looked over at Granny for help. "When Jeb and I married, I have to admit, Jackie Kennedy wore the nicest clothes, and I dreamt of wearing an outfit like hers on my wedding day."

"How did you see Jackie Kennedy? In a magazine?"

"In the newspapers. Her husband was killed a month before Jeb and I started to officially court. And lots of folks back then didn't have televisions and thirty or so people went to a house to watch the funeral." Granny sighed. "And I saw her and her small *kinner.*"

"Wasn't she dressed in all black?" Janice asked.

"*Jah*, she was. But, when I could get my hands on a magazine, I did." She looked over at Fannie. "And I compared myself with her beauty, wanting to look like her, and dress like her."

Fannie nodded. "That's why you were so against me looking at those glamour magazines like I did?"

"*Jah*. But I'm telling you this to help Colleen." Granny turned to the girl with honey-blonde hair who she took a liking to when they first met. "It's okay to think about nice clothes, but what's really important in a marriage?"

"The Bennett girls had inner beauty, and that captured the hearts of Mr. Darcy and Mr. Bingley," Fannie said. She turned to Marge. "Their inner beauty *secured* them."

Marge laughed. "Oh, I miss it up here. I always see what's important. Lavina's wedding didn't have a fancy gown, but they all start to look the same, anyhow. White, cream, ivory. And all the focus of the wedding was on God. Can't beat that. He's the one who holds the marriage together."

"But, no kissing after the vows?" Colleen exclaimed.

Lizzie scrunched her lips to one side. "Plenty of time for that after the wedding."

Granny chuckled. "And don't believe every Amish proverb you hear. Kissing does not wear out, and I'm seventy."

Colleen's eyes grew round. "What?"

Granny waved a hand like she was shooing a fly. "*Ach*, people say, 'Kissing wears out, cooking don't', but it's not true. I'll need kisses from Jeb until the day I die."

Laughter bounced around the room... all except Mona, who had her nose in her knitting. And Granny wondered what it was that hurt Mona. Was she in an unhappy marriage, or did her constant dripping make her husband spend too much time at work and choring?

~*~

Roman cut the cherry pie that Lizzie had made for the girls upon arriving home from school. She'd miss meeting them, being over at knitting circle, and once again, Roman had a hard time containing the love he had for his wife. She was a *mamm* to his *kinner*, but he prayed the Lord would open her womb and give her a boy. He never said this out loud to anyone, but just the thought of having a son follow him around the rocker shop, learning a trade, warmed his heart.

The UPS truck came barreling down the driveway, and he wanted to go out and shout at the man. Didn't he see all the buggies over at his *mamm*'s? The tree house and tire swing for the girls? Obviously, there were *kinner* and people about. No sooner had the truck come to a stop, the driver ran up the steps, threw a package next to the door, and was off.

Roman cringed. He'd have words with that new driver. The other driver had a good relationship with him, helping Roman ship his rockers across the country. He retrieved the package and it read *Amazon*. Roman chuckled at the thought of his parents thinking Suzy was ordering books from Central America, afraid she was paying extra shipping and not telling them.

But the package was addressed to Jenny Weaver? He called his oldest daughter over. "Looks like something came for you."

Her blonde braids sprang up and down as she bounced over to her *daed*. "I think Joe sent me another book on rabbits. Wish they hadn't moved..."

"You can go over and see Marge when the circle's over. Open your present so you can thank her."

Jenny ripped open the box and out slid two books, both entitled *Little Women*. "*Mamm* said I could read what the circle was reading if it was for little girls. Look, *Daed*. This one has pictures and not so many words, and this one has no pictures. The one with pictures is for me."

Roman laughed. "Calm down, Jenny. I'm sure your *mamm* has a plan to include Millie and Tillie."

"But they're only six, and can't read big words like me....now that I'm eight."

Roman stifled another laugh. "Well, maybe you can read it to the twins. Or me. I like a *goot* bedtime story."

Jenny leaned on her tip-toes and kissed her *daed* on his auburn beard. "*Daed*, I love *mamm* so. She does such nice things for us. But she looks sad at times."

"She has a lot on her mind. With her *daed* living next door in the *dawdyhaus*, well, she frets over him. "

"*Opa* Jonas is lonely since Amish camp is over." Her eyes grew round. "I could read to *Opa* Jonas."

"*Jah*, you could. He's in pain from arthritis or MS. Don't know which ones causing it, but your *mamm* feels his pain in her heart. So, help lift her heart by helping *Opa* Jonas."

Jenny scrunched her mouth to one side. "I have an idea…"

~*~

The women gawked at Suzy when she announced the next book would be *Little Women*. As she passed out copies, an awkward silence once again filled the room. Suzy, being used to teaching said, "Okay. Spill the beans."

Janice groaned. "It's a children's book."

"Have you ever read it?" Suzy asked.

Janice flipped through the pages. "Hey, it's over three hundred pages."

"Trust me," Suzy said. "It's the unabridged version. And the lessons learned in this book are... profound."

"I can't read a three-hundred-page book in a week," Ruth said. "I'm helping again with the Audubon bird count."

"And I'm busy with the store," Fannie gasped. "Melvin's clock sales are *goot* now since the English are starting to buy Christmas presents."

"It's November," Mona groaned. "I think it's ridiculous."

Fannie bit her lower lip, and then said, "We depend on the English for sales. Packaging them up is time consuming since we're shipping them out now. Just the wall clocks..."

"How do you advertise?" Janice asked.

Fannie looked over at Marge for help and soon found it. "Joe started posting Melvin's clocks on EBay. We get a percentage of the sale for his time."

"We're not supposed to use the internet," Mona pounced.

"You buy from those catalogs that come in the mail. What's the difference?"

Fannie's face was beet red, and Granny once again had to nod her head and pray for Mona. It was hard to be angry with someone she prayed for. "Suzy, can we have a few weeks to read this book? Maybe we can have Bible reading for next week and discuss it, but I'm not a fast reader." She looked down at her yarn and began to knit again. "And we need to talk about how big this circle is. When Lavina comes, we'll have ten."

"The more the merrier," Marge said with glee.

Everyone in the room nodded in agreement, and Granny's heart sank. How could she have more intimate talks the girls always appreciated, with so many girls? *Pie baking days.* The idea popped into her head, calming her heart. She'd met with Colleen and Lavina every week to make pies. With Jeb being busy with ministerial duties on Thursday, she could ask girls to bake on Thursdays.

Suzy stood up again. "How about we read a few chapters of the Gospel of John for next week, and meet at two. With daylight savings time, it gets dark at five, and I don't want anyone driving home in the dark when the snow flies."

"The Amish don't turn their clocks back," Janice said. "They don't follow all our silly rules."

"*Jah*, we do," Fannie said. "We have a clock set for English time, and another for Amish time. Our store hours are written on the door in English time."

Suzy shook her head. "I want to meet at one, English time, if that's alright. Then we can leave at three o'clock and get supper on. Everyone in agreement, raise your hands."

Granny had been to classes at Suzy's and marveled at how she commanded the classes with order, yet love. She raised her hand, as did all the women. She looked over at Colleen who seemed out of sorts… and went over to see if she could come over and help make pies for Forget-Me-Not Manor, the home for single mothers. The place where Colleen lived until she found out she had Amish roots right here in Smicksburg….and an Amish man she planned to marry. But something was amiss.

~*~

That night, Granny felt something lick her cheek, and she turned to see Bea, wiggling and giggling. It was time to take her out to be relieved. As much as Granny didn't want to get out from under the warm quilt, this dog never seemed a burden, since she loved her, maybe a little too much. She quickly put on her robe and slippers and went to the side door where Bea's leash hung from the pegboard.

Ice. Overnight, a misty rain covered everything with a thin coat of shiny ice. As the full moon made the reflections off the silhouette of trees in the yard, Granny stood in awe at the beauty. *What will heaven be like, if earth can be this glorious?*

Heaven. A place she and Jeb would mostly likely be in the not too distant future, but it was more natural a feeling than she thought. Truth be told, she yearned for it at times, but as long as the Good Lord gave her health, she'd be His hands and feet to a needy world.

And her mind turned to the girls in her circle and landed on Maryann. Was it her imagination, or was Maryann too pale, again? *Was* she cancer-free? It was exactly one year since her suspicions about Maryann's health surfaced, so was it just the weather and season that was playing on her mind? Granny would have to have her over to bake pies as well, maybe next week. Then she'd ask Maryann if she was taking the strengthening herbs Dan sold from his herb shop, and if she was keeping up with all her check-ups. Mothers always put their *kinner* first, and since Maryann had eight.... Well, for now, she'd just cast Maryann on God, and get back to a good night's sleep.

~*~

The next morning, Lizzie got up extra early to make a peach pie for the girls. They would be surprised, but what she had in store would pale in comparison. She lit an oil lamp to illuminate the kitchen, and quickly got a fire going in her cook stove. Then she got out her mixing bowl. The look on the girls' faces kept her moving as she quickly measured flour, salt, water, and butter and combined them to make her pastry dough.

Lizzie dusted the counter with flour and took half the dough to roll out. The other half would be the top. When she was finished, having put her canned peaches into the pie and topping it with a crust, she popped it into the oven, and then made coffee.

As it percolated in the coffee pot, the aroma itself seemed to make Lizzie wake up. She went to sit in a rocker in the living room for her morning devotions, but heard footsteps ascending the steps. Roman's footsteps.

His disheveled auburn hair got all the more scattered as he came over to her, scratching his head. "What's wrong? Why up so early?"

Lizzie held the Bible to her heart. "I have a surprise for the girls today."

He rubbed his eyes. "What?"

"We're celebrating Sister Day today. I have it all planned out."

"They have school. Why today?"

"Marge is off today to drive us. And we're going to an alpaca farm she knows about. Then out to lunch."

"What will Marge do the whole time?"

"Be my sister."

Roman lowered himself slowly into a chair opposite her. "Come again? I don't understand."

"I've been struggling with not having a sister to go out and celebrate with, and I just love Marge. The girls adore her, so we made plans."

Roman leaned forward and took her hands. "Lizzie, Marge is not Amish. Do you think you should be so close with an outsider?"

Lizzie knew Roman wasn't a demanding husband, never overbearing like some. She squeezed his hands. "If I'm tempted with English ways, I'll soon find out, and won't be... asking her to be like a sister."

Roman got up and pulled her out of her rocker, and embraced her tenderly. "Seems like that book you read has unsettled you."

"It opened my eyes to things lacking. I miss my *mamm* something awful."

"How does that book help?"

"The book's about a *mamm* with five daughters, so when reading it, I realized how much I miss not having her around. Discontentment floods me, but it's good for me."

Roman stroked her long brown hair. "How can that be *goot*?"

"It's like the refiners fire. The dross in my heart comes to the surface, and I see it for what it is, and let God skim it off."

"Making purer gold. I see." He cupped her cheeks in his hands and kissed her. "We're all in need of refining, but you're perfect to me."

Lizzie reveled in the love her husband had for her. It sunk deep into her soul, and she never tired of it. He kissed her again, and kissing was something she never got tired of either. Some women have sisters, but not so happy a marriage. She had Roman; could his love fill the cracks in her heart? As they continued to show deep love to each other, she started to think he could.

~*~

After sprinkling white flour on her kitchen counter, Granny took a quarter of the pastry dough from her stainless steel bowl, and plopped it down to roll out. From the corner of her eye, she could see Colleen was doing the same: making pies side by side... but miles apart. "Colleen, what ails you?"

Colleen rolled the dough out into a perfect circle, having been taught how to bake a pie from Granny all summer. "I don't know. Sometimes I think..."

"What?"

"I should have gone to pastry school, like I'd planned."

"But I can teach you anything those schools teach."

"Not fondant. Something I always wanted on my wedding cake..."

"What's fondant?" Granny asked, rolling her dough until it was too thin.

"It's icing that's like dough in a way. You roll it up and place it over the cake. It looks so elegant, but I'm sure I'm not supposed to think about anything... fancy."

The tone in Colleen's voice Granny knew well. It was the sound of being trapped into dead rules that didn't make sense. How Granny had had it out with other Amish women so legalistic with their rules that choked out love, joy and peace. She glanced over at Colleen. "Nothing's wrong with icing like that. I'd like to learn."

Colleen paused and she looked over at Granny. "Seriously?"

"Isn't there a cookbook for it? I mean, if I get a recipe, I'm sure I can figure it out."

Colleen held her head with one flour covered hand. "A fondant cake might look out of place with everything so plain around it." After wiping her hands on a tea towel, she went to Granny's oak table, and slowly sat down. "Granny, did the Amish wear plain clothes in the time of Jane Austen?"

Granny took her blue speckle ware teapot and filled it with water. "Well, I don't know. She was poor, and I suppose she wore whatever she could sew, like we do. And she was looked down on by rich folk."

Colleen leaned her head on one elbow and slouched. "I know it's vain, but I wanted to wear a long white gown on my wedding day. But it's not going to happen."

"But it's only one day, Colleen. Don't set your mind on trifles." Granny got up and took some cookies out of her cookie jar and placed them on the table.

"Is that an Amish proverb? If it is, it doesn't make sense." Colleen grabbed a cookie and took a bite.

"*Nee*, not a proverb, only old age speaking. With age comes wisdom, *jah*?" She chuckled. "And good books." Granny bit into a milk chocolate square. "Jeb reads as much as me now, since Jonas moved next door. Jonas reads really deep books on theology and has Jeb reading one by Brother Lawrence. A Catholic."

Colleen gasped. "Not a Protestant?"

"Weren't any Protestants in Lawrence's time. Anyhow, I'm getting sidetracked. This man wrote *The Practice of the Presence of God.* Lawrence was a monk who peeled potatoes and scrubbed floors, but folks were amazed by him, since he always seemed to show the fruits of the spirit all the time."

Colleen nodded, eager for Granny to go on.

"So people asked him his secret, and he wrote the book. He was elderly, full of wisdom," Granny winked, "and after reflecting over life, said that he feared trifles. You see, trifles are things that really don't matter. They're little things that make us stumble…."

"Like a wedding dress?"

"*Jah*, Colleen. It's only one day. Would your love for Hezekiah be sacrificed because for one day you didn't have a fancy dress?"

"Okay, I'm afraid I'll lose myself if I turn Amish."

"How so?"

"Well, I like fairytales, but they're forbidden by the Amish. I grew up on them…."

Granny swatted the air. "A trifle. You can read other things."

Colleen groaned. "What if the Ordnung said we could only read the Bible and no other books? Don't you ever fear that?"

Granny eyes mellowed. "*Ach*, you don't understand, do you? The *Ordnung* changes very slowly, when all are in agreement. We change at Easter, and won't even celebrate the holiday if we're not in agreement. Unity means more than anything, and love is what rules."

Colleen bit her lower lip. "Not sure I understand."

Granny rubbed the back of her neck. "Last year Jonas wanted a closed-in buggy, due to his MS and arthritis. But we Amish move as one, so after the Bishop said we couldn't have them, due to expense, he told Jonas he'd have an English driver all winter, and the *gmay* would pay for it."

Colleen's eyebrows flew up. "Wow, that's amazing."

Granny felt tears sting her eyes, so she turned to make tea. "Colleen, the older I get, and the more I see how the world changes, I feel ever so blessed to be Amish. I shudder to think I almost left."

Silence filled the room, only the sound of hot water being poured into mugs.

"Granny…?"

She could sense the question. "*Jah*, when the clothes drier became popular, the Mennonites had them, and I wanted one, too. Now I see it was a trifle. "

"But you spend so much time washing clothes. I don't think it's a trifle."

"Compared to the blessings I now enjoy being Amish, *jah*, it is a trifle." Granny turned and put two mugs on the table. "I made yours black, just how you like it." Granny saw the bewilderment in Colleen's eyes, and wondered how to explain what she meant. What Colleen needed to learn. She stared at the bowl of apples on the table, and slowly looked up. "Colleen, if you had to choose right now to have an apple or land to have an apple orchard, what would you pick?"

"What?"

"Just answer the question. Pretend you've been on a diet of cornmeal mush, with a tad of bacon, and you're hungry. Would you pick an apple to eat, or land to grow an orchard?"

Colleen took a deep breath. "Well, I like cornmeal and bacon, so I'd just take the land and make an orchard."

"But orchards take time, lots of patience and hard work."

"But I'd have lots of apples in the end."

Granny tapped the table with her fingers. "Do you see the connection?"

Colleen groaned again. "No."

Granny reached for her hand and squeezed it. "One apple will satisfy you for a minute or two. It's a trifle. But having an orchard takes years and you'll have good and bad times while growing it. An orchard isn't a trifle, some fleeting whim or passion."

Colleen squeezed Granny's hand. "I understand. A wedding dress is one day, like you said, an orchard is a long commitment, like marriage."

"Well, *jah*. You can fill your life with things that don't really matter that come easy, is what I meant, but marriage is like an orchard. You have dry times, harvest, planting again. *Ach*, Colleen, I didn't even see that."

"Granny, maybe it's why you like Jane Austen so much. One thing I won't be missing is sappy love stories I used to read. They fall in love on the first page and live happily after ever."

Granny grinned. "Like a fairytale?"

Colleen got up and ran around the table, hugging Granny from behind. "I'm so glad I have you. I feel so much better."

~*~

Granny was exhausted after Colleen left, and needed to rest her eyes before preparing the noon meal for Jeb. So, she went into her bedroom with some knitting in hand, knowing it relaxed her and she'd soon be asleep in her rocker.

She took the black yarn she'd spun from her black sheep, and started to make Jeb his special scarf for the months ahead, that would be freezing. Granny felt so full in her heart. Helping resolve some of Colleen's problems did her heart good. To help carry another's burden was a blessing not everyone knew about.

The image of Mona flashed before her. That woman did not know one was more blessed to give than receive. How many times had Mona stayed in her room while Fannie and Eliza put up half the harvest? And her poor husband, how could he live with such a woman?

Forgive me Lord. I need to recondition my mind about Mona. I do pray that when she reads Little Women, she'll see how wonderful a mamm the girls have; a selfless woman who puts others first.

And Lord, once again, I cast Maryann on you. I don't know why the fear of her cancer coming back keeps gnawing at me. I give all my knitting friends to you, Lord, for you care for them all.

In Jesus name,

Amen.

Dear Readers,

Thank you for joining Granny and her girls for their new knit lit circle. I leave my dear readers with a recipe for milk chocolate bars. Enjoy!

Milk Chocolate Bars

1 c. brown sugar
½ c. butter
½ c. milk
1 tsp. baking powder
2 eggs, beaten
1 ½ c. flour
1 tsp. salt
½ tsp. soda
1 pkg. chocolate chips
1 c. nuts

Mix all ingredients and bake at 350 degrees for twenty-five minutes.

EPISODE 2

◠◠◠◠◠

Little Women

Little Bea jumped up on Granny's lap and licked her face. "*Nee,* you sit on your little rug." She pointed to the rag rug she'd picked up at Emma Miller's Quilt Shop. If anyone knew it was for her little dog, she'd never hear the end of it. It was just an extra rug to scatter over the hardwood floors that grew cold in the winter, she convinced herself.

Bea put her bushy black tail between her legs and slowly made her way over to the blue rug.

"*Ach,* Deborah. She's afraid," Jeb said, getting up to retrieve the dog.

"She needs to learn her manners. Let her be."

Jeb leaned over the little black Pomeranian and pet her head. "Daed's got a treat for you later…"

Granny rolled her eyes and hoped Jeb would never slip and say such a thing when folks visited. Having a dog call you "*daed*". Ridiculous. But then, she had rocked the dog like a *mamm* would…

Jeb returned to the table and took a sip of coffee. "So, what are you doing today, besides having the circle?"

"Well, I'm volunteering at the Baptist Church, so we're having knitting at four o'clock today." Granny took a bite of oatmeal, but was shaken when Jeb started to cough….or choke? She sprang to her feet and slapped his back. "Jeb, you okay?"

After a coughing fit that seemed to last forever to Granny, Jeb sputtered, "You're getting involved in the Baptist Church? I must draw a line."

"*Ach*, Jeb. I'm not going to one of their Bible studies, although I hear Jerry preaches mighty *goot*. Don't you know what tomorrow is?"

"Thursday. I'm not daft, and Wednesday is the day the Baptist have their Bible study." He jabbed at his oatmeal. "Deborah, I just won't have it."

"Tomorrow's Thanksgiving, you old fool. And the Baptists are having a dinner for the needy at noon."

Jeb's eyes mellowed a bit. "Why not have it tomorrow?"

"So the families running it can eat Thanksgiving dinner with their own families."

Jeb pulled at his long gray beard. "Needy people around Smicksburg? I don't see any homeless here."

"Well, they're not homeless, but have fallen on such hard times, affording a nice turkey dinner is just too much for some."

Jeb gawked. "Really? We eat beef almost every night and chicken's like second best. *Ach*, I didn't know." He looked over at Bea. "We took in a starving dog, but never thought folks around here were hungry."

"And they don't have the support we have in the Amish community. Jerry and Janice do a fine job though, helping people whether they're Baptist or not."

Jeb put his spoon down. "What's that supposed to mean?"

"Just what I said. The Baptist help people —"

"It's your tone of voice. You're implying the Amish should be helping people outside our *Gmay*…"

"*Jah*, I am. "

The woodpecker who made its home at Granny's suet feeder tapped outside, out of sync with the pendulum clock.

"We give money to Christian Aid in Berlin, Ohio. And that money goes far. Have you read the latest newsletter, about how they helped the Hurricane Sandy victims?"

"*Ach*, Jeb, you're right. You write out the checks, so I forget at times that we are doing our part. But, there's other ways to help."

"How?"

"Well, do you know the English don't know how to do basic things to save money, like making sausage with a meat grinder? They pay top dollar at Punxsy-Mart for meat that's not even *goot* for them, not realizing they're wasting money."

"Why isn't the meat *goot*? Do they sell bad meat?"

"Well, Marge and Joe were surprised when they had their turkeys slaughtered, saying they didn't taste like chemicals. They'd never eaten organic meat before. So I was thinking that we could feed an extra beef cow all winter, and share it. Maybe even teach the men how to make jerky."

Jeb's eyes lit up. "I could show them the smoke house when the weather gets better. Teach them how to buy a pig at the auction to make hams." He took Granny's hand and kissed it. "You've got a heart big enough for two people. *Danki*."

The side door blew open and Jenny appeared, her nose red from the cold air. "*Oma*. I can't wait to go to go to the Baptist Church today and help. I'll be like one of the March girls in Little Women."

Granny's heart melted as her eight year old granddaughter said these words. The book Lizzie bought her, age appropriate, was bringing the best out in Jenny, just like good literature was supposed to do.

"A March girl?" Jeb teased. "Does she march?"

"*Nee, Opa*." Jenny giggled. "It's their last name in the book." She twirled around. "It's one of the best book's I've read. The March family almost seemed Amish."

"How so?" Granny asked.

Jenny came to the table and took a seat next to Jeb. "Well, they sewed their own clothes, made most of their food, rode on horses, and didn't have electricity. Lots of things."

Jeb patted her shoulder. "It's how people have been living for a long time. We haven't changed, the English have. People have never had so many conveniences. "

Jenny tilted her head to one side, as if deep in thought. "So why aren't people happy? The English have one face at Punxsy-Mart. It looks like this." Jenny furrowed her eyebrows and scrunched her lips.

Granny nodded. "They look anxious, Jenny. *Jah*, I know. Maybe all the modern things have taken them from the land and nature and make them nervous. That's what I think."

"Me too. And it's why I'm excited to go help today. *Mamm's* made so many mashed potatoes; my *daed's* going to have to help her load the buggy."

"Is there room for me?" Granny gasped, in an exaggerated tone, teasing Jenny.

Jenny got up and put her arm around Granny's neck. "We'll all squeeze in real tight. I love you *Oma*."

"And I love you."

~*~

Colleen admired the way Hezekiah could parallel park a horse and buggy. "I can't do this with a car." She leaned her head on his shoulder. "Are you sure you don't mind?"

"*Nee*. You go ahead on in. I'll walk up the road to see the smithy."

"Okay." She kissed his cheek and made her way out of the buggy, a thrill shooting through her heart to go shopping at Suzy's. Being able to buy colorful wool yarn to crochet rugs for her grandma's shop was the perfect solution to her feelings of…suffocation. But, the things she was learning to let go of to become Amish and marry Hezekiah were mere trifles, like Granny had told her. Colleen even had a trifle box given to her that Jeb made. Every little thing that didn't really matter in the long run, was a trifle and when she was upset about it, she'd write it on a scrap of paper, then stuff it in the little box. In a few days, she'd read her trifles, and they were all impulses, every one. Or worse yet, complaints. No, she would not let her life be run on impulses ever again.

When Colleen entered the shop the little bell rang as usual, adding charm to the shop. Suzy was at her desk, talking on the phone, so intent on her conversation, she almost didn't look up. But she did, and flashed Colleen a forced smile.

Lord, I cast Suzy on you. Something isn't right. Not only had she learned how to make fancy cake fondant with Granny over the past weeks, but also how to cast her cares on God, as soon as they came. She looked around at all the vibrant colors and was immediately drawn to the deep crimson chunky wool.

Colleen took the yarn off the shelf and looked at the price. Fair enough, knowing that it was real wool from a real sheep. And like Suzy always said, Life was too short to knit with cheap yarn. Colleen jumped when she heard the phone slam down. She twirled around to see Suzy, whose face was flushed. "What's wrong?"

Suzy pursed her lips and closed her eyes, and Colleen knew she was counting to ten mentally. When done she said very calmly, "Nothing's wrong. What makes you think something's wrong?"

Colleen made her way over to the desk. "You slammed the phone down."

"No. I dropped it." She wiped the sweat from her face. "I've been dying wool in the kitchen and am exhausted. Closing the shop tomorrow, so working double-time."

"Are you still volunteering over at the church dinner?"

"Dave is, but I need to keep at it here. " She sighed. "Sometimes I feel like Marmee in Little Women. People always calling me out, but I just don't have the time."

"But you just said you were staying here." Colleen looked into Suzy's eyes for her meaning, but found none.

Suzy got out the next knitting project she was on, having to knit every item in the store, and began to knit. "We have a shut-in list at the church. I'm one of the contact people. And someone just called to see if I could be assigned to a woman. "She shifted in her chair. "I am one person, and I simply said I could not get out today. She lives two miles out of town, and there's a chance of an ice storm. So, I simply said no…" Suzy looked up at Colleen distressed. "But I know Mrs. March would be going…"

Colleen took a seat by the desk. "Mrs. March isn't a real person."

"No, Louisa May Alcott wrote about her own mother when creating Mrs. March. Her mom was real, though."
Colleen fidgeted with the yarn in her hands. "Well, romanticized a bit though."

Suzy tried to conceal a grin, but couldn't, and smiled. "How'd you get so smart? Is it those baptism classes you're taking with Jeb?"

Colleen shook her head. "I'm like you. When we read Pride and Prejudice, it took me a week to get over not having a wedding gown. Reading makes you think, and sift through what's really important."

Suzy giggled. "Okay, it's not Jeb you're spending time with, it's Granny. She uses baking terms at times to get her point across."

"What?"

"Sifting. You said sifting through what's important."

Colleen knew she was changing from spending time with Granny and beamed. "Well, like I was saying, the more I read books, classic old books, I see how far we've gone away from normal. Look how simple Meg's wedding was? Aunt March was appalled, and I found myself laughing at her. Her big old house and fine furniture didn't make her very happy, either..."

"Like so many people losing their big homes. Their American Dream..." Suzy grabbed her phone off the receiver but put it back again. "It makes me so angry."

Colleen had only seen Suzy calm and steady and didn't know what to say. "Suzy, what's really wrong?"

Again, Suzy closed her eyes a few seconds and then exhaled audibly. "The new shut-in on the list. She's always put her nose up at Dave and me, living on top of our store. She's loaded, and used to come in and buy lots of yarn, but I'd rather have pleasant customers."

"So why is she on the shut-in list?"

"When her husband died a few years back, she developed agoraphobia. Now I am supposed to visit... Lord, help me!"

Colleen shook her head. "So, she's a rich snob who looked down on you, like Mrs. March and her girls were looked down on, right?"

Suzy slowly made eye contact with Colleen. "Exactly. Something about Mrs. March has gotten to me. She's too perfect and I am, 'hopelessly flawed'."

Colleen burst into laughter at Suzy's dramatics. "Everyone is. No one's perfect. " She got up and grabbed more of the crimson wool from the shelf. "Hezekiah will be here to pick me up any minute. How about you give me the lady's address and I can go see her."

"In your buggy?"

Colleen groaned. "I forgot. Will I ever be able to live without a car?" She set the yarn on the desk as Suzy wrote out her bill. "Agoraphobia is afraid of going out of your house, right?"

"Yes. I don't get it. The woman was the town gossip, and now she can't even get her own mail. Depended on her husband too much, I suppose." Suzy moaned. "But the church will help her. Yep, we Baptist are always there…."

~*~

Janice dipped a ladle into the turkey gravy to see its consistency. Perfect. Now the taste test. She poured the gravy into a bowl, grabbed a spoon and had herself gravy soup.

"Did it work?" Marge asked.

Janice licked her lips. "Yes, it did. Who would have thought basting a turkey with wine and butter." She put a finger to her mouth. "It's a secret, right? We know alcohol burns off, and we're only using it for taste."

Marge chuckled. "That's one thing about the Baptist I don't get. Jesus turned water into wine."

"I know, but we have the church rules to follow, and it's a small price to pay to be Baptist."

"Well, Joe and I were never drinkers, so it's not a problem. But I wonder if in a century from now, we'll look back and say that was too strict."

Janice narrowed her gaze. "We won't be here in a century. What are you getting at?"

"Well, Little Women was written a century ago, and we see how silly it is now that Jo couldn't be a writer, being a woman."

Janice took off her apron and plunked herself in a chair. "Well, what I got out of the book hit a little closer to home." She fidgeted with her wedding ring. "Jo moved away from home, and look what she found?"

"A husband?"

"Well, she found out what she was made of inside. The professor helped her, but you know what I mean. I just wonder…"

"What?"

"Well, you know how Jerry has his doctorate in theology now…he could teach at a seminary."

Marge slowly started to ladle mashed potatoes into serving bowls. "Go on…"

She cleared her throat, not wanting to unsettle a parishioner. She knew better. A pastor's wife had to keep things in confidence, even from her closest friends. "Well, maybe Jerry needs to move on to teaching…"

"Where?"

Janice knew several places he could teach, but they were all far from Smicksburg, down in the South…a place Jerry missed at times. She tried to twist her wedding ring off, but again, her knuckles were swollen. November and arthritis seemed to go together. She looked up to see Marge with fear etched all over her face. "What's wrong? Is something burning?"

"Where would you move?" Marge blurted.

"Oh. I'm just talking out loud. Most likely, we'll be here in Smicksburg until our dying day. We have burial plots bought at the cemetery. Jerry and I said there's no other place on earth like Smicksburg to be our final resting place. I mean, the cemetery view is gorgeous."

Marge rolled her eyes. "For Pete's sake, stop talking about dying! Are you alright?"

Janice slowly got up to pour gravy into the white gravy boats she'd gotten at the Dollar Tree. "Well, Beth died in the book; you know we all die sometime. But to be honest, there was something that really made me want to be more content with what I have, and be thriftier." She picked up a gravy boat. "Guess where I got this?"

"Wow, what a mystery. You and Jerry are those Craigslist people, so it was at an estate, in the parlor, with a knife."

"What?" Janice asked. "Hey, this wine in here. You didn't...."

"The game Clue? Haven't you ever played it?"

"No." She dismissed Marge's attempt at a joke. "The Dollar Tree. I buy everything there, and it really is a dollar. Not like all the other stores that have dollar in their name."

Janice handed the gravy boat to Marge. "Feel how heavy it is. Not cheap."

Marge reluctantly took the boat and held it. "Wonderful. Only a buck. Great."

"What's wrong?"

Now Marge sat down. "I don't know. These classic old-fashioned books we're reading are making us all so serious, don't you think? I mean, Fannie still slipped into her Jane Austen talk, and it's weird. 'I prefer to have a girl above all things'. She really said that."

"What's wrong with that? She wants a girl."

"It's how she said it. I tell you, it's a weird thing to hear an Amish woman talk British. She also keeps saying, 'In vain have I struggled'. "

"What's she struggling with?"

"Her mom again, but that's not the point. These old books are too deep sometimes."

"Well, I like them. It's hard to find good reading these days. And if we're being changed, then, well, it's good. I plan to be as frugal as Mrs. March, since this country's headed towards another recession. And giving is pretty low right now."

Marge shot up from her chair. "You're moving because the church isn't making it. Will the church have to close down? I've seen it before. Little churches aren't making it."

Janice held up a hand as if to shield herself from Marge's verbal barrage. "Hey, your imagination is running wild. The church is doing fine...but the budget for outreach is low. And that's why I want to tighten up, and be like Mrs. March. She was poor, but had enough to give to the Hummel's. There's lots of Hummels on the streets, and if I can help save a buck, I have more to give into that account."

Tears formed in Marge's eyes. "I feel the same way. Our house back in Indiana is big enough to take in a homeless family. Too big, in fact. I really miss our little *dawdyhaus*." Marge held onto the white chair and slowly sat back down. "That was odd."

"What?" Janice asked, but when she turned to see Marge's pale face made, her stomach tighten. "Marge, you're so white. Are you okay?"

Marge held out her hands. "I feel all shaky all of a sudden. Look at my hands."

Janice noticed she was visibly trembling. "Have you been around sick patients?"

"Bad flu going around."

Janice put her hand on Marge's forehead. "You feel warm. Best get Joe to take you home right now."

Marge shook her head but Janice insisted. "Granny will be here any minute, and I don't want her to catch this. She's old. I'm getting Joe."

~*~

Granny lugged her basket full of hot homemade bread into the kitchen, and was startled to hear Janice's voice in a panic. But when she made out what she said, her heart sank. "Granny will be here any minute, and I don't want her to catch this. She's old... Well, Janice wasn't young either, but she had two more decades on her. She remembered Janice's offer with the turkey. Did she think she was too old to make a decent meal for Jeb? Take leftovers from the church? Well, it was a special day, and she didn't need help.

Janice whizzed out of the kitchen eyes wide. "Have you seen Joe?"

Granny pointed across the fellowship hall. "He's over there, setting up tables."

Janice pointed a finger at Granny's face. "You stay here, and don't go into the kitchen. Marge is in there and...."

"I'm as old as dirt and you think it's dangerous for me to get sick. *Ach,* I got the flu last year and shook it right off."

Janice embraced Granny. "I'm sorry. Just concerned about you." She released Granny and ran over to get Joe.

Lizzie put her hand on Granny's shoulder. "You're hurt, aren't you?"

"*Nee.*" She lifted the basket to lean it on one hip. "Well, maybe. Makes me wonder sometimes if people view me like Aunt March."

Lizzie eyebrows creased. "But you're not grouchy."

"I'm opinionated, maybe a little too much. The Good Book says to only give advice when asked. But no, I seek out trouble."

"*Mamm*, it's your gift to see hurting people and help them. You've helped everyone in the knitting circle tremendously." She leaned over to embrace Granny. "You brought Roman and me together."

Joe soon darted past Granny, Lizzie and Jenny and went to see Marge in the kitchen. Granny heard Marge moan, and it pulled at her heart. She wanted to go in and help Marge, but would it make any real difference. Was she Aunt March, the outspoken nosey aunt in Little Women?

~*~

Fannie leaned her head against Melvin's chest. "Wish you didn't have to go back to work. I love you ardently." She felt his body jiggle, and then roar laughter escaped his lips. "I know. I talk funny since I've read Jane Austen."

He squeezed her tight. "Well, at least it makes me laugh. What's ardent mean? Something *goot* I hope."

"*Jah.* It means passionately…I think. Well, a lot. I love you a lot."

Melvin pulled her back and tilted her chin so their eyes met. "And I love you. Now, I need to get back to work, and hopefully we'll have more customers in the shop. Seems awfully slow."

"I think people miss Jonas running this place. He was so fun to talk to and I'm boring I suppose."

Melvin leaned down until their heads touched. "Do you need another compliment box for Christmas? What's gotten into you, always putting yourself down like you used to?"

Fannie pursed her lips, knowing what her husband wanted her to say. "I will praise thee; for I am fearfully and wonderfully made: marvelous are thy works; and that my soul knoweth right well. Psalm 139: 14...."

"That's my Fannie. Believe what God says about you, okay?"

The bell on the door jingled and soon all of Fannie confidence blew away. Her stomach turned when her mom had that shade of green in her eyes, the color of pond scum.

"I have been waiting and now we're late." Mona stood upright and tall, like a cat trying to defend itself.

Melvin put his arm around Fannie. "Mona, calm down. You see Fannie's pregnant and all. If she forgot or is late for something, I can take you. Now, where do you need to go?"

Fannie's heart leapt for joy. Since she told Melvin about her struggles with her *mamm*, he was more outspoken. She slipped her arm around him and rubbed his back.

Mona glared at Melvin. "We're late for knitting circle. *Ach,* Fannie, can't you get anything right?"

Fannie knew Mrs. March in Little Women would never speak to her daughters like this. And Granny never did either, making all her girls at the circle feel special.....equal.

She felt Melvin's back tense. "Mona, don't talk to Fannie like that. We all make mistakes, and love keeps no record of wrongs."

Fannie wanted to clap her hands, but contained herself. "*Mamm,* knitting circle is at four today.

Remember? It's Thanksgiving tomorrow and Granny's helping the Baptists feed the needy?"

Mona's mouth gaped. "The Baptists? *Ach,* she helps the Baptists but doesn't make quilts for the benefit auction…"

Fannie clenched her fist. "Granny makes crocheted rugs with Emma and Colleen. She doesn't like quilting bees because of all the gossip! And when was the last time you went to a quilting bee?"

Now Melvin was rubbing her back. "Mona, we all have different gifts, *jah*? I donate clocks to the auction, and not all Amish women like to quilt." He pulled at his stubbly beard. "What do you like to do?"

Mona put both hands on her hips, making her cape flow out like a bat. "I can jelly and sew aprons and whatnot. I do my part and-"

"Go to a quilting bee, then," Fannie blurted. "There're plenty around. Maybe the knitting circle isn't for you, since you and Granny don't see eye-to-eye."

Melvin kissed her on the cheek. "I need to get back to the shop. And don't worry about supper. I'll make something special for you. Have fun."

He made his way around the counter and tried to get out the front door, but Mona blocked his way. "You cook? That's a woman's job. Pretty soon Fannie will have you doing laundry," she huffed.

Melvin crossed his arms as if ready for battle. "Does your husband ever come out of that barn of yours?"

"What?"

"You heard me. Does he come in the house much?"

Mona turned as red as beets and said nothing, apparently shocked at Melvin's boldness.

Fannie had to admit she felt sorry for her *mamm*. "My *daed* never comes in much. He's so busy milking cows…."

Mona cleared her voice. "I don't see why you're asking about my husband's business."

Melvin looked back at Fannie, his eyes asking if he should continue, but she shook her head. She knew what he wanted to scream with all his might. Your husband's miserable since he can't do anything right in your eyes. So he lives in the barn.

Fannie thought of how the March girls lived for so long without their father around. But Mrs. March was so capable of running a household. Her *mamm* wasn't, for sure and for certain. But why?

~*~

Maryann felt fatigue wash over her as she carried the laundry basket up the stairs. Her heart pounded, echoing through her ears as she reached the top, so she sat down. Dear Lord. Help me. It's like last year. Is it the dreary weather making me tired, or is it…cancer again? Lord, you give good things to your children, so I'm believing it's the weather. I cast my care upon you…

Her oldest daughter, Becca, opened her bedroom door and rushed to her side. "*Mamm*, what happened?"

"Just taking a break. Actually, looking at the walls thinking they need a fresh coat of paint."

Becca bent down and took the laundry basket. "I'll finish up and you go have some tea."

Maryann knew it must be the weather affecting her, because she had to bid the tears to stay in check. The winter blues had gotten ahold of her. "*Danki*, Becca. But have tea with me."

"I'll make the tea and bring out some jam we made in the fall. What do you want? More apple butter or peach butter?"

"Don't we have any raspberry left?"

"*Nee*. The *kinner* ate it all up. It'll be peach, pear and apple butter all winter."

Maryann sighed. "I'll take apple butter." She got up and ascended the stairs, Becca close behind her. Did Becca know she was having dizzy spells again? Was she staying close in case she fell? Surely not. "Becca, don't you have papers to grade? Being the new school teacher takes time. I'll do the laundry."

"Well, tomorrow's Thanksgiving, and with so many *daed's* off work, there's no school. So, I'm free to help."

Maryann remembered how most Amish were farmers when she was growing up. Now it seemed like the Amish had to revolve their lives according to the English calendars. "Becca, don't you need a break, too?"

"I'm taking one now. Anyhow, I wanted to talk to you, alone." She quickly placed the laundry basket in the utility room, right off the kitchen, and then went to get the blue speckle ware teapot and filled it with water. "Gilbert's been asking me to go home from Sunday singings…"

"I noticed his buggy pulling in late at night."

Becca twirled around. "You did? But how can you tell it's Gilbert's?"

Maryann didn't want to admit she stayed up until Becca got home safely. A sixteen year old Amish girl had a right to attend singings and be in a courting buggy until all hours of the night. "Do you care for Gilbert?"

Becca got a jar of apple butter out of the pantry and bread from the breadbox and placed them on the table. "I think I love him. But how can I tell."

Love him! Maryann felt a dizzy again, but she was learning to hide them well. "*Ach,* you're too young."

"You knew *daed* was the one you'd marry when you were sixteen." Becca took a seat across the table. "I read

Little Women, you know. And somehow, I think Jo should have married Lawrence, not the professor."

"Why? Jo was young and didn't know her own mind. The professor helped her."

"But a woman isn't completed by a man, you've always said that."

Maryann took a piece of bread and smeared the jam on it. "*Jah*, I do say that. A man should complement, not complete a woman."

"But Lawrence complimented Jo all the time. I don't understand."

Maryann reached for Becca's hand, thankful that indeed her daughter was still young and needed her. "When I say complement, I don't mean someone saying something nice, like 'I like your new dress.' I mean complement, like something that brings out the best, like 'That dress complements your complexion.' Brings out the right colors on a woman's face. Understand?"

Becca slowly nodded. "So all these times you've said find someone who complements me, you meant someone who brings out the best, like the professor did for Jo?"

"*Jah*, exactly."

Becca squeezed her hand. "I'm so happy. Gilbert never compliments me, like saying how pretty my eyes are and all that stuff. But he brings out the best in me for sure…and that's how I know I love him."

Maryann looked at the beaming smile her daughter displayed, and wished she could make time stop. But life wasn't like that. It always went on, and children grew up, and loved ones passed on into eternity. Heaven. That's when it will all end, like Granny said last week at knitting circle. And when they hosted a singing in their barn, the youth sang a lively hymn

When we all get to heaven

What a day of rejoicing that will be
When we all see Jesus
We'll sing and shout for victory!

Maryann relished the thought, and squeezed Becca's hand tighter.

~*~

Granny jabbed the white cake with a toothpick to see if it was done. Janice arranged the turkey on a platter, along with mashed potatoes, gravy, stuffing, cranberry sauce and corn.

"When will Jeb be home?"

"Well, he can't call and let me know." Granny elbowed Janice playfully. "He said six, so just put the plate in the icebox."

Bea charged the door, so Granny knew the girls had arrived. She stomped her foot. "Beatrix. Come."

The little black dog put her tail between her legs and slowly pulled herself towards Granny with her front paws. Granny ran to the dog. "I didn't mean to scare you. Just want you to stop that yapping." She picked up Bea nuzzled her face against her long silky fur.

Mona opened the door and immediately clucked her tongue. But Fannie nudged her, and she only nodded at Granny, not making her usual complaints about the little dog.

"Come on in and get warmed up," Granny said. "Smells like snow."

"*Jah*, it does," Fannie said. "I like it when we meet earlier so I can drive home in daylight." Unwrapping her cap and hanging it on the pegboard, she rubbed her hands. "But it's always *goot* to be here. It's like my second home."

Mona's countenance dropped. "Your life revolves around knitting now. And being Amish, we should be quilting, like I said before."

Granny shot a quick prayer up. One for grace and strength. "We can quilt here, if you want. Just not on Wednesdays."

"Why? Going to the Baptist's church on Wednesdays now? Sunday with the Amish not enough?" Mona asked aloofly.

Fannie went to Granny and put her arm around her. "*Mamm*. She helped with their dinner today."

"And she was a big help," Janice shouted from the kitchen. "So were Lizzie and Jenny. My how the seniors loved Jenny talk about her caterpillar project. She's like a homeschooled kid."

Lizzie opened the door in time to hear Janice's remark. "We're going to homeschool soon."

Mona spun around and gawked at Lizzie. "Not send the girls to an Amish school?"

"Well, I'm looking into it. Jenny's more advanced than girls her age and should be sitting with the fifth graders, and feels bad about it, since she can't sit with her friends. Louisa May Alcott was homeschooled by her dad…."

"But Jenny is Amish," Mona blurted. "We pay taxes to build our own schools. What if every Amish family homeschooled? We wouldn't have our schools."

Granny sighed. "Mona, don't make a mountain of beans about it. Lizzie said she was thinking about it, and she is their *mamm* and knows best."

"But she isn't their *mamm*…." Mona pursed her lips.

Lizzie stepped closer to Mona and stood tall. "Abraham Lincoln had a *step-mamm* who he said was his best friend."

Janice joined the group. "So, you're reading the book about step parenting Suzy ordered?"

"*Jah*, and I just didn't know what an honor it truly is. It seems like stepmothers have gotten a bad name because of some English stories, like Snow White. I can see why we don't read fairy tales."

Janice grinned. "I love them and collect all the DVDs from Disney. But I'm not Amish, and don't see things like *yinz* do."

Granny shook her head. "In the important things, you do. Like helping the needy in town, like you did today. It all opened my eyes." When hearing chattering outside, she ran to the door. "Come on in where it's warm. No need to talk outside."

Suzy, Colleen and Ruth all entered, noses and cheeks red from the cold.

"I just watched the Weather Channel," Suzy said, "and it was saying we're in for a whopper of a storm. Maybe six inches of snow."

"The birds are all too quiet. Hiding in pine trees," Ruth added.

"Well, it won't snow until five-thirty." Suzy took off her black coat and orange hat and gloves. "So we have time for a short circle meeting."

Granny was always appalled at how much stock the English put in manmade devices to predict the weather. Didn't the Bible say God held back the wind? And why the uproar about snow? Didn't it say in Job that is was a treasure? "Come on in and have a slice of cake and hot chocolate."

"Thanks Granny, but we should skip dessert and start the circle. Don't *yinz* agree?"

All heads nodded nervously.

"Well, if you want hot chocolate it's simmering on the stove. Help yourselves."

"Okay girls, take a seat and let's knit and talk about Little Women. I need answers," Suzy said quickly.

"Answers to what?" Colleen grinned. "Are you giving us a quiz?"

"No. I just need advice about something. Something that surfaced in me while reading Little Women."

The women all took a seat to form a circle and Granny sat in her usual place. "What surfaced, Suzy?" she asked.

"Well, that Mrs. March is so good. I told Colleen when she visited the store this afternoon. I just can't do what Mrs. March does."

"Be a *mamm*?" Fannie asked.

"No. Not that. Going around town helping everyone. I have a store to run, but Mrs. March had four daughters with no husband around and she found time. So I did too. I went to Missy Prissy's."

Janice leaned forward. "I told you Jerry and I would do it tomorrow."

Suzy put a hand up. "No. I had to face her…."

Colleen knit with new blue yarn she decided to get in addition to all the crimson wool. "But you looked so tired when I saw you…."

"I'm beyond tired now! So, how did Mrs. March do it all so cheerfully?"

Granny took her black wool out of her basket and began to knit. "Can you back-up and tell us who Missy Prissy is?"

"Her real name is Missy Hopkins. She lives two miles outside of town. She has agoraphobia and can't leave the house."

"Is it contagious?" Ruth asked. "I've never heard of it."

Janice slowly rose her head to stare at Ruth. "Are you serious?"

"*Jah*, I am. What is it?"

"It's the fear of the marketplace, really. Fear of being in public, open spaces. Fear seems to cripple the person, making them unable to go out."

Suzy sighed and looked over at Colleen. "After you left, I got on my knees, literally. I know how I reacted to the telephone call said it all. I hold unforgiveness towards her and I needed to put feet to my faith, and serve her."

Granny put down her knitting needles. "Really? That's so…."

"Amish?" Suzy laughed. "We read the same Bible, *jah*?"

Snickers and warm mirth were heard throughout the room, and Granny nodded in agreement. "I didn't mean to say that, but with *goot* English friends, you understand what I mean. Not all English Christians act like you."

Suzy's shoulders slumped. "I know. Missy Prissy sure doesn't act like a Christian…"

"Is she?" Janice asked. "She depends on the church now, and we reach out to everyone in need. But I think she's an atheist." Janice's eyes grew round. "But so was Joe! And look at him now. We need to be real with Missy. That's what did it for Joe."

"How so?" Fannie asked. "And I thought little Jenny helped him believe in God, since she has childlike faith."

Lizzie spoke up. "It took my Jenny and others to help Joe see God, but I think what Janice is saying is that we were all real and transparent in front of Joe, and he saw the Lord working in our lives."

Fannie walked over to the window and looked out. "I don't see Marge's car. I thought maybe she and Joe were visiting with Roman and she'd come in later."

"She's sick. Left the church dinner," Granny said. "But where is Maryann?"

No one responded, and Granny took a deep breath. Maryann's health was a concern she had to cast on God continuously. Even getting up at night, worried over her dear friend. But she turned worry on its head and prayed instead. "Does anyone know if Maryann's alright?"

Mona finally spoke. "She and Becca stopped over and checked on me. Now that all my kids are grown....something she wouldn't have to bother with if Fannie came over more."

Fannie's head jerked up and her eyes were ablaze. "I've offered for you to live by us. We can't move the store to your place."

Suzy coughed loudly. "Ah, can we talk about Little Women? That's the purpose of this circle. How about we go around the room? Colleen, you start."

Colleen nodded. "I got a lot out of the book. The March girls were limited as to what they could wear, like I am now that I'm going to turn Amish. It's their inward beauty that really counted, and it took Amy a while to learn that, but she did." Colleen looked over at Ruth who sat next to her. "That's about it. How about you, Ruth?"

"Well, ever since we talked about *Pride and Prejudice*, I told *yinz* I was writing Luke love letters. What pricked my heart in Little Women was how much Jo liked to write, and I do too. But I don't know if being Amish, I can be a writer."

"*Jah*, you can." Granny quipped. "I've submitted things to *Family Life Magazine* and long ago, when I was a teacher, to *Blackboard Bulletin*." She looked over at Colleen. "No fairytales, only true stories, or parables so we learn a lesson, *jah*?"

Colleen nodded with a grin. "Even write poems?"

Laughter filled the room. "Of course you can write a poem," Granny said. "All of Psalms in the Bible is poetry. *Jah*, we love poetry."

Ruth craned her head forward. "I've been Amish my whole life, and I didn't know I could write for a magazine…."

"Maybe your *mamm* doesn't read much," Lizzie offered. "Does she read at all?"

Ruth shook her head. "Only her Bible."

Mona shifted in her seat. "Your *mamm* has common sense. No use reading things outside the Bible."

Granny tightened her grip on her yarn. Lord help me! Is there anyone as rude as Mona? She closed her eyes and prayed for strength, because she had an urge to throw her yarn at this woman who got under her skin so much it hurt.

"Mona, if you know Granny writes, how could you say something so rude? It takes lots of work to write."

Granny opened her eyes and slowly looked at Lizzie, who had dug in her heels and confronted Mona. She was becoming more like Roman, her husband, every day.

Mona shooed the air away from her. "It's my opinion, and I'm entitled to it. If someone gets hurt, it's not my fault."

Suzy stood up, put two fingers to her mouth, and blew a whistle loud enough to break glass. "Will you Amish stop this bickering? For pity sake. "She pointed to Fannie who sat next to Ruth. "Your turn."

Fannie's cheeks were red on her blush line. "What I got out of the book, was what kind of mamm I want to be." She looked down at her yarn. "Mrs. March had four daughters, all different in what they liked to do. And their personalities were different, but she loved them all the same, not having favorites." Her eyes glistened as tears formed. "Melvin and I want lots of *kinner,* and I hope I make all of them feel loved for who they are in here." She held her yarn up to her heart. "Colleen's right. It's what's in a person's heart that really matters. What makes them beautiful."

Granny knew she was seeing a miracle. For Fannie to say this in front of her *mamm* with such confidence, was one more step out of self-hatred and rejection she'd battled with. "*Danki* for sharing that, Fannie. You'll be a *wunderbar goot mamm.*"

"I fear I won't," Fannie said, almost in a whisper.

Silence. No one wanted to say the obvious. Fannie was afraid of being like her own *mamm*, a woman who had her favorites and even admitted it. Granny shot another prayer up, casting Fannie on God.

Suzy pointed to Mona. "How about you? What did you get out of the book?"

"Not much. Only that saving money is important. It showed the Civil War, and being Amish, and being a pacifist; I didn't see that the March's did the right thing, knitting for soldiers."

Fannie leaned towards her *mamm* and whispered loud enough that everyone heard, "The Baptists aren't pacifists. *Shh*"

Mona glared at Janice. "Your church believes in killing people?"

"Only in self-defense or to protect the liberties in this country that you enjoy. We have a church member in Iraq, and we're mighty proud of him, risking his life…"

Granny felt her emotions flapping like the cold laundry hanging on the porch. What made Mona so opinionated? As an Amish woman, she was to try to live at peace with others, not cause a war right in the middle of her knitting circle. Should she say something? Ask her to never come back? Every week Granny was on edge, not knowing what was coming out of Mona's mouth.

Mona's voice pierced the stillness. "Maybe I shouldn't read any more secular books and stick with the Bible. And stay home, not come anymore."

Granny took a deep breath, and relief settled upon her soul, until Lizzie spoke up. "Mona, I think you'll like the next book better. Anne of Green Gables doesn't have war and it's about an orphan girl being adopted. "

Janice clucked her tongue but quickly covered her mouth. "Oops. Sorry. But, isn't that a little kids book, too?"

Suzy cleared her throat. "Lizzie and I go online to make sure the books can be read by adults and children, since Jenny's reading the books for homeschooling. Now, Anne of Green Gables is over 300 pages." She turned to Janice and grinned. "And it's not exactly like the movie."

Janice stopped knitting in mid-air. "What's that supposed to mean?"

"You're always too busy to read, and you just watch the movies."

"How did you know?"

"Because when we talked about the book, you kept mixing Jo's name up with Winona Ryder, that's how."

Janice's bright smile flashed. "Busted. Suzy, you should be a detective. But I don't have time to read such long books, being a pastor's wife and running Forget-Me-Not-Manor, I fall asleep when I open a book."

Suzy leaned forward. "Why not have the girls at Forget-Me-Not read Anne of Green Gables out loud, in a group? They'd get a lot out of it."

"*Hmm.* That's an idea." Janice said. "Let me talk to the girls."

Suzy pointed to Granny. "Now, back to our discussion. What did you get out of Little Women?"

Granny didn't want to share something she feared, especially in front of Mona, who may make a snide remark. How could she say she feared she was a busy body, poking her nose into others business like Aunt Marge? No, she would deal with that between her and her Lord. "I liked how they knit for charity and gave so much to the Hummel family. Beth knew the risks of scarlet fever, but went over to help the family anyhow. No greater love than to lay down your life for a friend."

A buggy pulled up the driveway and Lizzie sprang up to see who it was. "Jeb's home early. Now, everybody knows what to do, *jah*?"

All heads nodded. Granny went into the kitchen and held the cake up so Jeb would see it when he opened the door. The girls all hid in the other room.

Jeb stomped his boots on the outside mat, then stepped inside. He appeared to not see Granny, as he bent down to untie his boot laces and remove his boots, putting them on the black rubber mat. "Anyone home?" he hollered.

"Old man, I'm right here. No need to yell."

He turned towards her and his jaw dropped. "*Ach,* is that for me?"

"*Jah*, Love. Happy Birthday."

He went over to her and leaned down to give her a kiss. "*Danki*, Love. You're married to an old man indeed."

Granny searched Jeb's eyes. Was he sad he was turning seventy-three? But his eyes were filled with mirth and she knew aging was a problem she dealt with, not him. She caressed his cheek. "A *wunderbar* old man."

Soon all the girls raced out of the living room, singing Happy Birthday. Janice ran to the icebox and retrieved a Thanksgiving platter, enough for two people. "*Yinz* have a birthday feast. Compliments of Smicksburg Baptist Church."

The girls all embraced Jeb, wishing him a happy birthday, but Janice kissed him on the cheek and gave him a present. "It's something I know you'll love," Janice said while bursting with enthusiasm.

Jeb blushed, obviously not used to having a woman besides his wife kiss his cheek, and Granny covered her mouth to hide her grin.

Jeb tore off the blue wrapping paper and held up a book. "A Charles Dickens Devotional? *Danki*. Is he a writer like Max Lucado?"

All the English women laughed, while the Amish women looked *furhoodled*. Granny had heard of this author, but couldn't recall what he wrote. When Janice mentioned that he was a classic writer and wrote the most wonderful Christmas story ever, and the children at the Baptist church were starting practice for a play written by this Dickens man, she wondered if she could go and watch it...but knew better than to push things concerning going into the Baptist church.

She knew Jeb was deeply touched by Janice's present, and looked around at all the happy faces. But where was Mona? Granny turned and literally stepped back in shock to see Mona in the next room, eyes sadder than a sick puppy.

~*~

Granny put her feet up on the little footstool Jeb made for her edema; swollen ankles and old age seemed to go together, although this was a recent development. Knitting by oil lamp, with Jeb next to her reading, in a nice snug home was something she treasured. And since she learned today how needy people really were, she gave praise to God. To think that some people couldn't afford their heating bills and keeping the house temperatures down to fifty was sad indeed. The cook stove and wood burning stove made their little house toasty.

Jeb handed her his magazine. "Do you like that walking stick?"

"For you? *Jah*, it's nice."

"It's for a woman. Has a butterfly carved on it."

Granny leaned closer. "I see them now. Are you thinking of making them to sell in the store?"

"I could. But do you like it?"

"Well, if I was in need of one, I suppose it's alright."

"So you don't like it?"

Granny moaned. "I didn't say that."

"So you'd use one, just like this?"

Granny looked into Jeb's searching eyes. "I don't need a cane, so if you make me one for Christmas, I wouldn't use it."

Jeb sighed. "I don't know what to make you this year. Last year you were real surprised, but this year I'm stumped."

"Make a donation to Christian Aid in my name. That's all I want." She sat back and began to knit. "You can buy a goat for *kinner* in poverty."

"But I always make you something for Christmas. Don't you care?"

Granny looked out the window. "If this snow keeps up, and we have a hard winter, I'll need snowshoes. I think we got eight inches, easily." As Granny continued to stare out the window, she noticed two lights moving down their driveway. Must be a car since buggy lights were smaller and dim, but in this snow, who could tell.

She soon saw Janice's van, and her heart picked up speed. "Something's wrong. Janice wouldn't drive in this snow unless it was an emergency.

Bea jumped off of Jeb's lap and ran to the door, barking as fierce as her little voice could get. Jeb went to retrieve her and soon Janice appeared at the door. "Come on in out of that cold." Jeb pet Bea to calm her.

Janice had been crying, Granny soon saw, as her puffy eyes came into focus. "What's wrong?"

"I, ah, got a call from Joe. Marge had a miscarriage."

Granny closed her eyes to hide the tears that welled up, and to pray a quick prayer for Marge. *Help her Lord. Carry her burden of loss, like you did for me when losing my girl.*

"She wants to see you," Janice said softly. "Will you go?"

"Now? In this weather?" Jeb huffed. "*Nee,* it's too cold out.'"

"I'll drive in my car to Indiana. There's lots of snow on the roads, but no ice." Janice said. "We'll be fine."

Jeb plopped down in his rocker. "Doesn't Marge have kin?"

Janice nodded. "She asked for Granny, though."

"Well, it can wait until morning," Jeb stroked Bea nervously. "Deborah could freeze outside, or worse yet, fall."

Granny asked Janice if she could have a few minutes with Jeb privately, and Janice went into the kitchen. Granny took Jeb's hand. "Turning seventy-three is hard, *jah?*"

"Don't know what you're talking about...."

"First the walking stick, and now I'm too frail an old woman to go out in the snow? Jeb, I'll be fine."

He rubbed the top of her hand with his thumb. How she loved it when he did this when courting and it never lost its appeal. It meant he was strong and wanted to protect her; he cherished her.

"*Jah*. Turning seventy-three seems more like seventy-five, and that's close to eighty...."

Granny got up and took Bea from his lap and sat in it. "I'll be fine. Marge needs me. What if you were called out as bishop?"

He squeezed her tight. "Bundle up, and tell Janice to drive slow if she speeds."

She kissed his cheek. "I will, love. But you just remember, you're still the young man with those turquoise eyes I fell in love with years ago."

"My eyes are hazel."

"When you're in a mood, they change. They're turquoise now." She leaned on his chest, hearing his heartbeat. "I might need to spend the night at the hospital, so don't wait up."

He said nothing, but squeezed her tighter.

~*~

Marge bit back tears when Granny entered her hospital room. But fear tightened like a noose around her heart. If she told Granny how she really felt, would she understand? Would she lose respect ? Would she scold her? When Granny came closer with outstretched arms, the wall she erected with others chipped. "So glad you came..."

"How are you?" Granny asked, bending down to embrace her. "Are you in pain?"

"Only a little. They're keeping me twenty-four hours for exams. Female exams."

Granny untied her cape strings and sat in a chair near the bed. "I lost a *kinner*, so I understand."

"You were so far along though, so it was different?"

"How so?"

"Well, you felt the baby kick. Move inside of you. I never did so...." Marge could not look Granny in the eyes, but she needed to tell someone. "I'm not as sad as some other women would be."

"Well, we all carry our grief differently, I suppose. Jeb planting those roses helped me heal. To see new life is *goot*, and every year when they bloom, I think of my girl in heaven."   Granny's eyes glistened. "She'll meet me up there, and so will your little one."

Marge pulled at the bed sheets. "Granny. I have to confess something horrible. Just don't know if I should. "

Granny stood up. "*Ach,* don't tell me you...." As quick as a person blushed, Granny's face turned white as snow. "You aborted the baby?"

Marge gawked. "No... " Marge covered her face with her hands. "But you say God looks at the heart, and it's just as bad."

Granny took her cape off her shoulders and sat back down. "Marge, speak plainly. I don't judge, unless it's something clearly forbidden in scripture. In that case, it's really God who's judging, not me. So...."

Marge wiped the tears that formed on her cheeks. "I didn't want the baby. And I had hateful thoughts though, wishing I'd have a miscarriage, and I did. And I'm not sad, so it's the same. God sees my heart and I'm a murderer."

"*Ach,* you're not a murderer. To hate is to murder, like the Good Book says, but God forgives, *jah*? Don't you think I struggle with hatred at times?"

Marge pushed the button to raise her bed. "You're just saying that to make me feel better."

"*Nee*, I don't do that. Ask Jeb. I hope I speak the truth, even if it hurts." Her eyes mellowed. "When I was pregnant, my emotions swayed like the wind. Some days I'd knit a blanket for the *boppli* inside of me, other times I wished I wasn't pregnant...at all. Understand?"

"So you felt the same way?"

"Well, when I lost my girl, she was still born. To see a child born with no breath isn't natural, and very sad." She got up and sat on the bed near Marge. "You're not sad because maybe you don't know what you lost, never being pregnant before?"

"I lost the baby and I'm glad. That's what's wrong with me. I'm materialistic to my core. And selfish, too. I kept complaining to Joe about how we can't afford a baby and I meant it."

Granny touched her hand. "Now, calm down and rest. Your hormones are all jumbled up, don't forget. And remember, God is merciful and forgiving. Rest...."

"But I feel so guilty... I am guilty. Oh, Granny I'm too afraid to say..."

Granny squeezed her hand. "Marge, what aren't you telling me?"

Marge felt a rage rise within her. The same rage she felt when she fell for the lie years ago. "Joe and I were so stupid. Joe and I weren't married, and I got pregnant, and we decided..." She couldn't say it. What would Granny think? What if Janice found out? She'd be thrown to the curb where she deserved to be.

"So, you had an abortion..." Granny grabbed her and pulled her to herself. "I'm so sorry, child. We all make mistakes."

Marge, in half shock, and half relief, sobbed uncontrollably. The guilt she and Joe carried for years haunted them to the point where they decided not to have children. And the fear she'd carried since she got pregnant...would she be a horrible mother since she killed her first born? And her own mother took her to the clinic at seventeen, and she didn't understand. How could she? Her own grandchild? And I was to say nothing to anyone, especially at church!

The more she cried and Granny held her, she felt a release of sorts that was foreign to her. Could God ever forgive such a thing? As Granny stroked her hair, hushing her, saying 'Mercy' and 'Grace on you' the warmth of God she felt in church hovered around her, seeping into the iron wall she'd built up around her heart that kept this horrible secret...and it was being lifted....

~*~

Granny felt Bea licking her face and she shooed her away. "Stop that." She heard a chuckle, opened one eye, and saw Jeb standing by the bed. Bea jumped with glee as she woke up to get her morning belly rub. "What time is it?"

"Ten. Was getting worried, but you came in late."

Ten? Amish women never slept until ten. She bolted up and glared at Jeb. "Why didn't you wake me up, old man?"

"Because you came in at two in the morning." He turned to retrieve a wooden tray he'd laid on their dresser. "Here, I made you breakfast."

The ornately carved tray was a beauty. Little songbirds flew across the top and birds' nests were on the bottom. "Jeb, did you make this?"

"*Jah.* We think they can sell in the store."

She rubbed her hands over the dark wood. "Is it pine?"

"*Nee,* solid walnut. Hard to find, so it's worth more. They had extra at the mill, scraps real cheap."

"Now, this is something I'd like for Christmas," Granny said, hoping Jeb would get the obvious message. She wanted to keep this tray.

Jeb winked. "*Nee*. You said you wanted snowshoes and snowshoes you will get."

"I didn't say that. Men wear snowshoes, not women."

"I heard it as plain as day, and Roman and I are working on them now." He chuckled and pointed towards the tray. "Now, eat your eggs and bacon before they get cold."

Granny, now awake, remembered Marge's sorrow last night. What the poor girl had been through, and what kind of mother did Marge have, encouraging an abortion?

Jeb sat on the bed. "Deborah, I was only kidding. You want this tray?"

She swallowed hard. "I'm fine. Just so sad about Marge."

"*Jah*, what you told me last night, it's a pity. But you helped Marge cry those cleansing tears, and showed her in scripture how she was forgiven? Made white as snow?"

"*Jah*, I did. So why am I so tired? Germs in the hospital. Might have caught something."

"You give out so much, and you need to rest…"

Granny remembered telling Marge to rest, but she had a hard time doing it herself. She planned to go to Maryann's to check on her today. But she just couldn't move. "Jeb, I feel so bad about Marge and that burden she carried, but I found something else out last night."

"What?"

"Well, in the book, Little Women, there's an aunt who is too opinionated and doesn't mind her business. And I kept wondering if I was like her, but these girls really do need me."

Jeb took her hand. "Of course they do. Who do they go to first to tell all their problems? Coming over here during the week to talk one-on-one? It's always you."

"*Nee*, I'm asking them to come over and bake pies…"

"You don't bake with Fannie and she's here nonetheless."

Granny smirked. "If you had a *mamm* like Mona, you'd come here, too, for a word of encouragement."

Jeb laughed. "*Ach*, Deborah, how can I help you carry such a heavy burden as that woman?"

Granny took a bite of eggs. "I best be eating…and have my morning devotions."

"I'm headed out to the shop. I'll take Bea with me." He kissed her forehead and scooped Bea up. "Come on, sweetie."

Granny felt fatigue wash over her, so she took a sip of coffee. Feeling that all too common feeling to unload her burdens at the foot of the cross, she prayed:

Lord,

I'm sorry I hold unkind thoughts towards Mona, but she's an awful hard woman, and treats Fannie so cruel it makes me sick. Really, Lord. You know how I get headaches after knitting circle now. Give me wisdom to know if I have to actually ask her not to come. When I started this circle, I wondered if the English wouldn't get a long, and now Mona has all the Amish on pins and needles.

And Lord, I don't know what's wrong with Maryann, but I have a sense it's not goot. Please let her know today she's loved. That I love and care for her. And do that for Marge too. Lord, heal her heart. Guilt is something you don't want us to carry, being the worst kind of burden. Let her know that even though her sin be as red as scarlet, she's white as snow and forgiven, because you took her place at the cross. You took the blame for her sin. And lead her to scriptures that will go from her head into her heart, that we are all

hopelessly flawed, like Jo feared in Little Women. And we need your grace...
In Jesus name
Amen.

~*~

My Dear Readers,

Thank you once again, for reading about Granny and her knitting friends. One of my favorite Bible verses is:

"Come now, let's settle this," says the LORD. "Though your sins are like scarlet, I will make them as white as snow. Though they are red like crimson, I will make them as white as wool." Isaiah 1:18 NLT

Guilt is a cruel master, and one God doesn't want us to follow. I have two friends who got abortions while in their teens, encouraged by their parents, and annually they grieve for the child they lost that day. And their guilt just doesn't seem to go away, even though the abortion was decades ago. But other women have told me that they were set free from guilt, understanding how deep the love of God really is. If you're a woman who needs to talk to someone about a guilt related issue, please contact me on my website, www.karenannavogel.com.

~*~

Basic White Cake

2½ c. flour
1 2/3 c. sugar
2/3 c. shortening
1 tsp. salt
¾ c. milk
4 ½ tsp. baking powder
5 eggs whites, unbeaten
½ c. milk
1 tsp. vanilla

Sift dry ingredients. Add shortening and milk and then beat. Add remaining ingredients. Bake at 350 for 30 minutes. Insert toothpick to see if done.

EPISODE 3

Anne Of Green Gables

"'God's in his heaven; all's right with the world,'" whispered Anne *softly.*

Granny held the book to her chest and took in the aroma of the morning coffee percolating in the blue speckle ware pot. *Lord, give me the confidence Anne has; after losing Matthew. She knows You are in control. Lord, I fear too much. Forgive me.*

The eggs sizzling in the skillet wafted a burnt scent, and she plunked the book on the table and ran to her stove, flipping the eggs over, just in time. Taking a mug, she poured a cup of coffee and sat down in the rocker near the window. The little snowbirds were back; the plain little gray and white birds, so gentle and timid. She wanted to go shoo the bluebirds that chased them from her feeder. Granny narrowed her gaze at a lone junco, and marveled at the book she'd just read, Anne of Green Gables. Anne had been like a helpless bird, but with love and community, along with her lack of self-pity, she was as beautiful as an indigo bunting or red finch. And Marilla, her adoptive mom, had learned to laugh and not be a crank. Could Mona learn this lesson?

Then she thought of Maryann, and the tests she needed to have tomorrow. Was 'All right with the world', as Anne bravely stated? The past few weeks had prompted Granny to put out more birdseed, since the feathered creatures calmed her nerves. Maryann's symptoms back, just like a nightmare. If her tests were positive tomorrow and the cancer had returned, would it mean more surgery, or worse? Was the cancer contained?

Granny massaged the back of her neck and tried to relax, but her mind wandered to the one on one talks she'd had with Marge while making pies. Her bubbly English friend unfolded such a wounded spirit, and it grieved Granny to her core. Guilt over an abortion she'd had while yet a young girl had plagued her to the point where everything Marge did was driven by guilt. Being a nurse wasn't her first choice, but saving lives to redeem herself for the little one she'd aborted, was not something the good Lord would want. And not wanting children, fearing she'd hurt or abuse her own child, guilt left such serious effects on her lovely friend. Granny didn't know what to say except scripture, since she knew it healed a heart, and set it free.

But for Granny to bare her soul to her Lord this morning, she needed to cast off her greatest care: Jeb. He was seventy-three now, and like he said, it seemed closer to seventy-five and that seemed like eighty. Matthew in Anne of Green Gables died over worry, really. Losing his money in a failed bank. Isn't that what Jeb and Roman talked about in hushed tones as if she couldn't hear? Sales were so slow for Christmas and the fiscal cliff that was feared by the Amish and English alike. Even Fannie had said that her store was slow, folks buying the bare minimum, hanging on to their purses.

Jeb would be out for his breakfast soon, Bea in tow, so she opened her Bible for her morning quiet time. Even though she'd memorized this scripture long ago, still she needed to read it at times:

For God hath not given us the spirit of fear; but of power, and of love, and of a sound mind. 1 Timothy 2:7

Granny clamped her eyes shut.

Lord, I am fearful and need to trust you. You put your power, love and a mind not given to worry in me through your Spirit. Help me, for it's just one of those days when I feel like hiding from the world, staying in bed reading a goot book, or knitting. But, I have knitting circle this afternoon, and I am your hands and feet to a hurting world, as feeble as they are.

Bea ran up to her, big brown eyes hopeful to get a belly rub. Granny scooped her up and held her like a baby, rocking her.

"I think she needs a friend," Jeb said, after a long yawn. "She tuckers me out."

"How so?"

"She's like a little *kinner,* always wanting attention. And getting up at night to let her out, well, it brings back memories…"

"Jeb, you never got up at night to tend to the *kinner.*"

"I heard the crying. And when you were too tired, *jah*, I did get up and help." He made his way over to the coffee pot. "Did you get some?"

"Jah, but could use another. These old bones…"

"I'm older, remember." He poured coffee into two mugs and set them on the table. "Come over here and tell me what you're fretting about."

Granny put Bea down, joined Jeb at the table, and sipped her coffee. "Who said I'm fretting? Lizzie?"

"*Nee*, you talked in your sleep last night. And you must have had a bad dream."

She gripped the mug. "I did. I was…"

"Throwing dirt on my coffin. Deborah, you threw dirt on me."

Jeb's attempt to make her laugh failed. "It was your funeral and it was red roses that I threw…since…"

Jeb reached across the table and took her hand. "Love, I hope we go at the same time, but most likely one of us will go first." He gripped her hand tighter. "But we're not to worry about tomorrow, *jah*? There's enough trouble in one day?"

Granny shook her head. "I can't help it. I never thought we'd get this old, and to think of you gone…"

"God gives his help when it's needed. We're still together, so we don't need it now. Remember when you saw your *mamm* going downhill, and you cried yourself to sleep a year before she passed?"

Granny nodded.

"Well, on the day she passed, you said it was as if God was lifting you, carrying you in a way you didn't expect."

Granny gave a faint smile.

"Trust God and don't go borrowing trouble…"

Granny pursed her lips and then met his eyes. "And you know I have a tendency to do that…"

"We all do, Love. We all do."

Bea hopped onto Granny's lap and nuzzled her face into Granny's bosom, fast asleep, not a care in the world. The little dog had learned to trust Jeb and her. By her age, why did she still not believe God would take care of her? Was it the human condition to fret about life, even until your dying day? Was there something in every heart that said, God I really don't think you care and I can manage on my own? Like the first sin in the Garden of Eden?

~*~

Ruth finished washing the morning dishes and started to wipe down the counters, but as fatigue washed over her, she had to make her way over to her rocker by the window and sit down. She noticed a downy woodpecker bobbing its head back and forth as it jabbed at the suet feeder, and for some reason she felt dizzy.

Luke came down the stairs and planted a kiss on her cheek before he left for work. "You feel warm." He put his lips on her forehead. "You have a fever, and you don't look *goot*."

Ruth put a hand up in protest. "I'm fine. Just resting for a spell."

Luke ran up the steps and soon returned with a thermometer. "You're pregnant and may need to see the doc. Open up."

Ruth obeyed as Luke placed the thermometer gently in her mouth. He pulled up a chair next to her and placed a hand on her shoulder. "We're not that busy at the woodshop. I can take care of you."

Her heart swelled with love for her dear husband. To think that last year this time, she left him for a few months. His cruel behavior towards her had made the elders and bishop get involved, and she thanked God daily for their intervention. How lovingly they'd restored her husband, and with some medical help for his anxiety disorder, he'd become the man she truly loved from her heart.

He took the thermometer out as it beeped. "*Ach*, you have a fever. It's one-hundred one." He helped her up out of her rocker and up the steps back into bed. "I'm staying home to keep an eye on you."

Ruth couldn't help but smile, but her throbbing head soon caused her to wince. "*Danki*. Can you lower the blinds? My eyes hurt."

Luke quickly lowered all the white shades in the room and soon darkness soothed Ruth's aching eyes. She pointed to their dresser. "Can you give me that book?"

"It's dark in here, and you're sick."

"I need to finish it by this afternoon. I have knitting circle."

"You're not going," Luke commanded gently. "You're carrying our *boppli,* and need to take care of the two of you."

She hated to miss knitting circle, but knew he was right.

Luke gave her a knowing look. "I'll read to you." He chuckled. "You're near the end and want to know what happens, *jah?*"

She nodded, and then relaxed on the bed as Luke opened the book to where she'd dog-eared the page. He cleared his throat and began to read:

"'Halfway down the hill a tall lad came whistling out of a gate before the Blythe homestead. It was Gilbert, and the whistle died on his lips as he recognized Anne. He lifted his cap courteously, but he would have passed on in silence, if Anne had not stopped and held out her hand.

"'Gilbert,' she said, with scarlet cheeks, "I want to thank you for giving up the school for me. It was very good of you--and I want you to know that I appreciate it."

"'Gilbert took the offered hand eagerly.

"'It wasn't particularly good of me at all, Anne. I was pleased to be able to do you some small service. Are we going to be friends after this? Have you really forgiven me my old fault?'

"Anne laughed and tried unsuccessfully to withdraw her hand.

"'I forgave you that day by the pond landing, although I didn't know it. What a stubborn little goose I was. I've been--I may as well make a complete confession--I've been sorry ever since.'"

Ruth quickly gasped for air as tears stung her eyes.

Luke put down the book. "What's wrong?"

She motioned for him to come near her, and he sat on the bed and took her hand. She kissed his hand and let tears fall on it. "I-I was a stubborn goose...all last winter."

Luke didn't say anything, but it seemed like healing had come from her words.

"I wasn't quick to forgive, like the Bible says to do. I knew you'd changed, but I made you sleep in Micah's room all winter, and I held such...bitterness towards you."

Luke sighed. "Ruth, we look forward, *jah?*"

"*Jah*, but when I read about Anne and how stubborn she was and how she outgrew it, I'm ashamed. I was a grown woman last winter and acted like a child."

"*Nee,* you acted like a hurting woman. I sinned and it left a scar on you."

"I sinned by wanting to punish you. I made your life miserable..."

Luke put his hand over her mouth to stop her from talking. "You rest now, and don't get all worked up over the past. We love each other, and love covers a multitude of sins." He felt her forehead again. "I'm getting you some medicine to bring this fever down and a cup of tea. If it doesn't come down, we're headed to the docs for sure."

He embraced her and cradled her head against his chest. "I love you so much," he whispered into her ear, and Ruth felt a weight lift off her heart. Confession was good for the soul.

~*~

Colleen hitched the horse to the post Suzy had outside her store. Still a little shaky about driving a buggy, she knew she'd find solace as she worked part-time in the yarn shop. Being around yarn all day, one day a week, would give Suzy time to teach spinning, dying and harder knitting techniques. While attending baptismal classes and studying the material Jeb gave as homework, Colleen found that the craft of knitting calmed her spirit enough to take in all the deep truths of scripture, and the book she was reading, Anne of Green Gables.

When she opened the door, the familiar bell rang and Suzy looked up cheerfully from her knitting. "Good morning, Colleen. So glad to have you here." She got up and went to Colleen, giving her a quick hug. "Can I take your...robe?"

"It's a cape," Colleen said with a wry smile. "And this is my new winter outer bonnet." She unlaced the black strings from under her chin and handed the heavy hat to Suzy.

Suzy made her way to the back of the shop to hang up the garments. "Colleen, don't you miss, well, dressing in style?"

Colleen shook her head. "No. Well, sometimes, but Granny helped me see that fashion is all a trifle."

"Isn't a trifle a dessert?"

"Yes, but it also means something not important." She placed her hands on her heart. "What really matters is in here: inner beauty."

Suzy lifted her hands up as if in surrender. "Can't say that I can go that far, since I design the garments I knit, but everyone has their own views." She pointed to the boxes on the floor. "You can start by unpacking the yarn and putting it on the shelves, and then I need things dusted."

Colleen went to work, if that's what it was called. Suzy had a tea break at ten, and when customers came in, Colleen was encouraged to talk to them, so they'd feel at home. No, she did not "work" at Suzy's; she enjoyed herself. Or was it that Amish ways were rubbing off on her? Work and pleasure were combined, as most Amish loved what they did for a living, finding their God given talents. Her mind turned again towards the book she'd just finished. "So, Suzy, did you like Anne of Green Gables?"

Suzy, who had continued her knitting, never looked up while engrossed in work. "I love that book. Rings true today as it did when it was written. Did you know it was a Sunday school paper first?"

"Really? It's not all that religious, though"

"Well, it's like a long parable of sorts. It shows a girl feeling totally alone in the world, wondering if God even saw her, and she ends up seeing that God was in control of her life. Understand?"

Colleen had felt alone in life, and flashbacks of her childhood were drudged up when she read the part about Anne having a window friend. She'd shared this with Hezekiah, and her grandma, but would Suzy think she was weird?

"What's on your mind?" Suzy asked.

"Oh, nothing really."

"Come on now…" Suzy prodded.

"Well, you know my parents were drug addicts, and I didn't have the happiest childhood." Colleen slowly placed more black yarn on a shelf. "I had window friends like Anne. I had no one else to talk to."

Suzy put her knitting down. "Want some tea? We can talk about this."

Colleen shook her head. "Tea is at ten, *jah?*" She attempted to make Suzy smile by using an Amish accent, but the compassion in Suzy's eyes made her want to find comfort. "I'll talk about it while I work."

Suzy nodded. "Well, you know there's always tea in the back, and I even got some fancy sugar cubes, just for our tea time. Our first Jane Austen tea."

Colleen went over to Suzy and hugged her from behind. "Thank you. I know you really care. Wish you were my mom…"

Suzy put one hand up to her eyes and started to fan vigorously. "Now, don't make me cry. I feel tears coming on."

After another squeeze, Colleen resumed her work. "Well, like I said, my parents were addicts. They had their druggy friends over, and I hid in the closet. So I had closet friends…like make believe friends I suppose…"

"And how old were you when you had these imaginary friends? Twelve, like Anne?"

She gripped the yarn, knowing there was healing in being transparent, but to verbalize her pain made her relive it. "Until I started cutting myself as a teenager. It made me feel…not dead. When I realized my imaginary friends weren't real, I felt too alone, and pretty numb. It's better to feel pain than feel dead."

Suzy pursed her lips, raised her eyebrows high, trying not to cry. "So, you were like Anne, and our church is like Matthew and Marilla?"

Colleen hadn't thought of this before. The very people who took her in as a single mom, she'd abandoned to be Amish. "I'll be forever grateful to the Baptist church, honestly."

"Oh, Colleen, everyone who has eyes can see you and Hezekiah were made for each other, and your grandma is Amish. But sometimes you work hard, reaching out in a church, and don't see much outcome. We're all thrilled for you. Remember, Amish and Baptists are both Christians, and that's what binds us, *jah*?"

Colleen grinned through tears that pooled in her eyes. "*Jah. Wir sind eins in dem Herrn* …

Suzy laughed. "I've picked up some German living here in Amish-land USA. "You're saying something about the Lord, *jah*?"

"Good," Colleen quipped. "I said, 'We are one in the Lord. My grandma and aunts only speak German in the home, and it's pretty easy to pick up." Her grandma's kindness only accentuated her own mother's cruelty. How could her grandma give birth to such a woman? "Suzy, since we're both plain old Christians, what do you think about forgiveness?"

Suzy cocked an eyebrow. "Correction. I am not plain or old." She winked. "But as far as forgiveness is concerned, the Lord doesn't give us much wiggle room."

"What do you mean?"

"Well, there's no way of getting out of it. Jesus said to forgive seventy times seven in one day! That's a lot of forgiving."

When Colleen thought of forgiving her mother and dad, her stomach turned into a knot. "So you agree with the Amish? About radical forgiveness?"

"I agree with the Bible about forgiveness. The Amish didn't invent it, but they practice it better than any Christian denomination I've seen. Seems like an option in most churches." Suzy looked down and knit quickly. "We all work on it. I have to visit Prissy sometime today, and let me tell you, I don't go skipping over there. Sometimes I wait until Dave has time to go because he drags me over. That woman…. Well, you see, forgiveness isn't a warm and fuzzy feeling. It's a verb."

"What's a verb again?" Colleen asked.

"An action. Like in a sentence, 'Suzy visited Prissy.' Visited is the verb. It's an action, not an emotion."

Colleen had heard Jeb explain this, but how Suzy described it helped her understand a little bit better. "It's a struggle for you to visit Prissy, so forgiveness is a struggle?"

"Well, it depends on how great the offense. I'd say with what you've been through, sweetie, yes, it will be a struggle."

"But I can't face my mom."

"Who said you had to?"

Colleen felt her rigid back relax. "No one. I just thought sooner or later I'd have to talk to her, if I really forgave her."

Suzy narrowed her eyes, as if deep in thought. "Well, Jesus forgave the people who did him wrong, but he chose his closest friends wisely. No one says you have to ever be good friends with your mom. To be honest, it might not be good for you."

"Really?"

"Well, you have a child to think about, and if they're on drugs, you can't expose Aurora to them."

Colleen wanted to jump for joy, but she only ran back over to Suzy and hugged her again. "I thought real forgiveness meant I needed to have a relationship with my parents. Thank you, Suzy." She squeezed her tight. "My family is within the Amish community…and the knitting circle."

"Yes, it is, my girl," Suzy said, "And we're all kindred spirits."

~*~

She passed the massive hollow tree, wondering when a good winter wind would blow it over, like other trees, pulled up by the roots. Truth be told, Mona was glad the old tree was still there, since she hadn't dared to drive a buggy past a certain point, always afraid to move further.

The accident that had happened in her teen years still gave her nightmares, but no one was killed, and for that she was thankful.

Mona spied Maryann's house down the road, off to the left. It was a crisp white color, not having a smidget of cracked paint, unlike hers. How many times had she'd begged Freeman to get a work crew together and have the house scraped and painted? A million? If she hadn't planted flowers outside around the mailbox, people driving by would think they were the strict Schwarsentruber Amish. But her husband was like her own dad, never paying attention to a word she'd said.

When it was time to cross the road, the familiar panic made her palms sweaty. It was a back country road, with no cars in sight, so why did she have such a fear of driving a buggy? It was embarrassing to turn down invitations to work frolics and canning bees of all kinds, and Mona knew people thought her mighty unkind. No, unsociable. If they only knew how hard she tried. And, like Fannie said, she was making progress, joining the dreaded knitting circle.

But Maryann was a few grades behind her in grade school and someone who she'd played with as a wee one. Knowing how upset the family was about the lump Maryann found in her breast just made her put on her boots, cape, bonnet, and force herself to bring words of comfort to her friend.

Mona pulled into the driveway, evenly plowed on both sides, breathed in the crisp winter air and let out a sigh. She'd come over to this house numerous times to pull taffy this time of year. Or pour maple syrup in the snow to let it harden into candy. How much she missed in life, like Marilla, by being afraid...and proud. Not admitting she needed people.

Soon Becca ran out of the side door. "Mona. So...happy to see you!"

"Surprised, *jah*? It's been a while."

"Let me take care of your horse." Becca smiled and took the reins from Mona.

"Danki. I appreciate that." Mona made her way up the walkway to the side door, and again, childhood memories flooded her. Maryann's parents were awfully nice, and never fought, it seemed. Unlike her own parents. She and Freeman rarely talked, but at least they didn't bicker, which was much better. Mona opened the door and walked into the kitchen, seeing Maryann sitting peacefully at the kitchen table, tea cup in hand. But when she saw Mona, she clasped her hand over her mouth. "What's wrong?"

Mona took off her outer bonnet and tapped her boots on the black rubber mat. "Nothing's wrong. Can't I come over and see my *goot* friend unannounced?"

Maryann slumped and grew pale. "Well, you haven't been to my house in decades. Not even when I had my *kinner*..."

"Well, I've been busy raising my own, and *ach,* well, I lost track of time." The excuse sounded lame even to her. "Maryann, I'm mighty concerned about your health, so thought I'd pay a visit."

"I get further testing tomorrow. It could be nothing, just a benign tumor. Has Marge said anything to you?"

"Marge? The *Englisher* that goes to our knitting circle?"

"*Jah*, she's a nurse and helped me through my surgery last year."

Mona shook her head. "Why would Marge say anything to me?"

Maryann fidgeted with the hem of her apron. "Just wondering. I have to say, Mona, your visit alarms me. You haven't been here in years, so I must look like death!"

Mona went to the table and took a seat. "*Nee,* you look fine."

"But, why come now?"

She tapped nervously on the oak table. "Well, to see how you are and to say…I'm sorry."

"For what?"

"We used to be bosom friends, like Anne and Diana. But I was opinionated and grouchy like Rachael Linn. I ruined it…" Maryann looked down, and it appeared to Mona that she hadn't gotten through. "I'm here for you now."

Maryann looked up and set her chin firm. "You want to clear your conscience just in case I do have cancer?"

Mona gasped. "How could you say such a thing?"

"Mona, you've treated me so unkind for years. Do you really think we can carry on our relationship as if nothing had happened? I've been so terribly hurt by you."

"What can I say to make it right?" Mona felt the blood rush down to her toes and a dizzy spell came on, but she would not give in.

"Mona, I forgive you. That you can depend on. But I don't trust you, understand? That needs to be earned."

For some reason, Mona wanted to scream at Maryann. It was mighty unchristian to act this way, and she didn't have the dream family like Maryann did. No, she had grouchy Freeman and only two daughters, not being blessed with more. And Maryann knew she was a nervous driver!

"Would you like some pie?" Maryann asked, with an obligatory smile.

Mona put a hand up. "I'll leave. It's clear that you don't want me here."

Maryann put her hand over her heart. "I guard myself here. Until you can show me you're sorry, I can't let my guard down. Understand?" Maryann paused, as if wondering if she should go on. "How many times had I made plans and you canceled? How many nights I'd cried, knowing I'd lost a friends who was like a sister. And I've stopped by your house, only to be treated rudely." Maryann looked at Mona with a glint of hope in her eyes. "I hope you understand."

"I most certainly do not. You are Amish, and we forgive." Mona spun around and retrieved her bonnet and flew out the door, bumping into Becca as she came in, and didn't even stop to say excuse me. This visit had not turned out to be what she expected. And the bitter pill to swallow was that Maryann was right. She'd ruined their kindred spirit relationship.

~*~

Janice closed her eyes as Linda, an excellent reader, finished Anne of Green Gables. The small group of single mothers who lived at Forget-Me-Not Manor wiped away tears, and one went over and sat next to Janice, leaning her head on her shoulder.

What was it that caused such a reaction from these girls? She needed to find out. "Girls, why all the tears?"

Paula, the girl next to her, said, "I'm so glad you were there for me."

"You took us in when no one wanted us," said another girl.

Janice had tried to get these girls to open up, but nothing seemed to work. "Girls, I have to say, I didn't expect this response to a book. You've read in the Bible about people being not wanted or abused by their families, right? *Yinz* had no reaction after reading about Joseph being sold into slavery by his own brother."

A shy red-haired girl who rarely spoke up in group conversations raised a hand.

"Yes," Janice said, urging her to speak.

"It… it w-was a long book. After a w-while, I felt like A-Anne."

Janice's heart swelled with emotion, since this stuttering girl's story was sadder than most. "So, longer books give you time to take it all in?"

She nodded. "When Anne g-got to stay at G-Green Gables, I felt sad."

"But how is that good?" Janice blurted.

"It m-made me realize I c-could never live here f-forever, and I c-cried. When Granny comes over with p-pies, she talks about cleansing t-tears."

Janice wanted to shake her head in confusion but restrained herself. "So, let me get this right. You read that Anne could stay at Green Gables, you're sad that you can't live here forever, you cried because of that, and you think the tears released your hurt."

All the girls nodded their heads, and Janice realized for the first time that a good book could take the reader to a place where they became the character, and helped them wade through their emotions. What a revelation! "Say, would you girls like to have a regular reading circle?"

The girls agreed in unison, looked at each other and laughed.

"So, what should we read?"

The girl with the red hair again put her hand up. "Can we r-read the book that c-comes after Anne of Green Gables?"

The blond-haired beauty that was cuddling her infant girl raised a hand. "It's listed in the back of the book. It's called Anne of Avonlea."

Janice could feel her smile spread from ear to ear. "Okay. I'll get the books, and we'll see what else we can learn from Anne."

~*~

Lizzie did not participate as Marge challenged the girls to a race to the book section at Punxsy-Mart. She actually held on to the twins' hands as Marge and Jenny ran.

When they arrived at the large book selection, Lizzie's eyes immediately went to books she had on her list for homeschooling. She hadn't taken Jenny out of school…yet. And today, the girls didn't go, instead going on a field trip to Rainbow Alpaca Farm to help feed the animals their breakfast and learn what all was entailed in having one of the beautiful creatures Tillie called 'half lamb, half llama.'

Marge came near her, downcast all of a sudden. "My life is a perfect graveyard of buried hopes."

Lizzie turned to meet her eyes. Marge had confessed the abortion she'd had as a teenager, and how it had haunted her ever since. Was she talking about this? Or her recent miscarriage? "Marge, just when I think you're in a *wunderbar goot* mood, you say such sad things."

"Anne said it in the book, and it's how I feel, here with you and the girls. I'm sorry for being selfish, but now that my closest Amish friends know about my…abortion…and their reaction, saying I was so young, a year older than Maryann's Becca, well, I'm finding healing."

Lizzie put a hand on her English friend's shoulder. "I'm glad. So why the sadness?"

Marge shrugged. "I guess I wanted the baby more than I thought. Guilt clouded my vision or something. But I'd long to have an Anne Girl."

Lizzie had to stifle a grin. Her animated friend did impulsive things, but at least she tried. Moving up to Smicksburg last year to live off the grid and failing was a lesson learned in knowing herself better. Now, reading a book about an orphan girl had Marge thinking she wanted a twelve year old girl with red hair and freckles. Truth be told, so did Lizzie. "I'd like that, too. To save a girl from a life of loneliness and give her a home. Every child deserves a home."

Marge's eyes narrowed and she snapped her fingers. "I've got it. Foster kids. It's like a trial run. It's not an adoption."

Lizzie looked around her, mentally counting three girls, and then thought about what Marge said. Foster children. "Is there a need for foster *kinner?*"

Marge gawked. "Sure is. There are so many kids in foster care; they have them in group homes. They're called orphanages in other countries, but we'd never admit we had orphans in America."

"Don't these *kinner* have any relatives? Some family member to take them in?"

Marge shook her head. "Look at Colleen. She was like a parent to her own folks, them being strung out on drugs. It's more common than you think. And I do home visits when working, and there's a family I need to report." She looked down and wrung her hands. "Problem is they're Amish."

Lizzie gasped. "Who?"

"Oh, the family lives south of here, past Indiana. I think they're Amish, but could be Old Order Mennonite."

"Maybe I know them. What's their last name?"

"Miller. Does that help?"

"*Nee*. First name?"

"Joe and Mary Miller."

Lizzie looked up, deep in thought. "But I know several Joe and Mary Millers that are married, where do I start?"

"By keeping the whole thing I just said under your bonnet. I can't prove it yet. But many kids in foster homes are there until they're eighteen."

"Do their foster parents get to keep them then?"

"Sadly, most go off on their own. Many join the military to get money and an education. So, they're pretty much on their own."

Lizzie took the book Jenny handed her, looked at the title and price, and then nodded her head in approval. "Do you mean all alone? No *kinner* at all?"

"Yes, and it makes me want an Anne-Girl."

"Why are you calling her Anne-Girl?"

"Because Aunt Josephine called her that, and it stuck. She wanted Anne to come and live with her in the fancy city, and be rich, but Anne knew what was important. L-O-V-E. What she found in Matthew and Marilla. I long to do that for a young girl."

Lizzie had a hard time absorbing all that was being said. She looked over at the girls talking cheerfully about what book to buy. They had each other, but it appeared that many didn't. To be totally alone in the world would be an awful feeling. It said in her Bible that the Lord put the lonely in families. Was this something they needed to be doing as a community? Lizzie admired how the Baptists opened a home for single mothers. Did the Amish need to open up homes for foster *kinner*?

Then she thought of Susanna Yoder in New York. Granny wrote to her regularly and gave updates as to her health, and the progress of the foster boys that were adopted by the Cherry Creek Amish. Is this something she needed to talk to Roman about? But he was struggling in the Rocker Shop, brainstorming for new wooden products to make, sales being low. "How can people afford foster *kinner?*" she asked Marge sheepishly.

"Oh, the government gives the foster parents enough money to raise them. It's only when they turn eighteen that they are no longer provided for and most likely why foster parents need to let them go. Not enough money to send them to college or learn a trade. The military does that." Marge peered into Lizzie's eyes like a hawk on prey. "Hey, what are you thinking?"

Lizzie smirked. "I think we're kindred spirits. We think alike."

Marge grabbed her shoulders. "If you look into it, I will, too. We can do it together." Marge was on her tiptoes now with delight, getting ready to do her jumping.

"I think I will…I wouldn't mind having an Anne Girl around…." Tillie pulled on her dress, bringing her back from imagining things…just like Anne. "What is it honey?"

"I can't wait any more. When are we going to the animal shelter?"

Lizzie knelt down to face Tillie. "Did you pick a book out on animals?"

Tillie held up a book on caring for kittens and held it up. "But I can't read it."

Lizzie wondered at times why God allowed her to raise such beautiful girls. She pulled Tillie to herself. "I'll read it to you. Do you want another kitten?"

"*Jah*, but we have a rabbit. Will a cat kill a rabbit?"

Lizzie nodded. "A cat in the house wouldn't be *goot*, but we have them in the barn."

"I wanted a pet for inside. To cuddle with at night."

Marge leaned towards Tillie. "Aw, honey, you have enough love in that heart of yours for two people." She rubbed the top of Tillie's bonnet playfully. "When we get to the animal shelter, another animal might grab at your big heart. One that gets along with rabbits.'

Lizzie looked up at Marge. "What gets along with a rabbit?"

"Anything but a cat, and we'll see lots of animals today, even rabbits. People can't seem to afford pet food anymore." Her eyes widened. "Maybe your rabbit would like a friend. How about another rabbit?"

Tillie's eyes misted. "Daed said I can't sleep with a rabbit on the bed, like Oma and Opa do with a dog." She looked hopefully at Lizzie. "Maybe we'll find a little dog."

Lizzie moaned.

~*~

Granny closed her eyes after she read the monthly newsletter from Christian Aid Ministries. She put her rocker to motion while the wind knocked to get inside. How many people were out on the streets in such weather? Why was she so blessed all her seventy years to live in such comfort, while others didn't have their basic needs met? Clean water and daily food. *Ach,* Lord, we do try to give as much as we can. And I'm knitting scarves, but it just doesn't seem enough.

The windows rattled and a draft swept through the room. Jeb opened the side door, inviting December winter to come on in and have a seat. Why didn't he close the door sooner? Old man....at seventy-three. Who knew how long he'd be with her or vice versa?

Feeling the cares of the world creep up on her, she quickly cast poverty in America on the Lord, knowing He was a big God who cared, and she was only one person. Then she lifted up the uncanny fear she had about being separated from Jeb that just wouldn't let her have any peace.

"Take a look, Deborah," Jeb said in hushed tones.

"What?" She opened her eyes and was glad she was sitting down. Jebediah Weaver, she wanted to scream. Another dog?

"Look, but be quiet. She's sleeping."

"Where'd you get that little dog, Jeb?"

"Lizzie and Marge rescued her today. Isn't she cute?"

"She's thin, poor thing."

"Doesn't weigh more than a little bag of flour from the store. Here, hold her."

As Jeb placed the shorthaired black dog on her lap, Granny's heart went out to the little critter. "Well, whose dog is it? Lizzie's or Marge's?"

Jeb sat in the rocker next to hers. "Tillie. They adopted her but Roman doesn't want a dog in the house..."

Granny stroked the dog's trembling body. "It's okay. Hush now."

"Well," Jeb continued, looking away from her. "I thought we'd keep her."

"What? Jebediah Weaver! We already have a dog in the house."

"*Ach*, Bea. I'll introduce them to each other."

To her shock, he went over to the blue rag rug near the woodstove and placed the little black dog next to Bea. "Bea, meet your new friend." Bea awoke and sniffed the dog, then, like a miracle, put one of her paws over it, as if trying to cuddle. "Will you look at that," Jeb beamed. "Bea. I'm so proud of you."

Granny reluctantly got up and went over to the stove, and had to admit she was touched. Bea is such a dear dog. She put her hand on Jeb's arm. "Old man. I know you like the dog and all, but dogs shed and I don't want two in the house. Most likely why Roman's putting up a fuss, since they already have a rabbit."

"He's just stubborn, is all. Tillie's a shy one, and needs a pet. They help bring you out of a shell." He picked up the little dog. "I know my dogs did for me."

How did Jeb do it? Pull at her heartstrings so? He'd been raised Schwartzentruber, the strictest of all Amish groups, and there were no end to the effects such nonsensical rules made. He'd even been told that to plant flowers was vanity and showed pride. Years ago, for him to plant her roses was a big step of freedom for him. "Jeb, let me pray on keeping the dog, so we're in agreement, *jah*?"

He bent down and kissed her cheek. "Of course. I thought you'd be real taken with her big brown eyes..."

She hadn't even noticed the dog's eyes, only Jeb's...so childlike and happy. He's still young inside, Granny thought. *Ach,* his body is old now, but he's still the man who won her heart so long ago. Not wanting to be impulsive, she just said, "I'll be thinking and praying about this real hard." To change the subject, she asked if he'd gotten the mail.

"Jah. Another letter from Nathan and Lavina. Having a *goot* time in Montana. Maybe a little too *goot.*"

"What does that mean?"

"Maybe they'll never come home..."

"*Ach*, Jeb. They bought the farm down the road." Just when his young side peeped out, his *ferhoodled* old-man-talk took over. What notions he'd been having lately. She went over to where the mail was placed and read all the letters, some circle letters, and some from pen pals.

~*~

Suzy pushed the button to release wiper fluid on her windshield as a passing Jeep spit up salt and ice onto her car. She spied her friend, Ginny, in the Jeep that had just passed. Ginny Rowland, her dear best friend and next door neighbor, had penciled her own name beside half of the church's shut-in list, and for that Suzy was thankful. But when Ginny said she needed to visit Prissy on a weekly basis, and 'love her enemies,' she wanted to throw a ball of yarn at her. And Colleen fears she'll be watched twenty-four-seven by the Amish? *Ha!* Suzy was scrutinized every day in a small town, and country gossip traveled as fast as the Amish grapevine.

She turned left and went down the steep hill that descended to Prissy's sprawling estate: thirty acres with a mansion in the middle, a black topped driveway that was maintained by her very own private gardener. *With the amount of money lavished on Prissy, a village in Haiti could be fed,* Suzy thought with a groan. Why would God freely give money to such a miser, never giving to any charities, yet living in a lap of luxury? Ginny wanted her to search her heart. *Was she jealous of Prissy? Surely she was not!*

As she drove near the entrance, Sammy was busy shoveling the sidewalk, snow falling too fast to keep up. The tall man looked up at her, and with his fur aviator style hat, Suzy thought he looked like a Viking. How ironic, she thought. Prissy can boss around a Viking. To her surprise, she started to chuckle, most likely letting off nervous energy, and Sammy came near the car. She opened the door and he asked for her keys.

"Thanks Sammy. Are you Prissy's...I mean Missy's valet service now?"

The kind, sensitive, elderly man's eyebrows shot up. "Making ends meet, is all."

"Oh, Sammy, I'm sorry. I'm kind of nervous to see...you know...the town miser herself."

Sammy took her keys. "If you knew her, you wouldn't say that."

"Why?"

"Well, it's not for me to say. I've just changed my mind about her."

With that Sammy got into the car and drove it towards the large detached garage on the side of the house. The garage that some suspected had a dozen antique cars housed in it, worth a fortune. Suzy felt her stomach flip. *Lord, the garage itself could house several Haitian families.* Ginny's son, now a missionary in Haiti, had written regularly and sent pictures back home, and the Baptists had given all they could, while not neglecting the needs of their own...in Smicksburg.

Suzy walked up to the door, gift bag in hand, and rang the doorbell. The door opened immediately, and a pretty young woman said hello and welcomed her in. Suzy suspected she was one of the maids, but the woman was a total stranger to her. She'd never seen her in town, but then again, Prissy lived two miles out of Smicksburg. Suzy followed the woman to a large living room she was sure she could fit her entire first floor of her house into. Windows from the high ceilings down to the plush rose colored carpet. Two overstuffed Victorian couches in shades of cream faced each other and burgundy leather Queen Anne chairs were dotted throughout the room. What luxury. But where was Prissy?

The woman she supposed was the maid had left her in the room, but to be by herself? "Maybe she had to put the crown on her royal highness and announce her arrival," Suzy said with a sigh.

"Excuse me?" said a voice behind Suzy but she didn't see anyone. "Hello?"

Soon a head popped up from the opposing couch. Prissy must have been lying on it, out of view. Suzy cleared her throat. "Why, ah, hi. Came here bearing gifts." She held up the pink gift bag.

Prissy, who was still in her silk white bathrobe, with a matching turban on her head, appeared to have just gotten up, but it was noon!

"I'm sorry, are you ill?" Suzy wondered.

"No. I don't go out much, and, well, stay in my lounge clothes."

The distance between them could have been a mile in many ways, but Suzy put one foot in front of the other and walked over and handed her the bag, and then took a seat on one of the burgundy chairs.

Prissy nodded, as if that was her way of saying thank you, and pulled the tissue paper out of the bag. She pulled up the shawl that Suzy had knit her; a prayer shawl.

"Oh, ah, thank you. A wide scarf."

Suzy's head jerked back as if hit in the face. "It's a shawl, not a scarf. Mighty wide to be a scarf."

"Oh, what I meant to say is stole. I have several mink stoles this wide and I do like how they keep my shoulders warn."

"Well, a shawl is like a stole, only made of yarn, not fur." Suzy cracked a knuckle, forcing herself to keep looking into the haughty pale blue eyes of Prissy. "I made it. It's called a Prayer Shawl. When I, ah, made it, I...prayed for you."

"Whatever for?" Prissy asked, snickering. "I have all of this," she said, as she picked up her dainty hand and swayed it around, pointing to the room.

Suzy looked at her watch. "Well, you lost your husband a while back, and are here alone. Just want you to know that you can call the Baptist church for anything you need."

Prissy stared at her. "But I have all I need."

Suzy pointed to the bag. "There's something else in there, on the bottom."

Prissy reached down and pulled out a book. "A Christmas Carol. How nice. I have several antique copies of Dickens works, but not A Christmas Carol."

"It's from Ginny Rowland. The children in our church are putting on a play in a few weeks. It's all based on A Christmas Carol, and we'd like for you to come."

Prissy rolled her eyes. "Poor Ginny Rowland. Someone should have helped her get through mid-life crisis better. Selling her big old farmhouse to live on top of her bookstore...."

Suzy jumped up, ready to defend her friend. "The Rowlands practically gave the church their house for homeless single moms. Surely you know the good that came out of them downsizing?"

Prissy clucked her tongue. "It's all ridiculous. We work hard for what we get to enjoy, not give it away to people who won't work."

Suzy feared she'd lose her temper, and promised Ginny that if Prissy said anything condescending about her living on top of her yarn shop, she'd only explain how happy she was, having a simpler life. "Ginny and James love living in four rooms, making life simpler. And they can give more to the orphanage their son helps run in Haiti..."

Prissy sniffed. "If you don't work, you don't eat. Isn't that somewhere in the Bible?"

Suzy wanted to scream, so she closed her eyes, and counted to ten, and then took a deep breath. "I best be going. The invitation to the Christmas play is in the bag. Have to run. Teaching a knitting class at one."

"In that puny little shop of yours? For heaven's sake, I would have continued taking lessons if we had room to sprawl out..."

An idea popped into Suzy's mind, but she dismissed it, knowing God would certainly not push her beyond what she could handle. But the impression came into her heart in a still small whisper. Teach Missy how to knit in her home...Suzy held her hand to her heart, realizing it must be the voice of God, because he knew His children by name. He called her Missy...not Prissy.

~*~

Granny felt heat rise into her cheeks when she saw all the women already seated for the knitting circle in her living room. Lizzie was busy at the kitchen table, cutting the raisin bars she'd made..."Ach, Lizzie, why didn't you wake me?"

"You looked too peaceful," Lizzie said. "And to sleep through all this howling wind, I figured you were bushed."

"I have been tired all day," she admitted. Getting old. Granny rubbed the back of her neck, and getting up to get some coffee and a bar cookie, she entered her living room. All the girls welcomed her, some concerned that she was sick, being in such a sound sleep. "*Ach, nee,* just fell asleep reading letters." She looked around the room after she took her seat. "Where's Ruth?"

Suzy spoke up while knitting. "Oh, I saw her in town with Luke. She had to see the doctor and can't make it."

"Well, she's pregnant." Granny said, concern noticeable in her voice. "Let's keep her in our prayers." Still feeling half asleep, she took a sip of coffee, and then noticed no one was eating. "Did everyone get raisin bars?"

"Jah," Fannie offered. "*Danki*, Granny. We devoured them…"

Suzy looked up and grinned at Granny. "I want that recipe for sure." She leaned towards Janice, seated next to her. "I think we can start discussing Anne of Green Gables now. Our Anne Girl seems to have helped the girls at Forget Me Not Manor."

Janice yawned. "Well, that book made some of the girls cry for the first time, or they spoke up about their past hurts. I've been spending lots of nights up counseling." Her shoulders slumped. "I am plumb exhausted."

"*Goot* literature changes us, *jah*?" Granny, now fully awake, chimed in.

"Yes," Janice continued, "but now they want to read Anne of Avonlea, and I can't keep up with the reading here." She flashed a smile at Marge. "Maybe I'll go back to watching the movies."

Marge giggled and Granny was glad to see it. How many days, and long into the night had she and Jeb talked to Marge and Joe about how God forgave them years ago? They were teenagers and not married yet when they were coaxed into aborting their child. How *goot* forgiveness is…

Suzy pointed at Colleen, fondly. "Tell the group what you got out of Anne of Green Gables."

Colleen put down her knitting and it was obvious she was fighting mighty hard to keep her tears from spilling down her cheeks. She stared at Janice, and then darted over to her, embracing her around the neck. "Thank you. I miss you."

Janice got up and held Colleen to herself. "What's wrong, Colleen?"

Colleen took the Kleenex Suzy offered, and blew her nose. "I realized that you and Jerry are my Matthew and Marilla. Thank you ever so much."

Janice cupped Colleen's cheeks. "You are so welcome. And we love you and want the best for you. No strings attached…*jah?*"

Colleen grinned when Janice used an Amish word. "So, you really aren't hurt that I'm not Baptist anymore? That I quit the program?"

Janice put two hands up, her palms up as if receiving something. "We take in our girls like this. It's with an open hand and heart, not one with a grip on you. We only want the Lord's hand on you. Understand?"

Colleen embraced her again. "I do now. But just so you know, you and Jerry are my Matthew and Marilla, saving me from a life filled with window friends."

"I needed to hear that." Janice admitted. "It's draining at times, helping the girls at the manor."

Suzy bellowed an '*Amen Sista*' and the room echoed with laughter as Janice and Colleen sat down and took up their knitting again. Suzy asked Granny what she got out of the book.

"Well, since we're talking from the heart… I'm worried for Jeb. Matthew died in the book because of financial problems. Sales are slow in the rocker shop…" She fiddled with her yarn. "Well, Jeb trusts God, but I'm embarrassed to say I'm struggling with it."

Lizzie groaned. "I feel the same way. I see Roman at the table at night, drawing up designs…"

"Well, why not put some little things for sale in my shop, and I'm sure I can make the connections to other stores." Suzy offered.

"What?" blurted Mona. "Depend on the English to make a living?"

Fannie nudged her. "*Mamm*, we've talked about this, *jah*? Melvin's clock shop wouldn't make it if it weren't for the English."

Mona pursed her lips and lifted her nose up in the air, for what seemed forever to Granny. I hope someone corrects her. Lord, let it be your will.

But the room was silent, all the women knitting away, appearing to concentrate a little too hard to make such easy scarves. Janice got out her phone and started to type away. "What are you doing?" Granny asked.

"Oh, adding to our prayer list. I just put in Jeb and Roman."

"Can you add Prissy? I mean Missy. Pray for me, too." Suzy said in a monotone voice as she knit at an even pace. "I'm visiting her and took her the prayer shawl I made. She called it a scarf, can you believe it?"

Janice chuckled. "Iron sharpens iron and that woman makes sparks fly, huh?"

Suzy kept knitting. "I am praying for her and this agoraphobia she has. It really is pitiful, but if Prissy were only nicer...But us Baptists, we're there to visit shut-ins come hail, sleet, or snow." Suzy laughed at her own dramatics, and looked over at Mona. "So, what did you get out of the book?"

Mona's eyes, dark and foreboding, simply said, "It's private."

Granny listened as rain pelted the window. *Drip, drip, drip.* Mona was a constant drip in her life, similar to the woman Suzy was visiting. And Granny was praying for

Mona, but…right now, most likely she wanted pity and for the circle to pry out of her what she got from the book. Self-pity was something Granny did not feed.

"Mona, did you like the book?" Suzy probed.

"It was alright."

Granny wanted to ask if she'd learned anything about cranky people being changed by the sweet tempered Anne. Was she ever affected by the sweet tempered Fannie, the daughter she ridiculed to no end? She stared at her knitting, shades of black and white making a unique pattern.

"Where's Maryann?" Janice asked, breaking the stillness.

"Getting herself prepared for tomorrow," Granny answered. "We're going to get that test done. *Ach,* another thing to pray about. Pray it's just a benign cyst."

"I have her on the list already. The whole church is praying for a good report," Janice said. Clearing her throat, she put a book up for all to see. "We're giving this book out for Christmas presents to shut-ins and I want *yinz* to have one. Actually, it would make my life easier if we could do it here, since the church is doing the play and…"

Suzy intervened. "What Janice is saying is that we're so busy the weeks leading up to Christmas, doing lots of outreach, so could we read A Christmas Carol next?"

Janice handed the paperback books out to all the women. Granny noticed Charles Dickens had written it. How much enjoyment Jeb was getting over the *Charles Dickens Devotional,* and she was sure he'd give her no questioning look when she showed him the book she was reading. She opened it to read, Marley was dead: to begin with. There is no doubt whatever about that.

What an odd way to start a book, Granny thought. "Janice, is this a sad book? About a man's funeral?"

"No, it's really like a long parable. You see, a miserly old man, Scrooge, is warned by his dead business partner that he needs to change his ways."

Granny gasped. "A dead business partner? Do you mean this is about talking to the dead?"

"No," Janice said. "It's about three ghosts who visit —"

Mona stood up tall. "Ghosts? We don't read about ghosts, or talking to the dead, or whatever you're trying to say."

Janice's head jerked back as if slapped. "It's called symbolism. The ghosts take Scrooge back in time to see his faults, then show him the future."

Granny could hardly believe she and Mona would both see eye-to-eye on anything. "Foretelling the future? It's forbidden in the Bible. Janice, I'm surprised your church is doing this as a play."

Janice's eyes got as round as saucers. "Charles Dickens was a Christian trying to teach a lesson through this book. It's kind of like a fantasy."

Colleen spoke up. "Granny, I've seen the movie. It's really wonderful, and I know you don't like fantasy, but it makes you change for the better."

Mona put her hand on her heart. "And you're going to be Amish. Well, this is a pretty kettle of fish."

Fannie started to laugh along with Marge.

Mona planted both hands on her hips. "What's so funny?"

"You are," Marge blurted, laughing harder. "You and Fannie. Fannie talks Jane Austen lines, and you just said something right out of Anne of Green Gables."

"I did not!"

Fannie held her middle and giggled. "Mamm, you've never said, 'This is a pretty kettle of fish' in my whole life. It's what Marilla says when she meets Anne."

Mona rolled her eyes and dismissed what Fannie said with the swoosh of her hand. "That's ridiculous." She spun around and glared at Granny. "Surely you won't allow this book to be read by real Amish folk." She glanced over at Colleen, nose up.

Granny put her head back on her rocker and closed her eyes. *Lord, I need wisdom. Help me.* As soon as she prayed, an idea popped into her head. She smiled and looked around the room. "What is the biggest sin?"

"What?" Mona snapped. "Not being obedient to the Bible."

"Not loving," Granny said, almost in a whisper. "We are to love each other, not seek our own way. We are all Christians and I'm thinking we need to respect others' convictions. If Janice has read this here book, and knows that its meaning will be helpful to point others to the straight and narrow, I say let's believe the best in her. Love thinks the best, *jah?* 1 Corinthians 13? But we Amish have to live by our *Ordnung* and no fantasy stories are allowed, especially ones with ghosts."

Suzy leaned forward. "That is so true. We all have different convictions about things. So what are we going to read that everyone agrees on?"

"Well," Granny continued, "*yinz* are busy at the Baptist church and are all reading this book. Since we know Charles Dickens was a good Christian man, is there another book that he wrote that we Amish can read?"

Marge gasped. "We can have a Dickens Christmas Party! Make desserts from his books. I always wanted to try figgie pudding."

"Well, I think that's a *goot* idea," Granny said. "I learned how to make fondant for Colleen's wedding cake, and I like a challenge." She looked over at Suzy. "So, what can we read?"

Suzy was looking straight ahead of her, deep in thought. "His books are long, very long. I'll have to go online and look to see if there are any less than four-hundred pages. He wrote some shorter stories, called novellas, so maybe I can find something."

"So, can we have a Dickens party?" Marge was on her toes, jumping, and Granny knew the weight of guilt the poor soul was trying to overcome. How Granny wanted to have a Christmas party, just to lend Marge her continued support. She found herself saying, yes.

Mona groaned.

~*~

Marge and Joe sat in their regular pew at the Smicksburg Baptist Church. Were they getting so stuck in their ways? Always sitting in the same place? Marge mused as she took Joe's hand and smiled. "I did it. I took Granny's advice and told Janice."

"And?"

"Not a smidgen of judgment. Can you believe it? Really, this is all such a shock."

Joe's eyes moistened. "And to think we kept it a secret all these years."

Marge nodded in agreement. "Confession is *goot* for the soul, as Granny says, and now we know first-hand. The guilt over that abortion, so long ago, when we didn't even know better...Well, I feel so much better."

"Me too. I thought for sure this church would kick us out or something."

Ginny Rowland got up, guitar in tow, and asked everyone to sing along with the words on the overhead projector. She introduced the song as Amazing Grace, but said that the real song's ending had been changed, and the original had been recently discovered.

She went on to say that John Newton, who wrote the lyrics, was a slave trader, and many lives were lost while he was in business. But when he became a Christian, he stopped what he was doing, became a pastor, and he was amazed at the forgiveness and grace God showed him.

Ginny asked if they could sing the first stanza, then skip down to the fourth and really think about the rest of the song. "Remember," she said, "this was a man responsible for many deaths and great cruelty. Think of how deep God's forgiveness really is."

She did a little guitar intro, then sang:

Amazing grace! how sweet the sound
That saved a wretch like me!
I once was lost, but now am found,
Was blind, but now I see.

The Lord has promised good to me,
His word my hope secures;
He will my shield and portion be,
As long as life endures.

Yes, when this flesh and heart shall fail,
And mortal life shall cease;
I shall possess, within the veil,
A life of joy and peace.

The earth shall soon dissolve like snow,
The sun forbear to shine;
But God, who called me here below,
Will be forever mine.

Marge wondered if Janice asked Ginny to do this song just for them. How light she felt, not carrying such a burden. And she lifted her hands and praised God for his forgiveness... and her knitting circle friends.

~*~

Jeb set the table and then put pure maple syrup out, since Deborah loved to bathe blueberry pancakes in it. He'd keep the pancakes hot on the cast iron skillet until she came in. Going over to the little blue rag rug, he knelt down to pet Bea and her new friend, Angel. That Deborah had held the dog, saying 'love doesn't seek its own way,' had touched him to no end, so this name she'd come up with, Angel, was gladly accepted. He hoped this little dog wouldn't be a burden, but a blessing to his dear wife. Jeb playfully rubbed the top of her small black head. "Angel, are you going to be a burden or blessing?"

He glanced over at the pendulum clock. *Noon?* Maryann's appointment was at seven. He got up and paced the floor, fearing they were delayed because they didn't get good news. He took a seat at his rocker and finished reading *Anne of Green Gables*. Helping homeschool Jenny was more educational and rewarding than he thought, since he was gaining so much insight from the books picked for knitting circle. But he could not have them read *A Christmas Carol*, and was glad Deborah had not tried to persuade him otherwise.

God's in his heaven; all's right with the world.

He reread the line again. *Jah*, no matter what the test results showed, God was in heaven and not taken by surprise. But Lord, please let it be nothing. Let Maryann be healthy for her *kinner*.

He heard the rumble of a car engine and soon saw the English driver they'd hired to take them to the hospital. Jeb squinted to see if Maryann was in the car, but he only saw Deborah, and ran out to the porch and quickly down the steps to make sure she didn't slip on any icy patches.

One look into her eyes told him volumes. The cancer was gone. *Maryann was well. Praise be.* He led her inside. "*Goot* news?"

"*Jah. Goot* news. The dizzy spells were all her nerves and anxiety, fearing the cancer had come back. She had calcium deposits in the breast, and those were the lumps." Granny looked over at Bea and Angel who were sound asleep. "Did you tire them out?"

Jeb nodded. "It's their noon nap time, like little *kinner*. Were Maryann's tests mighty long?"

"We went out to eat to celebrate after the *goot* news."

Jeb had waited patiently for hours, fearing the worst. "Well, you had the whole *Gmay* on pins and needles about the test results." His shoulders slumped and he went over to the peg to get his coat. "Best be going to tell the elders."

Granny ran towards him and grabbed his arm. "Jeb, what's wrong?"

"Nothing…"

"*Ach*, you're upset with me. I can see that."

Jeb knew how they talked about what love really was last night. It was patient and kind, not seeking his own. He felt unappreciated right now, since the table was set, and obviously Deborah saw the effort he made to make her a good meal. But his wife was so worried and now relieved, and she deserved to go out to eat. He pulled her to himself. "I made your favorite pancakes, but we'll warm them up for breakfast tomorrow."

"What pancakes?"

"The ones on the table…"

She pulled away and looked towards the table. "I don't see any pancakes. Looks like you left maple syrup on the table and plates…"

Jeb grinned. "*Ach*, love is not easily offended, and look at me. The pancakes are in the skillet."

Granny turned to him, got up on her tiptoes and kissed his cheek. "Jeb, you are the most *wunderbar* husband. *Danki* for thinking of me. I love you so."

He scooped her into his arms. "I love you, too."

~*~

Exhausted from the stressful morning, Granny sat in her rocker to knit after Jeb left to spread the good news. Maryann was cancer-free. *Praise be*!

She thought of the fears that Anne of Green Gables put in her heart concerning Jeb. Matthew had died, and Jeb would someday, too. And Maryann also, but most likely Granny wouldn't be around to see it.

She noticed the bird feeder was full of blue jays and cardinals, bigger birds that chased away the little sparrows. Sparrows. God kept his eyes on the sparrow, and he watched over Jeb. Over Maryann. Over her. Full of elation, she got up and sang the hymn she loved so well:

Why should I feel discouraged, why should the shadows come,
Why should my heart be lonely, and long for heaven and home,
When Jesus is my portion? My constant friend is He:
His eye is on the sparrow, and I know He watches me;
His eye is on the sparrow, and I know He watches me.

I sing because I'm happy,
I sing because I'm free,
For His eye is on the sparrow,
And I know He watches me.

"Let not your heart be troubled," His tender word I hear,
And resting on His goodness, I lose my doubts and fears;
Though by the path He leadeth, but one step I may see;
His eye is on the sparrow, and I know He watches me;
His eye is on the sparrow, and I know He watches me.

I sing because I'm happy,
I sing because I'm free,
For His eye is on the sparrow,
And I know He watches me.

Whenever I am tempted, whenever clouds arise,
When songs give place to sighing, when hope within me dies,
I draw the closer to Him, from care He sets me free;
His eye is on the sparrow, and I know He watches me;
His eye is on the sparrow, and I know He watches me.

Dear readers,

Are you worried about the future? I'll be the first to admit I do lots of casting off prayers daily, being a worry wart of sorts. But as an avid birdwatcher, I see the sparrows, and think of this scripture often:

What is the price of two sparrows—one copper coin? But not a single sparrow can fall to the ground without your Father knowing it. And the very hairs on your head are all numbered. So don't be afraid; you are more valuable to God than a whole flock of sparrows. Matthew 10: 29-31 NLT

Since many of you feel like you're part of Granny's knitting circle, why not sing the hymn Granny sang, and let its truth sink deep down into your heart?

I leave you all, once again, with an Amish recipe that Granny uses for dessert at knitting circle.

Raisin Bars

1 c. raisins
1 c. water
½ c. oil
½ c. brown sugar
½ c. sugar
1 egg
1 ¾ c. flour
1 tsp. cinnamon
1 tsp. nutmeg
 Pinch of salt
1 tsp. allspice
1 tsp. baking soda
½ tsp. ground cloves

Combine raisins and water in a pan and bring to gentle boil. Remove from heat when raisins are plump. Stir in oil and cool. Stir in sugar and egg. Sift dry ingredients and beat into mixture. Pour into greased 13 x 9 pan. Bake at 350 degrees for 25 minutes, or until done. Cut into squares when cool.

2/3 c. shortening
1 tsp. salt
¾ c. milk
4 ½ tsp. baking powder
5 eggs whites, unbeaten
½ c. milk
1 tsp. vanilla

Sift dry ingredients. Add shortening and milk and then beat. Add remaining ingredients. Bake at 350 for 30 minutes. Insert toothpick to see if done.

EPISODE 4

❧

Dickens Of A Tale

Jeb scooped scrambled eggs onto his plate. "*Danki*, Love. You make eggs the best."

Granny's eyebrows arched. "I'm the only one who's cooked for you in how long?" She bent over and kissed his cheek and gave him a playful hug around the neck, then took her place across the table from him. "Isn't this morning *wunderbar*? A sunny day in the middle of December is a treasure, for sure."

Jeb nodded. "*Jah*. A sunny day in December reminds me of our courting days. Seems like the *goot* lord was so happy we discovered we loved each other, He applauded from heaven."

Granny grinned. "That's mighty fancy talk, old man. You thinking of that Max Lucado book you're reading, Applause of Heaven?"

He took a sip of coffee. "*Jah*. Maybe. But I've been thinking about David Copperfield and my Dickens Devotional, too."

"Winter and reading go together mighty nice. And we haven't read a book out loud together in years."

"I have to read more, being the Bishop. Have to screen these books your circle's reading."

"Sorry, Love. Didn't think it would come to this. I never knew there were so many opinions on books. It's all such a trifle if you think of all the books you can read."

Jeb winked. "Like your Jane Austen said, 'Life seems but a quick succession of busy nothings'. *Jah*, a trifle."

Granny didn't understand his meaning. "Jeb, you don't have to look through any Jane Austen books. What are you talking about?"

His grin expanded into a broad smile, as he took a little package out of his pocket. "I got this for you, Love. You know I can never wait until Christmas to give you a present."

Granny felt heat rise in her cheeks, like a young teen. "*Ach. Danki*, Jeb." She took the little present, wrapped in white tissue paper, and saw A Little Book of Jane Austen Quotes. She opened it up to see that each page of the book was illustrated with pictures. Such pretty dresses, she thought. "I love it," she said, looking over at her dear husband.

He nodded. "I thought you would. I've been reading it, and what Austen said about life being busy with nothing, is true, *jah*?"

"If we let it. You thinking of Colleen?"

"*Jah*. She's struggling with following rules. But, let's not talk about my burdens this morning."

"I help carry them..."

He shook his head. "Not today. How about we decorate for Christmas?"

Granny's heart literally fluttered. *He wanted to put greenery and red candles in the window, reminiscent of their first Christmas together as a courting couple.* But soon the image of Mona broke through, and Granny felt her heart stop. No more fluttering, but panic set in. "Mona will criticize again!"

Jeb took a sip of coffee. "And you can tell her our story. Turn her critical remarks into a conversation. Maybe get to the woman's heart."

Granny took her fork and stabbed at the eggs in front of her. "If she has one!"

"Love. Come now. You can't hate."

Granny felt sweat forming on her forehead and her hands grew clammy. "Hates a strong word, Jebediah Weaver."

He waved one of his long crooked fingers at her. "Love your enemies."

Love Mona? The woman is downright spiteful. Granny closed her eyes and counted to ten, something Suzy did regularly, and she found her pulse slowing down. "Jeb, you're right. Now, let's decorate the windows and when Mona comes over for knitting circle and criticizes, I'll…" She put her hand over her heart, "try to dig deeper and maybe find a heart."

Jeb looked over at their two little dogs, Bea and Angel, both snuggling against each other, sharing the small blue rag rug. "I know, Deborah. Sometimes it's easier to get along with animals than some surly folk. Look at those two."

~*~

Colleen watched Aurora put gold glitter on the Christmas cards she was making for her new friends at the one-room Amish schoolhouse. Hezekiah squeezed her hand tighter. "We'll be a family in early spring, Lord willing." He stole a kiss on her cheek, and then caressed her hand. "I'm hopeful."

Colleen didn't know if she should wait until after Christmas to tell Hezekiah the truth. She was suffocating under the strict Amish rules.

"I'll plant a huge orchard in the spring, and add to Ella and Zach's pumpkin patch. And since corn did well last year, maybe have a corn maze just for fun."

She put her head on his shoulder. "Maybe."

"You want to do something else?"

Not be Amish, she wanted to scream, but instead said, "Hezekiah, I'm struggling again."

"With your baptismal classes?"

"No, I like them. So full of the Bible, but it's the rules. I don't know. It still bothers me that I couldn't read *A Christmas Carol*. I've seen the movie, and it's harmless."

"But there's ghosts in it."

"Well, they're called ghosts but they direct a man to better himself."

"Are they angels then?"

Colleen hadn't thought of that. "Maybe. But it doesn't matter. The 'angels' show the future as a lesson to a man, and the Amish see it as fortune telling."

Hezekiah withdrew his hand. "I don't like your tone. When you say 'Amish' you make it sound like something you despise."

Colleen put her head down. "I'm sorry. I'm afraid. Every concern I put in my trifle box I've realized in a few days it was no big deal. But not this time. "

Hezekiah fidgeted with the edge of his vest. "You have to have rules. I don't agree with them all, but I abide by them. Like when you used to drive a car, and said the speed limit was too low. You still obeyed the law, *jah?*"

Colleen nodded. "I just don't know why not being able to read A Christmas Carol bothers me still."

Aurora looked up at her, black eyes shining. "Mommy, see my card? This one's for Grandma."

Colleen smiled, but was baffled as to why she felt so sad. She should be happy that her child was in a warm home, not being out on the streets like last Christmas.

Hezekiah put his arm around her. "Colleen. What did you do for Christmas when you were a *kinner?* Did you make cards?"

Colleen's stomach tightened. "It's hard to talk about, really. I can't remember many happy times. Not many good memories, except books. I'd get my hands on any Christmas library book at school, and bury myself in them…"

"Honey, maybe that's why you're struggling with the book you can't read."

"What?"

"Books were a substitute for real friends, *jah*? You felt alone, so you daydreamed, living your life in books."

Colleen thought of Anne of Green Gables, her nose always in a book. Was she so similar? She even had window friends… "But I have lots of friends now. And a family."

Hezekiah peered over at the pendulum clock, and then looked at her with his blue eyes twinkling with delight. "Indiana County's called 'The Christmas Tree Capital of the World' by the English tourist," he whispered in her ear. "How about we take Aurora out on a sleigh ride and get a tree? We can start some new Christmas traditions, the three of us."

Tears stung Colleen's eyes, touched by how much he loved her daughter. "But the Amish don't have Christmas trees."

"We're getting a pine tree, not a Christmas tree. I want to show you something I did as a kid for fun."

"With a Christmas tree?"

"With a pine tree," he mused.

What she ever did to deserve such a man, she'd never know. He could pry her open so fast with his love and helped heal wounds. "Thank you so much," Colleen said.

"For a tree?"

"No, by listening and caring. I think I know why A Christmas Carol can now be taken out of my trifle box. I don't live through books anymore." Colleen asked Aurora to go check on her grandma to see if she needed help with the noon meal as an excuse to be alone with her wonderful fiancé. When Aurora was out of sight, she locked her arms around Hezekiah's neck, and kissed him until she was out of breath.

~*~

Maryann watched the snowflakes land on her black cape, and she thanked God she would be alive to see many more winters, Lord willing. The sun gleamed through puffy clouds, making streaks across open white fields, winter wheat peeping through.

Getting a clean bill of health, no cancer whatsoever found, was the white icing on the cake. The depth of concern her dear husband showed, saying he wanted to die if she did, that he needed her desperately, and not just to tend the eight *kinner*, well, she was a blessed woman, indeed.

And all her knitting circle friends' concern… even Mona's. How cold she'd been to her when visiting a few weeks back, but she was in shock, since Mona hadn't been to her house in decades. Hurt was more the word; they had been so close years ago. That her *kinner* didn't really know her, and Mona made no attempt to be friendly, only added to the wound she thought was long gone.

She pulled into Mona's place, the driveway slippery with ice and snow. Hadn't her husband plowed it? Maryann went as close to the side door as possible, found a place to hitch her horse, and lifted the basket with warm mincemeat pies out of the buggy. She walked inside, and as usual, no movement and all was dark. Blinds down in every window. Did Mona suffer from migraines and not tell anyone? No noon meal being prepared… was there no one home?

Maryann yelled a 'hello' loud enough for the cows in the barn to hear. The wind rattled the windows, making a din. Did she need to yell louder? "Hello!"

Not a peep. Maryann went to raise one of the kitchen blinds, and jumped when she heard movement in the utility room. Mice? *Ach,* there were too many cats in the barn for that. She wanted to jump on the table, but knew better. Instead, she continued to lift all the blinds in the kitchen, got a broom and opened the door to the utility room. She jumped back when she saw Mona. "What on earth are you doing in there? Didn't you hear me?"

Mona stared, eyes round. "*Nee.* I didn't."

Maryann looked about to see if Mona was doing laundry, but there was no sign of it. Was Mona hiding in the utility room, not answering the door on purpose? Feeling hurt, Maryann motioned to the basket. "I brought you some pies, but need to go. I have a shopping list a mile long to get over at Fannie's store."

She turned and made a beeline towards the side door, but Mona spoke up. "Wait."

Wait? How long do I have to wait for the old Mona to come back? The girl she'd been bosom friends with in school, only to be treated like a contagion. Maryann wanted to scream, tell her what she thought of her odd behavior, but then thought of *The Life of our Lord*, by Charles Dickens. He wasn't even Amish, yet believed in absolute forgiveness. *Forgive me Lord.*

She turned towards Mona. "I stopped by to say I was sorry for how coldly I received you when you came over. I was nervous, afraid the cancer had come back."

Mona walked out of the room, leaning on the counter for support. "I forgive you."

Maryann tightened her fist. You forgive me? After what you've done? She wanted to scream, but instead pursed her lips and said, "Thank you. I best be going now."

"Do you want something hot to drink? Coffee?"

"Do you have some made?"

Mona slowly made her way over to the black cook stove and lifted the speckle ware coffee pot. "Won't take but a minute. Sit down."

"Are you sick?" Maryann asked, afraid of the serious flu that was putting a record number of people in the hospital.

"*Nee,* I'm fine." Mona yanked at the hand pump, water pouring into the coffee pot.

Maryann took a seat at the long oak table. "I have so many *kinner* at home, I need to be careful."

Mona nodded, but stayed mum.

Maryann wished she was more passive, like some other Amish women, but she was as curious as a cat, Michael had always said. "Mona, what's wrong? You're moving so slow, and I do think you were hiding from visitors... from me."

Mona put the pot on the stove and took a seat. "I'm tired, Maryann."

"So you might be sick?"

"*Nee,* I'm tired of life. Tired of hiding... of being alone."

Maryann had never seen Mona this transparent, since she was a young girl. "What are you hiding from, Mona? And why do you say you're alone? You have two beautiful daughters and a husband —"

"Who despise me," Mona cut in. "Can't blame them…"

Mona was one of those people you had to yank something out, even a hello at times, but Maryann had a busy day ahead, making goodies for the knitting circle party. "Can you tell me what's wrong, Mona?"

Mona slowly folded her hands and placed them on the table. "When I heard Suzy talk about her friend having a fear of leaving the house, I now have a name for what's wrong with me."

"Agoraphobia?"

"Is that what Suzy's friend has?"

"I think. Suzy said it can happen after a tragedy."

Mona looked out the window, light shining on her face. "Remember the accident I was in, as a teen?"

"*Jah,* we all remember that. Buggy flipped a few times."

"Well, I was just getting my bearings on steering the family buggy. My *daed* and I were out, and I failed… again. He was furious."

"Furious? Because he had to get a new buggy?"

"That he had such a stupid *dochder.* He always said I didn't have the sense God gave geese."

Maryann thought of how afraid she was of Mona's *daed.* You never knew what was going to come out of his mouth. She remembered when he passed away, she felt relief, thinking she could go over to Mona's with ease. But… "Mona, your *daed* died shortly after the accident, *jah?*"

"*Jah.* Fell into the silo and buried to death. *Mamm* died shortly after, but it was all my fault."

"Your fault?"

"She said his mind was preoccupied with having such daft daughters, and couldn't pay attention to his work. *Mamm* died of grief."

Maryann knew Mona and her sisters were a handful, all five of them. And her *daed* had no help in the barn. "Mr. Bennett had five silly daughters, too."

Mona's head jerked back. "What?"

"In *Pride and Prejudice*. Mr. Bennett had five daughters that drove him mad. Could you imagine the *mamm* blaming one of the daughters if he died?"

Mona slowly shook her head. "*Nee*. That book was hard to read."

Maryann recalled how Mona had only read a few chapters, and her heart sank. How painful the book must have been, seeing close sisters and a *daed* that was strong, for the most part. "I want to help you," she found herself saying.

"I'm beyond help," Mona said, "but I appreciate the offer."

"Now why are you beyond help?"

"I'm old and I've ruined most of my life, with fear."

"You're not much older than I am. And believe me, I realize life is a gift and to be cherished. You're going to be an *oma* again soon. Fannie's *boppli* is due in a few months…" Maryann got up and sat next to Mona. "Whatever burden you have, I want to help lift it from you. And so do your friends."

"Friends? What friends?"

"Our knitting circle friends. Very few burdens are heavy if everyone lifts, Michael always says."

A tear slid down Mona's cheek. "You have a *goot* husband. Mine stays away…"

Maryann hugged Mona, her dear friend who had been a prisoner to her fears, brought on by guilt. *Ach,* if her parents were alive today, she'd give them an earful. But her mind soon turned to Fannie. History was repeating itself, Mona always putting her daughter down by harsh words.

As Mona openly wept on her shoulder, Maryann lifted her up to God, who was big enough to carry any burden, and make everything work out for the good. The black pieces on a bright quilt, was beautiful to behold, and the dark places in our lives, somehow, God used to make a beautiful pattern in our lives, Granny had always said.

~*~

Suzy pulled into the black-topped driveway of the sprawling mansion that Missy lived in... alone. With her maid service and 'butler,' she lived like one of the Crawley's on *Downton Abbey*. Was she one of Missy's servants, too? Suzy cringed but soon found herself ashamed of her attitude towards Miss Priss. Was she jealous of her? Surely not. No, Prissy was more like Miss Havisham, the offbeat character in Dickens' Great Expectations, and Suzy was like little Pip, the boy who came to amuse her, and then she kicked to the curb.

Suzy parked in the driveway and looked up into the sun peeping through the white cotton clouds. Lord, shine on me, and give me strength. I can't hide my heart from you, and you know I'm only made of dust and hopelessly flawed. Love Missy through me, because I just can't. And please help me with this anger I have towards her....

She encircled her neck with the new red scarf she made for Christmas to deck out her new green coat, and quickly made her way to the front door. The wind howled through the bare maple trees, and she jumped on her tiptoes to stay warm. Soon the door opened and Missy answered it. *Where's the maid?* Suzy wanted to ask, but instead just said hello and went inside.

"Can I take your coat?"

Suzy couldn't help but stare. Miss Priss was out of her lounge ware and dressed in a red sweater and blue jeans. *Blue jeans? With no designer labels?* Was she dressing down so Suzy would feel more comfortable? "Yes, just a minute."

Suzy took off her coat and Prissy seemed to admire it. "Nice coat. Where did you find it?"

"Uh, K-Mart. Up in Punxsy." She lowered her head. "It's my favorite store."

"Oh."

"My mom and I went shopping there all the time before God took her. Sometimes I think she'll come around the corner and say she found a blue light special," Suzy found herself chattering nervously. Why was she so embarrassed that she shopped at K-Mart?

"Come on into the main living room."

Like an obedient servant, she followed Missy into her grand living room where she received visitors. In the corner was a Christmas tree that could rival the Rockefeller tree in New York City. "Wow, now that's a tree."

"We do live in the best area for pines. I had it delivered and set up by Mussers Nursery. What fine people they are; so accommodating."

"And your silver ornaments are antiques. Stunning."

"Well, some were tarnished and needed polished. I like doing it myself, since my husband used to do it."

Suzy had been praying that Prissy would open up about the premature death of her husband, but now that it was happening, she didn't know what to say.

"I miss him now, but it's too late. I should have told him that I loved him." She swung her hand over her mouth and started to sob.

Suzy just gawked, and her tongue seemed frozen, unable to move. But she moved over to Miss Priss and put her arms around her and prayed. *Lord, help her.* She led her over to her sofa, and sat next to her. "Missy, can I help you?"

"You already have."

"How?"

She cleared her throat and tried to compose herself. "I read the book you gave me and it really did something to me, in here." She put her hands on her heart.

"You read the Bible?" Suzy blurted.

"No, not yet. *A Christmas Carol.* Remember how you brought it over as a gift from the church, along with the shawl you made? The prayer shawl?" She got up and opened the ottoman lid and got the shawl out and wrapped herself in it. "When I wear this, I feel like I'm getting a hug."

Suzy felt like she was in a dream. She'd heard this from other prayer shawl recipients, but thought Prissy didn't like it. "Well, I'm glad. And surprised."

"Because I didn't thank you properly? Well, now I am. I used to be a scrooge, but I'm intent on making things right."

Suzy noticed she was hardly breathing and gasped. "You a scrooge? Really?"

"You know I was, Suzy. I thought myself better than others. Remember how I treated you in your own store?"

"Well, you were being honest, is all. I do live above my shop..."

"I envy you. You're happy in that little place of yours, and here I am... and miserable. And trapped."

"Trapped? How so?"

Tears sprang to Missy's eyes again. "After Walter died, I didn't go out much. I know it's around town that I have agoraphobia, and I may have a little bit of fear, but the truth is, I can't drive. Never learned. Walter took me, or our driver."

Suzy somehow felt like she grew a foot. Here was the woman who had haunted her in her worst nightmares exposing how small she really was. A lonely woman that missed her husband, and wealth didn't make happy. Suzy also felt proud of herself, being a shop owner and independent. "I can teach you how to drive," she found herself saying

Missy wiped away a stray tear. "Sammy's doing that. We go up and down the driveway, over to the carriage house and back. I can't parallel park… or drive on the road. Too afraid, but I'm determined." She sat down and pulled the prayer shawl tight around her. "I'm such a mess. Sorry to unload on you."

"We're all hopelessly flawed," Suzy quipped. "Ever see *Little Women*?"

"I have all the versions of the movie on DVD."

"Well, you know how Jo tries and tries to do the right thing and then she realizes she's hopelessly flawed?"

"Yes."

"Well, it's the human condition. None of us are perfect, and we have faults." Suzy felt joy well within her. "It's why I love Christmas so much and I say Merry Christmas to everyone. Christ-mas, get it?"

"No."

"Oh, so you don't have any Catholic friends?"

"Yes, and I know they call church mass, but what's that got to do with Christmas?"

Suzy knew every time she talked about this she got too emotional, so she braced herself, lest she be sobbing, too. "Well, Christmas is a compound word, Christ and mass put together. And in the mass, the Catholics celebrate the breaking of the bread, the body of Christ. They celebrate his death…"

Missy sat up straight. "I don't think death is a pleasant topic to discuss at Christmas…"

"I talked about my mom and your husband. It's a part of life. And it's why Christ came to earth."

The wind rattled the large windows to a feverish pitch. "Does he want my attention?" Missy mused.

Suzy prodded. "Maybe he does. Want to go to the play tonight at church? I can pick you up."

Missy broke down again. Suzy embraced and rocked her. "It's all right."

"I'll start crying and ruin the play…"

"I'll be sitting next to you, sharing my box of Kleenex. I miss my mom something fierce." She tried to calm Missy down. As she continued to cry, Suzy noticed a warmth flow through her heart. Thank you, Lord, for loving this woman through me. We are all hopelessly flawed without your Holy Spirit in us, making us strong in our weaknesses.

~*~

Granny stirred the thick Figgie pudding mixture and slapped Jeb's hand as he tried to sneak a finger full. "Now, you wait until I'm done, old man."

"Wanted something tasty after reading the letter from Nathan." He put his hands on her shoulder, as if to support her. "Take a break now, and read it."

"I've never made this here recipe and I'm nervous. I'll read it later."

"Please?"

She turned to look into her husband's eyes. They were turquoise, not gray, which usually meant he had some high emotions. "Sure, Jeb. Is something wrong?"

"Don't know. It might be for the good, but I don't like it."

Granny braced herself, reaching for him, and found strength. "You don't like it? It's bad news…"

He put the letter in her hand, and she read:

Dear Oma and Opa,

Lavina and I are having a mighty good time here in Montana visiting my folks. Lavina loves it here, everything so open and free-like.

I'll come to the point, since my other letters fill you in on our daily life. We're hoping to move here. Last summer the bumper crop harvest made lots of money, and my dad bought more land. More land that needs farming, and someone to help. What I'm saying is that I can make a real living up here.

I said before Lavina feels free. Well, in more ways than one. She feels judged by her past in Smicksburg. She said it was a weight she carried she didn't realize. I didn't know it, either. But here, we can raise our kids without anyone even knowing about her having the twins out of wedlock.

Oma and Opa, I hope this doesn't upset you. I was hoping to settle right down the road, but this visit seems to have changed my mind. I'm sorry. I'll miss you. I'll be writing back to talk about all that I need to do to sell the farm and land and move up here.

Look for another letter soon.

Merry Christmas

Nathan

Granny swallowed hard the lump in her throat. First her sons moved away, all but Roman, and what hopes she had of having her closest grandson living down the road were dissolving.

"I'm sorry, Deborah. He's young and thoughtless. Should have waited until after Christmas to write such a thing."

Speechless, Granny turned to stir the Figgie pudding mixture. "It hasn't happened yet."

Jeb put his hands on her shoulders to massage them. "*Jah*, we live for today, not worried about tomorrow."

"No grace for tomorrow, yet. And I'll need it for this one." She cleared her throat. "For today, I have a knitting circle party to enjoy and when this is in the oven, we can put up the decorations."

"Porch is full of pine boughs waiting for us to put up," he said, pouring a cup of coffee that was always warming on the stove. "*Ach*, I can't wait." He set his mug down and ran out the door.

Granny continued to stare into the batter and realized she was Clara Peggotty and Nathan was David Copperfield. Peggotty, David's faithful nanny and friend, was weaved in and out of his life. But she was always there, ever faithful for Copperfield, and it made him a steady man. *Ach*, the whole book was about people being spun together by chance, and they were all stronger for it, just like the knitting circle.

Jeb came back in and ran over to Granny, putting a kiss on her cheek. "Here's another present."

She turned to see the carved tray he'd shown her a few weeks back, a scene with birds flying across the top, some perched on the bottom. She gazed into his eyes, and then wrapped her arms around his middle. "*Danki*, my leaning post. People come and go, but you're always here." Tears threatened to spill, but like she kept telling herself, today was a day to celebrate; she had a Dickens Christmas party to give as a gift to her knitting circle friends.

~*~

Fannie knocked on her *mamm's* door louder, but no one answered. *Ach, she's hiding again?* Maryann's 'news' she delivered about her *mamm* wasn't 'news' at all. Her *mamm* was cantankerous because she was mean spirited, not hurt. *She was hurt! Ach, to blame her bad attitude on opa was mighty low.*

Fannie opened the door and yelled, "Where are you, *Mamm?*"

As usual, not a sound, so she'd ascend the steps to her *mamm's* abode and have to beg her to come today, as usual, to knitting circle. And Maryann asked her to do just that: beg. Opening her door, Fannie saw the usual dark room, shades drawn. But she heard snoring, which surprised her, since her *mamm* usually slept in until eleven or so, then was up for the day.

Should she wake her up?

Fannie went inside and quietly took a seat in her *mamm's* rocker, watching her as she lay on the bed. Was she ill? Her *mamm* stirred and mumbled something, but Fannie couldn't make it out. "What?"

"I can't..."

"Can't what?" Fannie prodded, realizing she was talking in her sleep.

"Can't do the dishes right."

Fannie stifled a giggle. That's what her mamm always said to her. Curious enough to continue, she asked "Who said you can't do those dishes right?"

"*Mamm.* She's always mad. And Sherry's perfect."

Fannie froze. She had an Aunt Sherry, and really, her aunt was perfect in many ways. Was this a bad dream?

Fannie leaned forward. "Sherry isn't perfect..."

"*Daed* says she is. I'm a thorn...."

"A thorn?"

"In his side."

As Fannie's eyes adjusted to the room, she saw her *mamm* more clearly. Her face was contorted and she gripped the edge of her blanket to her chin. *Poor thing*, Fannie thought. *It's a nightmare based on truth. Should she wake her up?*

Fannie sat down again, being seven months pregnant and feeling rather heavy. "*Mamm*. Wake up. We need to go to knitting circle," she said loudly.

"You go. I have to do...dishes. Can't play."

Fannie, overwhelmed by the time crunch and the emotions emanating from her *mamm,* was baffled, so she shot up a prayer for wisdom, and looked out of one of the windows. She remembered Christmas long ago, when she was a little girl. Her *daed* had always helped build an igloo and snowmen, but *mamm* was always in the house... in this room. Eliza had always supervised Christmas dinner and they never had anything for Second Christmas, the next day. *Why?*

"Fannie, what are you doing?" her *mamm* said groggily.

"*Mamm*, are you awake?"

"My eyes are open..."

Fannie shifted in the chair. "You were talking in your sleep." She didn't want to pry but needed answers to her *mamm's* behavior. "You said something about Aunt Sherry."

"And what was that?"

"That your parents thought she was perfect... and you were... a thorn?"

Mona pushed back the covers and swung her legs out of bed, sitting up. "What time is it?"

"Twelve-thirty... and we need to leave for knitting circle."

Mona swung the covers back over her and said she was too tired to go.

~*~

Granny put on her best smile and opened the door to see Marge and Lizzie. "*Ach*, you're early."

"We came to get some ammo," Marge blurted.

Lizzie elbowed her. "We did not."

Granny tilted her head in wonder. "What's ammo? Something you need for your pies?"

Marge laughed. "We're done with making pies. Ammo's slang for ammunition... it means we need some advice so we can win a battle with Roman."

Granny scrunched her lips to one side, not to laugh out loud at her animated English friend. "Marge, just speak plainly. You and Lizzie have a seat, and we'll have some tea to warm you up." Granny went over to get her tea kettle and put water into it. "Now, tell me what you need advice about," Granny said as she took a seat opposite the table from them.

"Well," Lizzie started. "When we read *Anne of Green Gables*, well, it seemed like we got an idea. Marge says that foster homes are out of room, and I think it would be nice to take in an Anne Girl, I mean girl. I told Roman about it, and he's not for it."

Marge groaned. "He's a scrooge sometimes."

"What's a scrooge?" Granny asked.

"Oh, you're not allowed to read *A Christmas Carol*. I forgot. Scrooge is the miserly old man who —"

"Roman's not a miser," Lizzie was quick to say. "He's the most generous man I know. It's something else."

"And what is that?" Granny asked, noticing that Lizzie's face was growing crimson colored. She reached for her hand. "If it's not too personal."

Lizzie squeezed her hand. "Roman wants me to have *kinner,* but I just know I'm infertile. It's been seven months since we've wed, and besides that, I'm not grieving about it anymore. I'm content to be the *mamm* to the girls and have a yearning to love more."

Granny's heart swelled with love for this dear daughter-in-law of hers. "So homeschooling has nothing to do with feeling loss?"

"*Nee,* not at all. I believe God has given me the girls as a gift and I feel responsible to care for them. And Marge, well, she has her own story." Lizzie looked over at Marge, urging her to speak.

"Well, I know what you're going to say Granny. I feel guilty for the abortion long ago and want to pay my way into forgiveness with good deeds."

Granny put a hand up. "I wasn't going to say that at all. Go on."

"I feel the same way as Lizzie. Some people call it the Anne of Green Gables Syndrome, wanting to adopt or take in kids after reading the book, or watching the movie, which is awesome. But as a traveling nurse, I see things."

"Things like what?" Granny prodded.

"Well, we all know how Lavina came out of an abusive home, right? I helped her and want to help other girls."

Lavina. Granny remembered when she came to live with her last Old Christmas, having run away from home, and slowly finding the *daed* she longed for in Jeb. And a husband in her grandson, Nathan. "I got a letter from Nathan and he said Lavina's doing mighty fine. If you want to help girls like her, then why not do it?" Granny got up to put some cookies on a plate and make tea, but really wanted to hide the hurtful effects of the letter

Nathan sent. Thy will be done, Lord. She placed the sugar cookies and tea pot on the table.

Lizzie got three tea cups out of the cupboard and the sugar bowl. "But Roman wants his own children, and a boy at that," Lizzie explained.

"Then take in a boy," Granny quipped. "Just make sure there's no mix-up, *jah*? Like in the book?"

"Then we'd have a pretty kettle of fish," Marge blurted out, then laughed.

Lizzie still looked too solemn and Granny knew she felt defeated against her strong-willed son. "Lizzie, pray about it. If there's a need, Roman is sure to want to help. But you do have your *daed* to think about, too."

"*Ach*, remember how *Daed* had Amish Camp all summer? He loved talking to the kids. Actually, he's a pen pal to one. Charles, the boy who wore all black."

"Oh, the one with the dog collar?" Marge asked. "Just because he wears stuff like that doesn't mean he needs a home."

"I know," Lizzie said. "But he tells my daed things that aren't right, and it worries him. Wish we could help him."

"Do you have his address? I can track him down on my GPS."

Granny sipped some tea. "You best ask Jonas first. It's his pen pal and he's able to take care of the situation. He's a wise man, too." Granny took a cookie off the plate. "Now, it's almost one and I need to check on a few things before circle." She watched as Lizzie and Marge got up, hope springing in their steps. *Lord, you give and take away. Is it your will to take Nathan and Lavina far away to make room for hurting kinner? I will not fret, because your eye is on the sparrow... and my heart.*

~*~

Maryann entered the side door, followed by Fannie and Mona. "Merry Christmas, Granny. Here's two mincemeat pies." She placed them on the table.

Fannie ran over to Granny and kissed her cheek. "Merry Christmas. Hope you like it."

Fannie placed a package she'd had hidden behind her into Granny's hands. "*Danki*, Fannie. Something Melvin made?"

She nodded. "Open it up."

Granny obliged this dear girl who was like a daughter, and ripped the red and white striped paper and opened the box. "*Ach*, Fannie, it's too much."

"Not for you it isn't." Fannie put an arm around her. "Do you like it?"

Granny looked at the cuckoo clock that was adorned with carved birds. "I love it.... *Danki* ever so much."

Granny looked over at Mona. "Merry Christmas, Mona."

"Well, I don't know about that. Fannie and Maryann dragged me over here. I'm tired."

"Do you want some coffee?" Granny asked. "I make it strong."

Mona shook her head. "I'll just sit down and do what we're here for."

Maryann nudged Mona, and she quickly added, "Your decorations look nice."

Granny held on to Fannie, feeling faint. Mona always criticized how she and Jeb had put pine boughs around the windows and had red candles placed on the window sills. Confused, she asked, "You used to think it was too English looking. What changed your mind?"

Mona was silent, but Maryann nudged her again. "Well, it's a long story and like I said, I'm so tired."

Granny didn't know why Maryann kept elbowing Mona, but figured it was a cue for her to not ruin her Christmas knitting circle party. Or was it something else? Clenching her fists, she asked, "Mona, would you like to stop by tomorrow and help me make pies for Forget-Me-Not Manor?"

Mona was visibly taken back and fumbled for words. "I don't, ah, drive this far from home..."

"*Ach*, it's only a few miles. I can pick you up," Granny said. *Lord, have mercy, I am trying!* Granny thought. When will this woman ever stop this self-pity? Nonsense, she couldn't drive over...

Maryann put her arm around Mona. "You'll accept Granny's kind offer, *jah*?"

Mona slowly met Granny's eyes. "If it's not a bother."

"More hands make light work." Granny excused herself so she could greet the other girls coming in the kitchen, but she inwardly moaned. Nathan's letter, and now having to spend time with Mona tomorrow. Why did she ask her to come over?

~*~

When all the girls were seated around Granny's long oak table, Marge helped Granny place all the desserts on the table. "I can't wait to try some Figgie pudding. I've wanted to taste it all my life."

Granny laughed at Marge's dramatics and looked around the table. "Where's Ruth?"

Janice spoke up. "I stopped by to give her a ride, since she's so pregnant and it's cold, and can you believe she's still not better?"

"But she's been to *Gmay*, I mean, church," Granny said. "But she did look pale."

"Well," Mona griped. "We all know we can't miss going to meetings unless we're on death's door."

Granny took a deep breath. "Now, Jeb and the elders don't want a sick pregnant woman coming, for sure. Hope she's alright."

Suzy took a bite of mincemeat pie. "This is good. Oh, and Colleen will be late. Hezekiah took her and Aurora out on a sleigh ride to get a Christmas tree."

Maryann started to choke and coughed violently. Fannie hit her back, and she wiped her eyes with a handkerchief. "A Christmas tree? Are you sure?"

Suzy nodded. "She can tell *yinz* about it when she gets here."

"Amish don't have Christmas trees," Maryann continued. "It's not our way."

Granny put a hand up. "I'm sure Colleen will explain. Now, has everyone had a mug of wassail?"

"Tastes like spiced apple cider, Granny," Fannie said. "Why call it wassail?"

Granny grinned. "Well, I couldn't read *A Christmas Carol,* but I did get some library books out on what Charles Dickens would have had when he was alive."

"In Victorian times," Suzy added, a bit too chipper.

Janice laughed. "I think Suzy's still flying like a kite from her visit today."

"I am. Guilty as charged," she mused. "I had a great time visiting Prissy. I mean Missy. She read *A Christmas Carol* and boy did it help her. She thought of all her past Christmases with Walter, her husband, and she realized how much love they had in their marriage. Then she thought of her present state, and it made her realize she was being a scrooge with her money."

"A miser?" Granny asked.

"Yes. And, well, we talked about some changes she can make. Now that I see her every week for knitting lessons, she's not the woman I thought she was. Little by little, she's opening up, and I'm finding a real treasure."

Granny noticed Maryann put her arm around Mona, but Mona wiggled out of the embrace. *What on earth?*

Suzy clapped her hands playfully as if bringing her class into order. "Granny, I interrupted you. Now, what were you saying about Charles Dickens?"

Granny sat in Jeb's chair at the head of the table. "Well, they were frugal, using what they had to make *goot* food, but some went hungry. Actually, Jeb and I read *David Copperfield*, the book that's really Charles Dickens' story of his life. His life was very sad. When he was twelve, he had to work in a glue factory since the family went to debtor's prison."

Silence, almost a reverence, fell over the room. "I think it was mighty hard on him to write about his life, so he studied scripture and wrote *The Life of our Lord* when he wrote *David Copperfield*." Granny got up and got a blue hardcover book from her china closet drawer. Flipping through the pages, she reclined on her seat. "Now, this is only my opinion, but he starts this book with:

"My Dear Children, I am very anxious that you should know something about the History of Jesus Christ. For everybody ought to know about Him. No one ever lived who was so good, so kind, so gentle, and so sorry for all people who did wrong, or were in any way ill or miserable, as He was.

Granny eyed each girl, knowing the burdens they carried. "He was good, kind, gentle to all who did wrong or were miserable. That includes all of us, *jah?*"

All heads nodded in agreement, and to Granny's shock, Mona did, too. She held Mona's gaze and said, "Dickens read this to his children every year at Christmas as a reminder. Maybe some of us can read it on Christmas Day this year, making it a tradition."

"Is it long?" Janice asked. "Sorry, but like I've said, not much time to read."

"*Nee*, not at all. Mostly retells the New Testament so a child can understand it."

Lizzie sighed. "So he really cared about the education of his children. How *wunderbar*."

The door opened, bringing in a gust of wind. "So sorry I'm late. But Hezekiah and I, well, and Aurora too, we got a Christmas tree."

Granny noticed that Colleen glowed so bright, soon the room seemed to warm up. "Your *oma* allows you to have a Christmas tree in her *dawdyhaus*?"

She shook her head. "No, outside though." She lifted the large bag she brought in. "We decorated the pine tree we bought with food for the birds, and Hezekiah said the birds will find shelter in the pine tree." She squealed and spun around. "I love being Amish. Everything's so.... refreshing, being outside more."

Suzy laughed. "What's in the bag then?"

"Oh, bird ornaments."

"What?" Maryann asked, one eyebrow cocked.

Granny held her breath, praying Mona wouldn't say anything to spoil things. So far, she'd been unusually quiet.

Colleen whipped off her cape and bonnet and hung them on the peg, and then bent down and pulled a string of cranberries out of the bag. "This is the garland." She dug again in the bag and lifted up half an orange on a string. "See how it makes a bowl? You can fill it with seeds, but Orioles like oranges, so we left it empty to attract them. But my favorite one to make is the hearts and I made you each one." She lifted up a birdseed heart and smiled. "Merry Christmas."

"Sweetie, they're so cute. How'd you make them?" Marge asked.

"You put Crisco and birdseed together and mold them. It's super easy, but some seeds fall off, so I'll leave them in the bag."

She ran over and sat by Granny. "I am over being upset about not being able to read *A Christmas Carol*, but I'll tell you later. Enough about me."

Granny took Colleen's hand. "*Danki* for the gifts."

Colleen looked around the table. "Did you save some for me?"

"Aw, poor Tiny Tim," Janice said with a roar. "Don't give me that pathetic pout. Of course we saved you a few crumbs."

"Who's Tiny Tim?" Fannie asked.

"A little boy in *A Christmas Carol* that doesn't have enough to eat."

Granny leaned forward. "So, what happened to him?"

"Well, the man who was a miser changed and he helped the boy. Became like a second father to him."

Granny felt that usual itch to read something she couldn't. If she begged Jeb or told him they should read it together, he'd most likely allow it. But seeing Colleen so happy and twirling around in delight for the joy of being Amish, somehow made Granny not want to pursue it. There were rules, that she knew well, but so many possibilities to celebrate Christmas, she didn't want to squabble with Jeb.

"Is everyone done eating?" Marge asked.

The girls all nodded, except Colleen who was enjoying mincemeat pies.

Marge lifted a glassful of wassail in mid-air. "God bless us everyone."

Granny, although confused, lifted her glass and the girls followed. "God bless us, everyone."

~*~

Suzy sat next to Missy in the back pew, still stunned that she'd accepted her offer to come to church. Missy had always gone to church in Punxsutawney when Walter was alive. Did she miss it? Did the congregation miss her or her donations?

The children put on *A Christmas Carol* play, written a little different by Janice. The "ghost" of Christmas past represented a person with a strong belief in Christ, but life had worn them out, or riches had choked out the good seed. Suzy thought back to the day she finally surrendered to the blessed call, and put Jesus on the throne of her life.

How mean she was to the girls from Campus Crusade for Christ who came around with their Four Spiritual Laws tract. She'd told them to go away, accusing them of being a cult. But when she was on her back, sick with the flu, who showed up at her door? Patty, the one who freaked her out the most, always carrying her black Bible around campus, reading it openly in the cafeteria. But Patty brought her chicken soup, and simply loved her, helping nurse her back to help. *Love.* It really made a difference.

As the children portrayed Christmas Present, the main character was a prodigal, far from God, and Suzy vowed right then that she'd find Patty on Facebook and thank her, it being decades since She'd been that prodigal. To think that she graduated and left school not knowing what an impact Patty made on her life. Yes, she needed to find her.

Missy sat motionless throughout the play so far. Was she turned off by the message? Well, Jerry felt the Christmas message needed to tell why Christ came into the world, and not give a fluffy message, since the church was packed with "Christmas only" attenders. Would Missy walk out when Jerry got up to speak? Lord, help Missy really hear!

As the play went into the future, a life apart from Christ, Suzy gripped the pew, as heat rose into her cheeks. Suzy could tell Jerry was nervous, speaking to a packed house of two-hundred. *Lord, anyone having ears to hear, let them hear!*

"Boo! I'm the Ghost of Christmas Future," Jerry said with a chuckle. He loosened his red tie that he was obviously not used to wearing, his white shirt making his black skin look like ink. "Journey with me down a road, will you? Please open your Bibles to John 3:16. Some of you may have seen a book that simply has 3:16 on it. A wonderful book by Max Lucado. Anyone here a Max Lucado fan like me? I read him all the time. The Amish do, too. Did you know that?"

Suzy winced. Jerry was nervous, hopping off on bunny trails already. *Help him, Lord.*

"Anyhow, let's read John 3:16.

"For God loved the world so much that he gave his one and only Son, so that everyone who believes in him will not perish but have eternal life.

"Now, here's the thing you have to know. God loves you deeply. Don't miss that part. God loved the world. But we have a problem. Sin. An ugly word, but it's really just synonymous with having a shortcoming. And I think we can all agree we have shortcomings? We're not perfect, like God." He looked around the congregation. "Well, I know I'm not perfect. I mean, just this morning I was behind an Amish buggy and rage welled up in me. 'Pull over' I wanted to yell. Or even honk my horn. And *yinz* know how much I love the Amish, but man, those buggies go slow and I was in a hurry. Have things to do."

A nervous laugh escaped Jerry and Janice looked back to Suzy with a finger up. That was her cue to pray for her husband, and Suzy did.

Suzy bowed her head. *Lord, he's hopping again. Help him.*

"Anyone else have a problem with road rage?" he asked.

Suzy nudged Missy, who looked over at her with a smile. No, Missy was too afraid to drive, so no road rage.

"So, I have a shortcoming. Road rage. Right there and then, I sinned. Anger, verging on hate for the driver ahead of me, and an Amish person of all things. Well, it grew in me. I had to clamp my mouth shut so I didn't blurt out something I'd regret. I mean, I wasn't going to yell anything to the Amish man, but out loud in the car, and yell something God would hear. So, I still sin, miss the mark, so to speak."

He cleared his throat and wiped his forehead with his handkerchief. "Well, there's God up there in heaven, and here we are on the earth, imperfect. How do we talk to a perfect God?"

A silence fell over the church.

Jerry leaned on his podium. "I'll tell you how. Jesus took our time-out chair."

Suzy groaned. *What? Our time-out chair?*

"Ever see that nanny lady on television tell the naughty kids to sit in the time-out chair?"

Some heads nodded, while others just shook their heads.

"Well, we were bad, and Jesus went to the time-out chair for us." He walked over to the children who sat in the front row. "How relieved would you be if someone took your place at being grounded? Say you weren't allowed to go out for a week, and your friend says, 'I'll stay in your room for a week so you can go out and play.' Would you like that?"

The kids laughed and agreed.

"Okay, good." He met the eyes of the adults. "Let's say that chair is the electric chair. You're on death row and about to be executed for a crime. And up walks Jesus, tells the prison guard to let you go, that he'd take the electric chair for you. What would you say?"

Someone shouted "Amen," another "Glory!"

Jerry looked up. "I'd say, thank you. I'll accept your sacrifice. You must love me a lot." His eyes glistened. "And I told God that many Christmases ago. 'I accept your sacrifice, and in exchange, I'll go out of jail a free man.' I was declared innocent before God, because Jesus took my punishment, not in an electric chair, but at the cross."

He stepped back to his podium and thumbed through his Bible. "I said I was taking you down a road, but got sidetracked. Let me get back on that road called the Romans Road. You can Google it at home, but I want to get back to this closing scripture; Romans 10:13: *Everyone who calls on the name of the Lord will be saved.* In The Message Bible I love so well, it simply says, '*Everyone who calls, 'Help, God!' gets help.*'" Jerry laughed. "Can't get any simpler. How do we complicate things? Does anyone want God's help? If so, come on down to the front of the church and we'll have someone pray with you."

Missy got up, and Suzy was sure Jerry had done it again. Preaching a bold message on Christmas, not something warm and cozy, offending someone. To Suzy's shock, Missy went to the front, and Janice was right there, hugging her.

Suzy wanted to dance up and down the aisle, but this church wasn't Pentecostal, so she did a happy dance inside. She'd felt the burden of helping Missy, and now the woman was reaching out to others and God. She found herself saying, Praise be, under her breath, and then laughed, realizing she'd picked up that saying off the Amish.

~*~

Granny stroked Angel's short black fur as she heard Jeb's horse neigh. He'd gone over to pick up Mona to make pies, and with him on the verge of getting a nasty cold, it made her fuss all the more. Stuff and nonsense, as Marilla always said in *Anne of Green Gables*. Mona was in her forties and could surely drive herself over to their place.

Granny was going to hide the dogs in her bedroom, afraid Mona would again criticize her for having dogs in the house, but not today. She was feeling rather bold, ready to tackle Mona head-on. Like Jeb said, if she made a critical comment, she'd ask why and dig into the woman's heart to see what was ailing her. If she has a heart, Granny moaned internally, but quickly caught herself and asked the Lord to forgive her of having great disliking for Mona. Not hate, just a mighty big disliking. She thought of Fannie, and how she'd suffered having a *mamm* like Mona, but again, she dismissed the image and concentrated on the task at hand. Baking pies for the homeless women at Forget-Me-Not.

When Mona appeared in the doorway, she was actually smiling at Jeb, not down in the mouth as usual.

Praise be. Maybe she's in a *goot* mood. "Jeb, hurry on up and close that door. It's like an icebox in here."

Jeb flipped off his black wool hat and hung it on the peg, then collected Mona's cape and bonnet. "It's actually not too cold out there. No ice at all. Don't know why the boys can't come home for Christmas."

"Well, it's an expense, hiring a driver from Ohio and all." Granny put on a smile. "Hello, Mona. Ready to bake?"

"As ready as I'll ever been."

"Is something wrong?" Granny probed, remembering Jeb's advice. *Dig deeper.*

"*Nee,* I just can't bake all that well, is all. Don't have a knack for it."

Granny peered over at Jeb. "Pies. Best way to a man's heart. So, I'll help you."

Mona looked down, her cheeks pink. "Well, don't know about that."

Probe deeper. "Now why would you say that?"

"Because Freeman's on a diet and avoids pastries."

Granny turned to put water on and glared out the window to see the many birds at her birdfeeders. Finches did get along, like Ruth observed, but blue jays and cardinals fought. She groaned inwardly. She was a cardinal and Mona was a blue jay. Would they ever be able to sit at the same feeder in peace?

Remembering what the Bible had to say about hospitality, she turned with a smile. "Mona, I got some new tea. Ginger coconut, a gift from Marge. Want to try it?"

"Never heard of coconut tea before...."

"Well, Marge goes to a specialty tea shop in Monroeville Mall, when she gets her hair cut."

"She goes how many miles to get her hair cut?"

"*Ach*, maybe forty," Granny said, "But that's her business, *jah*?"

"Well, I don't travel much, as you know."

Granny felt her heart jump but she needed to open up this turtle of a woman. But why didn't Jeb stay? He'd gone off into the living room. "Mona, I go up to Punsxy-Mart often. Even thinking of getting a driver to take me to Cherry Creek, New York and see Susanna Yoder, my dear pen pal. Why not travel more?"

Mona looked down, and just mumbled, "It's expensive."

"*Ach*, you can come with me. I have a driver who's cheap. She goes out to eat, though, and we all pitch in to pay for the meal." Granny bit her lower lip. "Want to go shopping with me sometime?"

Mona sighed loudly. "Deborah, I know you think you need to help those girls at Forget-Me-Not, asking them to come over and make pies, but I don't need help."

"What?"

"You like to help people, but I'm fine, really. I like to stay at home."

Granny clenched her fists. "Fannie comes over to make pies, do you know that? And other women do, too."

"*Ach*, and I'm sure Fannie has stories to tell you that make you pity her…"

Granny closed her eyes. Lord, help! "Well, actually, Fannie doesn't wallow in any pity anymore since she reconditioned her mind."

"Her mind?"

"Well, *jah*. She thought she was fat, ugly and stupid, but she memorized scriptures that made her see what God thought of her. Then Melvin, as you know, made her a compliment box and his love healed a heart from –"

"*Ach*, Deborah, from what? Life is hard and Fannie needs to toughen up. I do, too."

Granny's eyes grew round. "Toughen up? Why would you do that for? I mean, aren't we to be tender-hearted, not tough?"

"You know what I mean. Take life's blows. I did, after…"

"After what?"

"After having a tough life, is all." Angel went over to Mona and sat her face down on her foot.

"Aw, will you look at that. That dog knows English, I declare. You just said you had a tough life, and here's Angel lending you strength.

Mona shooed Angel away. "*Ach,* Deborah. That's ridiculous."

Jeb came around the corner, coffee cup in hand. "Need more of this and black. I'm tired."

"Why not take Angel with you," Granny said as pleasantly as possible, feeling a tension headache coming on.

"Now look at that. She likes you, Mona."

Mona smiled at Jeb. "Your wife seems to think she can understand English."

"Come here, Angel," Jeb called, and Angel went to him. "*Jah*, she does. Want to see her beg for a treat?"

"Jeb we have pies to make. Mona, come on over and we'll start."

Jeb put a finger up. "Angel, dance."

Angel got up on her hind feet and tip toed around in a circle. "*Goot* dog. " Jeb scooped her up. "Here, Mona, hold her."

Before Mona could say no, Jeb had placed the little black dog in her arms. Granny noticed that the deep etches in Mona's forehead softened, and her shoulders relaxed. "She likes you," Granny forced herself to say.

Mona was silent, but held the dog, even stroked her back.

Jeb stood behind Mona and motioned for Granny to meet him in the living room. "*Ach*, Jeb, want to go over the mail real quick-like?"

"*Jah*, I suppose."

Granny excused herself and went into the next room with Jeb, who had a mischievous grin.

He whispered in her ear, "Remember when I said I was shy and my dogs pried me open? I think it'll work for Mona."

"What?"

"Let's give her Angel for a spell. She could help Mona, and if Mona's helped, she'll be less of a burden for you to carry."

Granny looked down. If love was a sacrifice, she'd be doing that for sure and certain. She'd become attached to the little dog. "You think so?"

"I know so," Jeb said.

"Only for a week or two. I'd miss Angel."

"I think Mona needs a long-term dog and..."

Granny held her middle. Thy will be done, Lord. "Most likely she won't want her anyhow."

Jeb winked at her and almost ran into the other room. Granny heard Jeb chat with Mona about keeping the dog for a while, for good company, and to Granny's shock, Mona agreed. What on earth! She'd criticized her for having a dog in the house, and now she was going to be doing the same. Granny sat in her chair, and Bea ran out of their bedroom, hopped on Granny's lap. Granny nuzzled her nose in Bea's long black fur. "You're staying here, not matter what," Granny whispered. "And I'll take you to visit Angel real regular-like." Her heart sank. "And that means me going over to Mona's... Lord have mercy."

~*~

When Mona finally left, Granny heard her knitting needles yelling to her to come get them and sit and knit. Upset with Jeb over being put on the spot concerning Angel, the dog he wanted in the first place, she got attached to in a few short weeks, and now was off to stay at Mona's? She was no spring chicken anymore, and with age, change came harder...for her. *Nee*, not for Jebediah Weaver!

She looked down at the beautiful shades of blues Suzy had dyed the yarn. Life was full of shades, some bright, some dull, some dark. All the pent up emotions she's been harboring since yesterday rose to the surface as she knit one, purled one. Knowing a headache was coming on if she didn't bow her head in prayer, Granny set her needles in her lap.

Lord,

How could Nathan be so insensitive to his oma? He knew I had my heart set on him living down the road, and now, even though it hasn't happened yet, I believe it will. Somehow, I just have this knowing. Lavina feels like a pure woman in Montana, and who am I to disagree? Lord, bless them in their new life, and fill the empty spot that will be in my heart.

And Lord, I know Angels a dog, but please help her live with Mona! She's a timid little thing, and Mona's well.....Mona! Ach, Lord, I can't hide my feeling from you. You see straight into my heart. Help me tolerate that woman!

And Lord, Danki for this Christmas season before me. In a few short days, we'll be having the two boys home from Ohio with their kinner and a full house over at Romans. Give Jeb and me the energy we need to keep up with the young ones.

In Jesus name,
Amen

Dear Readers,

No matter what time of year you're reading this, I'd like to say, *Merry Christmas*! Dickens' Scrooge said, "I will honor Christmas in my heart, and try to keep it all the year." All the books mentioned in this episode are real. *The Life of our Lord*, by Charles Dickens, can be purchased wherever books are sold, and well worth the reading.

I leave you all with a simple, thrifty recipe to make mincemeat pie, Amish style.

Mincemeat Pie

6 c. apples
2 c. COOKED ground meat
1 c. raisins
3 Tbsp. cider or vinegar
1 Tbsp. melted butter
1 ¾ c. sugar
1 tsp. cinnamon
1 tsp. allspice
Pinch of salt

Mix all ingredients and place in two unbaked pie shells.

Bake at 350 degrees for 30 minutes, or until done.

EPISODE 5

Jane Austen's Emma

Granny stroked Bea's long black fur, and then took another swig of coffee. "I can't help it, Jeb."

Jeb stabbed at his breakfast, a spread of potato pancakes, eggs and sausage, not looking up.

"Jeb, are you listening?"

"*Ach*, sorry, love. Hungry as a horse."

"Was it worth it?"

Jeb cocked an eyebrow. "Of course. Fasting on Old Christmas and reading scripture, *jah*. But today I'm famished."

Granny took Bea from off the bench and placed her on her lap. "Like I said. I can't help but think giving Angel to Mona was a mistake. Bea misses her; I can tell."

Jeb laughed. "Bea misses her? You miss her. Admit it."

"Jebediah Weaver. *Jah*, I miss her. Want me to admit anything else?"

Narrowing his eyes, a smirk slowly formed on his lips. "Okay, what Jane Austen character am I now? He must be cantankerous, *jah*?"

"Mr. Knightley. And he was always correcting Emma or…making her admit things."

"I thought she married him."

"She did," Granny moaned. "She did."

Jeb's eye misted. "Deborah, I don't like your tone."

"There you go again, Mr. Knightley."

He put up a hand. "I mean, I don't like the regret I hear in your voice." He jabbed at a piece of sausage with his fork. "Wish you would have done things differently?"

Granny looked down. "Sorry, old man. I got to thinking yesterday, having a whole day to sit and reflect. I have to admit I'm upset with you."

"Because I gave Angel to Mona?"

"*Jah.* I got attached to her in a short while. And you offered her to Mona by putting me on the spot? We should have discussed it."

"I'm mighty sorry, Deborah. I can go on over and fetch her back."

"*Nee,* from what Fannie tells me, the dog's been helping Mona cheer up, and open up, of all things."

"Dogs do that. But this here thing about Mr. Night, you have no regrets?"

"Mr. Knightley was his name. *Ach,* Jeb, we've been married for a coon's age. Why bring something like that up?"

"Because, seems like yesterday to me sometimes."

Granny continued to stroke Bea's fur. "Well, I have to admit you knocked sense into me, like Mr. Knightley did for Emma. He really helped her form her character, and you do that for me..."

"But?"

"But, at times, I wish I wasn't called to such a high standard. Being the bishop's wife now, well, so many eyes on us, and I'm afraid I'll slip..."

"And?"

"And disappoint you."

Jeb stopped his fork in midair. "Deborah, we all have feet of clay, especially me. I can fall and know it. Makes me bow my knee all the more. I needed to fast yesterday and repent."

"Of what?"

"Well, little foxes spoil the vine, *jah*? Small issues in my heart. My attitude about… being the bishop."

Granny got up, grabbed her speckle ware coffee pot and replenished Jeb's coffee. "Now this is news. What's ailing you about being bishop?"

Before she could leave, he grabbed her arm. "It's a burden, for sure. And I'm old. Mighty glad I have you to lean on."

Granny felt embarrassment flood her soul. How silly she'd been after finishing Emma yesterday. She'd read it before, but yesterday the gloom of the weather and lack of food, she saw the negative. What if she didn't marry someone with such a strict Schwarsentruber upbringing? Well, she would have backslid out of the Amish community, that's what. Almost leaving for Samuel, her first love. She kissed Jeb on the cheek. "Jeb, I need to confess something, too." She took her seat across the table from him. "I wallowed in self-pity after reading Emma. I kept thinking how I can't seem to get away with anything with you."

"What?" Jeb screamed like the wind outside. "You push every limit of the *Ordnung*. I'm just here reminding you there is one."

"What do you mean?"

"Well, how many Amish have such *goot* English friends? Wants to attend a Baptist service? Have a knitting circle with *Englishers*? Wants to read questionable books?"

Granny's mouth gaped. "Questionable books?"

"A Christmas Carol, with ghosts in it."

"I never pushed you on that matter."

Jeb was silent, and Granny feared she'd hurt his feelings. It was true; she couldn't get away with living a sloppy Christian life with Jeb as her husband. She reached for his hand. "Mr. Knightley, I'm sorry. I should be thankful you don't let me get away with anything. Like the Good Book says, 'Faithful are the wounds of a friend.'"

"*Ach,* love, I know what you mean. You keep me in my place, too, and sometimes sparks fly, *jah*? Iron against iron makes sparks."

"*Jah,* just need to see a horse shoe being made on an anvil to see that." She squeezed his hand. "I love you, old man, and am regretting nothing."

Jeb released her hand, ran over to retrieve her copy of Emma, and flipped towards the back of the book. He sat next to her and said, "'You hear nothing but truth from me. I have blamed you, and lectured you, and you have borne it as no other woman in England would have borne it.'"

Granny leaned her head on his shoulder and chuckled. "You read Emma?"

"*Jah,* but this part kicked me in the teeth. I have been hard, and you've borne it like no other woman in Smicksburg."

Granny felt her heart flutter like a school girl. The Jeb she fell in love with was strict yet always loving. Never preached anything he didn't practice. He was Mr. Knightley.

~*~

Mona sat across the table from Freeman, feeling hopeful. She's made his favorite breakfast: pie. After his fast yesterday, he dug in without a word of thanks, but he was a man of very few words. But he wouldn't be able to miss the romantic gesture in strawberry rhubarb pie.

After reading Emma, she wondered if Freeman was just so quiet around her because he was just like Mr. Knightley, who told Emma, if I loved you less, I might be able to talk about it more. Could it be true? Freeman rarely talked to her because he couldn't spit it out, so to speak? Share his feelings? His love?

After he finished off the pie, he went over to the stove to pour a second cup of coffee, and then headed towards the back door.

Mona spoke up, "Freeman, I was wondering…"

He turned to her, his black beard not yet speckled with gray, like her own hair. "What?"

"Well, if could go and visit Maryann and Michael sometime, like we used to…"

He grew pale. "Something wrong with Maryann?"

"*Nee.* Why does there have to be something wrong to visit friends?"

"Humph. Never do."

Mona felt her heart jump into her throat. "Can we talk?"

He glanced over at the clock and sat down in his chair. "*Jah.*"

"Did you like your pie?"

He nodded.

"I grow rhubarb because you like it." Silence seemed to scream at her, but she continued. "Can I ask you something?"

He nodded.

"Well, we hardly talk. Is it because you can't say how you feel?"

He nodded.

She knew it. He couldn't talk about his love for her. "Well, I'd like to hear it."

He shook his head and tapped his foot.

"Come on, Freeman. You can tell me what's going on inside…"

He set his jaw and looked up at the ceiling. After a few seconds he asked, "Can I go to the barn now?"

"What?"

"Didn't get all the cows milked."

"But I want to talk to you. We never do and I need to hear something..."

"What?"

She picked up Angel, the little black dog that had lived up to her name. "How do you feel about me?"

His eyes grew round and his face beet red, but he said nothing.

"Can't you say it?" Mona prodded.

"*Nee,* I can't."

"Why not?"

Freeman pounded his fist on the table, a rare display of temper. "Because I'm a Christian man."

"What?"

"*Jah.* I'll just keep it between me and the Lord how I feel about what I'm married to."

Mona stiffened and sat up straight. "And what is that?"

"A crabapple." He shot up, knocking his chair over, and stormed out the back door.

Mona gasped and held Angel close. Crabapple! Deep down it's what she feared. She wanted to run after him, tell him all she'd told Maryann about her past pain, and guilt all bottled up. But the chasm between them was too deep.

She wanted to go hide in her room and sob, but she picked up her journal notes on Emma instead.

I'm as selfish as Emma. She's better than I am, since she really cared for her *daed.* Really dedicated. I killed mine with worry, but Maryann said it wasn't my fault. That I carried too much guilt.

Mona didn't want to read this, so she flipped through her favorite passages.

I may have lost my heart, but not my self-control.

A sob escaped and a tear slid down her cheek onto Angel's fur. Cleansing tears, as Granny calls them, she thought. If only she could tell the woman how much she was being helped by her knitting circle. How she'd reconnected with Maryann, and making progress in being a better mother to Fannie, but she always thought Freeman loved her. By his look of distain when he spit out 'Crabapple,' she knew it was no longer true.

She read the quote again:

I may have lost my heart, but not my self-control.

Emma was much stronger than her because Mona let the tears flow freely, losing all composure, hanging on to Angel as if for dear life.

~*~

Fannie arched her back, and then rested her hands on her swelled middle. "*Ach*, Melvin, I can't wait to have this *boppli*. She's a kicker, that's for sure."

Melvin put more canned goods on one of the store's shelves. "Maybe it's *goot* that the store is slow…and the clock business."

"Why's that?"

"I can stock up and get orders in place before the wee one takes over our lives."

Fannie bit her lower lip. "Melvin, I've been meaning to talk to you about something."

Melvin stopped what he was doing, took Fannie's place at the scale and made her sit down. "*Okey Dokey*."

Fannie sighed. "Well, I've been thinking about that book, Emma, by Jane Austen."

Melvin looked over at her and winked. "Now I have two names, *jah*? Mr. Darcy and Mr. Knightley?"

"What?"

"You told me I was Mr. Knightley the other day. Most days you call me Mr. Darcy."

She nodded. "Well, Darcy, I'm being very serious now. So pay attention." She shifted on the chair. "Emma in the book, well she was spoiled in the beginning, but she grew up. And there's something I find lacking in my life compared to her…"

"She's a character in a book, not real, remember."

"I know. But you may not like what I have to say."

Melvin held a plastic bag in mid-air. "What?"

"Well, Emma had a *daed* who was a hypochondriac, like my own *mamm*. She was so nice to him, even when she was selfish. I'm so ashamed of how I've treated my folks."

Melvin's head spun around. "Your *mamm* should be ashamed of how she treats you. As for your *daed*, he hardly ever talks, so you can't really fault him."

"That's the thing. Maybe my *mamm* doesn't feel loved by anyone. She murmured something in her sleep a while back, and I think she's one hurting soul."

"Go on."

"Well, she hides in that house, you know. What if we built them a *dawdyhaus* in the back and –"

"*Nee.* I couldn't handle it."

"Melvin, it's our duty."

"Fannie, you get off on tangents with these books. First it was Pride and Prejudice, and you were mad at your *mamm* for not being like the *mamm* in the book. Now you want to have her live next door?"

"Well, lots of feelings surface when you read, like being in the refiners fire. God skims off the dross in our lives."

Melvin stopped weighing and took a chair next to her. "That sounds mighty spiritual. Been talking to Jonas about theology or Blacksmith Smitty?"

"Blacksmith Smitty. He said God turns the heat up in our lives to get out impurities, just like fire does to gold. And the heat makes us bendable, too."

Melvin took her hand. "Fannie, you're right. But you're also eight months pregnant, and emotional."

Fannie looked down at their intertwined hands. "I'm so burdened for *Mamm*. I know this sounds new, but Maryann asked me to try to see the hurting side of her, and I think I have, and want to help."

"Well, the *boppli* will be here, so how about she come stay for a week to help you? Let you get a taste of what it would be like."

Fannie noticed Melvin's face was contorted. "Mr. Darcy, you don't like this, do you?"

"*Nee.* I fear something…"

"What?"

"Your *mamm's* so critical, and if she criticizes our little one, I won't have it. She did enough damage to you."

Fannie straightened. It was one thing for her to criticize her *mamm*, but harder when Melvin did. Or was it that he was objective and could see things better? "Mr. Knightley, I agree. If *mamm* is critical of Deborah, she'll have to be put in her place. But can't you do what Maryann's asked? Try to see my *mamm's* hurt?"

"How?"

"I made a few pies. Can you take one over?"

Melvin snickered. "You mean you want me to go visit her? Make the arrangements for her to stay here only after the *boppli's* born only for a week?"

Fannie leaned forward and met him with a kiss. "*Jah.*"

~*~

Colleen sat with Suzy in the back room of the yarn shop, taking their ten o'clock Jane Austen Tea. "I'll take Earl Grey," she said, with her tea cup held up, her pinky finger extended in royal elegance.

Suzy bowed and poured tea into her cup. "That's what I brewed, me lady, since it's your favorite. And I bought some shortbread cookies, too."

Colleen squealed with delight. "I love shortbread."

"I know. You ate half the box last week." Suzy winked. "But that's what our little breaks are for. Eat up." She placed the plate of cookies on the table. "So, are you ready for circle today? Have you finished that boring book, Emma?"

"Boring? Are you serious?"

"Well, it wasn't about much. All they did was write letters, visit each other, hope to have balls. I liked Pride and Prejudice more."

"Well, I loved Emma. I think you're joking again."

"No, Janice said the same thing. The girls at Forget-Me-Not didn't get as much out of it as the Anne of Green Gables series."

Colleen put a cube of sugar in her tea. "I'm surprised. Emma is young, my age, and it shows her growing up…"

"But she was filthy rich, and married a rich man. So, many of us can't relate to all her sorrows."

"Well, Emma was lonely, remember? She had to learn how to reach out, like I did. The day I went to the Baptist mission in Pittsburgh is a day I can say I grew up, realizing I couldn't make it on my own."

Suzy sipped her tea. "I didn't see that in Emma. Good point."

"It also showed the social class thing, how Emma didn't want her friend to marry a farmer. I'm glad we don't have all those rules today, too."

"Wow, you're deep. Didn't see that either."

"But the thing that made me relieved that I live today, is that back in Jane's time, I'd be a fallen woman, since I had Aurora out of wedlock. Remember how Mr. Knightley was suspicious about Harriet's mother? Harriet was judged, and Aurora would be judged today." Colleen bit into a cookie. "Maybe some do and don't say anything…"

"Sweetie, no one says anything but praise about you. What else did you get out of that book?"

"Mr. Elton was a minister, and a real jerk. I think Jane had an ax to grind with ministers because she made Mr. Collins a fool in Pride and Prejudice, too."

Suzy's eyes narrowed. "You're right. But her dad was a minister, and she adored him. Have you read Mansfield Park?"

"No. Lavina has and she liked it."

"I love that one by Jane. She made Edmund Bertram, who became a minister in the end, perfect."

Colleen snapped her fingers. "I saw the movie. Johnny Lee Miller played him. What a dreamboat." She cupped her mouth. "Oops. I'm engaged."

Suzy laughed. "So. I saw the movie and can say Johnny is one mighty fine lookin' man, and I'm married. They couldn't have a gooney man play him, now could they?"

Colleen sighed. "I'll miss Lavina. She talked about that book, and we read The Secret Garden together. Can't believe she's up and moved to Montana."

"She felt judged here." Suzy shifted. "I'm not cutting down the Amish, but they're more old-fashioned, and Lavina had the twins out of wedlock. Most *Englishers* don't even bat an eye about it, since it's so common, but among the Amish, it's not."

Colleen knew her face was getting red, since perspiration was forming on her forehead. "And when I become Amish, will they look at me like a fallen woman? Hezekiah says no, but I really wonder sometimes."

"Hey, girlfriend, you asked God to forgive you, and as long as you're clean before God, that's all that matters. Do you struggle with guilt?"

She nodded. "Although, I couldn't live without my little girl, I do struggle."

"You gave her life. How precious is that in a day and age when you could have aborted her?"

"My parents wanted me to, but I just couldn't. Saw a special on PBS about how a baby's whole nervous system is developed at six weeks. No, I could never…"

"Well, there are women in our church who have. No one talks about it and it's all hush-hush, but it's there, none the same. And the guilt these women carry." Suzy sipped her tea. "I'm so proud of you that you gave us the gift of Aurora. She's a doll."

"Thank you, 'Mom.' Can I call you that once I'm Amish?"

Suzy smiled with a cookie in her mouth, her cheeks making her eyes turn into half-moons. After a swallow, she said, "I always wanted an Amish daughter." She chuckled. "So, what else did you get out of Emma? I must be dense."

Colleen swooshed the air. "You are not. Maybe I'm more like Emma than most. I did see she was insecure, comparing herself with Jane Fairfax."

"She was full of herself." Suzy grabbed her copy of the book off the counter, opened it and read, "Emma Woodhouse, handsome, clever, and rich, with a comfortable home and happy disposition seemed to unite some of the best blessings of existence; and had lived nearly twenty-one years in the world with very little to distress or vex her.'" She clamped the book shut. "See, a perfect snob."

Colleen sighed. "We can discuss this more at circle. I'll let others convince you."

Suzy poured more tea into her cup. "I could sit here all day, sipping tea. Maybe the Brits are on to something. I hear they still have tea breaks."

"We need to slow down and catch our breath in America, don't you think?"

"Hey, you objected to these teas at first saying, 'I don't want you to pay me for having fun.' Remember?"

Colleen nodded. "But now I see it's a good thing. Maybe we should have a half-hour tea."

Suzy laughed. "Nope. Fifteen minutes is all I can afford. Now, let's get back to work!"

~*~

Melvin warmed his hand on the pie plate as he banged on the side door of Mona's house. Not feeling comfortable just walking in, he took in a deep breath of crisp winter air. Not being windy, it didn't bite his cheeks and a tranquil hush was everywhere around him. He noticed some thawing snow making a rivulet down the side yard. Knowing a blustery February was ahead, he soaked up the calm.

He could only hear the mooing of cows and someone in the barn. Maybe Freeman needs a pie, he thought, and headed to the open barn door. "Freeman, you in here?"

"*Jah*, come in."

Melvin took a deep breath. Even though he was Amish and should be used to it, the smells of Freeman's barn made him nauseated. His *daed* was a clockmaker and farming didn't run in his blood. He liked the scent of newly cut wood, not cow manure. "Can you come on out?"

"Just a minute," he heard Freeman moan.

Could he handle having his father-in-law living next to him? Never knew where he stood concerning Freeman, him being a man of no words.

Freeman appeared at the barn door. "*Jah?*"

"I stopped by to deliver a pie from Fannie. Is Mona home?"

Freeman nodded and headed towards the house.

Melvin followed. "How you been, Freeman?"

"Can't complain. And you?"

"The same. Fannie's ready to be a *mamm* and me a *daed*. We're both real excited."

Freeman only nodded to acknowledge that he'd heard what was said.

"Don't have a boy name picked out yet."

Freeman shrugged. "Why not your daed's name?" He took off his boots and they entered the house.

"Well, if it's a girl we'll name her Deborah and if a boy, I'm thinking Jeb."

Freeman shot him a fiery glare. "Come again?"

"Deborah after Granny and Jeb after, well, Jeb Weaver."

"Why not Mona? That's Fannie's real *mamm's* name."

Melvin put the pie on the table. "I don't know. She's called her Deborah since she got pregnant. Nothing personal."

"Sit down."

Melvin obeyed, wondering why he felt so guilty all of a sudden. It was their *kinner's* name, for Pete's sake.

Freeman took a seat at the table and clasped his hands together, setting them on the table, as if to build a fortress between the two of them. Then, tears formed in his eyes. "Sorry, Melvin. I need to speak my mind."

"Go on..."

"Well, I don't say things much, but I think this whole business of naming the *boppli* after the Weavers had hurt Mona. She's awful moody lately."

Melvin's eyebrows shot up as if surprised. "Mona? Moody? Really?"

"Well, ever since she started reading those books. Those fiction books at the knitting group, she's been trying to pry things out of me."

"Fannie too, and since they're reading about romance a lot, I tell her I love her more."

"Huh?"

"*Jah*. I do. Tell her I love her. And do special things to make her life easier, being so pregnant and all."

Freeman scrunched his lips to one side, as if he'd just bit into a lemon. "Well, Mona's been such so crabby lately, it's a hard thing to say..."

"Women need it. Believe me. Do yourself a favor, tell your wife you love her and you'll be a happier man for it."

"How?"

"Well, you get back what you give, *jah?* If you don't give anything to your wife, you get nothing back."

He fidgeted with his fingers. "Well, I let her have the dog."

"And that's *goot*. But when was the last time you told her you loved her?"

Freeman readjusted the black wool hat on his head. "It's been a coon's age since I've done that. Silly."

Melvin frowned. "No, it's not."

"I work in that barn day in and day out. She knows I love her. Why tell her?"

"What's working in the barn got to do with anything?"

Freeman's eyes became fiery again. "I do it for her to show her that I..."

"Love her?"

"*Jah.* And she don't seem to appreciate it none. Most nights not even a hot meal."

Melvin took a deep breath. "Well, Fannie made you this pie. Why not have it for lunch?"

"I think I will. *Danki.*"

~*~

Mona stood at the top of the steps, hand over her heart. She'd heard every word Freeman said. He works in the barn because he loves me? And I thought it was to avoid me.

She went back into her room, wanting to finish Emma before the knitting circle. She sat in her chair, picked up Angel and her book, and then placed the book back down again Crabapple? Had she been crabby? And no hot meal in return for his hard work?

Why did she feel like crying again? Maybe these novels were making her lose her mind. She'd never thought so deeply about things in years. Ever since she'd read Anne of Green Gables, she'd been a mess. But then Charles Dickens Life of our Lord made her want to read her Bible more. And since Maryann said to read Psalms for her nerves, well, she was reading a lot. Was it bad to read so much, making her crabby?

Mona dismissed her silly notions and finished the last paragraph of her book:

The wedding was very much like other weddings, where the parties have no taste for finery or parade; and Mrs. Elton, from the particulars detailed by her husband, thought it all extremely shabby, and very inferior to her own.—"Very little white satin, very few lace veils; a most pitiful business!—Selina would stare when she heard of it."—But, in spite of these deficiencies, the wishes, the hopes, the confidence, the predictions of the small band of true friends who witnessed the ceremony, were fully answered in the perfect happiness of the union.

Mona read it again, and when she did, she did not like what she saw. Mona was Mrs. Elton, always finding fault. Very little white satin...then her eyes ran over 'small band of true friends'. Emma Woodhouse had matured and realized what was really important in life: relationships. Mona bowed her head and prayed out loud:

"Lord, it's me, Mona. I feel all jumbled up inside, and Granny said I can talk to you like a friend. Well, I'm thankful for getting a second chance in life, realizing that I'm a hermit and need to break out of my fears. Thank you for Maryann, my bosom friend, who listens to every word I say, and help me to be a better wife to Freeman.... We used to be so in love, a long time ago..."

She jumped up out of her chair when she realized Freeman was in the room. "*Ach,* you'll be the death of me yet, sneaking up on me like that!"

His eyes were mellow. "I love you, too. Even though I think you'll be the death of me sometimes."

Was she dreaming? Freeman was telling her he loved her? Why did she feel like springtime, when all the snow had melted and all was fresh and new? "*Ach,* Freeman, I love you, too."

He drew near and kissed her cheek. "I heard that there prayer. And I'm here, too. Not just Maryann. I know you have your fears."

She gasped for air, overwhelmed with wanting to cry and laugh at the same time. "*Danki.* I need help. I get so afraid when..."

"I know. And I'm going to help you more." He put his arm around her. "Fannie made us a pie. Let's have it for lunch."

"You had pie for breakfast." As soon as she said it, she kicked herself. "And you deserve another one for lunch."

~*~

Marge pulled into Lizzie's long driveway much slower, since Jeb had complained about her speeding.

"Will you come in for some tea or coffee?" Lizzie offered.

"I'd love that. And you need help with all these bags."

"*Jah.* I stock up when I see a big sale, and this month it's toilet paper."

Roman ran over from his shop, placed a kiss on Lizzie's cheek, and offered to take care of the bags. Lizzie stroked his auburn beard playfully, and Marge looked away. Newlyweds.

She followed Lizzie into the house. "How do you keep things so…spotless?"

"Jenny mopped the floors when you were gone, Lizzie," Roman said as he hauled in four large bags effortlessly. "The twins dusted, and well, did everything on the list."

"Where are they now?" Lizzie asked.

"Over at my parents. Visiting."

Marge put up her hands. "I need to go. Leave you lovebirds alone."

Roman chuckled. "*Nee,* you can stay."

"Well, I won't be long," Marge teased. "Only an hour or more."

Roman looked at Lizzie puzzled, and she grinned. "Marge's joking. Go on with you."

Roman nodded and went out the door. Lizzie escorted Marge into her large kitchen. "Coffee or tea?"

"Neither. Lizzie, I think Roman wants time alone with you. How about a glass of water?"

Lizzie shook her head. "You drove me up to Punxsy and I want to give you a treat." She turned to open her breadbox. "Want a homemade donut? Made them this morning."

"Homemade? How?"

"It's easy. I'll teach you sometime."

"Thanks, Lizzie. You're my Harriet."

"Come again?"

"You know, Harriet, in the book? Emma's friend?"

Lizzie smiled. "*Ach, danki.* I can't say you're Emma because she was selfish."

"You think so?"

"*Jah.* But the end made you think she'd grown up somehow."

"Oh, you should see the movie. It's great. Anyhow, what I want to say is, Harriet was a nice friend, always kind to Emma, even when her behavior wasn't so good. And Harriet brought the best out in Emma."

"Oh, you bring out the best in me, too."

Marge just stared at this woman she really didn't even feel worthy enough to be a friend to. "Well, I'll tell Joe that for laughs. Me, bring the best out in someone?"

"*Ach,* stop it. And Joe adores you."

Marge had to admit it was true. Her Joe did admire her despite how prickly she could be at times. "Well, Joe's a good man, not doubt about it. And I was thinking…is Jenny done with Little Men yet?"

"*Jah*, she's done with the *kinner* version. Why?" Lizzie placed a hot cup of tea on the table in front of Marge. "One or two donuts?"

"One. Need to watch my calories. Anyhow, I was thinking about the book, since I'm reading it too, being hooked on Louisa May Alcott. Wouldn't it be nice to have a homeless shelter for boys? We Baptist have one for girls, but not men? We need one."

Lizzie sat across from Marge, eyes wide. "I think you're right. So many boys in foster homes, as we found out."

"How long after filling out the paperwork will you get your home inspection?"

"The caseworker said she was real busy and would write to let us know. Roman's looking happy about it now. I don't mean to be a pushy wife, but those letters that *Daed* gets from Charles rip my heart out."

"And Roman reads them, too?"

"*Jah*, and wrote back to him. I think Charles planted the seed in Roman's heart to take in some boys. But they have to be younger than the twins."

"For good reason. I agree. But like I was saying, there's lots of boys who need a home. I told Janice how I felt, and she kind of brushed me off."

"Why?"

"Well, she probably thinks I'm a flake after trying to live off the grid and failing. Back and forth on things too much. I'm like Emma, can't finish a book, painting... my pregnancy..."

Lizzie leaned forward. "Marge, stop it. Quit putting yourself down. *Daed* says he read in one of his books that God didn't make junk. So, don't treat yourself like you are."

Marge raised her eye and stared at the ceiling. "The Lord your God is with you, he is mighty to save. He will take great delight in you, he will quiet you with his love, he will rejoice over you with singing. Zebediah 3:17."

Lizzie laughed. "*Goot*, but there's no Jebediah in the Bible, it's Zephaniah."

"*Ach*," Marge teased in an Amish accent. "I must have thought it rhymed with Jebediah. He's the one who told me to memorize it."

"Jeb? Not Granny?"

"No, Jeb. He's a kind soul and had self-worth issues growing up. It's why he let Mona have Angel."

Lizzie gawked. "Jeb? Well, you'd never know it."

"He reconditioned his mind and memorized that verse and told me to do the same. Think about it, Lizzie. God dances over us? Rejoices over us? How can we not do the same for some homeless boys?"

"You are a kindred spirit, Marge. I wish you were Amish," Lizzie blurted, then put a hand over her mouth.

"Why do you say that?"

"So you could go to my *Gmay*, I mean church."

"But I'd have to live by you."

Lizzie got up and put more donuts on a plate. "Nathan and Lavina aren't moving back. Staying in Montana."

"I know. Gossip vine goes faster than your Amish vine. But, I just can't live without electricity."

"It can be put in. *Englishers* buy Amish houses all the time."

"But it must be a fortune. The big farmhouse and my own little *dawdyhaus*. Man, do I miss that place."

Lizzie bit into a donut. "Pray about it. I just have a feeling about something."

Marge sighed. "Lizzie, I can't be Amish...for sure and for certain."

~*~

Granny lifted the baked apple filled with raisins and walnuts, and a dash of cinnamon to bring out all the flavors. She remembered how Miss Bates made a big deal about getting apples from Mr. Knightley in *Emma*. Was she so poor that even apples were a treat? Marge and Lizzie arrived with large bags. What on earth?

She met Lizzie's eyes, and who promptly said, "It's a surprise."

"Someone's birthday? Did I forget something?"

"*Nee, Mamm.* We'll talk about it when the circle arrives."

Marge's red cheeks told Granny how cold it was outside. "You *Englishers* never wear hats."

Lizzie leaned towards Marge. "She'd look *goot* in a bonnet, *jah*?"

Granny tilted her head. "I suppose, but Suzy makes such nice wool ones. Maybe take a peek at her new infinity scarves. You can wrap them around your head."

Soon Fannie, Mona, and Maryann entered the kitchen, and they put their capes and bonnets on the peg provided by the door. "How are you Granny?" Fannie asked, giving Granny a side hug. "I'm so huge. Little Deborah, or Little Debbie, will be out soon, though."

Granny slowly looked over at Mona, knowing this was a sore spot with her, Deborah being the *boppli's* name if a girl. But Mona had soft lines around her mouth and eyes and looked ten years younger. "Mona, you look well. Is Angel *goot* company?"

"*Jah*, to my surprise. I thought Jeb was just being daft to give her to me."

Granny clenched her fists. She could call Jeb 'daft' but not Mona, or any other person for that matter. "Jeb was helped by dogs his whole life. Thought you'd like one." She regretted her defensive tone as soon as she spit out these words.

Mona reached for Granny's hand. "*Ach*, I say wrong things. I meant at first I thought it an odd thing to have a dog in the house, as you know. But Angel lives up to her name, for sure."

Granny looked down at Mona's hand in hers. Praise be. This statue of a woman was pliable. Had Angel really done that much? *Ach*, Jeb's so wise.

Ruth appeared with Janice and Suzy, and Granny was overjoyed that Ruth was no longer ill, able to finally come back to the circle. She turned to Mona. "Can you help me pass out baked apples?"

Mona nodded, as she lilted over to the counter and picked up a tray. "In the living room?"

"*Jah*, put them on the coffee table. We can nibble on them as we knit."

Granny collected spoons and napkins and ambled herself into the living room. "Coffee's hot on the stove and baked apples are here on my new coffee table. Isn't it a beauty?"

"I love it," Marge said. "Something new Roman's making, right?"

"*Jah*," Lizzie said. "Bent wood coffee tables to match the rockers are selling like hotcakes."

"And I say 'Praise be' to that." Granny took a seat and picked up her yarn. "And the carved trays are doing *goot*, too. People buying after Christmas since the English give each other money."

Janice snickered. "*Ach*, we English are so materialistic, *jah*?"

Granny looked at Janice in wonder. "*Jah*, some are." She grinned. "Aren't you as chipper as the birds outside today."

Janice picked up her red yarn and began to knit. "I loved Emma and can't wait to talk about it."

Suzy shrugged. "Then you start. I'm clueless as to what Emma is all about, except a spoiled brat."

Janice got her copy of Emma out of her massive purse. "Well, it brought back memories for me." She opened the book and read:

"Dear Diary, Today I tried not to think about Mr. Knightly. I tried not to think about him when I discussed the menu with Cook... I tried not to think about him in the garden where I thrice plucked the petals off a daisy to ascertain his feelings for Harriet. I don't think we should keep daisies in the garden; they really are a drab little flower. And I tried not to think about him when I went to bed, but something had to be done."

Janice gazed around the circle. "I fell for Jerry back when dinosaurs roamed the earth, and forgot how I felt. This passage gave me such vivid flashbacks, my heart beat out of my chest." She looked at Colleen and then Fannie. "*Yinz* are so young, but when you become a fossil like me, and your heart skips a beat, you think it's love or a heart attack." She leaned over and howled. "Well, I knew it was love. Almost went to the doctor, though."

Laughter filled the room, and this made Granny glad. The English moved so fast, not taking time to reflect, and once again, she thanked God for her Amish heritage, especially Old Christmas, a day set apart just to be silent and revel in all life's blessings. Curiosity rose within her. "That's *wunderbar*, Janice. Don't the English reflect on Valentine's Day about love, though?"

"What?"

"Well, you said you hadn't thought of your first love for Jerry in a long time. What do the English do on Valentine's Day?"

"Eat chocolate," Janice quipped. "Jerry always gets me a heart-shaped box."

"What for?" Granny asked. "Is there some meaning in it?"

Janice put Emma back into her purse. "I don't understand the question, Granny."

"Well, do you take time to reflect or meditate?"

"Oh, no, it's a celebration time. But I suppose many couples reminisce about their lives together. Jerry and I are busy folks…so I guess we don't have time." She swallowed a lump. "Wow, never saw that before."

"A minister's work is never done." Granny tried to sympathize with her friend, but knew she and Jeb saw each other far more than Jerry and Janice.

"Too busy," Janice added.

Suzy groaned. "Ministers. It's another reason I don't like this book. Mr. Elton is a jerk and he's supposed to be a man of the cloth!"

All heads nodded in agreement.

Maryann spoke up. "I think Jane Austen makes fun of clergymen. Mr. Collins in Pride and Prejudice was *ferhoodled* in the brain, but I liked that book, overall. I didn't care for Emma. All they did was take walks and visit people."

"Oh," Colleen said. "It shows the beauty of a simple life. Emma didn't need fancy balls to be happy, even though they planned them. It was being happy with a small circle of friends." She looked across the room at Maryann. "Maybe you're so used to the slow pace of life, the community the Amish have, but this book makes most people envy Emma's life. So close with her father…" She pursed her lips. "Emma was so kind to the man, even though he was so grouchy and complained all the time."

"*Ach,* I agree," Lizzie said. "My *daed's* in real pain with MS, and rarely complains. If he did, like Mr. Woodhouse, it would be awful." She lowered her head back into her knitting. "Emma didn't have a *mamm,* and if people think she was selfish, I disagree. She was hiding her broken heart."

Silence hung over the room, knitting needles clicked. Granny wasn't expecting Lizzie to say this, and really didn't understand her meaning, so she probed. "Lizzie, what do you mean?"

Lizzie reached for her book, took out her paper book marker, and read:

"'I always deserve the best treatment because I never put up with any other.' She was guarding her heart from further pain. Losing a *mamm* makes you so isolated and… odd to others. You see girls with *mamm's* and you wonder if you did something wrong. You know, bad things happen to bad people, and all that…my *daed* helped me work it all out."

Suzy slowly put a hand up. "Lizzie, do you mean Emma was hurt?"

"*Jah. Daed* sees this in Charles, his English pen pal, who has an absent *daed*, one who's never home. Invited him up to visit and hopes to teach him what he taught me."

"Which is?" Marge asked, leaning forward.

"God is the father to the fatherless, like the Bible says, or in my case, a *mamm*. He has a special place in his heart for orphans, widows, and hurting folks." Lizzie's eyes misted. "We judged Charles by his black clothes, dog collar and piercings, but *daed* saw his heart."

Suzy put down her knitting. "We sure can misjudge people. Missy was a hurting person who hid it all by acting superior." She scratched her head. "I think I'll watch Emma, the new PBS movie, and see if I don't see her as a hurting person."

Colleen groaned. "I will miss television."

Suzy winked. "I can have the DVD player going while we have one of our tea breaks."

Granny wagged a finger. "*Nee*. Colleen will be baptized in a few months, so no television."

Colleen shook her head in agreement. "A trifle, right Granny?"

Granny beamed. How she loved this girl. "*Jah*, something not important in the long run." She turned to Fannie. "You're quiet. What did you get out of Emma?"

"I liked how Emma reached out to the poor. Miss Bates was my favorite character."

"You talk as much as her," Mona said, an attempt at a joke. No one laughed, but only looked sympathetically at Fannie whose face was read as beets.

Granny's heart plummeted. When would Mona learn to hold her tongue? Did she need to ask her to leave?

Mona slipped an arm stiffly around Fannie. "I'm sorry. I'm like Mrs. Elton, I suppose, always saying the wrong thing."

"Or," Lizzie offered, "like Emma, someone hurt deep down and covers it up. Making jokes at other's expenses, like Emma did with Miss Bates on Boxhill?"

Mona's head hung. "Can *yinz* pray for me? I have carried pain and hurt people…"

"Hurt people, hurt people," Janice said. "It's a rule of thumb in pastoral counseling. If you never felt loved, how can you give it out?"

Mona froze and Fannie took her hand. "We'll get through this together, *Mamm*."

Mona gasped, and reached awkwardly for Fannie, as if embracing someone was foreign to her. "*Danki*."

Granny looked out the window and saw finches pecking at thistle seed in the cylinder feeder. Lord, transform Mona into a finch, able to get along with others. Help her shed her blue jay ways…

As the room was still, Granny turned to Ruth, her bird-loving friend. "Ruth, how about you? Did you like Emma?"

"I thought it was written very well, and I liked Emma. She was strong. I saw she was hurting right away, and kept people at arm's length so they wouldn't see it. But I just don't understand Emma's comments about Robert Martin. She thinks a farmer is beneath her, and she's surprised he can write a *goot* letter." She beamed. "Luke started to write love letters to me after I started. Remember how I got the idea from Pride and Prejudice?"

All leaned forward, eager for more.

"Well, his letters melt my heart completely, and he was raised a farmer. Did Jane Austen think farmers were dumb?"

Marge groaned. "Some things never change. People look down on blue collar workers like they're not as smart as engineers, doctors or lawyers, but my Joe can fix anything, being so mechanically minded."

"So, people look down on other's professions in the English world?" Ruth asked. "Why? Everyone has their own talent."

"And some are more respectable than others," Marge added.

"*Ach*, 'Stuff and nonsense', like Marilla always said in Anne of Green Gables," Granny jested. "That's *ferhoodled*. Every person is equal, like the proverb says. 'He is the happiest, be he peasant or king, who finds peace at home.' That's what's important." She smiled around the room at the women she loved so well. "Isn't that the theme of Emma? Finding peace and community?"

All heads nodded. The wind whipped at the house, but the warmth within the room was unmistakable.

Lizzie stood up to get the bag she'd brought with her to the circle. "Don't mean to change the subject, but I want to share something with *yinz*." She turned to Marge. "Unless you want to ask."

"No, go on," Marge said.

"Well, I know we knit here, but Marge feels like Emma, not finishing things. Some of it's kind of personal, but I told her making a wedding quilt is something that takes real commitment." Lizzie smiled across the room at Colleen. "And we have an early spring wedding coming up, and we need help to make Colleen and Hezekiah's quilt. Can we count on *yinz*? We can meet at my place."

There was an enthusiastic cheer around the room, and Fannie stood up, clasping her hands. "Can we see the material you picked?"

"*Jah*," Lizzie said, "But, Colleen we want it to be a surprise, so can you move into the kitchen?"

Colleen nodded, eyes shining. "I found my little circle of friends, like Emma did. I love *yinz* so much." She went around the room embracing each woman quickly, and then ran into the kitchen.

~*~

Janice stared at the drip IV and then collapsed in a chair next to her husband. "Honey, something's got to give."

Jerry sat up in his hospital bed. "I agree. I need to get out of here so I can preach tonight."

Janice moaned. "Stop it. You're being admitted, and that's that. Dehydration and exhaustion, the doc said, remember?"

Jerry pursed his lips and laid back like an obedient child. Janice's heart skipped into her throat. "Sorry, honey. Don't mean to snap, just upset."

"I know. You think the church will kill me…"

"You need an assistant pastor, like I said a million times…"

"But we'd cut into our outreach money. What we need is a lay pastor, part-time."

Janice took her knitting out of her purse. "We need more money; it's the harsh cold reality. Not a sin to talk about it."

Jerry closed his eyes and mumbled, "We're holding our own. Small churches are dying…"

He closed his eyes and Janice let a tear trickle down onto the yarn. *Lord, we need help. So many in need and Jerry's big heart just can't turn people away.*

Suzy knocked gently on the door. "Can I come in?"

Janice nodded and Jerry woke up in a start. "What's wrong? Can't Andy lead Bible study tonight?"

"Yes. I didn't come to upset you. Please, calm down." Suzy took a seat in the hospital chair next to Janice. "I hope I came with some answers to your problem."

"You getting ordained?" Janice quipped.

"I wish," Suzy said. "But we women, we're the worker bees… overworked bees I might add, but we're about to get some relief."

Jerry bolted up. "Now, you have me curious. Spill the beans."

A broad smile slid across Suzy's face. "Well, maybe it's good you're in the hospital, because you might need treatment for shock. Guess what Missy did?"

"What?" Jerry and Janice blurted in unison.

"It's a secret, and no one can know."

A nurse came into the room to check Jerry's vitals. "Go on, Suzy."

Suzy shook her head, and pointed to the nurse.

"You feeling any better, Reverend Jackson?" the nurse asked.

"Oh, please, don't call me 'Reverend'. I'm no better than anyone else. It's just Jerry."

"Jerry, you're blood pressure's fine, but you need to rest." She turned to Suzy. "Don't get all tuckered out by visitors."

Suzy rolled her eyes. "We're family."

The nurse looked at Suzy, eyes narrow. Janice laughed as her dear friend always got people confused when she said this, which made Suzy do it all the more. How could they be related, Suzy a fair Irish woman, and Jerry and she African American? "We have a church family," Janice said to the nurse, then winked at Suzy.

The nurse exited the room. Janice leaned towards Suzy. "You're silly. Now, tell us what will 'shock' us."

Suzy's eyes lit up and she looked like a child opening presents under a Christmas tree. "Give and it shall be given unto you, is all I can say. Just guess."

"I can't. Just tell us," Jerry said evenly. "The suspense is making my blood pressure go up again."

"Okay, but I sure am glad you're sitting down. Missy is so grateful to the church outreach and well, the service that taught her about salvation. She said she was trying to help others, being jealous of Ginny Rowland."

"What for?" Janice asked.

"Giving up her house, or taking pennies for it, so Forget-Me-Not Manor could start. So she took in women in need, one by one. I thought one girl was a maid, but she was someone Missy was trying to help. She helped Sammy financially, too. But she only felt emptier."

Jerry's eyes were on her like a hawk on prey. "Well, she gave out of her lack, that's why. She got drained then?"

"Yes, but now she feels the love of God and isn't doing her 'good works' out of jealousy but out of appreciation of what Christ did for her on the cross. Or should I say, the Holy Spirit is filling..." Suzy cupped her mouth with her hands. "You'll never guess."

"What?" Janice felt exasperated now. This wasn't shocking news at all, and Jerry needed rest.

"She's selling all her antique cars and donating the money to our homeless ministry."

Jerry's eye misted and he took Janice's hands. "How many and how much are they worth?"

"I'm not finished. She's selling her house, too, and wants to live in town." Suzy laughed. "She's one nervous driver and needs to walk to stores. Anyhow, she said she has enough to live on forever, and the rest will go to the church."

Jerry's face contorted and then he bowed his head and sobbed like a baby.

Janice rose to her feet, lifted her hands, and shouted, "Thank you, Jesus."

Suzy got up and hugged Janice. "She does have one stipulation, though."

"What?" Janice asked.

"She wants the money invested to draw interest. And it will be enough to pay a part-time helper at the church."

"You mean a minister?" Jerry asked.

"Well, she said you looked 'ragged' but more like a person to be a paid deacon. Someone who can help in the homeless ministry."

Jerry put a hand up. "That was my specific prayer. Lord, I sure am glad I'm in the hospital because I think I am going into shock."

~*~

The next morning, Granny entered the hospital room with Marge, her driver. Jerry was smiling so much, she wondered if he hadn't received any visitors and was that lonely. "How are you, Jerry?"

"*Wunderbar goot!*" Jerry grinned.

Granny's brows furrowed. Was he on some kind of medicine for his nerves that made him a little too happy? "Well, we heard you collapsed at the pulpit, and Jeb sends his sympathies, saying he understands completely."

"Well, today's a new day with no mistakes in it, yet, as Janice says," Jerry said with mirth.

"She quotes Anne of Green Gables a lot, *jah*?"

"*Jah*, I suppose," Jerry said.

Why was Jerry using so many Amish words and making such light-hearted conversation, when he had what appeared to be an emotional breakdown, though mild? Was he now displaying symptoms of this? Granny took a seat, as did Marge.

"We missed you last night," Marge said, "but Andy did a good job preaching."

"Oh, I never had any concerns…"

Marge cocked an eyebrow. "Really?"

"Well, just a few concerns. I'm a control freak concerning sermons. Did the overhead projector work?"

"Yes, as usual." Marge looked over at Granny, concern registering on her face. "Why do you ask?"

"I think we need to switch to PowerPoint. Get some computers to update things into the modern world we live in." He glanced at Granny. "No offense to the Amish."

"No offense taken at all."

"But we can't afford computers and all that fancy stuff," Marge blurted, "and I like it simple."

Granny noticed Jerry had bloodshot eyes that protruded a little too much. "Jerry, is there anything we can do to help you? Make meals and take them over to Forget-Me-Not?"

Jerry snapped his fingers and laughed. "I need to tell someone or I'll bust"

"Tell us what?" Granny was now feeling shaken. Had Jerry lost his mind completely?

"We have an anonymous donor to the church. And it's not a little donation, but, well, more than the Amish auction brings in every August."

Granny got her yarn out of her satchel and started to knit to calm herself. Obviously Jerry was delusional and it pained her deeply.

Marge leaned forward. "How much does the Amish auction bring in?"

"Seventeen-thousand, last year," Granny said.

Jerry jerked his head from side to side, clapped his hands as if doing a happy dance. "Well, take that times ten…. at least."

Janice entered the room, a suitcase in her hand. "Morning everyone. Brought you some fresh stuff, honey."

"Is he staying long?" Granny asked.

"No, he'll be monitored until tomorrow, then free to go home."

Granny got up and took Janice by the elbow out into the hallway. "He needs to stay for a while, don't you think?"

Janice frowned. "The docs say he's fine…"

"But he's obviously not. Telling all kinds of stories and I'm concerned."

"What kind of stories?"

"Ridiculous things, like someone donating over a hundred-thousand dollars to your church."

Janice's face froze, and then she burst into laughter. "I see. You think he's gone off his rocker."

"*Jah*, and maybe you, too. You English work yourselves to no end. You need to rest on the Sabbath...."

Janice continued to laugh as she went into the hospital room. "Honey, Granny thinks we've gone nuts, telling such stories about money. Remember, the donor is anonymous. Don't go blabbing."

Marge got up and put her hands on her hips. "*Yinz* are making hairs on the back of my neck stand up. Are you both hallucinating?"

Janice wiped a tear and calmed herself down. "Sorry. We're overjoyed. Jerry did have to come in for IV treatments, being dehydrated and lacking minerals. He's been exhausted. But last night we got word about an anonymous donor to the church." She looked over at Jerry. "I talked to this donor this morning, and it's more than we thought... by a long shot. She has a lawyer involved..."

"That's fine. We need to be accountable." Jerry rested his head on his pillow. "How much more are we talking about?"

"Twice as much as we thought."

Jerry put his hand over his heart as if to protect it. "Thank you, Lord. Thank you, Lord..."

Marge jumped on her tiptoes and then took a seat. "What will the church do with the money?"

"It's earmarked for the homeless and other things. Jerry and I sat up late into the night, and we think a place for homeless men is needed. But we're obviously in shock, so we need to settle down, pray, talk to the elders."

"Safety in a multitude of counselors," Granny added.

"Absolutely. Jerry and I won't take any pay increase, that's for sure. With this much money, we might find ourselves discontent."

Marge's mouth gaped. "You deserve a raise."

"No, we have enough. Not rich, but not poor." Janice took Jerry's hand. "And this big lug gives away any extra anyhow."

Jerry smiled at Janice, and Granny soaked in this wonderful scene; a content English family.

The image of Nathan's farm flashed across her mind. Should she tell them it was for sale? Or was this all too much for Jerry? I'll wait, she decided. Maybe Nathan will change his mind and come home to Smicksburg... where he belongs.

~*~

That afternoon, Granny sipped piping hot tea as she sat in her rocker as close to the woodstove as she could without catching on fire. She thought back to Little Women and how Jo burnt the back of her dress, being too close to the fire, and delight flooded her soul. These classic books had been her treasures, and to share them with her 'circle of friends' made her joy overflow. But that it took some of the girls so long to understand the meaning behind Emma still baffled her. Emma was a work in progress, like every human being. It's what gives her such appeal, Granny thought.

She sipped her peppermint tea, good for sore throats. She'd felt ragged and a scratchy throat was a sign to rest. Granny's mind again went to Nathan's house. She could still walk to it, even at her age. Why was he staying in Montana? She bowed her head, sorry that she was being selfish. Her own son, Nathan Sr., of course would want to have his son raise a family near him. But... how she loved her grandson and Lavina. Your will be done, Lord.

Feeling a headache come on, Granny bowed her head and prayed:

Lord,

I am made of dust, as you well know. I have feet of clay, able to fall at any time. And I fear I'm being selfish concerning Nathan. I love him and want him living down the road, but have your way. He has his whole life ahead of him and I want the best for him... and you know best.

And Lord, thank you for the gift the anonymous donor is giving the Baptists. Give them wisdom on exactly how to use it, and bless their efforts to help those in need.

Lord, whatever has come over Mona, please continue to work in her heart. I feel like there's much I don't know, but Fannie and Maryann are your hands and feet to that woman. I used to have contempt for her, I admit, but now only pity. And you know I don't pity too many people, since we all have our cross to bear, as you did. But she seems mighty lost....

I give this day to you in Jesus name,

Amen.

Granny looked out the window and sunbeams burst through thick clouds, making rays glide over to the woods behind her house. She spotted something red coming down her driveway. As it got closer with rapid speed, she saw Marge's red sports car. *Ach,* she drives like a crazy person. Most likely she'd left something in the car and she was returning it, so why the rush?

Soon Marge slammed her door, ran up the porch steps and threw open her side door. "Fannie had a baby girl!"

"What? It's too early..."

"No, only three weeks. The baby's fine. A healthy baby girl."

Granny went over and embraced Marge. "That's *goot* news. And Fannie is okay?"

"Yes, she's beaming with joy."

Granny didn't know if Marge was exhausted from driving her to the hospital this morning, and then go off to work, but there was a shadow cast across her eyes. "Marge, what is it?"

"Nothing."

"Come on now..."

Marge's eyes pooled with tears. "I really wanted my baby. The miscarriage hits me at the oddest times. I'm selfish."

Granny led her by the elbow over to her kitchen table. "You're not selfish, just have a *mamm's* heart. You loved that wee one in you, who went home early to be with Jesus."

Marge sat at the table, head bowed. "But it hurts."

Granny reached for her hand across the table. "Hurt isn't all bad. I started the knitting circle because of pain."

"What?"

"*Jah,* many don't know how sad I was that all my *kinner* moved out of state except Roman. God took Abigail, his first wife, too, and I loved her so. God gives and takes away, as Job says in the Bible, blessed be the name of the Lord."

Marge sighed. "But I'm sure the knitting circle doesn't stop you from missing your kids."

Granny grinned. "*Ach,* it does. Somehow it does. And you and Lizzie wanting to take foster *kinner* might fill that longing in your heart for having *kinner.*"

Marge squeezed her hand. "Wish I was still your neighbor."

Granny thought again of Nathan's house. Marge used to live in the *dawdyhaus* in the back, and the farmhouse could be used for foster kids or homeless men. And maybe Marge and Joe could be the ones the Baptists hired to help. Her heart leapt for joy at the prospect, but she didn't mention anything to Marge. Granny knew she had a way of running ahead of God on making "His will happen." How many couples had she tried to pair up, being a matchmaker? Like Emma, she too had grown up.

Dear Readers,

I hope you enjoyed this episode of Amish Knit-Lit Circle. Emma continues to be one of my favorite books since it shows a flawed woman being transformed. We all know her journey isn't over, too, Emma being human. As I receive emails from readers, many of you can identify with Emma, feeling a little too blemished. Remember,

The Lord your God is with you, he is mighty to save. He will take great delight in you, he will quiet you with his love, he will rejoice over you with singing. Zephaniah 3:17.

I have a plaque with this verse written on it within view as I write. I too know I'm "hopelessly flawed" as Jo March puts it. But I also know God loves me, despite all my prickles. And He loves you, too, friends.

This recipe is appropriate to end Emma, since Robert Martin collected walnuts for Harriet, and Mr. Knightley supplied poor Miss Bates with apples. And my very own Mr. Knightley made it up! This is a secret (LOL), but my husband taught me how to cook! Enjoy!

Simple Baked Apples

Core as many apples as you want to serve and place in glass baking dish deep enough to cover
Fill each with equal parts chopped walnuts and raisins

Top with a tsp. of brown sugar.
Cover with aluminum foil to keep from drying.
Bake at 350 for 30-40 minutes or until tender.
Eat without guilt due to low fat and calories

EPISODE 6

∾

Black Beauty

Granny grabbed the coffeepot as Jeb cracked another knuckle. Slowly pouring the black liquid into his mug, she heard another sigh escape his lips. "Jeb, it will be alright. Believe me. I have a *mamm's* heart."

"Thought that would make it harder," he said, jabbing at his French toast.

"*Nee,* a *mamm* sees past all her *kinner's* faults, or handicaps."

"Mona doesn't, *jah*?"

"Well, most *mamms*. And Mona's changing, so don't be so harsh."

"You're defending Mona?" Jeb got up, raised his hands and shouted, "Hallelujah!"

Granny hit his arm. "Old man. Don't mock God."

"I'm not. I'm truly thankful."

"Your nerves are in a whirl ever since we got word about Ruth's *boppli*." Granny pulled at his sleeve as she sat down at the table, bringing Jeb down to his seat again. "Now, like I said, it will be fine."

Jeb groaned. "I'm not worried about Ruth. She's the predictable one. It's Luke…"

Granny bit her lower lip. "Hadn't thought much on that. But a *kinner* with down syndrome is what the Lord has blessed them with, and we can't change things."

He gripped her hand. "Be honest with me. This is going to be a long journey for them. They'll be caring for that child all their lives."

It was a rare time when Jeb fretted, Granny knew, so she just remained quiet until he released his concern.

Now being February, robins were spotted in yards all over Smicksburg. The braver robins, granny supposed, the hardy ones. Lord, bless Ruth and Luke as they continue to build their nest…"I learned something while reading Black Beauty. We really have no control over our lives, just like a horse."

"What?"

"Well, Black Beauty was a *goot* horse, but he was really at the mercy of his masters. And he had kind ones and not so kind. We have a master in heaven who's always *goot, jah*? And no matter how it looks we know everything can be worked out for the *goot*?"

Jeb's eyes mellowed a bit. "*Jah*. I suppose."

"You suppose?"

Jeb lowered his head and folded his hands in his lap. "I'm the bishop, so maybe I feel things more keenly. I'm praying for the right words to say when we visit, and I'm pretty stumped…"

Not knowing if she should interrupt his train of thought, Granny hesitated saying what she thought was really bothering him. "Can I help?"

"Pray I have the words to bring some comfort. Words of hope and practical ways to put our faith into action."

"Such as?"

"Well, I don't know. Does she need more tests? To confirm the diagnosis?"

"Well, that I don't know. We could always have a benefit auction."

"*Jah*, that would be *goot*." He looked over at her, eyes turquoise, deep with emotion. "And your knitting circle can make things for the *boppli*?"

Granny's brow wrinkled. "Make things? Like what?"

"I don't know. Those prayer shawls you make... make it a prayer blanket for the *boppli*."

"Ella did that for the twins. Okay, I can do that." She grabbed his hand. "Jeb, this is not the same as when we lost our girl. You're still mourning her loss, after all these years."

Jeb pursed his quivering lips. "*Nee,* I'm just concerned."

Tears brewed in Granny's eyes. "It's alright. I still think of her. When Black Beauty was taken away from his *mamm*, I thought I was *ferhoodled* in the head because I started to cry. Imagine that? And when Beauty thought back to happier times and his *mamm*, I wondered if our little one can see us from heaven. If she just can't wait to be with us."

Jeb cupped his face in his hands and let the tears flow. Granny sprang up and hugged him from behind. Leaning her chin on his shoulder, she whispered, "God will give them grace to carry them through, just like us. And they have a beautiful daughter, unique and special."

His shoulders trembled and Granny felt insecure. Jeb was her rock, her strong man. He'd been out tying up the roses onto the lattice that ran around the porch, making room to divide and plant yet another bush, an heirloom rose he bought for this year's planting. Did the pain of losing a *kinner* ever really go away? The Amish didn't plant flowers on the graves of their lost ones, yet she found such solace and peace in these roses that now encircled the house.

"You think Luke did everything he could? Get the midwife on time and all?"

Granny pat his shoulder. "*Jah.* Why?"

"Maybe they should have had the *kinner* at the hospital. Maybe we should have had our girl at the hospital. Maybe the English are right about the Amish…" Another sob escaped him as Jeb wiped his tears with a napkin. "Maybe we are stuck back in the Dark Ages."

Granny felt her heart jump into her throat, making it hard to talk. "Some *Englishers* say that, but Jeb, *kinner* die in the hospital, you know that. And lots of English have midwives deliver their *kinner* at home." She gripped his shoulders hard. "I listen to you correct me, Mr. Knightley, and now I'm going to do the same. Stop trying to carry a burden that's not yours. Only God has the strength to lift it. Remember in *Pilgrim's Progress* when Christian finds relief from the burden he carried on his back at the Cross? Leave it there, Jeb. Lay it down."

To her surprise his shoulders softened, and he pat her hand with his. After taking a deep breath, Jeb said, "You're right. And I know what I'm going to do, too."

"What's that?"

"Go over to Serenity Book Nook and buy a nice copy of *Pilgrim's Progress* for Ruth and Luke. They'll benefit from it like we did… and still do. *Danki*, love." He pulled her onto his lap and kissed her cheek.

Granny felt peace pour down into her soul and she leaned her head against his chest. "And anytime you miss our girl, remember, she's in heaven, awaiting us."

"*Jah.* I know. I stumble into doubt and self-pity, just like anyone else."

She heard his heart beat starting to slow down. He was the most selfless man she knew, yet slipped if he didn't have his eyes on the straight and narrow. She'd read *Pilgrim's Progress* to prepare her heart during the five weeks leading to Easter, and brought it up to the knitting circle, to see if they'd like to read it, too.

~*~

Mona put another piece of hot apple pie on Freeman's place and sat across from him. He nodded, but didn't say a word, only quickly ate his breakfast as usual… to get out into the barn… away from her.

"I'll not be going to knitting circle today."

"Huh?"

"I'll be babysitting Anna."

He nodded.

"What do you think of Fannie naming her Anna?"

He shrugged his shoulders.

"She thought I'd be upset if she named her Deborah, of all things…"

"I said something."

Mona tripped on her words. "What?"

"I said something to Melvin."

Mona grew impatient at times, as pulling words from Freeman's mouth was as tiresome as trying to catch a greased pig. "And what did you say?"

"That I thought it would bother you, her being called Deborah." He inhaled a piece of pie. "I told Melvin you'd be hurt."

"Really?" Mona said, putting her hand over her heart. He nodded.

"*Ach,* that was so… thoughtful. That you cared that I'd be hurt."

Freeman groaned. "Are you reading another romance novel?"

"*Nee.* Why do you ask?"

"Because ever since you're started reading them…" He glanced up at the clock. "I'm needed in the barn."

Mona grabbed for his hand. "Freeman, I have something to say." Her throat tightened. "A confession."

Freeman looked down at his hand covered by hers and froze. "Go on."

Mona squeezed his hand and got up to retrieve her copy of Black Beauty out of the China cupboard. Opening it to where her book marker laid, she read:

"There is no religion without love, and people may talk as much as they like about their religion, but if it does not teach them to be good and kind to man and beast it is all a sham - all a sham, James, and it won't stand when things come to be turned inside out and put down for what they are."

Mona sat down, and hugged the book. "I've been a bitter woman, Freeman, awful mad at my *daed* for being so mean. You knew him…"

Freeman nodded.

"Well, he was like one of the hard masters Black Beauty had so I always thought God was a master like him. Understand?"

He nodded again.

"Since I've been out more, making close friends again at the knitting circle, I've seen God to be loving. Don't be angry, but I learned it from the English."

Freeman cocked one eyebrow, then nodded.

"Suzy visited a woman she didn't like and she said 'God gave her his love for her' and I was taken back. Then Janice Jackson, pastor's wife at the Baptist church, said God gives her love for single homeless *mamms*. They openly talk like that, and it got me… searching."

Mona got up and lifted Angel from the little knit rug on the floor. "Then Jeb gave me Angel, saying dogs helped him, and somehow this little black dog, or maybe it was Jeb's gift, but I feel the love of God in my heart for the first time." She nuzzled Angel. "I held unforgiveness towards my *daed* and it blinded me or something. I couldn't see God as loving."

Freeman's eyes moistened. "But I've loved you, even though you've been a crabapple."

Mona stared at Freeman in disbelief. "Really?"

"*Jah*. Didn't you see it?"

Mona held Angel tight. "Sometimes…"

"I work in that barn day in and day out. Sometimes?"

"Well, I thought you hid in there to get away from me."

He set his jaw firm. "You stay in your room, avoiding me."

Mona couldn't deny the pain she saw in Freeman's eyes. "*Ach,* I'm so sorry."

Freeman nodded. "When we break bread together, at the noon meal, it means a lot to me."

Mona gasped. "And you thought I stayed upstairs to avoid you?"

He nodded...again.

"I was trying to give you some... peace. Having time alone. In peace."

He motioned for her to sit down. "I get lonely."

Mona put Angel down, sat next to him and reached for his hand again. "Me too. *Ach,* Freeman. It feels so *goot* to talk like this."

Freeman nodded and smiled and Mona thanked God she'd accepted Fannie's invitation to the knitting circle. Little did she know that it would begin to heal her marriage.

~*~

Colleen scanned the colorful yarn, neatly placed on the many shelves according to hue. "I like green the best, why?"

Suzy snapped her fingers. "I knew it. And it's a surprise. Amish women are making a quilt for you, and us Baptist need to keep up appearances." Suzy laughed. "I still can't believe you'll be getting married in two months, to an Amish man. *Ach, vell,* it was love at first sight, *jah?*"

Colleen grinned at Suzy's fake Dutch accent, and then went to the back of the store to resume winding yarn into spools. "Suzy, can I ask you something?"

"What's up?" Suzy asked as she shuffled papers around her desk.

"Well, after reading Black Beauty, I wondered if all horses were as nice as him. You know a lot about horses..."

"Well, Ginger had an attitude in the book. Many horses act like her. Nervous and jittery."

"But she wasn't treated right. When Black Beauty befriended her, she learned to trust."

Suzy looked up, her reading glasses teetering on the edge of her nose. "I have a feeling we're not talking about horses, but people."

Colleen shrugged. "Maybe I am. That book hit me in the heart about my dad. Anna Sewell sure wrote a lot about the dangers of drugs."

"Drugs?"

"Alcohol's a drug, and it almost killed Black Beauty and messed up a bunch of people in the story. And my life, too. But Beauty was always forgiving and loving..."

"He had no choice. He was a horse. Colleen, what's wrong? You have those droopy shoulders again."

Colleen straightened. "I'm tired."

"Hey, it's me. Your second mom, *jah*? And that better not change when you become Amish."

Change. Her whole life was change, Colleen thought, but she was setting roots in Smicksburg. "That will never change, Suzy. But I wonder if I should be reaching out to help my parents. That Mr. Smith who almost killed Beauty was a good man deep down."

Suzy darted up. "Almost killed Black Beauty, and Colleen, you did the right thing in getting your Black Beauty away from your parents."

"You mean Aurora?"

"Yes, honey. Oh, you are so hard on yourself at times. You just don't see yourself as others do... you're such a sweetheart and an overcomer."

"Overcomer?"

"Yes, you rescued yourself and daughter from a crack house. Don't ever forget that. What I saw in Black Beauty is a clear line between right and wrong. And when we live wrong, there's a price to pay."

A bell jangled, announcing someone was at the store door. Colleen turned to see a very stylish woman, decked out in all designer labels. Her Coach purse was huge, and Colleen prayed she had the cash to buy lots of yarn. Suzy, like all shop owners, was experiencing the winter slow months.

Suzy curtsied. "Thank you for entering my humble abode."

The woman smiled, then burst into laughter. "I drove over here, and I didn't hit one mailbox."

"Is Sammy out in the car?"

"No, I passed my driver's license. Thought I told you." She looked over at Colleen. "How nice. You have Amish working for you."

Suzy went over to Colleen and put her arm around her. "This is Colleen, the girl I told you about. Colleen, this is Missy, the one I've been giving knitting lessons to."

The woman who really changed, Colleen thought. "Nice to meet you."

"So, you're turning Amish then?" Missy asked. "Suzy's told me so much about you. When's the wedding?"

"In early May, before planting time," Colleen said. "I love it that the Amish live their lives around the seasons, don't you?"

Missy nodded. "They're smart. We *Englishers* try to cram too much into our lives. Suzy helped me see this." She looked at Suzy, love along with suspense written across her face. "I can't help it. I have to share something."

"What?" Suzy asked.

"I'm buying the big Victorian on Maple Street, and plan to have a tea shop on the first floor."

Suzy gawked. "That place is gorgeous. What happened to the other house you had your heart set on?"

"Well, after I read all your Jane Austen books, and thought about the little Jane Austen teas you and Colleen have at ten o'clock sharp. I knew I had to have a teahouse and sell things that Jane would approve of." She laughed and looked at her watch. "It's ten o'clock. What kind of establishment is this?"

Colleen knew how this woman got under every nerve of Suzy's being, and now she was here in the shop, chatting and being like a bosom friend. As she followed them into the back room where they had their teas, Colleen thought again of her wedding… without her mom being there. God changed Missy's life so radically in a short period of time. Could He do that for her parents?

~*~

Fannie leaned her head against the back of the rocker, thankful that Anna had stopped crying. *Why am I so impatient?* Guilt jabbed at her and she closed her eyes. *I am fearfully and wonderfully made….*

Melvin came over and sat in the chair next to her. "Tired?"

"*Jah*. Up a lot last night."

"Well, you relax over at Granny's today, and don't overdo it."

"I won't. But I don't know if I should leave Anna."

Melvin bit his lower lip. "I know what you mean. I fear your *mamm* won't be gentle with Anna, too."

"You know, Melvin. I'm afraid I'll be a horrible *mamm*, too."

"What?"

"*Jah*. How many women get impatient with an infant?"

"All of them? You're sleep deprived and the doc said your hormones will be jumbled for a while, just like Eliza's were. Depression after having a *boppli*?"

"Post-partum depression… it only lasted two weeks. I feel better."

Melvin slumped in his rocker. "Then why the blues?"

"I'm not sad."

"*Jah*, you are. Your fears kick in when you're down. And you're going to be a *goot mamm*."

Fannie knew Melvin always thought she got carried away with things learned in her novels, so should she even mention what she learned from Black Beauty? "Melvin, promise not to make fun of me."

"I never do. What's up?"

"Well, there was a horse in the book Black Beauty. Her name was Ginger, and she didn't get a *goot* start in life… and never really changed, not being able to trust people. She's skittish. And I fear that my upbringing will handicap me in a way. That I'll mess up Anna somehow."

Melvin looked over at her, his green eyes full of concern. "Fannie, I do think you have that depression. You're not yourself at all."

Men! How could she explain to him that she was afraid she'd be a horrible *mamm*, since she never had a *goot* example? How could she admit it to herself the rage she sometimes felt towards her upbringing? Her *mamm's* constant criticism and her *daed's* apathy. Never once had her *daed* stood up to her *mamm*, telling her to be kind. She was just like Ginger in the story, scarred for life because of cruel, ignorant or stupid people. How many times had Anna Sewell used stupid to describe people so accurately? No beating around the bush about it. And she liked the woman for it, bringing things out in the open about abused animals, and that's why she changed her mind to call her *boppli* Anna. And because my own stupid *mamm* would never give me any peace if I named her Deborah!

She looked over at Melvin... who was now asleep, mouth hanging open as he began to snore. Men! They have it so easy! They can sleep all night, and nap in the day, too! "Melvin!"

He jerked. "I was listening."

"I didn't say anything..."

"I'm sorry. Anna's crying in the middle of the night makes me tired all day."

"Me too. Now, about my *mamm* babysitting. Are you sure about it?"

"I'll stay nearby without being obvious. Let's give it a try. Who knows, maybe she'll be a better *oma* than a *mamm*?"

Fannie felt tension release in her neck. Maybe her *mamm* could redeem herself by being kind to Anna. Lord, I hope so!

~*~

Janice waved to Colleen up the street from Suzy's shop. "See you at one?" she yelled.

"See you at one," Colleen called back.

Janice took a deep breath, the cool air calming her. So much rested on this meeting that Jerry insisted on... so many lives. Lord, your will be done. Janice entered Suzy's shop, and knew enough to go around to the back room if Suzy was not in the shop. She heard laughter. Good, so far. Missy seems the same.... "Well, I thought I'd find you back here, sipping tea."

Suzy put one hand up in protest. "Our tea time is officially over. I need to get back to work."

Janice stared into Suzy's eyes, hoping she'd read into them that she needed to stay put. But Suzy smiled and went out to the store to resume work.

"So, Missy, how have you been?"

Missy got up from her seat at the little tea table and gave Janice a hug. "I'm doing almost too good."

"Too good to be true?" Janice blurted.

Missy slowly sat back down. "What do you mean?"

"Oh, I've never been one to be poised, not beating around the bush." She plunked herself on a chair opposite Missy. "I have to admit, Suzy called me and told me you were here, and I knew I had time to chat."

Missy frowned. "And what's wrong with that?"

"Well, it's church business, not just a chat." Janice arched her back and let out a sigh. "Missy, your offering to our church is something we're not used to. Jerry, being the man of integrity he is, wants to make sure you're not doing this out of impulse, obligation, or any other reason. Understand?"

"No." Missy tilted her head to one side.

"Well, many feel that they can buy their way to heaven, or get there by being good. You understand that God loves you just as much if you stay in your big house and don't give your money to the church, right?"

Missy looked over at her Coach purse and Janice prayed that the motive for giving was pure. *Lord, we could do so much with this money!*

"Walter's death roused me out of my slumber. I had deceived myself into thinking that we'd live forever and only lived for the here and now. And over the past few years, I've only felt emptier. No amount of things I could buy could fill this emptiness, except an eternal God. And I found him on Christmas Eve, at your church."

Janice thought of the Christmas Carol play the children put on, and how nervous Jerry was to preach that night, having a full house of two-hundred people. "That was some night, huh? I think Christmas has a way of making us think of what's important."

"Yes," Missy continued. "But this past Christmas I got the best present ever, Jesus in my heart. I never knew He could or would even want to live in someone like me."

Janice reached for her hand. "You should join our knitting circle. We read, too, as you know. We all learned from Little Women that we're all hopelessly flawed."

Missy began to blush. "Well, I haven't been the nicest person, putting my nose up at Suzy and Ginny next door. I was a snob, but it was all a masquerade. Behind my mask, I was a jealous woman. They had peace, and I didn't, and I despised them for it." A smile slid across Missy's face. "Now I have it too."

Janice put her head down, praying for strength. "Missy, I'm so happy for you, but have you had doubts about giving so much money to our church?"

"Well, it's for a shelter for homeless people, right? And someone to run it?"

"Oh, absolutely. Jerry won't touch a penny towards anything else. It's just that there's a place we have in mind to purchase. It's an Amish farm. Jerry has been in touch with your lawyer and things could happen really quickly and he's concerned that in a month or year from now, you'll regret giving away so much."

Missy got up and made her way over to the window, and gazed outside. "I made my mind up the week after Christmas. It's February now, and I have not one doubt. Actually, the house is sold, if everything goes through, and I made a bid on the Victorian house on Maple Street."

"It's a beauty," Janice said.

"I hope to serve people for the rest of my life, not live in isolation, away from the world. No, my tea will be top quality but cheap, as my profit will be in serving and speaking to my customers. I've wanted a teashop ever since I was a little girl, and my dream is about to come true."

Janice noticed that Missy looked younger, no rigid jaw line, or furrowed brow. Her whole countenance had changed. God had made her shine, and Janice had no doubts now that what she wanted to do came from her heart, and not as a way to pay back the church. But to be sure, she asked, "So, you want the total amount we talked about to go to a homeless ministry in our church, not out of any debt you feel you owe us?"

Missy looked at her sternly, wagging a finger. "Only one condition."

Janice's head jerked back. "What?"

"You become a regular at my teahouse."

Janice burst into laughter and relief washed over her. She thought back to A Christmas Carol and how quickly Scrooge had changed. Missy was like a modern day

Ebenezer, one who she was sure would be changing the whole town for the good. Giving to poor little Tiny Tim's, boys without homes.

~*~

Granny nervously clenched on to Jeb's wool coat as he opened the side door to Ruth and Luke's place. "Anyone home?" he yelled.

"Come on into the living room," Luke's voice was heard.

As they made their way into the living room, Granny couldn't help it. She ran to Luke, threw her arms around his neck, and embraced him. "Bless you. A new *boppli*. A *wee* girl."

Luke hugged her back. "*Jah*, and she's a sweet natured little thing at only three days old."

"We stayed away so Ruth could rest..." Granny looked back at Jeb who looked too serious. "But we're here now to bring some food, pies and other goodies."

Jeb took her cue to speak. "*Jah*, have it all out in the buggy."

"*Danki*. Hang up your hats and coats. Don't act like strangers."

Granny slipped off her cape and bonnet and Luke placed them on the pegboard out in the kitchen. "Jeb, you staying?"

Jeb was roused out of what appeared to be daydreaming. "*Ach, jah*." He took off his outer garments and hung them on the peg, too. But he took the book he had in his pocket out first. "This is for you. Best book I've ever read..."

Luke looked at the title. "*Pilgrim's Progress.* Can't say that I've read it. Is it a history book about the Mayflower Colony?"

Jeb shook his head. "*Nee,* it was written in a time of great persecution in Europe. John Bunyan was in jail when he wrote it, and it's like a journey through hard times."

Luke hit Jeb playfully on the shoulder. "You going to start a lit circle like the womenfolk?" He turned to Granny. "I'd say those books you picked are mighty helpful and Ruth feels she owes you a lot."

"Really?" Granny felt heat rise in her face. "We all pick the books. It's not anything special I do."

"*Nee,* you're wrong. The way you've taken the women under your wing like a mother hen has really affected Ruth."

Granny looked over at Jeb, her eyes pleading for him to inquire about Luke's odd behavior. Was he sleep deprived that he was being so sentimental? Or was the emotion of having a new daughter making him a little giddy?"

But Jeb said nothing.

"Well, can we see the *boppli?*"

Ruth appeared at the bottom of the steps. "*Jah,* you can see Debbie…" Ruth slowly walked over and placed the little girl in Granny's outstretched arms.

"We'll call her Little Debbie, like the snack we all love."

Pure love soared from Granny's heart to the little child in her arms. "She's so sweet, so naming her after a dessert's mighty appropriate."

Ruth put her arm around Granny. "She's named Deborah, after you."

"What? Why?" Granny knew her face was now beet red.

"We expect Debbie to be a model Proverbs 31 Woman, like you," Ruth continued. "At least, that's our vision for her future."

Granny's eyes stung as she tried to hold back tears. "Your vision?"

"*Jah*," Luke said. "We know Debbie has down syndrome, but she won't be handicapped when it comes to loving others." He glanced over at Jeb. "If it was a boy, we'd have named him Jeb, because you helped save our marriage by your love and concern. Example, too. We're aiming for Debbie to be a person who brings healing to others, like *yinz*."

A flock of Canada Geese flew overhead, their annual migration in full swing. Their honking made words incomprehensible, but the love in the room was undeniable. Granny looked down at Debbie. Maybe she would not be heard, like some folks, but her love would change lives. Praise be.

When the din passed, Luke showed Ruth the book Jeb gave him. "Maybe we can read this together."

Granny sat down and rocked Little Debbie. "I'd like for the circle to read it. Seems like Black Beauty drugged up some sad things in some of the girls. And since Easter is in five weeks, we can use it to prepare our hearts."

Jeb sat down in the chair next to Granny, admiring the *boppli*. "I read Little Debbie's won't be made anymore. Some kind of trouble with the company. But we'll have our very own right here."

Granny looked up and smiled at Jeb. As capable as he was at being a bishop, he didn't like to pry into folk's personal affairs, and he was stalling. Lord, help him.

"Would you like some coffee?" Luke asked. "Always have some warming on the stove."

Both Granny and Jeb shook their heads.

"I was wondering, Luke. Did you get your fishing license yet?"

"*Nee*. Trout season's a month away. Why?"

"*Ach,* just wondering…"

Granny bowed her head. Lord, help him.

Jeb cleared his throat. "Are *yinz* okay, really? Need anything from the *Gmay*?"

Ruth was now seated on the sofa, feet up on a foot rest. "We're fine. No needs at all."

"I, ah, mean for Debbie. Any further testing or special help?"

Ruth nodded. "Well, the visiting nurse will be helping me learn more about down syndrome and all, so lots of reading at first. But if there's something we need, we'll let you know."

Jeb sighed. "But how are *yinz*, really?"

Luke took a sip of his coffee before taking a seat. "Are we upset that our girl has a handicap? We were surprised; the first day, well, Ruth was upset. She wondered if being so sick for the past six weeks did something to our girl. But the nurse reassured her it wasn't anything she did. Then I remembered how much I struggled, thinking I was junk, and *yinz* told me God doesn't make junk." Emotion welled up in his voice and he coughed. "My Little Debbie may have some struggles like her *daed*, thinking she's not as *goot* as others, but it's all a lie, and I can tell her that. I believe she's really heaven-sent."

Jeb leaned forward. "The *goot* Lord goes before us, paving the way, *jah*? He knew exactly the right home for Little Debbie to be put in. One full of love and one I think God simply smiles down upon." He got up and shook Luke's hand. "I have to admit, I wasn't expecting this. I feared *yinz* would fight or blame each other for a so-called, 'not perfect' *boppli*. I can see your marriage is now too strong for such foolishness."

~*~

"He said cruelty was the devil's own trade-mark, and if we saw any one who took pleasure in cruelty we might know who he belonged to, for the devil was a murderer from the beginning, and a tormentor to the end. On the other hand, where we saw people who loved their neighbors, and were kind to man and beast, we might know that was God's mark."

Mona's eyes begged for understanding. "Fannie, I'm so sorry. I've been so bitter towards my own *daed*, when all the time, it wasn't him that was being mean to me. It was the devil."

Fannie turned her head in disbelief. The devil? Is she serious? And what about her behavior? It was like her own *daed's*? She thought back to Emma Woodhouse and how she pacified her father by listening, so she looked back over at her *mamm*, who was gently rocking Anna. "So, you think you were upset with the devil and not your *daed*?"

"Lend me your Bible."

Fannie moseyed over to her Bible on the desk, and placed it in her *mamm's* outstretched hand. She flipped it about and then it lay still in her hand. "Ephesians 6:10-12 says,

"Finally, my brethren, be strong in the Lord, and in the power of his might. Put on the whole armor of God, that ye may be able to stand against the wiles of the devil. For we wrestle not against flesh and blood, but against principalities, against powers, against the rulers of the darkness of this world, against spiritual wickedness in high places.

"There you have it. Something I never saw before. All the fighting is stirred up by the devil."

Fannie wanted to scream! Did her *mamm* ever take responsibility for her actions? She blamed her father, now the devil. Fannie mustered up courage and spit out, "How about all the verses about self-control? We aren't puppets on a string."

"I'm coming to that, Fannie. And this is hard for me, so be patient." She looked down at Anna. "When I read Emma, I prided myself on this line, 'I may have lost my heart, but not my self-control.' But the more I held my

Angel and fell apart, I realized that's exactly what I lacked: self-control. *Ach,* that little dog, my black beauty, has opened my eyes."

"Really?"

"*Jah.* She's skittish, and I remembered being that way." Tears welled in Mona's eyes. "And I see it in you sometimes. I've been an emotionally unstable *mamm* for years, and I'm ever so sorry."

Fannie looked around the room. Everything seemed surreal. The light filtering through the windows, the color of her tablecloth. Was she dreaming? She looked into her *mamm's* eyes; she was serious, and Fannie thought she saw real repentance. But as soon as her hopes soared, anger filled her. How many women of twenty-two had to listen to such nonsense? Her *mamm* was unloading a guilty conscience on her about words that should have never been spoken. Cruel words! And did she think that just by saying words, pain could be erased? Trust could instantly be given?

She met her *mamm's* eyes. "*Mamm,* I need to get ready for knitting. Give Anna only two ounces or she may spit-up."

"What? Fannie. Is that all you have to say? I'm asking for forgiveness…"

"And I'm tired to the bone. We can talk about this later…"

"When?"

Fannie stood tall. "When your actions consistently line up with your speech. You've belittled me my whole life, and I'm truly sorry if your *daed* did that to you. But the way I look at it, if you were so hurt by words, then why would you use them to hurt me, and not perfect little Eliza?"

Melvin ran into the room. "Everything alright? I heard shouting."

"I wasn't shouting."

"*Jah*, you were," Mona said, as she stood up. "Here, Melvin. I'm going home. You take Anna. I'm obviously not welcome here." Mona got her handkerchief from her apron pocket and wiped her eyes as she ran to get her cape and bonnet.

Melvin's eyes grew as round as a full moon.

Fannie shrugged her shoulders and yelled over to her *mamm*, not at the side door, "Make sure you close the door the whole way. It flies open sometimes."

"Fannie," Melvin blurted. "What happened?"

Fannie swooshed her hand into the air as if swatting a fly. "My *mamm*. Making more excuses for her behavior, which I'm not buying."

"What did she say?"

"*Ach,* she apologized for being a 'bad *mamm*' and she was mistreated growing up...blah, blah, blah. Words, they mean nothing unless backed up by action."

Melvin eyes got even bigger. "Fannie, out of the abundance of the mouth the heart speaks, like the Bible says. I think Mona was being sincere. She looked awful hurt."

Fannie groaned. "Can you watch Anna or should I stay home from circle?"

"*Nee,* you go to circle, and get some advice from Granny. I don't like what I'm seeing."

"And what is that?"

"Post-partum depression. Read another article on it and anger's another symptom."

Fannie clenched her fists and marched up the stairs... and slammed their bedroom door.

~*~

Granny was light on her feet, still in awe of the miracle she witnessed at Ruth's. How someone reacted was the real person, she always thought, and Luke was truly a healed man. He makes all things beautiful in His time, she mused.

She entered the living room with a tray full of fudgy brownies, and sat it on the coffee table. "There's hot water in the tea kettle and bags set out on the counter, so feel free to get a cup."

Suzy clapped her hands. "I can't wait to tell *yinz,* but guess what kind of new store we'll have in town?"

"A sewing store. One that sells lots of material."

Suzy shook her head. "No, something exciting."

Granny laughed. "We Amish would like a material store, not having to go up to Punxsy so much."

"But I have fun driving you when we go," Marge quipped.

"Will it be competition for our dry goods store?" Fannie asked.

Suzy playfully looked up. "Maybe. Maybe not."

"Maybe?" Fannie blurted. "Hope not!"

Granny took the seat next to Fannie. "Calm down, Fannie. I'm sure it's not a complete dry goods store."

"Well," Suzy continued to tease. "It kind of is all dry goods."

Fannie darted up. "*Ach,* just what I need. Are you serious?"

Granny pulled at Fannie's sleeve. "What's wrong with you today?"

Fannie face turned crimson. "Nothing. Nothing at all...."

"It's a tea shop!" Suzy clapped her hands again, and let out a whoop. "Right here in Smicksburg. Missy's going to own it and live on top. She bought the Victorian on Maple Street."

Marge put her hand on her heart. "That's my dream house. All those colors on one house, different shades of greens and pinks. It's kind of like a cottage on steroids." She picked up her knitting. "But Joe and I are learning to be content where we live right now."

Suzy looked around the room as usual before she started the book discussion. "Fannie, so good to have you back with us. You've missed the past two weeks, but you had a good reason."

Fannie knit nimbly and didn't look up. "I read Black Beauty though, and as we all know, I named my daughter after the author, Anna."

"I thought you were going to name her Deborah," Maryann said. "Why the change?"

"I'd rather not talk about it." She looked more intently at her yarn. "Like I said, I read the book and got a lot out of it. I could identify with Ginger, the poor horse who was never loved. She said to Black Beauty, 'If I had your bringing up I might have turned out like you…' I memorized that line… I've lived that line."

Suzy looked over at Granny with a quizzical gaze, as if she wanted her to step in and say something, but Granny was as stunned as everyone else. Fannie was never one to be moody or feel sorry for herself. Was she too tired to be here, too soon after having her *boppli*? "Fannie, we don't look back, *jah*? Like Lot's wife, lest we turn to salt and can't move forward?"

"*Jah*, I suppose," Fannie moaned. "Not easy to do sometimes."

"And you're awful tired. Having a *boppli* takes a lot out of you…"

"*Jah*, I'm sure you're right," Fannie said in a monotone voice.

Granny glanced over at Suzy and nodded towards Colleen, hoping she'd move on.

"Colleen, what did you get out of the book?"

"Well, when that drunk, Rueben Smith, made Beauty run home with one shoe, and then Beauty collapsed, Beauty stayed right beside him, in the rain. Beauty was loyal, even to an abusive drunk."

Suzy put down her knitting. "Colleen, do you want to share what you told me? Your idea?"

"Yes, actually I do need advice. Anna Sewell really shows the dangers of alcohol by many abusive horse owners being addicted to booze. But in this case, Reuben Smith was a good man." She opened her copy of the book. "Rueben's wife said after his death, 'He was so good; he was so good. It was that cursed drink.' I thought of my dad, and some happy times. He wasn't all that bad, and I'm thinking I should invite my parents to my wedding."

Granny had just taken a bite of a brownie and started to choke. Fannie hit her back, and Maryann raced to her with a glass of water. When she composed herself, Granny breathed heavy, her shoulders visibly heaving up and down. "Colleen. *Ach, nee.* You can't do that."

"Why not? And Granny, sorry if I almost gave you a heart attack."

Granny shook her head. "It went down the wrong pipe. But Colleen, there's safety in a multitude of counselors, *jah?* And I say you cannot expose your daughter or yourself to people who are drug addicts. I'm Amish, but I'm not ignorant to the dangers of that lifestyle."

"Really?" Colleen blurted, and then covered her mouth. "Sorry, I didn't mean that. It's just that the Amish don't even lock their doors at night."

"But Aurora is safe here. And how does your *oma* feel about seeing her prodigal daughter on such a happy day?"

Colleen's eyes narrowed. "I never thought of that. And she's going to so much trouble for my wedding… it's just hard sometimes, not having a mom."

"It's hard having a *mamm*, sometimes," Fannie mumbled loud enough only for Granny to hear. Lord, help Fannie. Something is ever so wrong.

"You best be talking to your grandma, Colleen," Janice chimed in. "I never counsel any of the girls to return to any abuse unless it's well monitored and… safe. You have to be as gentle as doves but as wise as a serpent."

"What a great saying," Marge said.

"Oh, that's in the Bible." Janice looked intently at Colleen. "I know your background, remember? I say, N-O. Have a day of celebration and on another day, if it's wise, then deal with your parents. Okay?"

"*Jah*, Colleen. Not everything has to be done on one day," Maryann added. "We can celebrate Christmas Eve the day before Christmas or a few days before. And sometimes we postpone Easter if the *Gmay* isn't in unity. Make your wedding day all about your love for Hezekiah and the wedding vow you'll make."

Colleen appeared more relaxed. "Thank you *all* so much. I never saw it that way. I guess this book made me feel something deep down for my dad somehow."

"Forgiveness, *jah*?" Granny pointed out. "You and Jeb are working on you forgiving your *daed* and some happy memories are slipping through."

"What do you mean?" Fannie asked.

"Well, unforgiveness blinds us of happy memories. But when we forgive, the blinders are taken off."

"Hmm," Fannie said under her breath.

"Maryann, did you like the book?" Suzy asked.

"I really did. Made me see our horses in a whole new way. I even talk to them now." She chuckled. "But it made me feel… normal out on the streets riding in a buggy. People have always driven buggies up until recently and I forget that when I see people whizzing by in their heated cars. I think the automobile started the downfall of civilization."

Janice let out a laugh. "Maryann, are you serious?"

"*Jah*, I am. The English make everything go so fast, and with new technology, we're always having to decide on this and that. It all clutters the mind, leaving less room for peace and simplicity."

Janice sighed. "Maybe you're right. We have maybe too many choices."

"Did you like Black Beauty, Janice?" Maryann asked.

"Oh, absolutely. Everything that was said about keeping the Sabbath was so right on. Obviously Anna Sewell had an ax to grind with employers who made people work on Sunday, since the one guy died because he worked on Sundays. What was his name?"

Colleen flipped through her book. "Seedy Sam. What an awful name."

Janice laughed. "I agree. But you see, Anna Sewell was a Quaker woman, and they're all into social justice and reform. It was the Quakers who were the first abolitionist, who really brought down slavery in America. George Fox, who wrote the Foxes Book of Martyrs, started the Quaker."

"I knew it," Granny said. "There's something about Black Beauty that seems Amish."

"I didn't say Amish, I said Quaker," Janice corrected.

"I know, but we both have roots back to Europe and religious persecution. Quakers are considered Plain people, like the Amish."

"So," Marge prodded. "What makes Black Beauty seem Amish?"

"Well, a clear distinction between right and wrong for one thing. And the easy way isn't always the right way to go. I suppose the emphasis on being kind and peace-loving, too."

"I think it's called a Christian worldview, Granny," Janice said. "It's found in older books, but not many modern. Seems like we have to apologize for saying there's right and wrong today."

"It's ridiculous," Marge continued. "That's why I like to watch Little House on television," Marge winked at Granny. "But we all know it's not so easy living off the grid."

"*Jah*, and you learned your lesson by trying, and that's a *goot* thing," Granny said warmly. She smiled at Marge. "So, did you like the book?"

Marge nodded. "I was surprised, it being considered a children's book and all. It had such deep meaning. Sad at times. Like when Beauty said he had the best stable and food, but not liberty. Made me feel sorry for him. But then there were parts that I thought had real spiritual depth." She fanned her face with one hand. "I get emotional when I talk about this, but Beauty knew his master's voice and followed him blindly, literally. When Beauty was afraid to leave the burning barn, he was calmed down by his master's voice and when a cloth was put over his eyes, he didn't resist being led out, all because he trusted that voice." She shook her head. "Why I resist the voice of God so much, when He's shown me time and time again that He's good and can be trusted, I'll never know."

The side door opened and Lizzie let in a gust of wind. "So sorry I'm late. I was working with Jenny on her schoolwork and fell asleep..."

"Homeschooling's hard work. Take a seat," Marge said, patting the chair next to her.

"Did I miss much?"

"*Nee,* we're getting ready to wrap up talking about *Black Beauty,*" Granny said. "Did you like the book?"

"Well, I read Jenny's *kinner* version, but, *jah,* I liked it. Sometimes Jenny thought it was sad when Beauty got whipped. She brought up the fact that Amish never whip their horses, and wondered why people do. I told her they must be in a rush."

"In too much a rush if you have to whip them," Suzy added.

"Suzy," Granny said. "You never said how you liked the book."

Suzy looked down and knit a little too fast. "It's one of my favorite books of all time, and that's why I wanted to read it. I'd love to have land for a horse like I did growing up. I think of my old horse sometimes, and it makes me miss her."

"*Ach,* so you had a horse?" Maryann asked.

"I jumped them. It made me feel like I could fly. When Beauty said she knew what it was like to be like one with his master, flying through the meadows, it gives me a lump in my throat." She placed a hand on her neck. "And I have a hard time talking... like... now. I get all choked... up."

"So you miss your horse?" Janice asked.

Suzy nodded, and then laughed as tears pooled in her eyes. "Makes me really emotional, even after all these years."

"Animals are *goot* for us. I believe Mona is enjoying having Angel around. Right, Fannie?"

"I suppose so."

Granny nudged Fannie and leaned towards her. "We need to talk."

"About what?"

"You. You're not yourself. Post-partum depression..."

Fannie darted up and started throwing yarn in her bag. "I need to get home."

Granny got up and took her arm. "Your *mamm's* watching Anna. You can stay for a while."

Fannie's lips trembled as she let Granny lead her out into the kitchen to talk.

"Fannie, you've got the blues real bad. Have you talked to an herbalist yet?"

"*Nee.* It's not post-partum depression like everyone thinks. It's that book, Black Beauty. It made so many emotions come to the surface. Things I need to forgive but can't."

"Your *mamm*," Granny said.

"*Jah*. I'm still kicking myself that I didn't name my *boppli* Deborah for fear that she'd be upset. Granny, I really wanted to name her after you."

Fannie's shoulders started to quake and Granny embraced her. "Now, now. You do the right thing and forgive your *mamm* even if you don't feel like it. God will bless you for it."

"She asked for forgiveness, saying Black Beauty helped her see she was a bitter woman, but sometimes I just wish that... you were my *mamm*."

Granny pat her back. "Well, God knows best. And He gave you the upbringing you had for a purpose. I don't think you'd be able to be so loving if you hadn't been so hurt."

Fannie pulled away and searched Granny's eyes. "What do you mean?"

"*Ach,* Fannie, you're as kind as they come, a friend to all, like Black Beauty. And how did you get that way?"

"I don't know..."

"By being broken, like the horse. And God is close to those who are broken, and well, He shines through you. Don't let unforgiveness or self-pity block His light."

"But it's so hard."

"God's grace is enough to help lift your burdens. And you have a *wunderbar* husband and a close circle of friends to help you, too."

Fannie kissed Granny's cheek and gave her a weak smile. "I love you."

"I love you, too."

~*~

That night at church, Janice had a hard time paying attention. Seeing Nathan's farmhouse tomorrow dominated her thoughts. Could you put plumbing in an Amish house? Electricity? And the Amish moved so much, what if they got to the lawyer's office to close on the house and Nathan decided he'd changed his mind?

She sat next to Suzy, notebook in hand, taking notes. Maybe she should take notes to keep her mind from wandering. Jerry was preaching on the prodigal son, and how the father had run up to him, seeing him a ways off, embracing him with the love of a father. A good father, not like Colleen's…

Janice took her notebook out of her massive new purse and set her face like flint to understand Jerry's sermon. She would stop fussing and turning around, counting numbers. The Christmas Eve service was packed out, but tonight the "thirty faithful" as she called them were the only ones here, and she wouldn't fret. Obviously they needed to hear this sermon….

The back door opened and Janice swung around to see who was coming in so late. Was this a joke? Some of the neighborhood kids up to a prank? For a teenager, with black clothing from head to toe swaggered in, as if he owned the place. When he got a little closer, she noticed his dog collar. Was this the kid who Jonas wrote to faithfully after meeting him at Amish Camp?

Janice made her way out of her pew and went to the back of the church, half the congregations' eyes on her. When she got closer, she knew it was the lad that was

Jonas' friend. But what was he doing in Smicksburg, in the bitter cold?

She sat next to him. "I think we've met before. Did you come up for Amish Camp?"

The shivering boy rubbed his hands together and shook. "*Ya.*"

Janice leaned closer and whispered. "How'd you get here?"

"I, h-hitchhiked. T-to c-cold, though."

Janice noticed his flushed face. Was he sick or just cold? If she put her hand on his forehead would he be upset, trying so hard to act tough? "Are you alright?"

"Y-yes. Well, no. Coming to live with Jonas."

"What? He agreed to that?"

"He doesn't know I'm here, yet. But this is where the bus started for camp, so I figured you knew the way…"

Janice knew she was bombarding him with question, but didn't care. Runaways needed to be reported. "How old are you?"

"Fourteen…"

"Do your parents know you're here?"

"No. They wouldn't miss me anyhow."

"What makes you say that?"

He looked up at her, black eyes sharp with pain. "It's the truth, that's why."

Janice looked aimlessly ahead. Lord, oh, we need your help.

~*~

Granny dosed off in her rocker, Bea lying on her lap, and her knitting lying on Bea. Lights flashed across the window, and she opened her eyes. Looking over at Jeb, who was reading *Pilgrim's Progress* next to her, she asked, "Does it lightning in February?"

"Huh?"

"I just saw a flash of lightning." As soon as she said this, she saw a car drive up with high beams on.

Jeb got up and looked out the window. "It's the Baptist church van. I wonder if something's wrong."

Soon footsteps were heard on the porch, and the door burst open. In walked Jerry and Janice... and a teenager. Granny noticed panic in Janice's eyes and got up to greet her. "What brings *yinz* here this time of night?"

"Sorry, but we saw a light on here, and not at Roman's."

"Come on in," Jeb offered. "Need something hot to drink?"

"No thank you. We'll get to the point." Jerry clamped his hand on the teenager's shoulder. "This is Charles. And he's hitchhiked the whole way up here from Pittsburgh to visit Jonas."

Granny took Charles' hand and shook it. "Charles, Lizzie talks about *yinz* the time."

"Who's Lizzie?"

"Jonas' daughter. Your Jonas' pen pal, *jah*?"

"Yes. He said to come up anytime, so here I am."

"Do you want to talk to Jonas?"

Jerry said after a yawn, "Charles, we can put you up for the night. These folk go to bed early, since they get up at the crack of dawn."

"*Nee,* before that," Jeb mused, trying to dispel the tension in the room. "I tell you what. Charles, you can stay here and see Jonas in the morning. All you'd have to do is walk across the yard. He lives right next door."

"Are you sure?" Janice exclaimed. "I mean, you don't know Charles."

Jeb put a hand up. "We have a spare bedroom, and it wouldn't be the first time we let someone stay here we didn't know. Remember Lavina? She's kin now, and she showed up on Old Christmas, an Amish runaway." He smiled at Charles. "I look at strangers as friends I just haven't met yet."

Charles eyes softened. "Thanks, sir."

"*Ach,* just call me Jeb, and this here's my wife Deborah, but everyone calls her Granny. You can, too."

Granny's heart swelled with love for this husband of hers. She thought back to the 1960's when she met Jeb. He'd taken in an African American hitchhiker and then sheltered him after the KKK beat him up. She slipped her arm thought Jeb's. "I'll get the room ready. Charles, do you want some hot chocolate?"

The edges of Charles' lips formed a hint of a smile. "Yes. Thank you."

~*~

By the noon meal the next day, Charles was still sleeping, and Granny wondered if he was exhausted from his trip. Jonas had come over to see him a few times, but didn't want to disturb him, saying the boy must need sleep. But a nasty flu was going around. What if he was sick? Granny peeped in Charles' room. "Are you alright in there?" The boy sat up, his black hair flat on one side and sticking out like a scarecrow on the other. Granny stifled a laugh. "I have lunch on the table. Hungry?"

He plunged back into bed, pulling the covers up over his head, and groaned.

"Are you sick?"

No answer. Just what Granny suspected, and she got the thermometer out of her apron pocket, and entered the room. "I need to take your temperature."

Charles mumbled something Granny couldn't make out from under the cover.

"What did you say?"

Charles unwrapped the covers he'd cocooned himself into, and sat up. "I'm not sick."

Granny felt his forehead. "Well, you feel cool to the touch. So, get yourself washed up and join us for the noon meal. Jonas will be here soon." She pointed to a pitcher and basin on a table near the window. "Let me know if you need anything else."

Charles swung his legs out of bed. Having slept in running shorts and a tee shirt, he went over to his backpack that hung from a pegboard.

Granny exited the room, and heard the scraping of Jonas' legs and crutches, and it was a wonderful sound. Jonas exercised, even though in pain, to keep what mobility he could maintain over the winter, having MS and arthritis. When Granny entered the kitchen, her heart once again leapt for love. Jeb was helping Jonas into his chair, not expecting him to sit on a backless bench. The regular seating places the Amish kept at their tables never changed, but Jeb gave Jonas his chair as he sat on the bench. Praise be.

"He's up now. Do the English sleep until noon, or do you think he's tired?"

Concern was etched on Jonas' face. "Lack of discipline in the home. Lack of a *daed*."

"He has a *daed*," Jeb quipped.

"He's never around and his *mamm* works full-time. Not a *goot* situation. I think he plays those games on television too much. Always mentions them in letters."

"*Ach,* we play Dutch Blitz late into the night on occasion, so maybe he's just having fun," Jeb said.

"By himself. *Nee,* I fear he's a lonely boy."

"How old is he?" Jeb asked.

"Fourteen. Such a hard age." Jonas grinned. "I think he needs more Amish camp. Maybe milk cows, clean stalls and whatnot. Feel useful…"

Granny put a spread of ham, scalloped potatoes, and pickled green beans on the table. Jeb got up to pour coffee into three mugs. Charles appeared in the doorway, his hair looking no different than when he woke up. "Charles, *ach,* I'm sorry. I didn't give you a comb," Granny said.

"Don't use one." He went directly over to Jonas and took his hand. "How are you, Jonas?"

"*Goot,* but mighty concerned about you. Hitch hiking's against the law for a reason."

Charles slowly sat on the bench near Jonas. "I had a buddy drive me most of the way. When we got to

Plumville his car stalled and I said I could manage from there. Only five miles or so."

"Do your parents know you're here?"

"No, but they wouldn't care. They took my sisters on a vacation to Florida." Darkness crept across his face. "They do it every year."

"And why aren't you in Florida with them?" Jonas asked, concern shaking his voice.

"You know why."

Jonas nodded, but anger shot from his eyes. "You're welcome to stay here a spell," he blurted.

Charles took a slice of ham from the platter. "Thanks, man. I appreciate it."

Jeb cleared his throat softly. "Charles, I'm the bishop and responsible for my flock. Not to rule them, but to serve them. My daughter-in-law homeschools her oldest. Do you have books to keep up with school?"

Charles nodded. "Brought them…."

"Won't your teachers miss you?" Granny asked. "I mean, they do take roll call, *jah*?"

"*Ya*, they do. But kids skip school all the time." His shoulders slumped. "I don't want to go back, really. Jonas told me if I was Amish, I'd be done with school, so I'm thinking of converting."

Agony worse than pain was now on Jonas' face. "You deserve better, Charles. I know your *daed's* driven you to this…"

Charles put his hand on Jonas' deformed one, and started to cry. And Jonas wept with him.

~*~

Granny felt rung out by the talk around the table, and an afternoon knitting session was needed.

Marge and Janice would be over to take down Charles' story, a horrid one of abuse. He was his *mamm's* son, but not his *daed's*, and how he'd suffered. Lizzie was a *wunderbar mamm* to *kinner* who weren't her own, and she had no doubts that she'd be accepted as a foster *mamm* along with Marge. The paperwork should be done soon, and God had perfect timing. But Lizzie couldn't take a *kinner* older than her own. Lord, you see this mess... help us all.

She picked up her black wool and began to knit. The feel of the yarn against her fingers brought comfort, as usual. In the spring, she planned to spin again, making more yarn for her growing circle as prices continued to increase. And her yarn was warm, made of wool, something she found the homeless really appreciated.

She saw out of her peripheral vision a red car darting down the driveway. Marge. Slow down! Granny always feared she'd hit her black Lab, Jack, as he was always chasing cars.

In no time, Marge and Janice flew through the side door. Marge was excited as she clapped her hands and danced on her tiptoes. "You'll never guess."

"What?"

Marge twirled around and Janice burst into laughter.

"Tell me," Granny moaned. "I need *goot* news."

Janice seated herself on the kitchen table bench. "Well, Jeb showed us Nathan's house and we're buying it."

"Yes," Marge screamed. "And guess who the church is hiring to take care of the homeless who come to live there?" She danced in a circle. "Joe and yours truly. And we're moving back into our *dawdyhaus*." She put her hand on her heart. "I could bust from joy!"

Granny couldn't help but laugh at animated Marge. "I'm supposing you'll have electricity, *jah*?"

"Yes, but we're keeping it simple. It will still look Amish, since I love the simplicity. Think it'll bring healing to the men."

"I agree. You English have things too crowded all over your walls."

"Yes we do," Janice said. Janice looked around the room. "Where's Charles?"

"Over at Jonas' place. Are you sure this is necessary?"

"From what Jeb told us, yes. He's awfully neglected," Janice said evenly. "Jeb said he doesn't even own a toothbrush?"

"*Nee*, but maybe he forgot to pack it. Hard to believe his *mamm* wouldn't buy him something for a dollar. I know he doesn't have a comb, that's for sure."

"A comb?" Marge asked. "How do you know?"

"His hair. It sticks straight out from his head, but then again, he said he liked it that way. It's sad."

"It's the fashion," Marge giggled. "It's called bed head, or something like that. The kids do it on purpose."

"Fashion, my eye," Janice said. "The kid wears black all the time because he probably doesn't have many clothes. As for his hair, if he doesn't have a toothbrush, he probably has little else." Janice clenched her teeth and shook her head. "My eyes are wide open ever since we opened Forget-Me-Not Manor. Parents care as much about their kids as their dogs."

Granny felt tears well up. "When I heard Charles open up about his life, I thought of Joe, the man who eventually cared for him. Are we like Joe, the one who will care for Charles? I'd hate to see him go off to a foster home, into a place where he knows no one…"

Janice bit her lower lip. "Charles isn't a horse who can't speak up, right? Thank God he can tell others about his treatment."

Marge broke in then. "I'm going to do everything in my power to get Charles as a foster child. I can homeschool him, since it's the middle of the school year, and —"

"One step at a time," Janice said, cutting Marge short. "Let's go talk to Charles."

Granny made her way over to her China closet. "Here. Take this over to Charles. Maybe the book will help him open up."

"I'm sure Charles can relate to Black Beauty."

"And we'll all need to be reading *Pilgrim's Progress* over the next few weeks," Janice said. "We're on a journey into the unknown, just like Christian in the book."

Marge got up on her tiptoes again. "A journey I'm more than willing to make. Moving back to Smicksburg." She ran over and kissed Granny on the cheek. "We'll be neighbors again."

~*~

Granny continued to knit, as her little black dog, Bea, warmed her feet. But as she knit one, purled one, she felt the loss of Nathan topple into her heart. *Ach,* I will miss him, and Lavina so much. Did Lavina come from a home as bad as Charles? Would Charles be their new Lavina to love and see healed?

As her mind raced, she put down her knitting needles, picked Bea up, holding her close, and prayed:

Lord Jesus,

You've come to heal the brokenhearted and bring peace into our hearts. A peace that passes human understanding. I'm needing it now. You give and take away, and I know you're God and know best, but I'm heartsick. Hope deferred makes the heart sick, as your Word says. And I had high hopes of Nathan and Lavina living right down the road. Heal my heart, Lord.

And Father, help Charles. Is he like Black Beauty, a broken boy? A teen that had no one who brushed his fur or put a blanket on him when cold, like a good master did for a horse? Pave the way for justice to be done, and please let Marge be his foster mamm.

And Lord, danki for this new home for unloved, misplaced boys. Charles Dickens spoke out against the cruel treatment of children in his books, and the Quakers continue to do so to this day. Help us all do our part to speak up for those who have no voice.

In Jesus name,
Amen

Dear Readers,

I hope you enjoyed this episode of Amish Knit Lit Circle. As I read Black Beauty, I thought of all the hurt going on in this world we live in, and as usual, pray to find out what is my part in bringing healing. For my husband, Tim, and me, it has been sponsoring children through Compassion International and New Missions. If you go to my website, www.karenannavogel.com there are links to both ministries. We also are looking to take in another rescue dog, most likely a big old Lab like our Jack was. (R.I.P. old friend). I continue to make prayer shawls for the terminally ill, also.

But God has made us all different. I'm not a cat person, but maybe you are and there are stray cats you can adopt. Or maybe you're a better cook than me, (most likely, you are) and can take meals to ailing people. The causes are endless and so is our time and energy, but I know God uses willing hearts and will lead.

God bless you all, my friends!

Fudgy Brownies

4 square unsweetened chocolate

2 sticks of butter, cubed

4 eggs

1 ½ c. sugar

1 tsp. vanilla

1 c. flour

1 c. chocolate chips

1 c. chopped nuts

Melt chocolate and butter until smooth. Beat eggs, sugar and vanilla for two minutes (by hand) and combine with chocolate mixture. Fold in flour, not overbeating. Pour into a greased pan. Sprinkle with chocolate chips and nuts. Bake at 350 degrees for 30 minutes.

EPISODE 7

Pilgrim's Progress

Granny sipped her morning coffee, glimpsing outside to see a magenta sky, a glorious sunrise. Having so many people coming over today, it being three weeks before Easter and unity key to celebrate without delay, she and Jeb had to do what Bishop Mast and Sarah had to do last year... help people with unforgiveness towards someone in the *Gmay*. To wash each other's feet on Easter during their day-long service, ill will would ruin this peaceful day.

Jeb sauntered over to the table, Bea in tow. "*Goot* morning."

"You look awful."

"It's hard to sleep when you're wrestling with God..."

Granny knew Jeb sometimes begrudged the fact that he was bishop at his age, and had words with God. They 'reasoned together' like the Good Book said to do until understanding was given. "Are you ready for the visitors?"

"*Jah*, I am. *'Tis goot* to be a servant of God and help mend fences between folks." He sat Bea down on her little blue rug. "Do you think she's lonely? Missing Angel?"

"*Nee,* she's fine. Janice is talking about having pet therapy at the new house of boys." She sighed. "When I go past that place, I picture Nathan and Lavina living there with lots of *kinner*. But, it just won't be." Granny got up, opened her black oven door, took out a platter full of eggs, bacon, and English muffins and placed it in front of Jeb.

"*Danki,*" he said. "We may not see Nathan's *kinner* grow up, but we'll see Charles, once he moves in. And so many other young men in need."

Granny slowly poured herself another cup of coffee and sat down. "And Clark's back. He'll run it along with Joe."

"What happened to his landscaping? Didn't he go to college for that?"

"*Jah,* but Janice and Jerry think he'd be *goot* to teach the boys how to grow their own food and raise animals and whatnot...." Tears pooled in Granny's eyes and she swatted at them. "So tired of these sore throats. Choking back tears makes me –"

Jeb gripped her hand. "Deborah, love, I know this whole thing with the Baptist buying Nathan's house has you sad, but we move on, *jah*? Forward?"

Granny groaned. "Well, truth be told, I finished Pilgrim's Progress this morning and you're right; it's *goot.* But no rest for the weary..."

"What?"

"Well, Christian goes on and on, falling into harm, pain, suffering. It's life I suppose."

Jeb poked at his eggs with his fork. "But there were resting places all along the journey. Didn't you notice that?"

Granny shook her head. "Seemed like one uphill climb to me."

"*Ach,* one of my favorite parts is when Pilgrim goes up Difficulty Hill and rests at the arbor the Lord provided."

Granny's brow furrowed. "It's such a short time though. And only a few sentences describe it."

"It doesn't say how long Christian stayed there, but it was enough for him to be refreshed." He grinned. "I'm preaching to myself. I need rest for today, and I plan to take breaks and go to the arbor God put in my heart. Stay and dine with the Lord for a while." He got up and grabbed his Bible from the China closet door. Flipping though, Jeb found his place and read:

"Behold, I stand at the door, and knock: if any man hear my voice, and open the door, I will come in to him, and will sup with him, and he with me. Revelation 3:20." He lifted his hands in praise. "Deborah Weaver, I thank God for you."

"Why?"

"Because you pick me up."

"How?"

"Well, you're my leaning post, *jah*? I'm yours. You're struggling about missing Nathan and it makes me try to help you. But in helping you, I help myself."

"You mean you feel blessed to help someone else?"

"*Nee,* you fret so much, it makes me find scriptures to comfort you, and they help me, too."

Granny's eyes narrowed. "You fret, too… old man."

He groaned. "I know. Just 'playing with your head,' or kidding, like the English say?"

Granny didn't even try hiding her smile. "Marge and Joe say the oddest things, don't they?"

"*Jah*, they do, but we sound funny to them." Jeb took a long swig of coffee. "Mona will be here soon. Best get to praying."

Granny took his hand. "She's not a burden anymore, you know."

"*Jah*, from what I hear, she's in need of help. So, let's pray."

~*~

Colleen hit the nail with the hammer five times and then turned and smirked. "See, women can pound a nail in as well as a guy." She giggled. "It's fun having you back with us, Clark."

"And I'll be able to live here, rent-free, since Nathan sold it all so cheap."

"You and Joe will have your hands full, helping the foster boys." She looked up at his jet black hair. "You're salt and pepper now, white paint everywhere." Colleen grabbed a rag. "Bend down. There's a glob I can get out right now."

Clark obeyed and Colleen wiped paint from his hair.

"So, us two former homeless bums will both be settling in Smicksburg."

Colleen pulled at one of his long locks of hair. "Speak for yourself." She turned him around to get the paint off the back of his head. "You know I found my Amish grandma and all. And I'm turning plain."

"Well, it's not Halloween, so I figured that much."

"Halloween?"

"You're in plain clothes. And Jerry and Janice told me all about it. About Hezekiah, too…"

The lilt in his voice fell, and Colleen's heart leapt into her throat. She'd known that Clark had liked her in the past, but she figured it was a fleeting thing.

He turned to her. "Are you sure about Hezekiah?"

Colleen hesitated, not wanting to hurt him. She looked into his dark eyes. Eyes that were now confident, having gotten his degree in horticulture, no longer homeless, and something else. What was it?

"I'll take that as a 'no.'"

"What?"

"I just asked you if you're sure about Hezekiah and you said nothing. "

She clasped her hands and placed them on her heart. "Oh, I love him. No doubts at all. I just don't want to..."

"Hurt me?" Clark reached for her hand. "We had so many *goot* talks and I thought you felt something for me. You wrote."

"I write to everyone now, since I don't have a phone." She withdrew her hand. "I'm sorry, Clark, if you took it a different way."

Clark tilted his head to one side, eyeing her clothing. "Colleen, seriously, you have no doubts about being Amish?"

"I've lived plain for months now, and will be baptized on Sunday. I'll take my vow to the church. I love everything about the Amish."

Clark sidestepped over to the corner of the room, as if dancing, and put a CD into his boom box and soon a light Jazz song rang out. Clark knew she loved Kenny G. Did he purposefully bring this CD they'd often listened to in his car to tempt her?

"I can't be listening to that anymore," she protested. "There's all kinds of music here. We can sing in harmony and I'm going to learn to play the harmonica."

Clark laughed. "How about a juice harp while you're at it? How about a scrub board. Hey, you can have a dishpan band with all the things in your Amish house."

Colleen giggled. Carl was a real jokester at times, and really got her going. Memories of meeting him for the first time flooded her. He was so lonely, a homeless hippy –type guy hitchhiking through town, until he met Jerry and Janice and they took him in. He couldn't stay at Forget-Me-Not, it being full of girls, but he came over often and he'd played a part in helping her open up. Indeed, he was so different now.

"Clark, the right girl will come along for you." She'd learned to be frank from the Amish. "I'm Hezekiah's girl, and I love him deeply."

Their eyes locked again.

"You don't convince me, Colleen. You may be Amish for a year or two, like some who've converted, but you'll get tired of it all." He bowed, drew her into himself and started to sway. "Dance with me. For old times' sake?"

Being in Clark's embrace made her heart flip. Why? Fear gripped Colleen around the throat as doubts about Hezekiah entered her mind. She pulled away, flustered, and then excused herself, saying she forgot to do something in the barn. As she ran towards the door, she bumped into Hezekiah, hurt etched in his eyes.

~*~

Mona's hands trembled the further she got from home, and closer to Granny and Jeb's place, but she was determined to get over her ridiculous fears. Mud slashed up against the buggy and soon Jack barked loudly, announcing her arrival. "Shoo. Now don't get too close to the horse… or buggy," she yelled at the huge dog. Jack only continued at her horse's hooves, jumping into potholes full of water, sending water into her buggy. "Now, Jack, shoo!"

Jeb ran out on the porch, called the dog, which immediately ran to his side. "Sorry," he yelled. "Gets excited, is all."

Mona couldn't help but smile at Jeb, the kindest man she knew. When he gave her Angel, she'd thought him daft, but now she realized that a dog was *goot* for the nerves and emotions. When she knit now, Angel sat on her lap, her face on her knees, keeping her warm. How did she ever manage without her?

Jeb took the reins and after tying them to a post, helped Mona out of the buggy. "You should have brought Angel for a visit."

"Freeman's watching her…"

"Really?"

"*Jah.* He likes the little critter."

Jeb took her elbow, leading her inside, taking her wraps, and asking her if she needed anything hot to drink. Jeb was a gentleman from out of one of the classics they'd been reading, with old fashioned manners. But then again, Freeman had been so attentive lately, and their hearts were melding into one. So, why was Fannie so cantankerous?

Mona saw Granny knitting in her rocker. "How many scarves do you make in a week?"

"*Ach,* several," Granny quipped. "If I have yarn, I knit. And I'm sure hoping to spin a lot this summer. Nothing like spinning amongst the roses."

Mona now knew why so many were drawn to Deborah Weaver. The many talks they'd had before or after knitting circle had helped her become more transparent towards others, taking off her mask. 'No one can help you if they can't see the real you,' Granny had said.

Jeb poured hot water into the tea kettle and placed it on the stove. "Sit down, Mona. Now, how can I help you?"

Mona looked over at Granny, needing support, and she took her cue, scooting her rocker near the table.

"Well, with Easter coming and all, I have to admit I'm mighty upset with Fannie."

"What did she do?" Granny asked.

"*Ach,* she's become so rude. When I try to talk to her, she's like Apollyon in Pilgrim's Progress!"

Jeb's body shook as he laughed. "Apollyon's the monster, *jah*? Isn't that taking things a little too far?"

"*Ach,* she rages on and on…"

Granny put down her knitting. "Has Fannie told you why she's angry?"

Mona bowed her head and fidgeted with the end of Granny's blue and white checkered tablecloth. "*Jah*, but I asked for forgiveness."

"For what?" Granny prodded.

"Well, I've been a grouchy *mamm*. And neglectful, too. Fears have kept me pent up, but I've changed. Everyone sees it, but Fannie just is so unchristian, not forgiving."

Jeb scratched his head. "You read Pilgrim's Progress?"

"*Jah*. It was *goot*."

"Well, I've read it several times and recommended it for a reason: to prepare hearts for Easter. This is my first year as bishop on Easter and all, and I thought I'd let John Bunyan do some plowing for me."

"Plowing?" Mona asked.

"You know, dig up folk's hearts to the Word of God so it can fall on *goot* soil, so it can grow. Now, I've been thinking about you, and see something that applies."

Mona prayed for grace, hoping Jeb wouldn't yell at her or break her heart with guilt, like Fannie was doing. "What do you see?"

"If I don't stay on the straight and narrow, I too can fall into the Slough of Despond, like our pilgrim in the story did."

"Really? You?"

"*Jah*, we all have feet of clay at times. But Pilgrim called out in the story and Helper came to help pull him out." He looked over at Granny. "She's my helper, along with the *goot* Lord, along with many others. Pilgrim was never alone on his journey, was he?"

"*Nee,* he wasn't. Or if he was he needed help."

"Do you know what the Slough of Despond is?"

"A place that keeps us from moving on the path?"

"Despond means depression, hopelessness, misery."

Mona met his turquoise eyes. "You think I'm weak then?" Shame filled her and she knew she was starting to blush.

Jeb opened his Bible that sat on the table. "Now, we're all weak. It's basic to the Christian message. We all miss the mark, not being perfect like God and not at the Celestial City yet. But God expects us to fight."

"We're pacifists," Mona blurted, astonished.

Jeb skimmed though his Bible, put up a finger and read:

"Beat your plowshares into swords

"And your pruning hooks into spears;

"Let the weak say, 'I am strong.'

"That's Job 3:10." He flipped through his Bible towards the back, put his hand up and then jumped up and ran into the living room.

Mona looked over at Granny, who shrugged, obviously not knowing what was wrong.

Jeb ran back with another book lifted above his head. "I'm going to read this out of my new Bible. The King James is beautiful and all, but I like several translations."

Mona knew one of her faults was being a know-it-all, but most Amish knew they only read the King James Version. Would the church be voting on changing the *Ordnung*? She closed her eyes and clamped her mouth shut.

"Put on all of God's armor so that you will be able to stand firm against all strategies of the devil. For we are not fighting against flesh-and-blood enemies, but against evil rulers and authorities of the unseen world, against mighty powers in this dark world, and against evil spirits in the heavenly places." Jeb paused. "Now right here it says we're not fighting against people. Understand?"

Mona leaned forward and nodded, surprisingly interested.

"And you know it later goes on to say put your armor on?"

Mona looked up, deep in thought. After a deep breath, she said, "We have to dress for battle. *Ach,* and in the story, when Pilgrim is attacked there's no armor to protect his back if he turned and ran."

"Amen," Jeb bellowed. "Do you see?" He raised his Bible to his heart. "This here Book gives us strength. It's called a sword."

"And Pilgrim almost got crushed to death by the monster because his sword fell out of his hand."

"*Jah!* The Enemy of our soul likes to press into us. Oppress us."

"*Ach,* Jeb. That's the word for how I feel. Oppressed. Sometimes I feel like I'm being suffocated by fear itself."

Jeb reached for her hands. "God has not given you a spirit of fear, but power, love, and a sound mind. He loves you, wants to give you power and a mind free from worry. But as we know from the book, it doesn't happen overnight. Pilgrim goes through many trials, but is never alone."

Mona felt a painful yet sweet softening in her heart. This is what she needed, yet had been denied most of her life: love. Someone who would help her. But then again, she'd erected a wall so no one could get in. Granny got up and sat next to her on the bench, and tears fell down her cheeks. Jeb clenched her hands tighter and Granny rubbed her back.

Jeb then withdrew his hands to flip through his Bible again. "We all fall into pits in life. Mine might not look like yours, but it's still a pit. And Kind David fell into one. He even wrote a song about it, here in Psalm 40: I'll just read two lines though:

"He lifted me out of the pit of despair, out of the mud and the mire.

He set my feet on solid ground and steadied me as I walked along.

He has given me a new song to sing, a hymn of praise to our God.

Many will see what he has done and be amazed. They will put their trust in the Lord.

Jeb slowly met Mona's gaze. "Now, I believe God's lifting you out of your pit, but Fannie doesn't see it... yet. But when you start to sing a new song, one of happiness and not gloom, she'll take notice and be amazed... and she'll believe you're sincere. Understand?"

Mona felt free for the first time in her life. No amount of doubt from Fannie or anyone else was going to steal this precious feeling from her.

~*~

Suzy lingered in her heated, leather seat, not wanting to get out of Missy's luxurious car. She thought she loved Jeeps the most, but not now. Well, a Jeep with heated seats would do just fine, she mused.

"It's back here," Missy said, waving over towards the barn near the *dawdyhaus* that Joe and Marge were moving back into.

"In the barn?" Suzy clenched her fist. She would not get her hopes up. This surprise was probably the animals that Missy anonymously bought for the farm: goats, chickens, and other animals so the boys would learn farming and living close to nature.

She hopped out of the car, zipped up her winter jacket, and pulled the new mint green scarf she just made over her face. What a pair they were, Missy with a long fur coat on, and her in her plain old black down jacket.

"Hurry up, I can't wait to see your face," Missy called back.

Suzy dodged mud puddles as she ran down the dirt road and caught up with Missy. "You're in good shape for your age. How old are you?"

"Your age," Missy said with a wry smile.

"I'm still twenty-nine. Okay, thirty-nine."

"Me, too." Missy slid the barn door open and pushed Suzy inside. "They're all yours."

Suzy shook her head, trying to wake up. She pinched herself, but no, she was not dreaming. In newly made stalls, there were four alpacas, all a different color: black, white, cream, brown. She remembered as a little girl wanting one of these gentle creatures as a pet, but now she wanted them for spinning their fur. Suzy spun around and saw Missy, a smile shining from her eyes. "I don't know what to say. Thank you."

Missy beamed. "No, thank you. If you hadn't obeyed that prompting God gave you to visit a grouchy old woman who was demeaning and arrogant, I'd still be in prison in that big old mansion."

Suzy laughed. "Correction. You are not old. And you're not grouchy anymore."

Missy went over to Suzy and embraced her. "My chains are gone, just like the song says. My money is too, not that it's a bad thing, but the love of it sure is."

Suzy jumped when she heard a rustling sound come from the back of the barn. "Oh, man. I think we need some cats."

"Why?"

Suzy groaned. "I hate mice or rodents of any kind. Marge got that little kitten from the shelter, and maybe it will help. Just the scent of a cat around makes the mice flee."

Suzy went towards the sound, but Missy froze where she stood. "Why get close to them?"

"Just curious. That was too loud for a rat."

"A rat!"

"Could be chipmunks or squirrels, which can do damage to a place in no time." Suzy continued toward the sound, and jumped when Colleen popped her head above a stall. "Goodness. You almost gave me a heart attack."

"Sorry. Just back here needing time alone. And taking measurements for the Amish work crew coming over."

Suzy put her hands on her hips. "Fess up. Amish men do their own measuring. Why are you out here?" She turned back to Missy. "It's Colleen. You go ahead inside and I'll see you there."

After Missy left, she turned to Colleen. "You look as white as a ghost. What's wrong?"

Colleen let out a sigh, vapor rising out of her mouth. "Remember how we quote Jo March all the time, saying we're hopelessly flawed? Well, I'm beyond hopeless. I'm flawed through and through." She stomped one foot. "Just when things were going so right!"

Suzy gaped. "No. He wouldn't do that. Not Hezekiah. He's Amish!"

"What are you talking about?"

"I'll wring his neck. He broke things off, didn't he?"

"No," Colleen blurted. "But I've messed things up horribly. I may as well just take off these plain clothes and put on jeans again."

Suzy shook her head. "Well, whatever happened?"

Colleen shook her head like a bobble doll. "I've made such a mess of things. I hurt Hezekiah. He'll never forgive me," she said in staccato phrases. "It was a dream. That a man like him would want me."

Suzy led Colleen to a nearby bench. "Tell me what happened."

Just then, Janice called in from the barn door, "Suzy, are you in here?"

"Yes. Why?" Suzy sprang up. "Do you need something?"

"Oh, you silly. I want to see your expression. Can you believe these alpacas Missy bought, and for you. "

Suzy waved her hand vigorously. Missy wanted to remain anonymous, and with Colleen sitting behind the stall...

"Why are you waving at me, Suzy?" Janice chuckled as she drew near, but stopped short when Colleen came into view. "Oops. Guess the cat's out of the bag."

Colleen stood up. "I won't tell anyone, although everyone assumes it's Missy anyhow. Who else has that kind of money around here?"

"Who said it was someone here who gave the money?" Janice asked.

"Everyone in town," Colleen said. "The country gossip vine runs faster than the Amish..."

Janice gave Colleen a pensive look. "Colleen. What's wrong? Where's my sunshine girl?"

When Colleen didn't speak, Suzy put her arm around her. "Tell us, honey."

"Well, I've been talking a lot to Clark ever since he got back. We were good friends, and the more we talk, I'm tempted."

"Define tempted," Janice said evenly.

"I miss music for starters. When I left Forget-Me-Not to live with my grandma, I loved the quiet. Clark's been playing all kinds of stuff on his boom box and I find myself wanting to dance. Actually, I did dance."

"Dancing isn't a sin," Suzy said. "Some Amish square dance."

"I danced with Clark in the living room. He took my hand and we started dancing to the music. And of course, as my luck would have it, Hezekiah walked in. And the shock and hurt on his face... it was horrible."

"But Hezekiah is so understanding. Did you explain to him what happened?"

Colleen scrunched her lips to one side and shook her head. "He stood there one minute, then charged out of the house."

Suzy took her hand. "Colleen, the Amish do that. They calm down before speaking, or at least try to. When he comes back, just explain to him what happened, like you just did to us."

"I miss dancing. I miss music other than Gregorian chants." She stomped her foot again. "Who am I kidding? I miss wearing jeans."

"Oh, honey. You need to talk to Granny."

"Granny?"

"Yes. That trifle box she told you about, where you put things in that bug you and wait a few days, then see if it was really nothing. I know Clark being around has been a shock to you, and you do know he has a crush on you, right?" Janice asked.

"No, I didn't. Not until this morning. He told me and I think Hezekiah may have overheard."

"Oh, Lord," Janice said. She grabbed Suzy and Colleen's hands. "Let's pray. I smell a rat."

Colleen cocked her head back. "There's no rats in here. What are you talking about?"

"It's a code," Suzy said. "It means we think Old Lucifer's up to something."

~*~

Even though it was bitterly cold outside, Ruth sweat profusely and took a handkerchief out of her apron pocket and wiped her forehead. She met Jeb's eyes, then Granny's, and once again, shame flooded her. "Like I said, this is hard, but confession is *goot* for the soul, *jah*?"

"*Jah*," Granny said. "Hard to believe you have something so serious to confess that you can't partake in communion."

"Well, I do. I hurt my *boppli*."

Granny leaned back. "What? *Ach*, Ruth. You couldn't."

"Not on purpose. It was my stupid obsession with birds."

Jeb shook his head. "I'm *ferhoodled*. Make your meaning clear."

Ruth wrung her hands and her lips went pencil thin. "You know how sick I was the months leading to Debbie coming into this world. Well, I didn't listen to Luke, but instead went out and filled the birdfeeders."

"And?" Jeb prodded

"Well, I also didn't stop feeding the birds by hand. They're half-starved in January, so I took my seeds out and stood like a statue out in the cold, and let birds eat from my palms."

Granny looked at Jeb, confusion etched on her face. "I think it's nice you care for birds."

"But Luke didn't want me out there. Birds carry diseases, and well, I hurt Debbie."

"How?" Jeb asked, pulling at his long gray beard.

"I must have gotten sick from the birds, *jah*? And it hurt Debbie…"

Granny poured more hot water from her tea pot into Ruth's cup. "But Debbie isn't sick. I don't understand your meaning."

Ruth clenched her tea cup. "Don't you see? It's my fault she has Down Syndrome!"

Granny ran around the table and embraced Ruth. "Debbie's not sick. She's special and God let a very special couple have her."

"What do you mean?" Ruth asked, mechanically.

"Well," Granny continued, "you're tenderhearted, and an overcomer. Luke and you, both. You had a mountain to climb last year, but you did it, and have a *goot* marriage. I'd say it's a firm foundation for a happy family."

Jeb cut in. "Ruth, your Debbie has angels."

"What?" Ruth and Granny asked in unison.

Jeb opened Pilgrim's Progress that sat next to his Bible. Thumbing through and pulling at his beard harder, he finally said, "*Ach*, it's right here. The Shining Ones, the three celestial creatures who clothe Christian with new garments and give him the certificate. These Shining Ones act as guardians who help Pilgrim."

"But isn't that just a story?" Ruth asked.

"*Ach*, maybe so. But the Bible says that wee ones have angels that ever behold the face of God." He opened his Bible, scanned through, and then put up a finger, as if to hush them. "Baby's angels ever behold the face of God. Listen to Matthew 18:10: 'Beware that you don't look down on any of these little ones. For I tell you that in heaven their angels are always in the presence of my heavenly Father.'"

Ruth didn't know if she was tired, hungry from fasting or maybe just stressed, but she didn't understand why Jeb was bringing up this scripture, as if it was as profound as Luther's Ninety-Five Theses. She was relieved when Granny said she was confused, too.

Jeb cocked his head. "From what I understand, Debbie will always be like a *kinner* inside, *jah?*"

Ruth nodded. "The doctor said she won't advance more than a five, maybe up to eight year old."

Jeb raised his hands in praise. "Don't you see? She'll always be a *kinner* inside, and will have angels that are always facing the Throne of God. Some say that angels here means 'spirit,' but it's still all *goot.* Debbie's spirit will ever behold God in a special way. *Ach,* remember when you're a *kinner,* you forget about who offended you yesterday; you're not troubled by half the things that bog down adults?" He paused, eyes shining. "The happiest days in my life were when I was a *kinner.* How about you, Ruth?"

Ruth slowly shook her head, but she was still thinking about what Jeb said about Debbie having a special relationship with God. So, Debbie was blessed? Special in a way that never dawned upon her. Her delayed reaction to Debbie's condition had given room to some awful thoughts, but this was beautiful.

"*Danki,* Jeb. You're the wisest bishop I've ever had."

Jeb lifted up the two books. "I read a lot. Fill my head with *goot* books." He winked. "I even read Jane Austen, but that stays between us, *jah?*"

Ruth laughed. "*Jah.*"

~*~

When Fannie opened Granny's storm door, she hesitated. Through the glass she could see that Ruth was having a mighty serious discussion with Bishop Jeb. Ruth? She was a saint. What would she have to confess?

Fannie rolled her eyes. When would she ever stop comparing herself to others, always feeling inferior? Lately, no amount of memorizing scripture or reading little compliments from her box Melvin gave her had any lasting effect. Maybe for a few hours, but then she plunged down into negative thoughts again.

She noticed Ruth was laughing now, so maybe this was just a friendly visit. Odd, though, since Jeb had church members lined up to confess any disunity or sin before breaking bread on Easter. Fannie saw that Granny was coming to the door, so she opened it.

"Now, don't act English and knock. Why not just come in?" Granny asked.

"I, ah, well, thought I was intruding."

Granny touched Fannie's cheek. "You never intrude. *Jah*, Jeb is busy, but I'd just have you sit in the living room."

"Is Ruth done? I mean, visiting and all."

Granny gave a wry smile. "She has her problems too, not just you. Come on in. Jeb knows you're coming."

Fannie stepped back. "Maybe I can just tell Lizzie my problems? Jeb looks tired, and you do, too."

Granny pulled Fannie inside. "Jeb would be hurt. He's your bishop."

For that Fannie was grateful, but she knew that Jeb had been unusually fond of her *mamm* lately, giving her a dog, picking her up to go places... anything for attention, Fannie moaned internally. And with her *mamm's* wagging tongue, she wondered what she'd told Jeb about her.

Post-partum depression had been her *mamm's* excuse to justify her normal behavior!

Ruth gave her a quick hug. "See you in an hour or so?"

"*Jah*, I think. If I can get away from Anna. Melvin's sitting with her now and he's busy turning sod and spreading manure."

"So soon?"

"It is March," Fannie said. "And we're growing some organic things for the store. How's Little Debbie?"

Ruth slipped her arm through Granny's. "She's fine. Real special little girl."

Ruth's beaming face only magnified Fannie's weaknesses, and she recoiled. A woman who gives birth to a handicapped *boppli* and not a care in the world. Why did she let her *mamm* get to her so much? Because she was so weak, Fannie thought, unlike Ruth who is a rock.

Fannie rolled her eyes again. Don't compare yourself to Ruth.

"Well," Ruth cut into her thought, "I think Debbie is mighty special at least."

"What?" Fannie asked in a monotone voice.

"You can roll your eyes if you want, but Debbie is a special little girl."

Fannie gasped, and then embraced Ruth. "*Ach,* I know that. I was thinking of something else." She stomped her foot. "I'm a mess. Can't even concentrate lately."

Ruth pat her back. "It's called post-partum depression, *jah*? I have it a little bit, too. Sorry for snapping."

Fannie stiffened. She did not have a depression problem.

Ruth gave her a quick squeeze and then turned to get her cape and bonnet off the peg near the door. "I best be getting home. *Mamm's* watching Mica and Debbie, but I got to gabbing too much. Need to run."

A dart of jealousy hit Fannie's heart. Ruth had help with her *kinner*, but she didn't. Well, she did, but didn't want it from her *mamm*.

"Give me your wraps and go over and have some tea," Granny said, her lips thin. "Are you alright?"

"*Nee*, that's why I'm here." She staggered over to sit across from Jeb. "I'm here to confess, but you look too tired."

Jeb, who had his nose in a book, looked up. "*Jah*, I am. But this black tea's keeping me going. What ails you, dear one?"

Dear one? He never called her that. Did he feel sorry for her? Did she look that bad? She blurted out, "My *mamm* is Obstinate in Pilgrim's Progress, and I don't want anything to do with her."

Granny sat next to her. "What on earth?"

"It's in that book." Fannie pointed to Jeb's copy of Pilgrim's Progress. "Best book on freedom I've ever read. Pilgrim leaves the City of Destruction with all the horrible people, and I'm making a break from my *mamm*, Obstinate. Pilgrim did the right thing in leaving, cutting ties. And I —"

"Hold on!" Jeb cut her off. "Fannie, now listen here. You read just the first part of the book for knitting circle, *jah*?"

"Is there a part two?"

"*Jah*," Jeb said. "It's about Pilgrim's wife, Christiana, who leaves the City of Destruction after pondering his words."

"So Christian, or Pilgrim, or whatever his name is, goes back to the City of Destruction? I thought he died and went to heaven."

"He did," Granny said. "No, he didn't go back."

Fannie knew Jeb was too tired to listen and she'd most likely be told about her depression and need to forgive her *mamm*.

"Pilgrim didn't go back, but God did."

"What?" Fannie asked.

"Well, Jesus lived in the Celestial City before he came to earth, which is what the City of Destruction symbolizes. Not the beautiful world God created, but the fallen human condition, understand?"

Fannie just stared into Jeb's grayish blue eyes. "Wow, I never thought of that. The City of Destruction was a horrible place."

"Well, if we're to imitate our Lord, we need to do the same. But your *mamm* doesn't live in the City of Destruction, since she's a believer. She's struggling on her path to the Celestial City like we all are. And remember, Christian lost his burden when he stood in the shadow of the cross." He took Fannie's hand. "Let it go."

Fannie's chin quivered. "How can I? When I see my *mamm* doting over Anna, I want to shake her. There, I said it. She never showed me the affection she's showing my Anna. Why?"

"*Grandkinner* are so easy to love. You don't have the responsibility of caring day and night, and the exhaustion, either. And with age comes wisdom, *jah*? Maybe your *mamm* has regrets over how she's raised you and wants to make things right with Anna?"

Granny put her arm around Fannie. "You have to forgive your *mamm*. We've been over this again and again.

It's for your own *goot*. I think it's the depression talking here."

Fannie shook her head. "I'm not depressed!"

"Take it from a *mamm* of six, *jah*, you are."

"Six?"

"Five boys here and one girl waiting to meet us in heaven."

Fannie's countenance dropped. "I'm sorry. I forget."

"You're looking inward too much," Jeb said. "Can't see others very clear that way."

Is that what was wrong with her? Had she only looked at her own problems… and is this what postpartum depression did?

~*~

Granny took the remaining oatmeal muffins she'd served to visitors all morning, to the coffee table in the living room. "Help yourselves, and like usual, there's coffee and tea hot on the stove." She wiped her brow and looked at Janice. "Being a bishop's wife is hard work."

Janice looked up from her knitting, one eyebrow cocked. "Yep, sure is. But we don't have such strict rules for Easter as you do."

"What do you mean?" Suzy asked.

"Well, you won't have communion unless everyone's in unity, right? No unforgiveness?"

"*Jah*," Granny said. "You don't?"

Janice groaned. "I've lived in Smicksburg for decades, and yet, I'm still rethinking things. We should stress forgiveness and unity before communion. We have it once a month, though, and *yinz* have it once a year, right?"

Granny nodded. "Some have it twice, but we have it at Easter. I think the spring weather, and the sun, whenever it does come out, makes folks more chipper and apt to get along." She looked around the circle. "Jeb and I have been using Pilgrim's Progress to help the flock. Sure is a helpful book."

Mona groaned. "Hope it helped Fannie…"

Suzy cleared her throat. "We don't talk about members if they're not here. No gossip."

"I wasn't gossiping," Mona huffed.

Suzy slumped in her seat. "Where's Lizzie?"

"I brought Charles over to visit Jonas, and she's spoiling him with homemade goodies," Janice said with appreciation. "That kid needs some doting on."

Suzy nodded in agreement and then pointed to Mona. "What did you get out of Pilgrim's Progress?"

Mona straightened. "Well, I could relate about having burdens on my back and was happy for Pilgrim when they fell off. But what's a wicket gate? Anyone know? A 'fancy' name for a gate?"

"It's a narrow gate, sometimes a smaller door within a larger door," Janice said.

"My, aren't we smart," Marge laughed. "You watched the movie, didn't you?"

Janice pursed her lips and then grinned. "We have been so busy with the farm that, yes I did." She looked over at Mona. "It's a narrow gate. Go on Mona, sorry to interrupt."

Mona looked down at her yarn. "I didn't see it as a narrow gate. I suppose it's a reminder to stay on the straight and narrow. Now if I remember right, wasn't the path that led to the Celestial City narrow, too?"

Granny shot a prayer up for Mona. She was seeing things she'd never seen before. Opening up like crocuses outside. "Mona, what do you like about the narrow gate and path?"

Mona bit her lower lip and then her rigid face relaxed. "Pilgrim was never alone on the path. As scared as he was, he was never alone." She shyly looked around the room. "I've tried to stay on the straight and narrow, but fell. Fell into depression, fears, and bitterness. I see now it's not *goot* to be alone." She held her throat as if what she was going to say next was painful. "I'm mighty glad I was invited to this here knitting circle. I have *yinz* all to walk the path with. Helped me as I fall all the time."

Granny got up and nearly ran to Mona. "*Ach,* bless you. We all fall. Pilgrim fell." She leaned over and hugged Mona, who hugged her back. "You have us all to pick you up. We're knit-pickers, *jah*?"

Mona laughed. "*Jah. Danki* Granny."

Granny stepped back. "You called me Granny. Praise be."

Laughter filled the room.

Mona tried to hide her laughter. "I'm too old to call you that, though."

Granny cupped Mona's cheek. "You call me Granny anyhow, understand?"

"*Jah*, Granny," Mona quipped.

Granny went back to her seat, a lilt in her step. Praise be. Mona's a new woman. She's learning the need for fellowship. Women are stronger spun together, like wool. Praise be! Granny sat next to Colleen and pat her knee. "You're quiet today. Tired from all the work over at the farm?"

Colleen shifted. "*Jah*. I suppose."

Granny knew something was amiss, as Colleen was not her calm, good-natured self. Had the book upset her? "Colleen, did you like Pilgrim's Progress?"

"Well, I remember in Little Women that the girls read this book, and pretended to carry burdens. I liked that."

"Why?" Granny prodded.

"Because I like *Little Women*. It's my favorite book, next to The Secret Garden."

Granny did not like the way Colleen was acting English, beating around the bush, as Jeb always called it. The Amish talked plain and straight forward.

Robins chirped and called to each other, something Granny loved about these spring birds. Birds were predictable, and so far, so had Colleen been. What was wrong?

"Maryann, how about you? Did you like the book?" Suzy asked.

"*Ach*, so much. Too much to tell. But I'm ever so thankful for the light God gives us on a journey. When I was battling cancer, it was the only stable thing to me. Fear, anger, all kinds of emotions washed away when the light of God's Word, or God with skin on, as Marge called it. Someone who you could feel, a human, who just held me." She looked over at Marge. "You were there for me, body, mind, and spirit. You were like Hopeful and Faithful all wrapped into one." She glanced around the circle. "Marge was my nurse, so I saw her the most. But *yinz* did, in some way, give me light." Maryann took Mona's hand. "Or if I didn't see you, I knew you were praying."

Marge gasped for air. "Maryann, I'm going to blow."

"What?"

"I'm going to gush out in tears." She fanned her face with one hand. "Maryann, you helped me see God more clearly. Joe too. And what about Lavina? You were a great light and help to that girl."

"*Ach,*" Maryann said. "I'll miss her. I don't mean to be questioning the ways of God, but I didn't see that coming. Becca is so sad."

"Me too," Colleen spoke up.

Granny took Colleen's hand. "Is that what's ailing you, Colleen? Because you're in *goot* company. I'm tired of always moving forward on the path to the Celestial City. But Pilgrim always moved on. Nothing stays the same." She sighed. "Wish I could bottle moments up, preserve them forever. "

Colleen said nothing, but Granny felt her hand harden. "Colleen... are you nervous about your baptism this Sunday?"

She nodded. "Can we talk about this later? In private?"

The fear, no guilt, in Colleen's eyes made Granny realize that she might have some things to confess before communion. "I'm sorry, Colleen. *Jah*, of course. Want to see Jeb after circle?"

"*Nee,* no time today. But tomorrow?"

"Okay. That'll be fine." Granny looked over at Suzy to divert the attention from Colleen. "Suzy, what did you get out of the book."

"Well, Vanity Fair was made out to be an awful place, full of money-hungry, greedy folks. Pilgrim stood out like a sore thumb, and it made me realize so do I. And Ginny Rowland, too. And boy did it help Missy. Missy said she'd never seen people so happy who lived on top of their stores." Suzy chuckled. "And now Missy's going to be doing it in her new tea shop."

"She's like Hopeful," Maryann blurted. "Hopeful saw something different in Pilgrim and started on the narrow road with him. *Ach,* that's *wunderbar.*"

"I'm sure glad she went on the straight and narrow," Janice said, "or we wouldn't have the farm."

"Janice!" Suzy chided. "What are you talking about? The person who gave us the money for the farm was called Anonymous."

Janice's eyes were round as buttons. "Oh, *yinz* can't tell anyone. Missy wants to be an anonymous donor."

"Why?" Mona asked.

Suzy spoke up. "She doesn't want to be loved for what she can give. She's not used to being loved for who she is."

"She needs to come to knitting circle," Mona quipped. "Lots of love here."

"I'll do that," Suzy said. "But the word is mum about her being the donor, understand?"

All heads nodded in agreement.

Suzy took an oatmeal muffin off the table and placed it on a napkin. "Granny, I'm curious what you got out of the book, or is it old hat to you."

"Old hat?"

"Yes, something you've read so many times you don't get much out of it anymore."

Granny shook her head. "Jeb's the one who's read it over and over. Not me. But I simply love it. And I needed it, especially the part about the lions. Poor Pilgrim was so afraid, but the lions were on chains and as long as he stayed on the lighted path, they couldn't get to him. Mighty powerful parable of sorts."

"I agree," Janice said. "And if you see the movie on YouTube, it'll stick in your mind."

Suzy let out an exasperated sigh. "Janice, did you check your brains out at the door? First you tell us who the donor is, and now you're telling the Amish to watch YouTube?"

Janice eyed Suzy. "We've had a stressful day at the farm, have we not? And I'm tired. I do make mistakes."

"I'm sorry." Suzy bit into her muffin. "You're overworked with this whole project." She grabbed a muffin and gave it to Janice. "Here, have one. Oatmeal's good for you."

Janice took the muffin with a smile that slid across her face. "Thanks… Obstinate."

Suzy took a ball of yarn out of her basket and threw it at Janice. "That's the worst character in the book!" She ran over and got another muffin and threatened to throw it at Janice's face. "Take that back."

Janice set a face bold towards Suzy. "Make me."

Suzy stooped down, got a ball of yarn, and flung it at Janice, but missed her and hit a framed picture on the wall. Granny gasped, as Marge braced it as it swung, almost falling to pieces. Granny shot up. "Now don't act like *kinner*. You almost broke my family tree."

Suzy quickly sat down. "Sorry, Granny. I know that picture means a lot." She lowered her head and slowly knit. "Thanks for keeping me on the straight and narrow. I do stray at times."

"*Ach,* I'm not against having fun," Granny said. "But we need to wrap up this discussion. We have more confessors coming over soon and Marge hasn't shared what she got out of the book."

Marge clapped her hands. "Well, I felt like I was Pilgrim. Going on the path, straying on the path, but ending up at the Celestial City in the end. Joe and I have been on a journey, moving to Smicksburg, then back to Indiana, and now back to the Celestial City."

Maryann gawked. "Smicksburg? The Celestial City? *Nee,* Heaven is."

"And Smicksburg," Marge explained, "is the next best thing. I call it my slice of heaven. I'm so happy to be back."

"And it's *wunderbar* to have my old neighbor back," Granny said. "I'll miss Nathan and Lavina, for sure and for certain, but we move forward, *jah*?"

Echoes of '*jah*'s' and 'yeses' bounced around the walls of Granny's heart, making her glad.

~*~

Marge snuggled closer to Joe on the church pew. "Can you believe we'll only be two miles from church again?"

He beamed. "Never knew becoming a Christian could be this much fun. Not a sappy religion for pansies at all."

Jerry mounted to his pulpit, looked around at the "Faithful Forty", as he called them: the Wednesday night church goers. "Well, it's good to see you all. Tonight will be different, since I have some announcements to make, and then we'll have a special time of worship for what God has done." He lifted up Pilgrim's Progress. "This here book has helped many a Pilgrim on his journey; his Christian walk. Everyone seems to get something different out of it, depending on what they're facing in real life. But, first of all, I want to tell you that the author, John Bunyan, was a good Baptist." He chuckled. "Okay, the real truth is, he was Baptist, but preferred to be called simply as 'Christian'. Is it any wonder that his main character, the Pilgrim, is named Christian?"

Heads in the congregation shook and one woman yelled an 'amen' from the back.

"Now Bunyan lived in poverty, and when old enough to have an occupation, became a tinker, a mender of pots and pans. So he was always traveling, just like the main character in his book. I found that interesting. So, Bunyan was always on a journey, and not shying from it like a Hobbit." He shifted. "Sometimes I see folks in small towns as Hobbits, J.R.R. Tolkien's midget characters in the Lord of the Rings Trilogy." Jerry looked down at Janice who sat in the front pew next to Charles. "I know. I'm on a bunny trail again, but did you all see the new movie?"

Some heads nodded, while others looked at each other in bewilderment.

"Well, I get a lot out of those movies that take us on journeys, full of danger, booby-traps and all that stuff. But this time through Pilgrim's Progress, I wasn't taken with the action parts as much as the soul parts.

"Let me explain. What I saw as the main action was fellowship and looking out for each other. Pilgrim is never alone, for one thing. And when he falls into trouble, when he calls out, there's help from mostly other travelers. I really liked the part when his friend, Hopeful, comes along in the story. Hopeful was stuck living in Vanity Fair, a carnal, money-loving place. When he met Christian, he saw something different in him. A joy not attached to material possessions. So, he becomes his companion, meaning he becomes a believer on the road to the Celestial City. But this younger friend ends up saving Pilgrim.

"There's a rough road that the two have to travel on, and Pilgrim's feet start to hurt so badly, that he wants to take a short cut. Hopeful warns him they need to stay on the straight and narrow, but no, Pilgrim is older and wiser and thinks he knows best. They end up being taken prisoner at Doubting Castle. They almost die by the hand of Giant Despair, but, now get this, Hopeful keeps saying words of, well, hope, and this hope breaks through despair and they're free." Jerry clapped his hands and shouted, "Hallelujah. Isn't that so true? Hope kills despair, right?"

All heads nodded, and Marge leaned her head on Joe's shoulder, whispering in his ear, "Now isn't that the truth."

Jerry walked down from the altar and pulled Charles up to his feet. "You've all met Charles, but if not, this is a new addition to our family for a while. He's become a source of hope to Janice and myself, in a most unlikely way. And you may ask why. Well, we were thinking that maybe I should take a job down south as a professor in a Bible college."

Gasps echoed throughout the church.

"We're not going anywhere, though. And it's because Charles gave us hope, and hope moves us in a different direction. Sit down, Son," Jerry said to Charles, after squeezing his shoulder. "You see, this young man, Charles, made a dangerous journey to visit an Amish friend, not unlike Pilgrim. He was fleeing from his own City of Destruction, and that takes courage. Now, from all he's told us, we know there's a real need for foster homes right here in the USA." He motioned for Janice to come stand by him, and when she did, he took her hand. "We want to announce that we'll be opening a foster house, being connected with a Christian foster care agency here in Pennsylvania. It's approved by the state and all. And we're happy to say that it's on Peach Street in an Amish farm turned modern." He motioned for Marge and Joe to stand up, which they did. "Marge and Joe will move back into their old *dawdyhaus*, with electricity this time," he chuckled, "and we'll have a working farm for foster boys to learn to bond with animals and whatnot. Also cuts costs." He motioned for Marge and Joe to sit down, and Janice also took her seat. "Are there any questions?"

A man shot up from the back pew. "Who's paying for all this? We can barely make the payment to the orphanage in Haiti."

Jerry shoved his hands in his pockets. "We got a large donation that will cover all the costs."

Chatter and fingers pointing to wealthier members ensued. Suzy looked back at Marge, finger to her lips, and Marge nodded. It would be hard not to slip up someday and spill the beans, that Suzy's knitting pupil was the mystery woman. Marge knew she'd have to be extra careful, living at the house behind the main farmhouse.

Another hand arose. "Is anyone going to live in the farm? Joe and Marge will live in a separate house, leaving them to themselves?"

Jerry struck his forehead. "Duh, I forgot. Clark, stand up."

Clark stood up, flicked back his chin-length black hair, and gave a playful bow to the congregation.

"*Yinz* remember Clark, right? He lived with us, got schooling up in Punxsy. Well, he's going to live with the boys as soon as his papers clear, and he'll be teaching horticulture and all that fancy stuff you learn in college about plants."

The congregation started with one person clapping, and then the whole church followed, welcoming Clark back into their church. "Can't find a better man than Clark," someone yelled. Clark curtsied, making everyone roar with laughter.

"I think Clark has the sense of humor, and can connect with the boys, since he was homeless when he came to us, and found a family with us." Jerry's face contorted. "You see, these boys will be adoptable. They'll need families. They're at the point of no return, understand? No parents fit for them to go home to."

A mourning dove softly cooed outside. Marge nudged Joe, and then whispered in his ear, "Did you know this?"

He cupped his hand over his mouth to muffle the sound. "No, but you know what this means don't you?"

"No."

"God sees us fit to be parents to a bunch of kids. Man, the guilt we had over the abortion sure blinded us."

Jerry asked Ginny Rowland to come forward to lead the church in a new hymn.

Ginny flung the guitar strap over her shoulder. "Seems like the whole town's reading Pilgrim's Progress. I've sold so many copies from my bookstore; I'm out of stock." She tuned up her guitar as she talked into the microphone. "I did some digging, and John Bunyan wrote a hymn called, To be a Pilgrim. The words are on the overhead projector, and let's sing it first, and then discuss a new name for the foster home.

He who would valiant be 'gainst all disaster,
Let him in constancy follow the Master.
There's no discouragement shall make him once relent
His first avowed intent to be a pilgrim.

Who so beset him round with dismal stories
Do but themselves confound - his strength the more is.
No foes shall stay his might; though he with giants fight,
He will make good his right to be a pilgrim.

Since, Lord, Thou dost defend us with Thy Spirit,
We know we at the end, shall life inherit.
Then fancies flee away! I'll fear not what men say,
I'll labor night and day to be a pilgrim.

Marge wiped a tear as the slow, meditative hymn came to a close. Though the words and meaning seemed antiquated, they were filled with hope. She reread the last line: I'll labor night and day to be a pilgrim. That she would do, being faithful to the call to care for these boys that were in need of good parents. People like her, of all people. Joy filled her as she realized she was free from guilt, and could with confidence be a foster parent.

Joe's voice broke into her train of thought. "How about we call it Arbor Creek? Pilgrim went to an arbor for rest and to take a drink of water." His cheeks colored. "Yeah, I read the book." He leaned on one foot, and then the other. "Water symbolizes the Holy Spirit and there's a creek in the back of the property."

Marge pushed her lips together tight, to not show how very proud she was of Joe. Looking at the other church members, heads nodding in amazement, she pat Joe's back. "I love it!"

Ginny strummed her guitar as if a drumroll. "I think we have a name. Do *yinz* agree?"

"Amen," Janice shouted, and everyone clapped.

Marge stood up and did a happy dance, right out in the aisle, not able to contain herself.

~*~

Jeb stared into his morning coffee, and Colleen didn't know how to read this expression. Was he thinking deeply about what she said, angry, or both?

Granny put her arm around her. "Anything else you need to confess?"

"No, I don't think so."

Jeb cleared his throat loudly, looked up aimlessly, and then met her eyes. "Colleen, this changes everything, *jah*?"

Not able to speak, Colleen remained silent.

Granny squeezed Colleen shoulder. "Did you put all this in your trifle box?"

"Yes, but it's been less than twenty-four hours…"

"Come again?" Jeb asked. "Don't know your meaning."

"Remember," Granny chimed in, "Colleen writes things that aren't really important, trifles, in her little box."

"*Ach, jah.*" Jeb pounded the table with his tapping fingers. "Then in a few days you see they were fleeting nothings." Jeb cracked a knuckle and leaned back in his chair. "I've been thinking about something. Colleen, you've been mighty faithful throughout baptismal classes and proving time and this came on sudden-like. Do you think you're going through the Valley of the Shadow of Death?"

Colleen grunted. "You can say that again."

"I mean the part in Pilgrim's Progress, where Pilgrim is tempted by base thoughts in the valley, and Pilgrim thinks it's him. But it's not…"

"What do you mean?"

"Any thought can fly into our heads; it's only when you entertain it, give it a room in your heart and let it live there, that's when it's sin, as I look at it. A fleeting thought isn't sin."

Colleen groaned. "But I feel so guilty, thinking such thoughts about Clark. I was unfaithful in my mind. The Bible says if you look at someone with lust, you've committed the act."

"Christ was tempted," Jeb interjected, "but without sin."

"*Jah,*" Granny said. "Remember when he was tempted for forty days and forty nights in the wilderness?

Satan whispered things in His ears trying to get him to act on it. He didn't turn a stone into bread, or jump off a cliff to see if angels would catch him, or bow down to Satan so he could have everything he owned."

"Bow down to Satan? Really?" Colleen had known Satan worshippers out on the streets, and could never understand how anyone could do such a thing.

"A thought isn't a sin," Jeb said kindly. "Think about it like this. A seed falls in your flower patch. It's a thistle seed and you don't want thistles in your garden. So, when you see a thistle seed fall in, you simply take it out. If it makes a little seedling, you pull it out. Sin's like that. It's a little thing, a thought. Don't let it take root."

Colleen felt a heavy stone of guilt come off her heart. But as soon as she found reprieve from her dilemma, Hezekiah's face appeared before her. "I understand, I think. But I hurt Hezekiah."

"Have you talked with him?" Granny asked.

"No. I'm too ashamed. He left, pretty angry and hurt."

"And this was yesterday?" Jeb asked.

Colleen nodded.

"Why'd you let the sun go down on your anger?" Jeb asked.

"We can go over and visit him now," Granny advised. "He loves you and will forgive."

Jeb took a swig of his coffee. "He's not home."

"How do you know?" Granny asked.

"Word has it he went out to Ohio yesterday."

"Why?" Colleen knew she was in a nightmare while wide awake. She'd lost him. How could she be so stupid? "He didn't even tell me."

"But he needs to be here on Sunday for Easter," Granny said.

"It's only Thursday, Deborah. Don't get your dander up." Jeb raked his fingers through his gray hair. "Colleen, are you willing to be Amish if Hezekiah's not ready to wed?"

Colleen didn't think her heart could sink so low. She'd never pondered an Amish life without Hezekiah. It all came so naturally, him helping her over rough patches of doubts and teaching her so many things about the Amish. She couldn't think of life without him at all. "Do you know where in Ohio he went?"

"Millersburg, I suppose," Granny said. "We have lots of kin out there in Holmes County. Why?"

"I need to see him. Maybe Suzy will drive me out. I just can't let him…" She covered her face with her hands.

"Now, now," Jeb said. "This may take more time, but it will all work out. The Lord's will be done."

"What will take more time?" Colleen blurted.

"Well, possibly your baptism and wedding. You didn't answer my question about being Amish without Hezekiah, and I have a hankering you're doing it for him. Now, that's alright. Not finding fault in that, but when you vow to be Amish, it's a vow as serious as a marriage vow. You can have no doubts or be double-minded about it. And it's only three days away." He sighed loudly. "Let's seek God over these next few days and see what unfolds."

"*Jah*," Granny said, "And don't lose hope. We have a saying. 'Some may see a hopeless end, but as a believer we rejoice in an endless hope.'"

~*~

Granny's slowly opened her eyes. She had fallen asleep again while knitting after the noon meal. So many visitors, church members who needed to confess sins or needed counsel had her nerves on edge so she took a break to knit. But she soon dozed off.

But she had Colleen heavy on her heart as she was knitting, and the dear girl weighed on her again. What was wrong with this girl she loved so? Was she having serious doubts about becoming Amish, since her baptism was to take place in a few days?

She leaned her head against the back of her Amish rocker as other concerns flooded her mind. She would not worry and fret, but pray. She closed her eyes:

Dear Jesus,

You know me through and through, and for that I am so thankful. And you know Colleen through and through, too. Only you know if she would be happy being Amish. You see her down the road of life, as an elderly woman. Would she be fulfilled being Hezekiah's wife with many grandkinner running underfoot? As much as I see this being possible, you know best, so your will be done.

And Lord, Hezekiah taking off and going to Ohio is not like him. He's as steady as they come. Be with him, Lord. If he's upset with Colleen, give him the grace to forgive. He saw her dancing with Clark, of all things. Lord, he needs your grace for sure.

Also, Fannie and Mona have such a bad mother-daughter relationship. I understand Mona now and I pray Fannie will someday. Give her strength to forgive and help her understand that we're all made of dust, hopelessly flawed.

I ask all this in Jesus name,
Amen.

Dear Readers,

I hope you enjoyed this episode of Amish Knit Lit Circle. *Pilgrim's Progress* is a classic book that some claim is second in sales to the Bible, the Bible being the all-time best- selling book. I think Pilgrims Progress is worth reading at different times in life, if you're in The Valley of the Shadow of Death, or resting at an arbor. The book is free public domain and is available on all eBook devices.

I leave you again with a recipe for Amish oatmeal muffins, something you can eat all day, be it breakfast, a mid-afternoon snack, or for dessert.

Oatmeal Muffins

1 c. rolled oats
1 c. milk
1/3 c. shortening
½ c. brown sugar
1 egg
1 c. flour
½ tsp. baking soda
1 tsp. baking powder
1 tsp. salt

Mix oats and milk together, then add remaining ingredients. Fill greased or paper-lined muffin cups 2/3rds full. Bake at 375 degrees for 20 minutes. Insert toothpick. If clean, the muffins are done. If not clean, bake a few minutes longer.

EPISODE 8

The Secret Garden

Granny thought her eyeballs would come out of their sockets, so shocked that Jeb didn't have the same reaction to the news they'd received through the Amish grapevine. "Jebediah Weaver, Hezekiah came back from Ohio with a woman! Understand? And she's living at his house."

"And?"

"So he got married out in Ohio…"

"*Jah*, I suppose."

Granny scooped scrambled eggs out of her cast iron skillet, slapped them on a plate and jostled it in front of Jeb. "I suppose? He's broken Colleen's heart is what I suppose!"

Jeb leaned back, hands up as if in surrender. "Colleen's a faithful one, for sure and for certain. Going through her baptismal vows with Hezekiah not even there to witness it."

"He should be horse whipped," Granny blurted. "Why on earth has he treated Colleen so terrible? *Ach,* she really is Mary Lennox."

"Mary who?"

"Mary Lennox, the main character in The Secret Garden. She had a wretched life. A very lonely life."

"But Colleen's found her Amish relations and has the knitting circle friends. I think she'll be fine."

Granny sat down and glared at Jeb.

"I think I'll be having a busy day today," Jeb said massaging his temples.

"Busy as in going over to Hezekiah's?"

He nodded. "Need to ask a few questions."

"Can I go?"

"You're watching the *kinner* aren't you? Lizzie and Roman are helping Marge and Joe move in."

Granny tapped her fingers on the table. "I could ask Becca to babysit."

"*Ach, nee.* I need to have one-on-one words with Hezekiah, man to man." Jeb frowned, knitting his eyebrows together a little too tight.

"You don't fool me. You don't want me to go."

He reached over and pat her shoulder. "Don't know if you could handle it, old woman."

Old woman? He hadn't called her that in a long time. When Jeb got nervous he said odd things, so what was he hiding?

"Did you see the roses? Blooming mighty fine," Jeb said.

"*Jah*, I told you I was out clipping them yesterday." Granny sighed. "If you won't tell me, maybe it's that bad. *Ach,* I had such hopes for Colleen."

Jeb took her hand and rubbed the top of it with his thumb. "Things turn out alright in the end, *jay*? Remember our courting days?"

Granny felt tension drain out of her back. "*Jah*, and I took the road less traveled…"

"And it's made all the difference," Jeb finished. "Are you reading Robert Frost again?"

"*Jah.* Always do in spring. His poems have more meaning now. Hard to read about flowers and blueberries and whatnot when the earth is covered in snow."

"Unless you read his snow poems…"

Granny bit her lower lip. "Poems soothe me. Don't know how or why, but they do. And I've been baffled lately about Colleen's situation. She was headed down a path that was so sure, but now it's so uncertain."

Jeb motioned for Bea to come up on his lap. "Don't fret so, love. You care too much at times."

"I know. Can't help it, having a *mamm's* heart and all."

Jeb lifted up Bea, putting her face up to his. "I want to show you something. Come around the back of me."

Granny obeyed, even though she knew Jeb was changing the subject and she wanted to fret out loud a bit more concerning Colleen.

"Now, watch this," Jeb said. "Bea, look at your *daed.*"

Bea's timid eyes had always looked away, Granny knew. The dog didn't trust people and couldn't look anyone in the eyes. But to her astonishment, Bea slowly and with great timidity, made her big brown eyes meet Jeb's.

"That's my girl, Bea. See, I won't hurt you." Jeb nuzzled his face into Bea's long fur. "You're loved and trust me, *jah?*"

Granny swallowed the lump that formed in her throat. "Now, I'll be. I never thought she'd do that."

Jeb turned to look at Granny. "Look to God, Deborah, and trust him. It will all turn out right."

Granny hugged him around the neck and kissed his cheek. "I see your meaning. I need to trust, not fret."

Jeb grabbed her hand. "How about we say casting off prayers together? Right here and now."

Granny squeezed his hand. "I'd like that. And need it. Colleen will be over today for knitting circle and I don't know what to say."

Jeb bowed his head, and Granny took his cue and bowed hers, too.

~*~

Colleen smoothed her wrinkled black apron, having been too distracted to think of ironing. Was she presentable for work? And now she needed this little job more than ever, not having an Amish husband for support, as she thought.

When she opened the door to the yarn shop, the little bell jingled, and it calmed her heart a tad. Some things never changed: yarn shops. Yes, having something to lace in between her fingers to make a pattern was something she had control over. Life, she did not.

"Morning, doll face," Suzy nearly sang as she appeared from the back room.

"Yes, it is a good morning. I see your daffodils and tulips are up."

Suzy plunked herself at her desk and began shuffling through paperwork. "Those flowers always tell me something. Do you know what?"

"What?"

"Clean your house and shop. It's spring cleaning time." Suzy chuckled. "And having a real Amish woman to help me clean, what more could I want?" Suzy's eyes met Colleen's and her face dropped into concern. "I'm sorry. Being cheerful around someone who's going through a hard time is like serving them vinegar to drink."

Colleen pursed her lips. "Well, I've had a bitter blow, but I look forward, as the Amish do. This place is not our home…"

Suzy pat the chair next to her. "Sit down and knit the rest of this scarf. I can't keep them in stock."

"You don't want me to clean?"

"No," Suzy insisted. "I need scarves made. Spring scarves are all the rage, you know."

Colleen knew Suzy had been trying to make her work pleasant, but she didn't know that work was now something she did with pleasure. Something about the Amish way of life, combining work with fellowship, was something she looked forward to. But, of course, knitting was her best stress buster yet.

"No word from Hezekiah?"

Colleen shook her head. "Of course you've heard the rumors."

"No. I only hear English gossip. The Amish are pretty mum about their own affairs."

When Colleen heard the word 'affair,' she felt the life drain from her. Is that what Hezekiah had been doing? Colleen's arms felt limp and she set the green yarn in her lap. "Hezekiah came home from Ohio with a woman."

Suzy leaned back in her chair, mouth gaping in shock.

"Word has it he married her out in Ohio."

"Seriously? I don't believe it!" Suzy blurted.

"Who else could she be?"

"Maybe it's his sister."

"He doesn't have a sister...."

"Well, how about another female relative? Like an aunt or cousin?"

Colleen shook her head. "To be honest, I did something horrible. Since no one's heard from him, I went over to his house to tidy-up, get his mail and all. And there were lots of letters from a woman named Lottie, and a heart was always drawn on the back of the envelopes."

"What?" Suzy pounded the desk. "What a jerk! And he's Amish, for Pete's sake. And I thought Amish were upright and Hezekiah a man of honor!"

Colleen could hold in the tears no more, and let them fall on the scarf, half knit. "He was the first man I trusted in a romantic way, too."

Suzy shot up. "You watch the shop. I'm going over and having words with him."

Colleen put up an arm, blocking Suzy in the corner. "No. We Amish don't settle things like that."

"I am not Amish." Suzy took Colleen's shoulders and squeezed them. "And honey, you have a heart. One that is broken. Why are you acting so pious? Like a martyr?"

Colleen stomped one foot as more tears fell. "Because I'm learning to be a pacifist and right now, I want to go over and slap him." A nervous twitch kept her left eyelid fluttering. "I'm trying to accept that I am Mary Lennox, a girl not wanted by her parents and tries to find happiness in a new place..."

She shook uncontrollably and soon felt Suzy's embrace. "I'm so sorry. I bet The Secret Garden was hard for you to read while going through this." She took Colleen's hands. "Sit down, honey. Want some tea?"

Colleen obeyed but declined tea and resumed her knitting, very mechanically. "Hezekiah was as sweet as Dickon in the book. Everything about him was so sincere."

"Well, it's all very shocking," Suzy said. "Did he ever try to contact you?"

Colleen shook her head. "No, not one letter."

Suzy leaned forward, eyes pensive. "This doesn't make any sense. If he was upset that you and Clark were dancing, getting the wrong idea, Granny would say that that reaction meant jealousy. I'm thinking he got mad because he loves you. But then he's writing to another woman?"

Colleen put a hand up. "Can we change the subject? I mean, the more I talk about it, it hurts."

"Alright, honey. But do you mind if I go over and talk to Hezekiah? Remember, even though you're Amish, I'm still like your mom, *jah*?"

Colleen gave a faint smile as Suzy used an Amish accent. "You are like my mom. And because of that, you can be like a mother bear and might hurt him. So, no, don't go over. Let's just move forward."

~*~

Fannie plunged the hand spade into the soil and dropped in three seeds. Zucchini always needed to be planted with three seeds, and for the first time, she wondered why. Was there some type of scientific reason? She stared at the seeds, and thought what the Bible said about a three strand cord being not easily broken. Granny had told her this over and over, that women were like thin strands of string, able to break, but when spun together, strong.

She felt pressure rise into her cheeks as she recalled the advice Granny gave to her and her *mamm* concerning their strained relationship. "Where you tend a rose, a thistle cannot grow." This line from The Secret Garden had made Fannie cringe at first and get rather defensive, thinking Granny had deserted her and was on her *mamm's* side. But, as usual, Granny saw through her and reaffirmed her love for her.

Fannie turned to see her *mamm* holding Anna, her precious baby girl, as they made their way out into the hot spring morning. "Does she need to nurse?" Fannie asked.

"*Nee,* we just thought we'd come out and keep you company," Mona said.

Fannie looked again at the three seeds in the hole. Lord, help me. I'm willing to obey. "*Mamm,* have you planted many zucchini this year?"

"*Ach, nee.* I don't have a green thumb, like you."

Fannie remembered all the years she and her sister tended the garden while her *mamm* hid herself upstairs in her bedroom, too depressed to leave it. She had a green thumb out of necessity. But, maybe she wouldn't have such a knack with plants if her *mamm* was as capable as others. "*Mamm*, why don't we share a garden? I'll be Dickon, the one who could make anything grow, and you could be Mary…" Fannie almost said, Mary Mary quite contrary, but held her tongue. Such a joke would not be taken well.

"I'd like that, but only if you can put up with a contrary Mary."

Fannie slowly turned and looked up at her *mamm*. "You know I didn't mean to imply that."

"I know. But Dickon did help Mary, and she was a self-centered little girl. I've been a self-centered old woman."

"You're not even fifty."

"You get my meaning, Fannie."

Fannie didn't know if the awkwardness around her *mamm* would ever end, but they were on a new path, and hopefully with new results. The thought of her sister, Eliza, her *mamm's* favorite daughter, came to Fannie. "Do you want to include Eliza in this garden? We have lots of room and she doesn't live far."

Mona kissed her *grandkinner's* cheek. "*Nee,* just you and me. We have some thistles to pull out, *jah?* And I can see Anna more. Have one on one time with her." She kissed Anna again. "Fannie, I was thinking that with you having the store and all, I could watch her more often."

Self-pity threatened to dig into Fannie. The love she'd always wanted from her *mamm* was given to her *kinner* so freely, but with her, it was work. She thought of Mary Lennox, the poor unloved girl in The Secret Garden. Fannie had such pity for her and understood why she was unable to love others. Her *mamm's* story was so similar, so why couldn't Fannie pity her? Granny said it was hurt and pride mixed together. *Jah*, she was hurt and needed time to grieve the fact that she basically raised her own *mamm*. But pride because she thought if she was in her *mamm's* shoes, she'd have acted better. Not been so indulgent into her own wants and needs, not even paying attention to her, only Eliza. Would this pain ever go away?

"Well, you talk it over with Melvin," Mona said in a defeated tone.

"What?"

"You didn't say anything when I asked about babysitting Anna while you helped in the store."

Fannie covered the seeds with soil and stood up. "*Mamm*, I'd be happy for your help. And since you make pies better than Granny, how about you help me bake for the benefit auction?"

Mona's eyes became so soft and tender, Fannie was taken back. She'd never seen such an emotion come from her *mamm's* heart out through her eyes. Was it love?

"Honey, I should have taught you many things, but I was like Scrooge, only thinking of myself."

"Who's Scrooge?" Fannie asked.

Mona gasped. "*Ach,* don't tell Jeb, but I read A Christmas Carol. I know he didn't want us to, since there's ghosts in it and all, but when I saw the change it made in Missy, I knew I had to read it. Serenity Book Nook lent me a copy."

Fannie looked at her *mamm* who tried to appear perfect in all ways to others, and for some reason, she seemed so much more human for revealing this secret. Fannie suddenly couldn't hide her mirth, and started to laugh.

"Promise you won't tell Jeb!" Mona said evenly. "I've never disobeyed one iota of what a Bishop has said, and I'll repent if necessary, but I just had to read it."

Fannie looked at the woman who she tried to please her whole life, and she saw a flawed woman. "*Ach, mamm,* we're all hopelessly flawed, like Jo in Little Women."

Mona looked at her demurely. "So you won't tell? And you don't think less of me?"

Fannie ran over to embrace her *mamm.* "You're being transparent, *Mamm. Ach,* how can I love or even know someone who can't confide in me their faults? It's why Granny and I are so close."

Mona kissed Fannie's cheek. "Well, I'm not jealous of Deborah, I mean, Granny, anymore. But you can tell me your faults and I'll share all mine. Enough to fill a wheelbarrow, I dare say."

As Fannie held her *mamm's* embrace, her heart became as warm as this fine spring morning.

~*~

Ruth watched a robin laden with hay in her beak, making a nest in the tree between her house and her parents. She thought of Mary Lennox being led by a robin into a secret garden, which eventually led her to true friends. People who really loved her.

Her eyes scanned the vast backyard and she noticed her *mamm* was hanging laundry. Her *mamm.* A woman who had been helping with her Little Debbie. And when others implied that it was somehow a sad thing to have a Down Syndrome granddaughter, how her *mamm* would go on and on about how very special Debbie was.

But have I ever told my *mamm* how special she is? Taking us into their *dawdyhaus* so that Luke could be watched, having been so verbally abusive. How patiently they waited for him to change and never bringing up his past sins? Her *daed* teaching Luke carpentry so they could work side-by-side...No, she never actually said thank you. The English did all the time, but the Amish just showed their love, not being so verbal.

Ruth observed her *mamm* was headed back to her house, and she called out to her, "*Mamm*, do you have time for some pie?"

"*Ach, jah.* For a few minutes. I wanted to get in some plants in my kitchen garden."

As her *mamm* walked towards her, she thought of poor Mary Lennox, a girl who was never loved by her parents. The new foster home the Baptists were opening was something she'd like to be involved in. Give the love she'd received so freely from her parents to others in need. Would Jeb allow it? Ruth stifled a laugh. Of course he would. He was married to Granny, who regularly took pies to Forget-Me-Not Manor, and stayed and talked to the homeless mothers.

"Is everything alright, Ruth? Need to talk?" her *mamm* asked.

"*Jah*, I do. Come on in and have some strawberry rhubarb pie. Fresh from the garden."

"Now, that's a treat."

Ruth motioned for her *mamm* to sit down at her table and took the pie out of her icebox. "Want me to warm it up?"

"*Nee.* Such a bother to get the stove stoked." She grinned. "We don't have those fancy microwaves like the English, *jah*?"

"It's not any trouble. The oven's still warm from breakfast."

"Okay. Have any vanilla ice cream while you're pampering me so?"

Ruth turned and tears filled her eyes. "*Mamm*. I have something to tell you, but I can't find words."

"Something is wrong with Debbie?"

Ruth slid the stoneware plate into the oven and sat across from her *mamm*. "I've been seeing things lately. Mona was jealous of Fannie's relationship with Granny, until she got to know Granny better."

"Which I find odd, to say the least."

Ruth shifted. "*Jah*, me too. But it seems like Mona's been hiding some problems she's had for a long while and it all surfaced at the circle."

"Well, we don't judge, *jah*? Now, what did you want to tell me?"

Ruth felt her hands grow sweaty. Why was it so hard to tell someone so close that you loved them? She took a deep breath, looked into her *mamm's* eyes, and said, "*Mamm*, I love you."

The crow's feet around her *mamm's* eyes, indented all the more into laugh lines. The joy on her *mamm's* face was undeniable. "*Ach,* Ruth, *danki*."

Ruth grabbed her hands. "I'm sorry I've never said it before. Or thank you for helping me with Luke and now Debbie."

Tears were now sliding down her *mamm's* cheeks, so she withdrew her handkerchief from her apron pocket and covered her face.

"I didn't want to make you cry," Ruth said. "I know, I should have said it sooner."

Her *mamm* blotted both eyes and then beamed. "I'm sorry. Wasn't expecting such praise."

Ruth got the pie out of the oven and placed it in front of her *mamm*. "*Mamm*, I've learned so much from Granny and my English friends. We Amish don't say what we feel, always trying to show it."

Ruth's *mamm* grinned. "Maybe I should join this knitting circle of yours. You used to be like a little bird, never really leaving the nest. I had to shoo you out as a *kinner*, remember?"

Ruth laughed. "*Jah*, I was a timid one."

"You're a deep, sensitive woman who has become my..."

"What?"

"Best friend."

Ruth ran around the table and embraced her *mamm*. "And you're my best friend." She squeezed her tight.

"We sound so English, *jah*?"

"*Jah*, we do, but it feels *goot*," Ruth said, her heart brimming over with happiness.

~*~

Marge stomped into one of the five upstairs bedrooms of the farmhouse being remodeled by the Baptists, and upon seeing Clark, growled, "Can we talk?"

The electrician, who was bent over, working on an outlet, slowly stood up, eyes wide as saucers. "Should I leave?"

"Unless you want to witness a murder," Marge fumed.

Clark rolled his eyes. "Marge, I told you, I cannot be two people. Can't paint and plow up fields at the same time."

"This has nothing to do with... work!"

The electrician put up both hands as if in a stick up. "I'm out of here. Let me know when it's safe to return." At that he darted from the room.

"Marge, why the dramatics?" Clark asked wryly.

Marge clenched her fists and remembered she was a good Christian woman, and closed her eyes and tried to count to ten, but only made it to five. "You ruined Colleen's life! Lizzie just told me all about it."

"About what? Hey, she's the one who chose to be Amish."

"I'm not talking about Colleen becoming Amish. And there's nothing wrong with being Amish. Well, except when you're a complete wimp."

Clark's dark eyes registered complete confusion. He got two chairs, sat in one and patted the other. "Sit down. Calm down. And slow down! I don't know what you're even talking about."

Marge reluctantly obeyed. "Lizzie told me she doubts that Colleen and Hezekiah will be getting married."

Clark rubbed his clean-shaven chin. "I didn't think it would work."

"You made it not work!"

"Now how did I do that?"

Marge gripped the bottom of her chair. "You flirted with Colleen and Hezekiah saw it. *Yinz* dancing to jazz. Remember?"

Clark looked up, staring at the ceiling. "Vaguely. I mean, Colleen and I goofed around a lot."

"Well Amish people don't. And Hezekiah ran like a girl. A wimp!"

Clark smirked. "Where to?"

"Ohio, to a sweetheart I guess, because she's living here now."

"And?"

"And the Amish don't live together before marriage, like we don't. Hello, they got married!"

A glint crossed Clark's face. "So, Colleen's not engaged anymore."

"She's an Amish heartbroken girl is what."

Clark fidgeted his fingers. "Now, I don't like to hear that."

"Really?"

"Really. Colleen and I got real close, both having similar struggles. I care about her, Marge. Just too much and she didn't feel it in a romantic way, like I did." He got up and started to pace the floor. "Is there anything I can do?"

Marge looked at Clark with new eyes. He really did care for Colleen in an unselfish way. Marge got up and put a hand on his shoulder. "I judged you wrongly. You do care for her."

"Sure do. She's pure goodness. And when I hitchhiked up here, she was my first real friend. And when you're on the road, being homeless, loneliness can be the most painful thing, not the cold and lack of food."

Marge went to one of the windows, looking down at the vacant yard. Was this true? Loneliness was worse than being hungry or cold? Being a mother figure for the boys who came to the house really was important. She looked over at Clark. "Do you think we'll make a difference in the children's lives that come here?"

Clark met her at the window and looked out, too. "They need stability." He elbowed her playfully. "You'll need to work on that."

"Oh, hush up. I was upset."

"You scared the electrician right out of here..."

Marge pursed her lips to hide her grin. Clark did have a way of joking that lightened life up. No wonder Colleen was attached to him. Marge looked over at Clark and wondered what he'd look like in Amish clothes and a beard. Was he the one for Colleen? Would he convert for her? Would Colleen forsake her baptismal vows and become English again? People do make mistakes....

"What are you thinking?" Clark asked.

"Of a plan. I think Granny's rubbing off on me."

"In what way?"

"Oh, ah, she likes to see people happy and… spun together, as she calls it."

~*~

As much as Granny loved watching her granddaughters, she was relieved when she saw Lizzie and Roman's buggy coming down her long driveway. Granny went out on her porch and waved. Roman brought the buggy to a halt. "Isn't *Daed* back yet?"

"*Nee.* It's rather odd, but so is this whole ordeal with Hezekiah. You didn't find out anything further?"

Lizzie and Roman both shook their heads.

"Jeb left after breakfast, and now it's almost time for knitting circle."

"Which road did he take?" Roman asked.

"His usual, I suppose. But then again, it's spring and he does like to stroll around on dirt roads."

"But it's so muddy. *Ach,* maybe he got stuck or broke a wheel." Roman put his hand on Lizzie's back. "I need to go search for him."

Lizzie kissed his cheek, and got out of the buggy. "*Mamm,* are you alright?"

Granny was always amazed at how selfless Lizzie was. Not only had she become a *wunderbar goot* stepmother, but one who took care of her handicapped *daed,* and now, hovering over Jeb and herself in their old age. "I'm fine. You go on and tend to the girls."

"Are you sure?"

"*Jah.* I have some casting off to do."

Concern etched all over Lizzie's face. "Me, too. When I woke up this morning, I had a foreboding type feeling I just can't chase away. Awfully concerned about Colleen and I need to cast her on Him."

"*Jah,*" Granny agreed. "And that's what I need to do, too." She gave Lizzie a faint smile and went back into her house. With the blackberry cobbler made for knitting circle along with cold root beer, she went over to her rocker and closed her eyes.

Lord,

Something is not right and I feel it so keenly. The sweet scent of my roses don't even cheer me up. I'm so concerned for Colleen. I've watched her over these past few weeks, being a baptized member of our Gmay. She's so faithful, and You honor those who honor You. How can this be if Hezekiah's gone off to marry someone else?

Lord, I really don't feel like having knitting circle today, but going back to bed. But I am Your hands and feet to serve anywhere You see fit, and for some reason, You've chosen for me to be hospitable and loving to my women friends. To make us stronger together. For that I'm thankful, but I just am so tired, and need Your strength and a mind free from fretting. Help me, Lord.

Amen

~*~

Granny looked around the circle, feeling comfort as Marge started to share what she got out of The Secret Garden. Feeling totally forgiven and whole inside, being haunted by an abortion she had while a teen, made her aspire to be like Susan Sowerby, the saintly woman who had a cottage full of children, yet became like a mother to other children in need. Granny was watching a miracle, and she gave thanks.

But she couldn't help but meet Colleen's eyes. Colleen looked like a wounded bird, one wing broken. And Lizzie's absence, having to stay home to watch the girls, only highlighted the fact that Roman wasn't home yet. So, something happened to Jeb.

Suzy nodded to Granny. "What did you get out of the book?"

Granny knit a few stitches before looking around the room. "Well, we're led in little steps is what I got. Mary Lennox was a hurt child who couldn't trust anyone, but she started to trust a robin, of all things. She also found healing in the garden, seeing all of God's creation. It's almost like she could see the nature of God, well, through nature." She resumed her knitting. "So animals and nature are *goot* for people."

Suzy spoke up, a lilt in her voice. "I agree. Spring is a time when I'm outside a lot getting colors for my yarn. Who's a better artist than God? And, like you said, it shows His nature." She looked over at Ruth. "You look like you have something to say about that robin, you bird lover."

Ruth grinned. "I liked how real the robin was made out to be, as if it has a personality of its own." She opened her book to where the bookmark lay. "Listen to this:

"The robin flew from his swinging spray of ivy on to the top of the wall and he opened his beak and sang a loud, lovely trill, merely to show off. Nothing in the world is quite as adorably lovely as a robin when he shows off - and they are nearly always doing it."

Praise for spring, bird's nests being built all around Smicksburg, and new baby farm animals resonated around the room. All seemed to be euphoric about the season, except Colleen, who never lifted her eyes from her knitting.

"Oh," Janice said, "I think the Doxology being sung by Collin when he couldn't explain why he was so happy at the end, floored me."

"What's the Doxology?" Fannie asked.

"Oh, you know." Janice sang in her deep mellow voice.

"Praise God, from Whom all blessings flow;
"Praise Him, all creatures here below;
"Praise Him above, ye heavenly host;
"Praise Father, Son, and Holy Ghost."

Hands clapped when she finished and Mona swiped a tear. "That was beautiful. And I see life that way now, too, not being a hypochondriac." She put her arm around Fannie. "It took this girl to show me that. She was like Mary Lennox telling Collin, 'You don't have a lump in your back. You won't be a hunchback. Get outside and enjoy life." Mona turned to Fannie. "Hysterics makes lumps."

Fannie was clearly shocked. "What?"

"You know, in the book when Collin thinks he'll die from being a hunchback and Mary examines his back, saying he has no lumps, no sign of being a hunchback. Well, you got this hysterical woman who was afraid of life to come to this circle." Mona's chin started to quiver and then her body followed suit. She grabbed Fannie around the neck. "*Danki*, my dear daughter."

Granny noticed tears in Fannie's eyes. Cleansing tears. Praise be.

Again, Granny eyed Colleen who didn't say a word. "Colleen, you didn't like the book the second time you read it?"

She shook her head. "Made me realize I am Mary Lennox. The part in the book that said her mother and father had no time for her, only going to parties, well, that's my life."

Suzy nudged Colleen who sat next to her. "Remember, I'm your mom…"

Janice leaned forward. "Yes, Colleen. You have many mothers here, although Suzy thinks she owns you." She winked at Suzy. "Even though you're Amish now, I'm still here for you."

"And everyone in the *Gmay* is there for you as well," Granny added. "We are family, *jah*?"

Colleen shrugged her shoulders. "Yes, I suppose."

Maryann put her yarn down in her lap. "Colleen, count your blessings."

Colleen's head snapped up, her eyes narrow. "Count my blessings? When I thought I was going to get married and my fiancé loves another woman?"

Suzy defended Colleen. "Yes, Maryann, she needs to mourn, not count her blessings."

Undaunted, Maryann opened her book and read:

"At that moment a very good thing was happening to her. Four good things had happened to her, in fact, since she came to Misselthwaite Manor. She had felt as if she had understood a robin and that he had understood her; she had run in the wind until her blood had grown warm; she had been healthily hungry for the first time in her life; and she had found out what it was to be sorry for someone.

"Colleen, while battling cancer I had no appetite and now I thank God that I do. I didn't see anything to be thankful for until I was reminded by some in this circle that giving thanks, counting blessings, is the most powerful thing to do. Yes, it is hard, but the more you give thanks, the more things you notice to give thanks for." Maryann's eyes welled with tears. "I am so sorry things didn't work out with Hezekiah and you are in my prayers, but do try to see what God is trying to say during this valley you're in."

The air seemed fragile after Maryann's words and no one wanted to break the silence.

Colleen attempted a smile. "Maybe you're right, Maryann. I thank God for you all."

A horse neighed and Granny jumped from her chair and ran to the window. "Praise be, it's Jeb and he's alright."

"Was he in danger?" Suzy asked.

"Well, he was out all day and didn't come home for the noon meal."

"You need a cell phone," Janice stated offhandedly. "Oops," she was quick to say. "Sorry, I forget sometimes you're Amish.

~*~

Jeb ran into the knitting circle, pulling Colleen into the kitchen, motioning Granny to join him. What on earth? Granny excused herself and joined Jeb and Colleen. Jeb's eyes were swollen and she knew he had been crying. "Jeb, what's wrong?"

Jeb, obviously shaken, took his chair at the head of the table. Granny ran to the icebox and put a glass of iced tea in front of him.

Jeb patted the table, asking Colleen to sit down. After Colleen obeyed, he took her hand. "Dear one, Hezekiah has been in a mighty bad car accident. He got word that there was a fire in Millersburg, and left without saying a word to anyone."

"What? When did it happen? Is he alright?" Colleen demanded in rapid succession.

"Well, he came out of a coma, but his memory isn't working. Didn't know me."

"Does he have any broken bones?" Granny asked. "I mean, was his head the only thing hurt?"

"He has busted ribs, but thank God no internal bleeding. He wasn't wearing a seatbelt and flew through the front window, head first."

"Oh my!" Colleen nearly screamed. "Can I see him?"

"That's why I came over. Knew you'd be here. Maybe he'll recognize you. Like I said, he doesn't know me." Jeb blinked rapidly as tears fell onto his cheeks.

Colleen looked over at Granny as if in shock, then reached for her and Granny ran to her as Colleen collapsed into her arms and wept.

~*~

Colleen trembled as she got out of Jeb's buggy, and Granny undergirded her with one arm. A beautiful woman greeted them at the door, her eyes blue as forget-me-nots, a twist of strawberry-red hair curling out from under her *kapp*. Colleen's stomach flipped as she wondered who this woman was. Obviously, Lottie, the woman from Millersburg who sent him letters with hearts on the back.

"*Goot* to see you again," she said to Jeb.

Jeb tipped his straw hat. "Lottie, this is my wife, Deborah, and this is Colleen, the girl you asked for."

Lottie gripped Colleen's hand. "*Ach,* Hezekiah has written to me about you."

Colleen put her head down, said a quick prayer for strength. She was here to help Hezekiah, whether he cared for her or not. Colleen met Lottie's sad eyes. "Can I see Hezekiah?"

"Come on in. He may be sleeping, but rest will help him, I'm sure."

She motioned for them to go back to the first floor bedroom, off the living room. Hezekiah lay in the twin bed pushed up against a window, the white curtains fluttering as a breeze filled the room with the scent of lilacs. As they walked closer to the bed, Hezekiah did not turn his head, but stared at the ceiling.

"Talk to him," Lottie said, bringing up a wooden chair near the bed.

"Will he hear me?"

"The doctors said they don't know," Lottie explained, "but he needs all the stimulation he can get. I read to him at night, not knowing if he understands."

Colleen brushed away the jealous feeling she had towards Lottie and sat in the chair. What she wanted to say, she didn't want others to hear, so she asked if they could leave and she could be alone with him. After they exited the room, she got up, kissed his cheek, his forehead, his mouth. "I will always love you, Hezekiah. You are still the gentlest man I've ever known. You know all about my past, as you so patiently pulled it out of me. Every time I told you another story, your listening ears helped me release the poison in my soul, and I will always love you for that."

He showed no movement. A fly landed on his cheek and he didn't flinch.

"Hezekiah, do you smell the lilacs outside? Remember when you helped me plant all those flowers in our secret garden, and you said lilacs need sun? So we planted bleeding hearts, hostas, and creeping myrtle? Remember when we talked about the bleeding hearts, which led to our talk about me cutting myself to feel alive?" She bit back tears. "I feel alive now, in so many ways. I know God loves me but it took lots of people to help me see that. You helped me the most, along with Granny and Jeb."

Colleen slumped in her chair and sorrow soon filled her until she wept again. She took her black apron up to her face to catch her tears, and let out all the agony in her heart. After a few minutes, she thought back to Pilgrim's Progress, when Pilgrim was in the Valley of the Shadow of Death. Pilgrim had to continue going through the valley until he saw the light again, and that's just what she'd have to do, no matter how painful. Like Granny said, some squares on a quilt are black, but when combined with others, it made a nice pattern. This was a black spot in her life, but it wouldn't last forever. One of her favorite Bible verses had become, Weeping may last through the night, but joy comes with the morning. She said it over and over in her mind, meditating on each word, until she fell asleep in the chair.

~*~

Colleen jumped when someone touched her shoulder. When she opened her eyes, she saw Lottie leaning over her. "Do you want some tea? Something to drink?"

"No, I'm fine. Really."

"Well, Jeb and Granny want to come in. Want to take a walk? Such a nice day."

Colleen had just come out of a wonderful dream. She was marrying Hezekiah, who was healthy, and strong, and didn't have a redheaded beauty hovering over him. "I'm really tired today. Don't really feel like taking a walk."

Lottie pulled her up by one hand. "Come on. It's a surprise."

Colleen resisted, but this woman had muscles. Was she a dairy farmer who hand-milked cows? Her grip was like a man's. "Okay, if you insist."

Lottie nearly skipped through the room and Colleen followed. Well, at least one of us is happy, Colleen thought.

When they got outside, Lottie stared down at her feet. "Aren't you going to take them off?"

Colleen looked down. "On, no. I'm new to the Amish faith and all, but I wear shoes. Bees sting."

Lottie laughed. "Come on. Take them off. It's our way."

Colleen wanted to turn around and run back into the house. Why was this woman so excited and acting so odd? "I'll keep my shoes on."

Lottie shrugged and then took her hand, pulling her around to the backyard. "Wait a minute. Can we walk?" Colleen asked.

"*Ach, jah*, we can. I get excited. *Mamm* says I'm mighty high-spirited, but Hezekiah always liked that about me."

"Oh," Colleen said, feeling her heart sink into her feet. "Have you known Hezekiah long?"

"Since I was in diapers. We grew up like brother and sister. Hezekiah doesn't have a sister, so he adopted me as one when we were wee ones. He never told you about me?"

"No," Colleen said evenly, wondering how much more she could endure this conversation.

"But we write back and forth. I'm surprised..." Lottie took her hand again and pulled her. "Let's run."

Colleen had no choice as she felt her arm would pull from its socket if she resisted. They ran down a path in the woods behind Hezekiah's and they soon came to a large rock garden. Colleen put her hand over her heart. "Oh, it's full of shade plants. How beautiful."

"We have more bulbs and plants to put in."

This remark bit Colleen, so she bit back. "Does Hezekiah make gardens with all his girls?"

Lottie frowned. "I don't know. But I know this one is for you."

Colleen searched Lottie's blue eyes. "What are you saying?"

"He's been working on this forever. Said it was a wedding present for you. I've sent him so many of my heirloom seeds, he said I should try selling them. I always put a heart on the back of each envelope so he knows it's from me and contains precious seeds. One time he threw out the little pouch I enclosed, not seeing it."

Colleen raised a hand to stop her chatter. "Wait. Why are you saying that this garden is for me?"

Lottie's eyes narrowed. "Colleen, I have a feeling there's a big misunderstanding. I'm Hezekiah's cousin and I know you're new to the Amish and all, but we don't marry first cousins, like the English think."

Colleen stared at her. "His cousin? But you put hearts on his letters?"

"Like I said. We don't marry cousins and –"

"I know that." Colleen let out a gasp. "Oh, so you're his cousin with the green thumb. Yes, he has talked about you."

Lottie smiled. "You thought I was his girl?"

"Yes, I did."

Lottie leaned over and laughed. "*Ach,* I needed some *goot* humor. *Nee,* he's like my brother." She looped her arm through Colleen's. "He loves you ever so much and wanted to marry you in a garden. Most unusual, but he said it was something between you two."

Colleen gulped as her mouth grew dry. "Hezekiah, he is too good for me."

Granny ran towards them, and then put both hands on her knees, leaning over, gasping for air.

"What's wrong?" Colleen squealed.

"Hezekiah's trying to talk."

~*~

Colleen ran into Hezekiah's room, quick to notice that his eyes were moving around, ever so slightly. "Hezekiah, I'm here." She took his hand, kissed his cheek and smiled at him. "I'm here."

His eyes portrayed little emotion, but Colleen thought she saw fear. He attempted to talk, but could only make out guttural sounds.

"I saw the garden," Colleen said, impervious to what she saw before her. Faith is the evidence of things not seen. She would talk to Hezekiah until he was whole again. "The garden is so beautiful, and I see you had many bleeding hearts planted." She kissed his cheek, and then the story of Sleeping Beauty and Snow White came to her mind. Even though she was Amish and could no longer read fairy tales, she had them memorized. A kiss by their true love had woken them up...

She turned to Jeb who was in the room. "Could you leave us alone for a while?"

Jeb nodded and left the room, closing the door behind him.

Colleen planted her lips on Hezekiah's, hoping they would wake him up so they could have a fairy tale happily ever after life together.

~*~

The next morning, at the crack of dawn, Janice pulled into Hezekiah's farm, and the women from the knitting circle spilled out. Colleen directed them to the back of the house where the garden shed stood and told them all to take a hand spade, shovel, hoe or whatever they could find. Lottie ran out to meet them, and when Granny saw the girl, she marveled at her beautiful red hair. With no men around, it hung down her back, her head only covered with a plain black bandana.

Lottie chattered on about the new garden as she led them through the path and into the area where they would spend the morning planting, weeding, and watering. A dry spell had left some areas nearly brown, even in the shade. "I smell rain," Lottie said, as she went from plant to plant, saying its name, function in herbal medicine if it had one. Granny wondered if the girl had time to breathe she babbled on so. *And this is Hezekiah's cousin? Calm and cool Hezekiah?* Granny thought.

She decided to take a chance when Lottie paused to speak. "Is Hezekiah showing any signs of improvement today?"

"*Ach,* a little. Seems like the more time Colleen spends time with him, he becomes more aware." She put her hands on her hips. "Don't know what her secret is."

Suzy let out a giggle and everyone turned to her.

"What's so funny?" Janice asked.

Suzy scrunched her lips to one side. "Well, we can't talk about fairy tales now can we."

"What?" Fannie asked. "What's a book got to do with this?"

"Hello," Suzy said. "How do Sleeping Beauty and Snow White wake up?"

Marge started to jiggle around the middle and then laughter erupted. "Oh, that's funny."

"I don't' get it," Granny said. "Is there a tonic or something good for comas in the book?"

Marge doubled over laughing. "Kissing! Prince Charming kisses Sleeping Beauty and she wakes up. Oh, remember when Colleen brought Snow White to circle and Jenny got afraid of stepmothers?"

"Yes," Lizzie said, "and ran away to your place. *Ach,* she thought I was wicked…. How far we've come."

"I hardly notice she's your stepdaughter," Marge said with admiration.

Lottie leaned on a shovel. "So this is the knitting circle Colleen told me about."

"Yes," Suzy said. "Guilty as charged." She pointed to Granny. "She started it. Was all Amish at first and then Granny opened it up to us Baptists and that's how Colleen met us all. I'm her 'English *Mamm.*'"

Lottie glanced around at all the women. "I don't knit, but I quilt. Have a quilt shop back home in Millersburg."

"Oh," Granny said with admiration. "I had a quilt shop, but I gave it up a few years back. I guess I am retired, as the English put it. I spin and knit now."

Lottie pursed her lips. "Did someone take over your shop?"

"*Nee,* just gave it up is all. Why?"

Lottie's cheeks turned pink. "My parents are hoping I'll stay here. Move my shop here."

Marge slapped her hands on her cheeks. "You don't think Hezekiah will need care for long, do you? As a nurse, I know they come out of comas and all."

"We're hoping he has a full recovery. *Nee,* I'm twenty and not married. My parents said maybe I need to move away to meet someone."

Granny smiled. "I'm from Millersburg and I met my husband here in 1963, when this settlement started."

Fannie put an arm around Granny. "If you're looking for a husband, this woman will help you. She's the town matchmaker."

Granny slapped Fannie playfully. "I am not."

Fannie leaned in close to Granny. "Emma."

"Emma is my *mamm's* name," Lottie quipped. "I'll remember your name."

"My name is Deborah, not Emma. We read books and knit and read a lot of Jane Austen."

Lottie put her hand on her heart. "Oh, I love all her books. I'm a bookworm, too, much to my parents' dismay. By the time I work at the shop and read books, it leaves little time for men."

Mona spoke up. "Well, you're a real pretty girl. I'm sure you've had your chances?"

Lottie nodded. "Well, yes I did, but he found someone else." Sorrow filled her eyes. "I was engaged, but my fiancé left the Amish and now lives in sin, living with a woman. I keep hoping he'll come back."

"That's a pretty kettle of fish," Mona barked. "He doesn't deserve you."

"Here, here," Janice said, clapping. "You deserve better. And if a man will leave you for another woman, he just was not into you."

"What?" Lottie asked.

"He didn't love you enough. Not the kind of love you deserve," Janice said. "Take a look at Colleen and Hezekiah. That man loves a single mother with all his heart. Treats Aurora like his own daughter because he loves Colleen unconditionally. You need a man like that."

Heads nodded and Marge shouted an 'Amen.' Lottie stared at the women. "Are you all so...I don't know. Confident?"

Fannie put her arm around Granny again. "I am now, thanks to this woman and all my knitting friends. I really think you belong here."

Lottie, who now seemed speechless, said, "Maybe I do...."

~*~

Later that day, after Jeb and Joe placed Hezekiah in a wheelchair, strapping him up for support, they wheeled him out to the secret garden that was all neatly planted with seeds, bulbs, bushes, and plants.

They left Hezekiah alone with Colleen at her request, and she sat on a grassy spot in front of his wheelchair. She picked up her book, The Secret Garden, the book she was reading when she first started to court her beloved. It had several pieces of paper stuck in it as book markers, and she flipped the book open and began to quote her favorite passages.

"If you look the right way, you can see that the whole world is a garden."

"'Is the spring coming?' he said. 'What is it like?'...'It is the sun shining on the rain and the rain falling on the sunshine...'"

"It made her think that it was curious how much nicer a person looked when he smiled. She had not thought of it before."

Colleen looked up and gasped. Hezekiah was smiling? She ran to him, kissed him once again. "Oh, you remember. You told me that I looked better when I smiled. My love, are you waking up?"

He didn't speak but his blue eyes sparkled. The eyes that seemed to be able to pull poison out of Colleen's soul, eyes that waited patiently as she poured out past hurts that threatened to grow like a cancer within her. "I'll be here, with you, until you are recovered, even if I'm old and gray. I'll never leave you, ever."

Three weeks later

Colleen smoothed the new white apron after Aurora hugged her around the middle. Aurora had on her plain clothes, but was allowed to wear flowers in her hair. No, the Amish didn't have flower girls, but in Colleen's mind,

Aurora was one. It wasn't a sin to have a flower girl. Neither was it allowed to have an *Englisher* be an attendant, but she wanted Suzy by her side, so in her mind, Suzy was a bridesmaid. Yes, this was not your typical Amish wedding. Even to have a wedding in the middle of planting season was unusual, let alone one outside in a garden, but Jeb said mercy and love were more important than any traditions. He was also pretty sure no other Amish woman would ask such things, being brought up to think a certain way on weddings, so he made more allowances with Colleen.

Colleen thought back to when she almost wanted to leave the Amish because she wanted a fancy dress, like the dresses in Pride and Prejudice she used to watch over and over. Granny had told her it was a trifle, and she was right. Because today, as she was in a mint green dress, a white apron and *kapp*, she felt like royalty. After all, she was marrying her prince.

Suzy's mint green plain dress to match Lottie's had been made in a few days by Lottie, someone with a real talent for sewing. Colleen tried not to laugh at Suzy as she wore a black eyelet scarf over her hair, as did other *Englishers* in attendance.

Suzy held her at arm's length. "You look beautiful, my dear daughter." A sob escaped Suzy and she quickly started to laugh as tears slid down her cheeks. "I promised Janice I'd show self-control today. But this is so unusual."

Granny poked her head into the bedroom. "Jeb said he's ready. I've never seen a bride walk down an aisle with her *daed*." She clasped her hands together. "I think it's a *goot* idea."

Fear gripped Colleen. "Granny, no one else is here from church, I mean *Gmay*, right? Only my family,

Hezekiah's, and the knitting circle? This is not your average Amish wedding and I don't want to offend."

Granny walked over to Colleen and grabbed her hands. "This is what you English call an immediate family only wedding, *jah*?"

"Yes, small and intimate. And you know, because of Hezekiah's condition."

Granny nodded. "I'm an old woman who's seen lots of change in her day. Believe me, some of it is for the *goot*." She winked. "Don't tell the bishop that."

Colleen covered her mouth to hide laughter. "No, never. Our bishop is so strict."

Granny turned to go but looked back, eyes misted. "I knew the day I met you over at Forget-Me-Not Manor that you were a kindred spirit. I love you so."

"And I love you…"

~*~

After looping her arm through Jeb's, they followed Aurora as she ambled her way down the stone path to the garden. Jeb kissed Colleen's cheek, and then left her next to Hezekiah's wheelchair.

Hezekiah gripped her hand as Jeb stood before them. He asked them if they would vow to be faithful unto death and they both made the commitment. Colleen knew that Hezekiah's slurred speech would improve over time. His latest MRI showed no permanent damage, but even if it had, she had no desire to be with anyone else.

After their vows were said and Jeb gave the blessing, a whistle was heard and everyone's heads darted to the back of the small gathering. Colleen at first was aghast that Joe and Marge had clapped and whistled, but then the whole small circle of friends and family joined in with laughter, and clapped as well, another thing unusual for an Amish wedding.

The wedding ceremony ended and soon everyone started to put up tables for a dinner, all prepared by the knitting circle. Granny told her to close her eyes as she led her over to a small table, just for the couple. When she was allowed to look, Colleen saw a beautiful two-tiered wedding cake in fondant, paste yellow roses and candy bees that appeared to be flying buzzing around it. She blushed. "I love it. It's so beautiful. And the bees are... unique."

Jeb clasped his hands. "It's part of the surprise."

Granny, eyes wide, exclaimed, "Jebediah Weaver, it's a secret. Let them eat their meal first."

Hezekiah sat in his wheelchair, not restrained as he was able to sit up. "*Danki.*"

Jeb tapped his foot. "Food can wait. I want to tell you about the surprise." He unlocked the break on Hezekiah's wheel chair and started to push him on the grass, towards the back to the property.

"Old man, get some help. You're not a teenager anymore."

"*Nee,* but as strong as one."

Granny groaned but slid her arm around Colleen's waist. "Do you remember when I met you I said you had honey-colored eyes and honey-colored hair?"

"Yes. That was such a compliment."

"And I also said I thought you were as sweet as honey, right?"

Confused, Colleen leaned her head to one side. "Yes. What are you trying to say? My cake is honey flavored?"

Granny squeezed her. "*Nee,* much better than that."

As they followed Jeb and Hezekiah, Colleen heard buzzing in the back orchard. "Bees. Run!"

She pulled at Granny but Granny stood her ground. "Yes, bees."

Colleen held her cheeks, wanting to scream. "Bees are all over the apple trees."

Jeb and Granny laughed. "They're getting used to their new home."

"What?"

"You have twenty bee hives back here, enough to start a honey business." Jeb looked down at Hezekiah. "Your cousin told me you always wanted an apiary."

Hezekiah leaned forward, and pulled himself up. "*Danki.*"

Colleen screamed. "You're standing! Oh, Lord! You're standing!"

"I a-am," he beamed.

Granny took a handkerchief out of her apron pocket and buried her face in it, sobbing. Jeb went over to her, leaning her against him.

Colleen held on to Hezekiah arms. "Can you try to walk?"

He nodded, and slowly put one foot in front of the other. He looked down at her. "Far enough?"

"It's one step." She buried her face in his chest and wept.

Soon voices were heard and the whole circle of close friends and family met them in the orchard. Some screamed about hearing bees, but Jeb explained that the Amish community didn't know if Hezekiah would ever recover enough to be a farmer, so they made him bee hives. Something Colleen could do for income.

Then Hezekiah took a few steps and waved at the crowd. "*Danki.* Friends."

Hezekiah's parents ran to him along with other family members from Millersburg. The knitting circle ran to Colleen, the *Englishers* saying, "Oh, God hears when the Baptist pray, and hallelujah God healed him"; the

Amish saying "the Amish have been fasting and praying for a miracle and God heard us." Colleen laughed, and then they all did. They were all heard by God, their many casting off prayers for Hezekiah, and God had heard. They joined hands, while Granny led in prayer.

"*Lord,*

"*What a blessed day. What a blessed, miraculous day. I thank you for these girls of mine. Bless Colleen and Hezekiah as they start their new life together. Bless all the changes spring has brought upon us, the home at Arbor Creek accepting unwanted boys to adopt. And we look forward to the many summer days together as you have brought us Lottie here, to teach us all how to be better seamstresses, but of course we'll still be faithful to knit for the homeless.*

She paused and looked around the circle, tired of the jokes that she was Emma, the matchmaker.

"*And Lord, Lottie is single. Bring the right man to her, right here in Smicksburg, without my assistance. You are the matchmaker who brought Colleen and Hezekiah together, a match made in heaven.*

"*In Jesus name,*

"*Amen.*"

Everyone said amen, hugged each other and headed down to where the food was set up. After all, they had a wedding feast to enjoy this day.

Dear Reader,

Oh, thank you for patiently following this series. My love for classic literature along with the Amish made this the most enjoyable writing experience to date. As you can see, there's a new character, Lottie, who's introduced in this last episode. Well, she sews and will appear in the next series, Amish Knit & Stitch Circle, coming out in 2014. I've written *Amish Knitting Circle, Amish Friends*

Knitting Circle and Amish Knit Lit Circle while having four weddings! Yes, God has a sense of humor. All four of my kids got married over the past three years. So, I need a little break before launching *Amish Knit & Stitch Circle.*

Thank you all for keeping Granny Weaver alive. From results on Facebook at my author page, you shouted out that she must live. *Danki.* I love to write about her.

I leave you, as usual, with this recipe:

Blackberry or Blueberry Cobbler

3 Tbsp. butter
1 egg
½ tsp. salt
2 Tbsp. apple cider vinegar
¼ c. berry juice
2/3 c. blackberries or blue berries
¾ c. sugar
1½ c. flour
1 tsp. soda
½ tsp. cinnamon
½ tsp. ground cloves

Cream butter and sugar. Add egg and beat until fluffy. Add dry ingredients along with berries, juice and vinegar. Bake in 8 inch square pan at 350 degrees.

RECIPE INDEX

ABOUT THE AUTHOR

Karen Anna Vogel is the author of the popular Amish Knitting Circle series. She goes straight to the Amish grapevine for inspiration, having many Amish friends in Western Pennsylvania. To date she has five novels: *Amish Knitting Circle: Smicksburg Tales 1, Amish Friends Knitting Circle: Smicksburg Tales 2, Amish Knit Lit Circle: Smicksburg Tales 3, Knit Together, The Amish Doll, Granny & Jeb's Love Story, and Amish Pen Pals: Rachael's Confession.*

Karen lives in a century old farmhouse with her husband Tim, where they enjoy homesteading. They have four married children and a granddaughter, who they spoil rotten. Visit her blog, *Amish Crossings,* www.karenannavogel.blogspot.com or her Facebook author page at www. https://www.facebook.com/VogelReaders to celebrate the simple life. See hundreds of her Amish pictures, swap gardening tips and thrifty recipes, meet fellow knitters and crochets', and leave prayer requests.

HOW TO KNOW GOD

God so loved the world, that He gave His only Son, that whoever believes in Him should not perish but have eternal life. John 3:16

God so loved the world

God loves you!

"I have loved you with an everlasting love." — Jeremiah 31:3

"Indeed the very hairs of your head are numbered." — Luke 12:7

That He gave His only Son

Who is God's son?

"Jesus answered, 'I am the way and the truth and the life. No one comes to the Father except through me.'" — John 14:6

That whoever believes in Him

Whosoever? Even me?

No matter what you've done, God will receive you into His family. He will change you, so come as you are.

"I am the Lord, the God of all mankind. Is anything too hard for me?"

— Jeremiah 32:27

"The Spirit of the Lord will come upon you in power, … and you will be changed into a different person." — 1 Samuel 10:6

Should not perish but have eternal life

Can I have that "blessed hope" of spending eternity with God?

"I write these things to you who believe in the name of Son of God so that you may know that you have eternal life." - 1 John 5:13

To know Jesus, come as you are and humbly admit you're a sinner. A sinner is someone who has missed the target of God's perfect holiness. I think we all qualify to be sinners. Open the door of your heart and let Christ in. He'll cleanse you from all sins. He says he stands at the door of your heart and knocks. Let Him in. Talk to Jesus like a friend...because when you open the door of your heart, you have a friend eager to come inside. Bless you!

Thank you for taking the time to read this series. We hope you enjoyed it. You may also enjoy other works by Karen Anna Vogel published by Lamb Books www.lambbooks.com

Amish Knitting Circle: Smicksburg Tales 1
Amish Knitting Circle: Smicksburg Tales 2
Amish Knit Lit Circle: Smicksburg Tales 3
Coming in 2014: Amish Knit & Stitch Circle: Smicksburg Tales 4
Full length novels:
Knit Together: An Amish Knitting Novel
The Amish Doll: An Amish Knitting Novel
Novellas:
Amish Knitting Circle Christmas: Granny & Jeb's Love Story
Amish Pen Pals: Rachael's Confession
Christmas Union: Quaker Abolitionist of Chester County, PA

Made in the USA
Columbia, SC
06 January 2019